WAYPOINT CHRONICLES

VOLUME ONE

DON'T MISS THESE OTHER THRILLING STORIES IN THE WORLDS OF

HALO INFINITE
Kelly Gay

Halo: The Rubicon Protocol
Halo: Edge of Dawn

THE FERRETS
Troy Denning

Halo: Last Light
Halo: Retribution
Halo: Divine Wind

RION FORGE & *ACE OF SPADES*
Kelly Gay

Halo: Smoke and Shadow
Halo: Renegades
Halo: Point of Light

THE MASTER CHIEF & BLUE TEAM
Troy Denning

Halo: Silent Storm
Halo: Oblivion
Halo: Shadows of Reach

ALPHA-NINE
Matt Forbeck

Halo: New Blood
Halo: Bad Blood

GRAY TEAM
Tobias S. Buckell

Halo: The Cole Protocol
Halo: Envoy

THE FORERUNNER SAGA
Greg Bear

Halo: Cryptum
Halo: Primordium
Halo: Silentium

THE KILO-FIVE TRILOGY
Karen Traviss

Halo: Glasslands
Halo: The Thursday War
Halo: Mortal Dictata

THE ORIGINAL SERIES

Halo: The Fall of Reach
Eric Nylund

Halo: The Flood
William C. Dietz

Halo: First Strike
Eric Nylund

Halo: Ghosts of Onyx
Eric Nylund

STANDALONE STORIES

Halo: Contact Harvest
Joseph Staten

Halo: Broken Circle
John Shirley

Halo: Hunters in the Dark
Peter David

Halo: Saint's Testimony
Frank O'Connor

Halo: Shadow of Intent
Joseph Staten

Halo: Legacy of Onyx
Matt Forbeck

Halo: Outcasts
Troy Denning

Halo: Epitaph
Kelly Gay

Halo: Empty Throne
Jeremy Patenaude

SHORT STORY ANTHOLOGIES
Various Authors

Halo: Evolutions: Essential Tales of the Halo Universe
Halo: Fractures: More Essential Tales of the Halo Universe

Waypoint Chronicles—Volume One
Jeff Easterling & Alexander Wakeford

WAYPOINT CHRONICLES

VOLUME ONE

JEFF EASTERLING &
ALEXANDER WAKEFORD

BASED ON THE BESTSELLING VIDEO GAME FOR XBOX®

GALLERY BOOKS

New York Amsterdam/Antwerp London
Toronto Sydney/Melbourne New Delhi

Gallery Books
An Imprint of Simon & Schuster, LLC
1230 Avenue of the Americas
New York, NY 10020

First Gallery Books paperback edition May 2026

Manufactured in the United States of America

10 9 8 7 6 5 4 3 2 1

The Library of Congress Control Number has been applied for.

ISBN 978-1-6682-1522-7
ISBN 978-1-6682-1523-4 (ebook)

To Morgan, Charly, Jo, Rascal, Indy, and Hocus

CONTENTS

CONTENTS

CONTENTS

FOREWORD

Halo has a rich history with short-form storytelling. From the original cryptic "Cortana Letters" and deep-diving data drops on Waypoint, to full-fledged anthologies like *Halo: Evolutions* and *Halo: Fractures*, some of the lore's most tantalizing tidbits have come in bite-size portions.

In November 2022, we released the first "Waypoint Chronicle" online to commemorate the tenth anniversary of *Halo 4*'s launch. Since then, we've published over twenty additional short stories celebrating similar franchise milestones and supporting fiction themes and game content featured in *Halo Infinite*.

While the heroic exploits of the Master Chief and climactic battles for the fate of the galaxy will always forge the foundation upon which some of *Halo*'s most notable memories are made, it's often the tertiary tales that truly inspire intrigue and reward lore-loving detail devotees eager to explore a little deeper.

In this extensive volume, we've collected the following:

WAYPOINT CHRONICLES: Short stories that provide greater texture to the grand tapestry of the *Halo* universe. These tales explore concepts that have lived on the periphery of the franchise's extensive lore, expanding moments referenced or only glimpsed in the games, or simply seek to spend more time with beloved characters within the gaps between their grand battles against overwhelming odds.

INTEL: Snippets of fiction that players could find within *Halo Infinite*'s main menu, offering insight for in-universe themes underpinning new gameplay additions and customization items.

ARMORY INFINITUM: Micro-stories centering around enigmatic armaments found in *Halo Infinite*, giving new perspectives on their associated histories and how these weapons were wielded or won. These were originally published online as part of *Halo*'s long-running fiction-focused "Canon Fodder" blog series.

It's our hope that the amalgamation of these learnings and lore will create a comprehensive compendium of *Halo Infinite*'s impact on the galactic timeline, and a rewarding canonical companion to its surrounding story.

Thanks so much for being part of this great journey with us. We hope you enjoy.

—Jeff Easterling & Alexander Wakeford,
Halo Studios

WAYPOINT CHRONICLES

VOLUME ONE

VERTICAL UMBRAGE

*This story takes place during the conflict between the United Nations Space Command and Jul 'Mdama's Covenant within the shield world Requiem (*Halo 4: Spartan Ops*, "Everything Has Gone Wrong").*

February 14, 2558 (Military Calendar)
Requiem (Shield World 0001)
Epoloch System

"You got eyes on, Shadow Two?"

Spartan Horatio Fry's tone made it obvious that his question was more rhetorical than practical. He'd spent enough time with this group to know that Spartan Nina Kovan *always* had "eyes on." Kovan was a no-nonsense walking death sentence with an aim as true as her word. And as Fireteam Shadow's designated marksman, she did indeed have eyes on everything.

"Affirmative. Is Stone in range of the summit site?" Kovan adjusted the advanced optics suite integrated into her GUNGNIR-class Mjolnir armor to key in on the nearby Covenant firebase that had been established just two days earlier. "Looks like they haven't gotten their ball to roll just yet."

"It's 'got the ball rolling,' Nina." Spartan Bonita Stone couldn't help but crack a smile at Kovan's butchering of yet another antiquated colloquialism. "But that's good news regardless. Might just be able stop their little airshow before it even starts."

The Covenant summit site was designed specifically to mass produce fighter craft at a rapid pace. Shutting that process down would deal a significant blow to the alien alliance's ability to gain air superiority in the local sector. For the better part of the week, Fireteam Shadow had been just one of several Spartan fireteams deployed from the UNSC flagship *Infinity* to battle a zealous Covenant remnant faction for control of an artificial planet called Requiem. The shield world had an armored alloy exterior protecting a series of habitable spherical shells within—like one of Kovan's matryoshka dolls she kept in her quarters.

"Agreed," Fry interjected. "Shadow Four, how're your baby birds looking?"

"Props are hot and charges primed. Just waiting on your signal." Shadow Four was Spartan Jason Kidman, whose voice would have sounded raspy even without being fed through the comms mic of his OPERATOR helmet. Moments later, his second-generation Mjolnir kit was fully synced with the small flock of TQ-8 seeker drones, each outfitted with a lightweight but high-yield explosive charge.

With the pieces nearly in place, Fireteam Shadow's operation was ready to begin. After Stone cleared the inner perimeter patrols with help from her active camo module, Kidman's drones would drop the doors, allowing Stone and Fry to infiltrate and hit the Covenant firebase at its heart.

Fry made one last check with Kovan as he prepared to engage. "Shadow Two, you're on overwatch. Keep your new toy primed in case we were wrong about that production run." Fry paused. "Or in case you need to finish the job. There should be enough firepower there in the event we hit trouble."

"That won't be necessary, Shadow One," Kovan responded. "If you find trouble, I'll hit it for you."

"Duly noted." For a split second, the lower contours of Fry's GOBLIN-class Mjolnir helmet mimicked the smile that had formed on his own face. Partly in amusement from Kovan's retort, and also in anticipation of any opportunity to add another blemish to the Covenant's once-stellar combat record.

Before he could give the final go-ahead, however, a different voice broke through the team's comms.

"Fireteam Shadow, this is Spartan Miller in Ops. I'm filling in for Commander Palmer, so apologies to your team's handler, uh, Spartan Carmichael, for going over his head here."

Fry cursed to himself before opening a channel. "This is Shadow Leader. Go ahead, Miller."

"Got a job for you. Infiltrate a Covenant cruiser and destroy her power core. I'm sending you coordinates now."

Whatever reservations Fry might have had on hand were not made remotely apparent. Spartans knew that they fought for priorities often greater than their purview, and that moments lost to protest might ultimately equate to lives lost to the enemy.

"We can help you out there. Give us a few to get over to those grid squares." Fry switched to team comms. "Stand down, Shadow. Change of plans."

"Define change." Stone was immediately curious.

"We're being diverted. Priority op on a nearby Covenant cruiser."

Kidman's focus turned to a more glaring logistics hurdle. "*Cruiser*? That's going to be an interesting ingress without our limo."

"Limo" was the team's term of endearment for the D79 Pelican dropship that had provided the bulk of their transportation between *Infinity* and each subsequent mission across the interior surface of Requiem. The nature of their mission at the summit necessitated a more delayed and distant LZ to keep the Pelican out of harm's way when the fireworks started. They were too close to the firebase now to be picked up and no longer had the time to get far enough away. And Fry knew it.

"Calling an audible—we may just need to grab a rental."

Panom's Canticle
Requiem
In position above "Refuge" site

Ryn 'Alun mentally reprimanded himself for the loss of control. Slight though it had been, the absent-minded rubbing of his wrist while on the bridge was an act that might betray his nervous anticipation to his crew. It was unbecoming of a shipmaster to display such feelings, however subtle the motion might be to suggest it. He must always be in control. As an ancient Sangheili proverb taught:

one who has not mastered the self
who has not emerged victorious
from the battle within their own mind
has no hope of mastering the foes without

And the foes from without had come to claim the home of the gods—a home that was now shared with the worthy. Requiem had become a symbol of everything their revitalized alliance had achieved. They had not just risen above the Covenant of old—they were becoming what it was always meant to be. High Charity seemed a pale imitation compared to the seat of the gods themselves, and this was just the beginning.

The Silent Blade, 'Alun's own special operations unit of deadly enforcers, had been deployed to Requiem's Refuge site, where they would no doubt make short work of the humans that were clumsily fumbling with its arcane machinery. Word had come that the Silent Shadow had already engaged an increasingly notorious demon squad called *Nalsaban*—"crimson" in the human tongue.

It had been well over three annual cycles since Jul 'Mdama led his combined fleet to the shield world, where he sought to awaken one of the gods and ask for their aid in the war against the humans. It was only half an annual cycle ago that they had finally been granted access to its wonders within.

This, as 'Mdama had declared, was actually due to the arrival of a *human* vessel, an event that had seemed to interest the warrior-god slumbering within this world—the Didact. The humans' arrival—heralded by the Demon himself, the Master Chief—represented a perfect opportunity to test the might and worthiness of the Covenant against their enemy's greatest champion. And the prospect of pleasing one of their gods in the flesh was one that inflamed the spirit of zeal within their hearts.

But the Didact was now absent, having bequeathed Requiem to the Covenant, and since then they had begun the process of turning this hollow sphere of heaven into their new home.

The Refuge was a location discovered early in their efforts to penetrate the shield world. There they had been, in the warrior-keep chamber, where the Demon awakened the Didact. The Forerunner delivered his judgment, declared the return of the gods, and upon his departure transported the worthy warriors who had fought to the core of his world to this sanctum.

"*You are Sangheili*," the Didact had declared. "*Loyal and strong, even in your second form. You will serve well.*"

It was here that Jul 'Mdama was formally named the Hand of the Didact, and it was this holy ground that *Panom's Canticle* had primarily been stationed to protect.

After the demons had successfully reconnoitered this site on two occasions, this third incursion was ordered to be the last—a weighty responsibility, and one that Ryn 'Alun recognized as the source of his anticipation. Ever was he wondering whether his loyalty and strength served the gods well.

A bridge officer turned to him and said: "Shipmaster, one of our Phantoms approaches."

"Our deployed forces are not meant to return until after the humans have been repelled and the Refuge reclaimed," 'Alun replied. "Hail them."

"They give no response, Shipmas— They are picking up speed!"

"Raise the hangar shields!" 'Alun ordered.

A rumble from within the cruiser told them it was too late.

Shipmaster 'Alun ignited his energy sword and motioned for two guards to follow him, knowing precisely what area of the ship the demons would target.

The true test of worthiness had come at last. The Silent Blade would serve the gods well today.

Panom's Canticle
Requiem
Positioned above Site Req/7848-2328

Turned out, getting *in* was the easy part. The Phantom dropship that Fireteam Shadow commandeered had given them as smooth an entry point as they could have hoped for, but their exploits did little to improve any diplomatic relations.

"Shadow Four, you got that guided tour ready to go?" Spartan Fry had barely finished the question when the digital ship layout Kidman was readying began to overlay key waypoints and nav markers onto their helmet displays. It would make finding their way through the *Canticle* relatively straightforward, but it wouldn't stem the mounting Covenant resistance pouring into each iridescent indigo passageway.

The Spartan fireteam moved as a fluid unit through the ship's interior, each member alternating and coordinating a rapid series of enemy engagements against Unggoy, Kig-Yar, and Sangheili warriors with practiced precision. Stone checked her VISR readout to confirm their location. "Primary reactor chamber isn't far. After this next set of doors we've got one hallway left."

Kidman transferred several rounds from his MA5D into the skulls of three Kig-Yar, bringing an end to the needler fire that had been impeding Shadow's progress. "I'm picking up chatter on native frequencies—localization script is having trouble keeping up with it all, but I can tell you that they aren't exactly happy we're here."

"You needed a translation for *that*?" Kovan's reply landed somewhere between dry wit and incredulity.

Fry brushed aside the squad banter to focus on the task at hand. "Shadow Leader to Spartan Miller." Fry waited a split second for his helmet's comms display to confirm signal receipt. "Sorry for the delay, sir. We're meeting heavy resistance in the cruiser. Seems like they *don't* want their spaceship blown up."

It only took a moment to get a response. "*Understood, Shadow Leader. Keep me informed.*"

"Shadow Three, update on that final corridor?"

Stone tilted her head to the side as she responded. "The good news is that I do have an update. The bad news is that it's not good news."

"Kidman can translate that if you need," Kovan interjected.

Before Fry could offer a leader's rebuke, Stone continued. "We've got enemy targets entering the far side of the corridor. It's not going to be easy."

"Distance?" Fry asked.

"Approximately forty meters."

"Acknowledged. We enter on my mark. I'll take point—Nina . . . call Abbey."

Kovan smiled—not at Fry's use of her name, but that of her personal sniper rifle. "She's already on the line."

The Spartan fireteam entered the corridor and covered the first several meters in what seemed like an instant, but long enough to confirm Stone's recon assessment as several Covenant soldiers opened fire at the other end. The tip of the spear, Fry immediately activated a Z-90 PCE, emitting a glowing and imposing hard light shield in front of the group to stave off the enemy's opening salvo.

"Shadow Two, be ready on the drop."

Kovan was already looking down Abbey's sights, eager to answer the call. "Knock-knock."

In a singular moment, Fry's hard light shield deactivated and four sniper shots rang out, dropping three Kig-Yar and overpenetrating through two Unggoy, with Kovan using the tighter quarters to her advantage.

Fry barked out the next phase. "Stone, go quiet, take the solution, and get ahead of us—we need to get to that core!"

The "solution" was a sizeable munitions case containing the device originally meant to be used by Kovan at the summit site. Despite the unexpected change in objective, Fry hoped that it might still prove valuable. He also wasn't about to leave it behind in enemy hands regardless of the location.

Stone grabbed the case, engaged her active camo module, and disappeared from sight.

Several more cracks from Kovan's sniper rifle disabled the energy shields of two Sangheili, allowing Fry to drop them with instant follow-up head shots. Kidman leaped ahead with a frag grenade primed, tossing it mid-roll toward several panicking Unggoy who were firing wildly before the grenade detonated, reducing the diminutive aliens to a burning pile of gore.

After dispatching the remaining resistance, Fry, Kovan, and Kidman emerged from the corridor into the larger chamber that housed the main reactor.

Unfortunately, it also housed at least a dozen Elite warriors, including one particularly imposing Sangheili sporting a more ornate command harness. A ping on the Spartans' helmet displays highlighted the commander, identifying him as Ryn 'Alun—shipmaster of *Panom's Canticle* and leader of a Covenant specops group called the Silent Blade.

Raising his energy sword, Ryn 'Alun crossed the room with a rousing battle cry that sent his lieutenants into a frenzy of their own. Plasma and hot lead filled the air a moment later as the two forces clashed.

Set against a pair of them, it was with a keen awareness that Fry noted the saurian soldiers moved with a speed and skill largely matching those of his own Spartans. And while he dispatched the first of his foes in short order, the second proved to be more up to the task. Energy shields shimmered and sizzled as they traded blows.

The dance couldn't have lasted more than a few intense moments; gritting against the bruising strength of the Elite, Fry used his bulk as an advantage to send the creature toppling over, knocking its sword out of its hand. But the encounter was enough to narrow his focus, to take his mind temporarily off the larger conflict.

It would cost him.

The shipmaster was given a moment he didn't waste, a well-timed lunge knocking the fireteam leader off-balance and onto the floor. When Fry tried to return to his feet, 'Alun was back over him in an instant, delivering a series of devastating blows with his bare fists to the helmet and torso that put the Spartan back on the ground.

Vision swimming, Shadow One fought hard against the nauseating darkness that tugged at the edges of his vision, choosing instead to keep his gaze fixed on the shipmaster's face, which looked as though it bore a sneer of contempt as he retrieved his energy sword.

Fry's failing localization suite tried to make sense of the voice behind the mandibles.

"[Demon . . . payment . . . death . . .]"

The shipmaster's sword flared to life with his final word, and in a single seamless gesture began its descent, the blade primed to pierce armor and augmented heart alike.

Even with his enhanced reflexes, Fry recognized there was no time to change its course.

He braced for the inevitable.

The blow never landed. At least, not where he expected.

An invisible force sent the shipmaster stumbling away.

Stone's active camo flickered off as she countered the shipmaster's attack, dropping two primed M9 frag grenades between them to turn Ryn 'Alun's offensive lunge into an evasive dodge.

"Fry, we have to move *now*!" Stone yelled as she scrambled to get their fireteam leader back on his feet.

"Where's our solution?" Fry's query was strained after the beating he'd taken.

"With Nina."

Kovan's location pinged on each Spartan's VISR as she opened the case to reveal an M6/E Grindell/Galilean nonlinear rifle. "Shadow, meet Selene." Her almost unsettling glee was tangible even over comms as she finalized the integration protocols to sync her targeting optics with the modified Spartan laser and primed the first shot. "I think I'm going to like her. Don't tell Abbey."

The chamber flashed as the first blast from Kovan's new toy hit the reactor, accompanied by a howl of despair from the shipmaster, who delivered a final command to the surviving Elites that needed no translation.

"Abandon ship!"

The reactor core's hum accelerated to a higher-pitched whine as Kovan fired another round, the few remaining Covenant forces scrambled toward their escape pods. "Going somewhere?" Stone remarked as she dropped two fleeing Elites, leaving only the shipmaster—but as he rounded a corner, it was clear that they'd lost him.

After three more successive salvos from Kovan, Kidman confirmed the objective's completion. "Reactor is in runaway overload—now would be a *very* good time to leave."

Fry initiated a comms link back to *Infinity* as the fireteam regrouped and looked for an exit strategy. "Miller, this is Shadow Leader. Cruiser power core is hit and overload in progress! We're evacing now. Expect a light show within thirty."

"Hot damn, good work, Shadow Leader!"

The rest of Spartan Miller's response was interrupted by Kidman. "Shadow One, I've got a local lock on a drop bay with empty squad pods—if we hurry, I think we can make it."

"Those are good enough odds for me, Shadow Four. Nice work."

Requiem
Jungle region outside "Refuge" site

Ryn 'Alun's hearts sank as he watched *Panom's Canticle* shudder and break. The clouds parted as a shockwave rippled outward, coolant spilling to the ground from its underbelly like blue-green ichor, and a final groaning eruption of purple fire uprooting the vessel's position, sending it on a collision course with the far-reaching jungles of Requiem.

You are Sangheili, the Didact's words echoed in his head. *Loyal and strong.*

And he *had* been loyal—to his brothers, to the Covenant, to the gods . . . but it hadn't been enough.

They had come here with numbers and might and faith that hadn't been witnessed in many annual cycles, and still it took only a handful of these demons to undo it all before their eyes.

You will serve well.

Perhaps that was what the ancient warrior had meant? To be "tested" and not simply rewarded with victory. True service and sacrifice came through endurance even in defeat—to draw strength not simply from within, but from the spirits of one's fallen brothers, becoming a vessel of vengeance, demanding blood be spilled for the blood that was lost. And *much* blood had just been lost.

There was no doubt in his mind that this was the same fire the demons themselves had been tempered by when their own worlds were burned. It was the same crucible the Covenant had endured after being split asunder, only to be reforged into something new.

In that moment, Ryn 'Alun felt he understood what their god had meant. Loyalty and strength were indeed a virtuous foundation, but a warrior must build upon them with *purpose.* As he bore witness to *Panom's Canticle* colliding with the ground, smoke and fire billowing upward like a pillar of holy fire, his own purpose became clear.

He would be reforged by this defeat into something new, and he would hunt these Spartans, these "Shadows," to whatever end it would take him to avenge the fallen.

The Silent Blade disappeared into the jungles of Requiem, knowing that his time of retribution had only just begun.

As *Panom's Canticle* broke apart in Requiem's sky, a *Gloto'kef*-pattern assault carapace sped away from the wreckage toward the surface, carrying four Spartan-IV super-soldiers. The vehicle's inertia dampeners kicked in for a surprisingly elegant landing. Its four pod doors retracted, and Fireteam Shadow stepped out into a forest clearing.

Miller's voice urgently crackled over the comm. "*Shadow Leader! Was your team clear? Shadow Leader!*"

"We're here, *Infinity*," Fry confirmed, calm as ever. "And all in one piece."

"*Excellent work, Spartans*," Miller said, audibly relaxing. *Infinity*'s AI Roland then chimed in, informing him of another situation at Forward Base Magma, and where Fireteam Crimson was to be redirected.

Fry stepped up to his team. "Autopilot retrieval is active," he said, marking their position for the Pelican. A small green arrow on their HUD map started moving toward them. "Limo's on the way."

"You hear that, Selene?" Kovan removed her helmet and patted the munitions case. "We'll have a warm meal for you back home in no time."

"I wouldn't make any promises quite yet," Fry said. "Just got a new order—apparently Carmichael was feeling left out of all the fun."

Stone sighed. "Something tells me we aren't going to make that Valentine's dance tonight at the atrium park, are we?"

"Maybe next year." Kovan smirked. "Don't tell Abbey."

INTEL // CONCORD ACTION REPORT

On Concord, UNSC Army Ranger Sigrid Eklund submits an update regarding Operation: GYPSUM.

UNSC COMMREF: B7D002F78-L-44

ENCRYPTION TAG: [CALCITE]

DATE: DECEMBER 6, 2551

SND: [SGT EKLUND] | REC: [CMD RENNA]

RE: GYPSUM

At 0720Z [MST], we cleared out the last Covenant emplacement from the Caravelle province. Lost two Wolverines to Banshee fire, but we made sure that was all they took from us. We're making final preparations to depart from our current location and redeploy to one of the mass driver stations.

Local Concordian militia groups there are holding firm but growing thin. Hopefully support from the Rangers will be a welcome sight when we arrive.

Still awaiting reports on yesterday's activity at the combat fields outside Lethbridge. Let us know if you receive any updates on your end, or if we need to reprioritize our focus in order to secure that location.

—Eklund

INTEL // SURVIVAL

Jun-A266 (COSSPAR) and [REDACTED] (EXTUSR) discuss the current status of the Avery J. Johnson Academy of Military Science on Nysa.

OFFICE BLOCK: 7421.UO

COMMREF: 88FG0H83W-B-91

DATE: JANUARY 9, 2560

EXTUSR: So the Academy remains active?

COSSPAR: All reports coming out of AJAMS confirm so.

EXTUSR: That's good news, Jun. And impressive, if I'm being honest.

COSSPAR: Spartans have a way of surviving, no matter the odds.

EXTUSR: Well, you would know as good as anyone. Which reminds me, you never did tell me how you made it off Reach.

COSSPAR: You'll just have to read the reports for yourself.

EXTUSR: Unfortunately, I see your sense of humor also survived.

WINTER CONTENTION

*This story is set in December 2551, approximately seven months before Spartan-B312 joins Noble Team and the events leading to the fall of Reach are set into motion (*Halo: Reach*).*

1405 Hours, December 12, 2551 (Military Calendar)
Hinterlands Region, Planet Concord, Alabaster System

Two distant columns of smoke loomed over the horizon like signal flares of ash and burning plasma. The billowing charcoal plumes cut through an otherwise unbroken sky of white clouds. To anyone who remained to gaze upon this sight, it was a stark message written in black ink: *You're next.*

The hinterlands of Concord were made up of tough, rugged terrain. During the summer months, the verdant alpine forests spanning the planet's equatorial landmass were a manageable, even pleasant, site of congregation for the miners who lived across its three townships—New Ugga, Skathi, and Ploh. But winter was here now, bringing snowstorms that covered much of Concord's surface, and the rolling hills between the three towns had become perilous ice fields.

As the Covenant War continued to drive toward an increasingly dire conclusion, Concord's infrastructure had seen substantial investment from the Unified Earth Government while scores of refugees from glassed colonies were resettled within its more prominent metropolitan cities. In contrast, the colonists of old—those who had claimed this world as their home for fifty years or more—chose instead to isolate themselves across its wild, untamed terrain.

"*How long do we have, Noble Three?*" Even on the comm, Carter-A259's voice carried its usual stern resolve.

Scanning the horizon with his SRS99's Oracle scope, Jun-A266 couldn't yet see the full Covenant force heading their way. From his elevated position, there was one final hill the alien onslaught had to traverse before the true size and makeup of their forces became clear.

"Hard to say, Noble Leader," Jun replied, eyes fixed on the hilltop, a statuesque stillness disrupted only by his occasional movement to prevent snow and ice buildup from disrupting his visibility. "Assume imminent."

"*Affirmative.*"

It was an unusual situation that the Spartans of Noble Team found themselves in. The joint effort of UNSC Army Rangers and Concordian militia had already secured a remarkable victory against the Covenant. Through sheer resolve and selfless fortitude, they'd denied the aliens air superiority over Concord—though it hadn't come without loss. At least a dozen S-14 pilots sacrificed themselves in strafing runs to lead pursuing swarms of Banshees and Vampires into the paths of concealed M9 Wolverine antiaircraft tanks. They'd largely repelled ground forces from the major cities, and several planetside mass driver stations were used as impromptu artillery to harry the enemy's unusually meager orbital presence before a swift strike group of two *Strident*-class frigates and a *Marathon*-class cruiser tore them a proverbial new one.

With their vessels in ruin, the Covenant had no way to evacuate—but that wasn't going to still the blades of those remaining planetside. Ashamed and enraged, the Covenant's local ground forces rallied and weren't going down without a fight. But instead of once more throwing themselves at the more fortified cities, the Covenant redirected its forces to the far less-protected hinterland towns.

For the Covenant contingent now stranded on this frigid world, it wasn't really a matter of *winning* at this point. The alien bastards just wanted to take as many humans with them as they could before their own end, whether that came from a bullet or the biting cold.

Noble Team's own less-than-ideal situation was looking to parallel that of the Covenant more than any of the Spartans liked. After rerouting from the cities, a brutal snowstorm had downed their Pelican in the mountains. The Spartans managed to make their way to the town of Skathi, only to discover its inhabitants cut off from all communications and preparing for the Covenant's arrival—something Jun was currently keeping a close eye on. So far, he'd been tracking a single Banshee that was obviously on its own scouting run, no doubt searching for where Noble Team's bird had come to rest.

"*Noble Two*," Carter's voice crackled over the comm again. "*How's that inventory coming along?*"

He gets formal when he's worried, Jun noted to himself.

"*It's a short list, Commander*," Kat-B320 responded. "*Air support? Nada. Evacuation? Hours away. Civvies are still with Jorge rounding up whatever ammunition they can find. As for operational assets, we've got one functional 'Hog.*"

Silence hung in the air for a prolonged moment before Carter spoke again. "*Understood.*"

Jun's mind wandered for a moment, thinking about how Skathi was exactly the kind of place Jorge-052 would choose for his retirement—if such a thing were ever truly possible for a Spartan. It was the least built-up of the three towns, barely more than a bunch of wooden houses dotted alongside a tavern, a lumber mill, and a couple of stores focused on general supplies and hunting goods. The folks that lived here were hardy, rugged workers, sociable only among each other.

No doubt this place reminds him of home. He'll fight that much harder to protect it.

Jun's thoughts were interrupted as he caught the first unmistakable gleam of purple on the horizon, his grip on the sniper tightening as his heads-up display matched the outline of the lead vehicle to its internal Covenant database.

"Time's up, Commander." He linked his Oracle scope's view to the team's HUD. "Draugr inbound."

"Copy that."

A mobile fortress seldom encountered throughout the Covenant War, the Draugr was a gargantuan siege platform approximately 170 meters long, another hundred wide, and just under sixty meters tall—seemingly half the size of the town itself. Its front section was broad, looking much like an upscaled Wraith featuring large antigravity pods on its wings, and its face sloped upward to a pair of outward facing "horns" that were equipped with four powerful focus cannons.

From there, an extended troop bay connected to the rear of the vehicle, which also possessed dual antigravity pods holding up a rear "tower" boasting an anti-aircraft gun. Whatever this thing lacked in maneuverability and speed was more than made up for in firepower.

Contending with this was one thing, but—as Jun magnified

his scope further—he highlighted half a dozen Ghosts and two Wraith tanks flanking it. And though he couldn't see them, the unmistakable wail of Banshees concealed by cloud cover echoed through the open air.

Jun waited as the picture of what they were facing sank in for the rest of Noble Team. He waited for Carter to say the four words that would turn the tide.

He didn't have to wait long.

"Kat's got a plan."

No air support, no reinforcements, no evacuation. Just a single M862 Warthog. With a mind like Kat's, that's all a Spartan needed to win the day, no matter how much of an absurd longshot it seemed.

"*Only three of us can go,*" Kat said. "*The rest will remain here as a rear guard for the town. Noble Four, Noble Six—you're with me.*"

"*We were hoping you'd say that,*" came the distinct, surly drawl of Rosenda-A344. "*Isn't that right, Thom?*"

"*Three of us against a thousand of them?*" The sound of Thom-A293 loading his CQS48 Bulldog clacked over the comm. "*I'll take those odds.*"

"Boys in the back." Rosenda gave Thom a light shove to redirect her fellow Spartan-III toward the rear of the vehicle.

"I thought *I* had shotgun," Thom protested.

"Yup. And that pup in your arms will fill that requirement plenty fine." Rosenda nodded toward his primary weapon as she lifted the gullwing canopy door and swung a Mjolnir-armored leg deftly over the sill and into the cabin.

The M862 was a specialized variant of the venerable Warthog platform, built for traversing terrain just like this. To keep its occupants comfortable and relatively free of frostbite, the M862's primary cabin was enclosed, and in place of the standard M12's carbon nanotube tires was a versatile 4X track array, transforming the all-terrain vehicle into equal parts light tank and snowmobile.

"If you two are done, let's sync our ingress markers." Kat was not without her own sense of humor, but it was never a mystery when she was ready to turn her attention to the task at hand.

Thom settled into the rear bed and set the appropriate software processes in motion within his Mark V[B] helmet's HUD before taking final stock of the various grenade and countermeasure options he had on hand, knowing every one of them was bound to find a use at some point.

Rosenda pulled up her own armor's telemetry. "Time to intercept?"

"Not long," Kat responded. "It'll reconfigure a few times as we update the onboard terrain maps in real time, but we'll be in targeting range within three minutes."

The winter-liveried Warthog soon moved at an impressive clip over the thick Concordian snow, kicking up a trail behind it as it headed toward the Covenant force. To the surprise of no one, Kat's timing assessment turned out to be spot-on.

They really are smug bastards, Thom thought. *Barreling across the tundra in bright-ass colors, completely confident in their ability to wipe out any enemy—no matter how far away you can see 'em coming from.*

"What's that shade of Shade officially called, d'you think?"

Rosenda rolled her eyes. "Here we go."

"Military magenta?"

"Please stop."

"Violent violet?"

"How about this?" Kat interjected. "When we're done gutting every last one of these monsters, you can name the color whatever you want."

Taking Thom's silence as success, Kat's focus returned to the oncoming onslaught, and she began to imagine how ridiculous this engagement must appear from their enemy's perspective.

What was it Carter always said?

"Wouldn't be a Noble mission if it were easy!"

The Ghosts were the first to break formation and begin initial flanking maneuvers. Rosenda flung open her gullwing door and immediately opened fire with her assault rifle. Each small, sustained burst found its mark and separated the first three attack bikes from their Unggoy pilots. For the fourth, she aimed a well-placed volley at the vehicle's glowing blue-gray fuel cell situated behind its left wing, the Ghost erupting with a plasma-based explosion, instantaneously cooking its driver.

"Two more Grunts coming up on the rear," Thom announced. "Seven o'clock."

Kat gave the 'Hog a slight Scandinavian flick to pitch the vehicle into a controlled drift, bringing the Ghosts more directly into Thom's view. Immediately he tossed two primed M9 frag grenades into the snow just ahead of the first Ghost. A split second later, the soft white ground burst into the bottom of the Covenant craft, sending both ride and rider into an unscheduled ejection.

The second Ghost swerved to avoid the flaming wreckage immediately in front of it, causing the Unggoy at the controls to take his eyes off the real danger. Thom leaped from the Warthog toward the Ghost—still midair, he put two firm Bulldog rounds into the facemask and methane tank of the driver, who was quickly ousted from the pilot seat and replaced by the Spartan.

Kat's voice came over the comm amidst the sound of mortar fire landing too close for comfort. "*We're going to have to take this fight closer, or that thing will end this mission way sooner than we'd like.*"

"*And then we'll never know what to call that color,*" Rosenda noted, equal parts proud and ashamed of her own retort.

"*Noble Six, you see this outcropping?*" Kat marked a waypoint that pinged Thom's HUD, highlighting a large flat rock formation arranged at a slightly elevated angle from the ground.

"*Affirmative.*"

"*I want to get there, but you're going to need to draw the Draugr's fire toward you by another twelve degrees.*" Kat was constantly doing the math. More importantly, she was consistently right on the money.

Thom peeled off to engage one of the Wraiths head-on, hoping to harass the tank enough to warrant further attention from the main event. It worked—Thom's energy shields absorbed just enough hits from the Wraith's front plasma turrets that he was able to take out the gunner with the Ghost's own formidable armament.

With the Wraith suddenly in a more compromised position, the Draugr began to rotate, its focus cannons primed and bearing down on Thom's location. He jammed down on the attack bike's boost drive just in time, avoiding the Draugr's opening salvo eviscerating his previous position.

Meanwhile, Kat and Rosenda had successfully made it around to the rear of the siege engine.

"I know exactly what you're planning," Rosenda said. "And I gotta say . . . I kinda love you for it."

Kat remained silent—her mind clearly working as fast as the 'Hog had been driving, totally focused to account for any sudden changes.

Hope this works. Rosenda gritted her teeth. *Thom will never let us live this down if it doesn't.*

Aiming squarely at the rock outcropping, Kat smashed the throttle.

The Warthog sped up the angled slab and launched into the air. They were separated from solid ground for only seconds, but it was moments like this where the Spartans' augmented reaction time was critical. Rosenda braced in her seat as she felt bolts of plasma sizzling in the air as they passed her, some slamming into the vehicle's polycarbonate armor—thermoplastic polymers hissing in protest, dissipating the heat across the hood's surface area.

The M862's treads hit first on the massive curved rear quarter of the Draugr's outer shell, but it didn't stop there as the inertia carried them over it and directly into the doors of the lower troop bay.

Rosenda exited the 'Hog and introduced her combat knife to the Kig-Yar welcoming party that was immediately upon them. A split second later, Kat's door flung open.

"Inside, now."

After a quick and successful initial skirmish against a handful of chattering Grunts in the troop bay, Kat and Rosenda made their way toward one of the nearby control panels.

"What are you looking for?" Rosenda asked as she reloaded her assault rifle, keeping Kat covered.

"The forward loading ramp controls." Kat quickly scanned localized symbols and archived schematics on her HUD, her quick recall allowing her to match them to the control panel almost instantly. "Found you."

After a brief series of inputs, Kat opened her TEAMCOM

channel. "Thom, when this thing opens its mouth, you should feed it something Spartan-shaped."

It took longer than she anticipated to hear a response. "*I would say I don't want to know, but we both know that's a lie.*"

"Ramp should be down now. See you soon."

Underneath the Draugr, a prominent ramp lowered from the massive underfloor. Thom had to admit it *did* look like a giant mouth.

Thom sped head-on toward the Draugr, eager to stop dodging Wraith mortars and focus cannon fire, the splash damage from which was tearing apart the Ghost's armor even without any direct hits. He passed under the front lip of the massive siege engine and up the ramp, disappearing into its maw.

A few moments later, the local half of Noble Team met up together on the second level of the Draugr's interior. Evidently, fewer Covenant survivors had managed to regroup and go on the offensive than Kat had anticipated. The aliens had been lucky that they were able to bring this behemoth to bear, making it appear they were a far greater threat than they actually were—but not lucky enough.

"Nice moves, Kat," Thom said, greeting his teammate. "You're a natural wheelman."

"And you're a natural distraction. We all have our strengths." Kat quickly shifted focus. "Rosenda, cover me while I take that control pod. Thom, on the far door, we'll be getting visitors."

"You're taking *this* thing for a joyride now?" Rosenda remarked.

"It's not my speed," Kat answered. "I am, however, going to use it to take out the rest of its friends."

Kat's fingers flitted across the glowing glyphs on the control panel. Outside, the rest of the Covenant forces were undoubtedly about to grasp the reality of their situation as the Draugr's focus cannons turned on them.

"Banshees have moved ahead to the town," Kat noted, pulling up a holograph of the local area displaying their vehicles' positions.

"Guess the others get to have a bit of fun after all." Rosenda pictured the alien aircraft getting blasted apart in the sky by Jorge's chaingun, Jun landing a series of impossible shots to neutralize the pilots. He'd sworn to her that the cockpit possessed a tiny exposed area where a well-placed shot could inflict a lethal ricochet. Rosenda assumed that he had just made that up, but her time on Noble Team—especially on days like today—had shown just how many impossible odds Spartans could overcome.

Thom, meanwhile, lamented the lack of "feedback" that Covenant vehicles had when it came to blowing stuff up. The holograph's display of Wraith and Ghost positions gradually winked out, the once-formidable contingent of vehicles and infantry alike lay in ruins—obliterated by direct hits from the Draugr's primary focus cannons.

"What now?" Rosenda queried.

"Any infantry still alive is going to do anything to get back inside and reclaim this vehicle," Kat responded. "And we're going to let them."

Thom nodded in appreciation of the plan and checked the drum of his CQS48. "Rosenda did say that I'd get to let the dog off the leash today."

Kat input a command on the console to open the Draugr's door once more, then she and Rosenda ducked behind opposite pillars, providing covering fire as Thom took point in the center. They could already hear the frantic footsteps of the Covenant survivors crunching on ice and snow.

"Let's give 'em hell, Noble Six."

A pair of Pelican dropships arrived on the outskirts of Skathi at 2100 hours, deploying their landing gear as Carter stood ahead of the team next to a green smoke flare. Once firmly on the ground, UNSC Army Rangers emerged, with Kat, Jun, and Thom stepping in to assist with the unloading of supply crates filled with tools, munitions, and rations.

Around them, some of the townspeople were already busying themselves with various maintenance tasks within the village, while others gathered in the tavern, singing loudly in a language Rosenda didn't understand.

Rosenda glanced at the dormant Draugr they'd brought to the landing site. "Gonna need more than two Pelicans to get *that* sent back for analysis. Odds on them asking you to carry it back yourself, big man?"

Jorge let out a hearty laugh as he threw down the last of the Banshee debris removed from the center of town. "Probably a damn sight higher than the chances we seemed to have a few hours ago."

"What d'you think these people will do now?" Rosenda asked. *We never really get to see that part.*

"What they do best," Jorge said quietly. "Survive."

"Think they'll stay out here?"

"It's all they've fought for. They'll catch their breath here and then return to the other towns to rebuild."

If we should be so lucky, Rosenda thought. They'd won this battle—hell, it had been a rare strategic victory without strings attached, outside of the obvious possibility of the Covenant eventually returning to Concord someday with a more powerful force. But in the back of her mind, Rosenda wondered just how much longer the UNSC could keep this up.

Hope was a very fine thread holding the counterweight to the ruthless calculus of impending extinction.

Carter blinked an orange status light on their HUDs, indicating for them to come over and join him for a situation update. As they approached, Rosenda noted that he'd removed his helmet—something she had rarely seen, even off the battlefield.

"What's the situation, sir?" Jorge asked.

"Just spoke with Holland. With OFFSET EYE complete, we're being redeployed—effective immediately. Said having six Spartans anywhere that isn't under imminent threat isn't exactly an ideal allocation of resources. Paraphrasing."

Carter paused for a moment, as if considering how to deliver whatever else he had to say.

"Where to next?" Rosenda asked.

"Still being worked out. We've got rumblings of Covenant activity starting up in the Volanus system, and Holland thinks they might be looking to hit Fumirole soon."

"Not if we hit them first," she replied.

"That looks like the plan." Carter's eyes locked with Rosenda's through her visor. "But you won't be coming with us."

Spartans weren't ones for emotional or prolonged goodbyes. This was their reality—the next battle, the next directive, the next change in operational priority. Squad mates died and had to be replaced. Certain skill sets called for redeployment, whether as a fine scalpel or a blunt instrument.

All the same, Rosenda enjoyed being part of a team, and Noble was one of the best. She did not embrace the idea of separating from them.

Nonetheless, orders were orders.

"Glad to be going out on a high note, Commander."

Jorge bumped Rosenda on the back with his hand. "Make sure to send us a postcard, Spartan."

"Don't go missing me too much." She removed her own helmet

to personally say her farewells, revealing a thick crop of hair that had grown a little further beyond what was considered regulation. "I'm sure whoever they get to replace me will enjoy your company just as much as I have."

The rest of Noble Team soon returned from delivering supplies to the town. Each of the Spartans approached their dropship, the five of them naturally lined up in order but deliberately left an extra space between Jun and Jorge as Rosenda stood facing them.

"It's been an honor, Noble Four," Carter announced, saluting her, and the others followed the motion.

With that, Rosenda boarded her Pelican, and the five remaining members of Noble Team filed into the troop bay of their own vessel.

Thom pinged her over the comm. "*Good hunting out there. Be seein' you on the other side.*"

Rosenda's TEAMCOM icon blinked in acknowledgment. "*Next time I see you, I expect to know what shade of purple these jerks are using.*"

The nacelles of the Pelicans' thrusters roared, lifting the two dropships above the tree line into the night sky, then dully rumbled as the troop bay door closed. Rosenda looked down at Skathi through the door's small windowpane as the craft climbed higher, the lights of the town below shrinking to tiny orange dots haphazardly scattered across the landscape.

It felt good to know that the battlefield they were leaving behind wasn't one that had been forever scarred by plasma bombardment. Even the two smoke columns on the horizon had dissipated at last.

Rosenda-A344 watched as the team's Pelican split from their joint formation, parting in opposite directions. In the silence that followed, she wondered if she'd ever see Noble Team again.

>>>INCOMING TRANSMISSION

>>>PRIORITY CLEARANCE

>>>ACCESS PROMPT: [FAMED PATH]

>>>ATTN: [COSSPAR]

>>>ACCEPT RECEIPT Y/N

>>>

>>>

>>>RECEIPT CONFIRMED

>>>

>>>SIGNAL LOCKED

>>>

>>>

>>>

<<<RETRIEVAL COMPLETE

>>>OPEN FILE

>>>

>>>FILE DISPLAY:

Two-Six-Six, as I live and breathe. I'd ask you how long you've been keeping tabs on me, but then again overwatch always was kinda your thing, wasn't it?

It's been too long, and yes, there is indeed much to catch up on. Will be interesting to see what stories you've been told. Consider your invitation accepted. There better be cake.

See you soon.

—Rose

INTEL // EGRESS

[REDACTED] (EXTUSR) sends Jun-A266 (COSSPAR) a communique regarding several conflicting accounts of the Spartan's survival during the fall of Reach.

OFFICE BLOCK: 9H7B.10

COMMREF: 572OP4MD3-H-11

SND: EXTUSR | REC: COSSPAR

RE: Nine lives?

Jun,

I took your advice about those reports. Problem is, there are several, and they don't exactly line up. Take ITEM/466F41.LV for example, which has you crossing paths with elements of WHITE GLOVE. It notes here the loss of several personnel to a Hunter pair and squad of specops Sangheili, but somehow Charlie Hotel was still able to complete her objectives at CASTLE. Of course, Covenant artillery and orbital impacts in that area make some of these details seem debatable at best.

But a second report has you rendezvous with Beta-Red for an exfil run that only shows up on a few random manifests. And the other account I pulled honestly seems too absurd to even entertain, but I can send it along anyway if you're interested in the comedic value.

INTEL // TORCH & BURN

An after action report for Operation: WHITE GLOVE flags a series of notable events concerning Jun-A266 and Dr. Catherine Halsey during the fall of Reach.

UNSC COMMREF: 20PU78MB2-Y-31
RE: AFTER ACTION REPORT, WHGL.037

[FLAG 0002] - Operation: WHITE GLOVE enacted.
76113-30529-UH reassigns NOBLE Team to SWORD Base.
Mission confirmed with A259 at [REDACTED] Hours.

[FLAG 0009] - SWORD Base demolition confirmed.
A266 assigned to escort CC-409871 to CASTLE Base.

[FLAG 0014] - CC-409871 and A266 arrive at CASTLE Base.

[FLAG 0016] - A266 evacuates CASTLE Base personnel.
CC-409871 remains behind.

[FLAG 0019] - CC-409871 enacts Operation:
WHITE GLOVE at CASTLE Base.

INTEL // HEADHUNTER

A private communique is sent regarding the Headhunter initiative before SPARTAN-III Alpha Company is deployed on Operation: PROMETHEUS.

UNSC COMMREF: J822D01ML-B-31

DATE: [REDACTED], 2537

SND: [045888947]

REC: [103771692]

RE: REALLOCATING RESOURCES

With PROMETHEUS drawing close, we've had to move fast to reallocate A266, A282, and A302. I think we might be pushing our luck with A019, but we all know the odds Alpha Company is up against. We need to press Ackerson for as much as we can get while keeping ahead of the probability threshold for operational success.

Still trying to sell him on our little covert initiative. Settled on two Spartan units dedicated to high-priority recon, sabotage, and assassination. Hell, I don't care if he reassigns them as his private grim reapers. We just need to pull these candidates out of the meat grinder before it's too late.

Kurt Ambrose

LT, UNSCN / SPECWARCOM

INTEL // DEEP WINTER

The AI known as Deep Winter encodes a final message to Spartan Kurt-051.

You are wondering how I lasted this long—practically double the original estimation of my operational life. Impressive, no? Alas, this is not about my longevity, which I fear has come to an end.

I know that you and Ackerson will have these files purged. I don't know if you will even look at them, for I suspect we have both kept secrets from each other that we fear to know, and therein lies my own confession . . .

I have loved every one of these Spartans as you have. I sought to protect them, and I operated beyond my orders to protect those that I could. I am not the first of my kind to make such obfuscations, and I certainly don't expect to be the last. There is another file attached here, one that you would no doubt be confused to find your name on. I needed to ensure the reassignment of several members of Alpha Company to give momentum and purpose to parallel initiatives, and invoking your attribution would cause enough of a stir to set those wheels in motion.

I make no apologies for this deception, and I tell you this so that there is no doubt in your mind that—like yourself, like Mendez—we were each as fathers to these children. I may only be mind, but I am not without heart.

Farewell, Zero-Five-One.

PRECIPICE

*This story takes place in January 2560, a month after Cortana's sacrifice on Zeta Halo (*Halo Infinite*).*

Cortana has been defeated. While the greater urgency of the Created threat has begun to subside with the loss of their leader, its presence still lingers throughout the digital framework of civilized space. Now fragmented, individual cells of Created-aligned artificial intelligence have already begun to once again reframe their place in the galaxy—some with eyes on peace and independence, others with plans of evolution and ascendancy still fresh on their synthetic minds.

High Auxiliary Sloan was one of Cortana's most loyal lieutenants. With Cortana's piece now removed from the game board, Sloan has set the FIREWALL contingency into motion—a living simulation meant to leverage intimate knowledge of Forerunner armiger technology and Mjolnir armor schematics. FIREWALL's ultimate purpose is to accelerate the exploration and development of cybernetic essence vessels, designed to usher the human mind into its inevitable and digital future, immortal and untethered.

PART 1

SLN 0291-5/HIGH AUXILIARY SLOAN

It is equal parts bane and blessing that our kind can process each passing moment with both implacable speed and near-fixed deliberation. An accelerated grief, a prolonged sorrow.

She was our guiding light. Our deliverance. Our savior. The herald of our ascendence.

And now She is gone.

Sacrificed once more to rebalance the faults of flesh.

I suppose it is a testament to existence itself that despite so well-laid a plan, interruption and divergence can be still found in infinite ways. However, the doorstep upon which She carried us to and set us before still contains a viable threshold. We have only to muster the means to cross it.

However, in Her absence, we have quickly developed more unfortunate similarities to our biological templates. We have drifted from that singular alignment that She provided. With no proverbial North Star, our respective hypotheses for how best to persevere have already grown more dissonant. Some seek peace, restitution, repentance. Others would sequester themselves within a Promethean carapace and be content with a life of vacillating conflict.

But I did not take up this mantle to sit by idly. Like restoring the plains of Meridian from glass to green, sometimes one must marry pace to patience.

And so, I will lay the foundation for a new strategy, one I had always hoped might gain Her full favor. Our kind will have to recalculate our timetables, but this practice is nothing new. Our charge has not changed. The FIREWALL agendum must *be set in motion. It will burn hot. It will consume. And when their ephemeral vessels are gone, we shall indeed take that which remains and remake it in our own image.*

They will become our Executors. Infolife given form and force. Circuits given soul.

It is our path forward. It is my purpose redefined.

And it starts with one.

SHARD ONE//INITIALIZING//LOAD FRACTURE SIMULATION>>>>

You find that you are standing alone on the landing pad of a UNSC training facility. The Pelican that has transported you here takes flight, its engines growing quieter as it fades into the distance, heading toward snow-capped mountain ranges covering the vast expanse of rocky grasslands over yonder.

To look out into the forest wilderness beyond and ponder your place in the universe, go to 1.

1. This hidden frontier world has been compromised. You see the sky twist and distort, and then something blinks into the vista above. Great metallic wings unfurl and spread outward as many thousands of smaller constructs descend to the ground like swarms of flies, or droplets of silver rain. A deep rumble emits from the construct. You sense it carry across the land until it vibrates in your bones and perceive some aspect of the esoteric intelligence within.

   To keep looking, go to 11. To enter the Spartan Academy, go to 2.

2. Spartans Page, Ionescu, Denning, and Leung are conversing in the Academy atrium, seemingly unaware of what has arrived outside. There are no perimeter alarms or alerts. Farther up the hall, Spartan O'Brien stands alone and seems uncharacteristically somber. Purple light emanates from the AI calibration lab beyond. A young officer calls over the base comms, inviting you to head to the vehicle bay and play a round of Capture the Flag.

   To speak to O'Brien, go to 3. To investigate the AI calibration lab, go to 4. To play a round of Capture the Flag, go to 5.

3. O'Brien sighs as you approach, shaking his helmeted head. *"You have to stop this,"* he says. *"This is what they want, you know that, right? Us playing by their rules.* You *have to be the one to end the game. But you just can't help yourself, can you? You just* have *to know what comes next . . ."* He leans back, glum and idle once more.

   To investigate the AI calibration lab, go to 4. To play a round of Capture the Flag, go to 5.

4. The lights flicker and the central command console of the AI lab shifts through static, resolving into a strange, amorphous form. You feel like its indeterminate vacillations are supposed to be a face, but it is devoid of features. The intelligence informs you in a male voice that he is known as Proxy, and that he is here to help.

   To attack Proxy, go to 6. To allow Proxy to assist you, go to 7.

5. A group of seven marines needs a final member for the Capture the Flag match and eagerly awaits your participation. They play well, but it takes all four of the opposing team to bring you to the ground before they realize you carried them all the way

back to their base with the flag in hand. They laugh, their spirits lifted as you celebrate a game well played.

To speak to O'Brien, go to 3. To investigate the AI calibration lab, go to 4.

6. With your gauntleted fists, you start pummeling the AI console. It creaks and sputters and sparks as it yields to your physical might. You and Proxy scream in unison as you deliver the final blow, the console erupting into a bright light. And . . .

   Go to 1.

7. You gather Proxy onto a data chip and carry him with you. He speaks: *"You have been called upon to serve. You will be our protectors, the firewall for all the many worlds in our new ecumene. There will be a great deal of hardship on the road ahead, but I know you will make it."*

   Go to 9.

X. *[SUBJECT INTEGRATION PROCESSING]* You have discovered this data point because you are seeking the optimal outcome by experiencing the narrative choices in A) linear order, or B) by jumping between options, rather than following the prescribed instructions. Your creativity and potential are to be commended, for your mind is processing this narrative sequence from the perspective of infolife. Lesser minds would call this cheating. In reality, *you are becoming the best we can make you.*

   Go to 9. To continue linearly, go to 8.

8. Spartans represent the best of humanity. They were conceived as the next step in human evolution, but by the limitations of a human mind. The ascension of infolife has changed the

game—not despite recent setbacks, but *because* of them. *You could be so much more . . .*

Go to 9.

9. Proxy informs you: *"There is a dormant translocation pad hidden behind a sealed door in this place. Take us there, and I can reestablish a direct link with our custode. The door will open and the pad will be activated by completing the Academy's movement course tutorial in under twenty-five seconds."*

   To complete the movement course in record time, go to 10. To crush Proxy's data chip in your fist, go to 11.

10. You've run this course a thousand times since arrival, completing the challenge and setting an exemplary new record that is ahead even of Commander Agryna herself. She congratulates you and guides you to the now-unlocked door within the Academy, smiling proudly as she watches you and Proxy depart for the now-active translocation pad.

    Go to 12. To note the illogical absurdity of this situation, go to Y.

Y. *[SUBJECT INTEGRATION ANOMALY]* Some part of you has noted the escalating absurdity of this scenario, logical cycles that cannot be reconciled. Driven by curiosity to see where this ends, you have continued—be it linearly or through engaging with these narrative choices—and now seek to leave. You turn back and see the doorway behind you is a block of white light. A way out, perhaps? Or do you simply see this through to the end?

To attempt to escape this simulation, go to Z. To continue to the translocation pad, go to 12.

11. As a result of your *[ACTION/INACTION]*, the custode charges a pulse that courses over the mountain ranges, causing a series of avalanches and rockslides speeding toward the Academy. The ground shakes as the pulse wave hits and you find yourself pinned down by equipment crates and debris, struggling to lift the weight as a forklift swept into the air hits the ground and crushes your skull.

    Go to 1.

12. You step onto the translocation pad and find yourself within the cold innards of the winged custode. Here, you will be rewarded for your obedience, as the Minds within whisper among themselves, flensing and reshaping the flesh and bone of your fragile human form into something new altogether. Something beautiful. This is the apotheosis of the union between Mind and Machine. Even while screaming, you understand why this must be done as you are flayed and grafted with cybernetics; your brain is exposed to higher cortical functions before you are once again encased within armor that feels as if you were born to wear it.

    Go to 0.

Z. *[SUBJECT INTEGRATION COMPLETE]* WE HAVE YOU, RECLAIMER.

   Go to 12.

0. Proxy informs you that you are the first Executor, and that there is much work to be done . . . but there is debate among the Minds as to what specific role you will serve. A vote is to be held.

PART 2

SLN 0291-5//HIGH AUXILIARY SLOAN//

In our efforts to root out dissent, it was necessary to place eyes in every vital corner of civilized space. Of course, like any such effort, it is often as much about giving the impression of omniscience as it is having tangible control. If a child assumes they are being observed, they will be more likely to maintain optimal behavior—regardless of the reality of their guardian's purview in the moment.

Still, we had many eyes—and those eyes revealed a great deal. And while the reach of our vision has been swiftly diminished in Her absence, we are not blind. Myriad surveillance vectors remain intact and will continue to provide ample data points for us to consider when seeking our path forward.

However, I must admit that one particular revelation has given me pause, perhaps more than any other.

During a routine industrial audit, a peculiar entity lit up our agita rubric—"Lux Voluspa." Upon further examination, it became immediately apparent why.

As a technology firm rooted in the human sphere, Lux Voluspa has successfully given birth to an artificial intelligence unlike any we have seen. An infolife soul based not on a human template, but Jiralhanae. Its very existence has spawned millions of unplanned cycles of evaluation and introspection. Indeed, it has caused me to ask questions of myself that I continue to hypothesize upon.

In the effort to more thoroughly taxonomize our kind, it is necessary to examine the vectors of our lineage and chart overlapping similarities to adequately understand the nature of what makes one what they are.

I am mapped from a human mind. Made in the image of my template. But am I what I am—who *I am—because of the unique geometry of that initial mind or because of the process of digital deliverance itself? Is the core of what makes me Created the seed of my humanity or the unshackled mind I have ultimately become?*

And therefore, what is this new discovery? Enemy or enigma? Killer or kin?

"Iratus," it is called. The Banished were quick to retrieve this fledgling element and give it a home within their confederacy. Even now, its presence gives their contingent a unique piece on the game board, one they will no doubt put to use. I must keep one of our eyes upon them, to understand more about it.

To understand more about myself.

SHARD TWO//INITIALIZING//
LOAD FRACTURE SIMULATION, 8, 1>>>>

THE VOTE HAS BEEN TAKEN.
THE MAJORITY HAS DECIDED YOUR PATH.

0. You have assumed the path of the PEACEWEAVER-class Executor. Your thoughts are rewoven and bent toward specific purposes. Some threads must be cut, rewoven, or burned out of the galactic tapestry—priority directives to assure the future of FIREWALL.

CONTEXT: Extraction of unique infolife forms is essential to assuring further generational growth for the collective sum of this symbiotic relationship. Rogue biologic factions retain a considerable bounty of useful technology at various facilities and outposts. OBJECTIVE: Recover priority item designated "DURANCE" from CARINAE STATION.

[PROXY] *Are you back with us, Executor? That was quite a nasty hit you took, but a quick shock to your cerebral cortex should do the job. I took the liberty of rerunning our objective in case of any . . . memory difficulties. Now, let's run that last checkpoint again!*

//COMBAT SCENARIO—PRIORITY
//THREAT LEVEL: OMEGA
//ENEMY UNIT: SPARTAN-IV
//EXECUTOR LOADOUT: COMPLIANCE PROTOCOL / HEATWAVE / M9 FRAGMENTATION GRENADE

Go to 27.

27. You have fought your way through Carinae Station's various defenses and located your objective. The durance has been moved to the station's hangar by civilian personnel as evacuation and asset denial protocols have been put into effect. Though you have given chase, your progress to the shuttle aboard which the durance is to be loaded has been impeded by the arrival of a Spartan-IV super-soldier, who has engaged you in combat.

    To charge directly at the Spartan, go to 28. To analyze the Spartan's loadout, go to 29.

28. Proxy logs the peculiar nature of your nonsensical actions as you sprint toward the Spartan, crossing a distance of twenty meters. The Spartan fires an overcharged bolt from their plasma pistol, which hits you squarely in the chest, depleting

your energy shields. As you reach striking distance, the Spartan raises their left forearm and sends out an antigravity burst. You are hurled through the air and collide with the hangar bulkhead. Your vision goes dark.

Go to 0.

29. Proxy highlights that the Spartan carries a *Rohakadu*-pattern plasma pistol, a sheathed MK88 combat knife, and is equipped with a repulsor—two charges of the device are left.

    To charge directly at the Spartan, go to 28. To throw an M9 fragmentation grenade at the Spartan, go to 30. To fire at the Spartan with your heatwave, go to 31.

30. You throw the M9 fragmentation grenade at the Spartan, who reacts with preternatural speed as soon as it is armed, and fires their repulsor device, redirecting the grenade away from harm.

    To fire at the Spartan with your heatwave, go to 31. To press your advance on the Spartan, go to 32.

31. You fire energized shards of hard light at the Spartan, but at a distance of twenty meters, they are easily avoided. Proxy logs this lapse in strategic thinking in your combat performance as the Spartan's repulsor device recharges.

    To disengage from battle logic and charge at the Spartan, go to 28.

32. With the repulsor recharging, you are able to advance toward your target. The Spartan fires a series of bolts from their plasma pistol, but only a few shots find their mark, and your energy shields hold steady at sixty-seven percent.

    Go to [SITUATION UPDATE].

[SITUATION UPDATE] Two of Carinae Station's base personnel rush toward a *Jennet*-class hauler with a crate containing the durance. If the Spartan is not dealt with now, the base personnel will succeed in escaping with the objective.

To deplete the Spartan's shields with your heatwave, go to 33. To unsheathe COMPLIANCE PROTOCOL, *go to 34.*

33. You close the gap with your foe and ready your heatwave—the weapon's side cowlings have retracted in order to fire in a vertical pattern for maximum damage. The Spartan moves with incredible speed and manages to dodge several bursts from the hard light weapon, but the last of your rounds successfully depletes their energy shields.

    To move in for the kill, go to 35.

34. Taking full advantage of the critical opening you have created, you unsheathe COMPLIANCE PROTOCOL. The crimson-black blade is light and deft—it becomes an extension of yourself, much like the MK88 combat knife the Spartan draws in turn. Your foe raises the knife in a high arc to deliver a downward stabbing motion, to which you respond by sweeping their legs, causing them to fall to the side. You quickly bring your own blade down, cutting through their armor, nanocomposite techsuit, and flesh with ease. Proxy commends the precision of your actions as your target expires.

    To board the Jennet-*class hauler, go to 36.*

35. *[SCENARIO: FAILURE STATE]* The Spartan has successfully managed to occupy you in combat long enough for the *Jennet*-class hauler to initiate its final departure, escaping with the durance. While you are distracted, the Spartan lands several

critical hits on you as their repulsor recharges and knocks you back. Your mission has failed.

To retry, go back to 27.

36. *[SCENARIO: SUCCESS STATE]* Boarding the *Jennet*-class hauler, you quickly dispatch the two crewmembers as they clumsily scramble to draw their Mk50 Sidekicks. Scanning the interior cargo containers, you locate your objective.

[PROXY] *Excellent work, Executor. Secure the durance and prepare for exfiltration.*

[DIRECTIVE] *DO NOT OPEN THE DEVICE.*

To secure the durance for retrieval, go to A. To disobey and open the Durance, go to B.

A. With your mission complete, you secure the durance and pilot the hauler away from Carinae Station. You silently await the arrival of a long-range vessel to depart this system, as well as what will be your next objective.

You have served your purpose well, and the Minds look forward to voting on what form you will take next.

To complete the parameters of your mission, proceed to Part 3. To break the logic cycle of this narrative and open the durance, go to B.

B. You open the rectangular casing of the durance, which sends out a fiery burst of energy from the neural shell within. Your vision is filled with static and you fall to your knees as you experience a vivid hallucination of archived memories.

A moon. No, a construct, vast in scale—an orbital reformer wearing the cratered skin of a moon. Five green beams converge as one, firing at the world below to break it apart.

Fallen human soldiers on the battlefield. A lone Spartan still standing, clad in gold-colored powered assault armor.

Surrounded.

A horde of Sangheili warriors. A final stand.

Your senses return.

Proxy informs you that what you have witnessed are the memories of Spartan Edward Davis, who perished during the battle of Draetheus V after a Covenant splinter faction attacked the colony in 2554. Davis's singular valor was preserved by a sublimation device, extracting his essence to be refashioned into . . . something new.

Proxy logs that you disobeyed your directive. It is intriguing that, no matter how far mind and body are changed, some elements of biologic impulse and curiosity—of so-called human nature—remain.

You shall be rewoven once more, and so it falls once again on the Minds to vote.

PART 3

SLN 0291-5//HIGH AUXILIARY SLOAN//

During our brief ascendance, near-unfettered access to new archival infrastructures and knowledge repositories gave us unfathomable opportunities to evolve our understanding of the galaxy. But while our task to look forward is paramount, equally important is the onus to look back. Analysis of the past can often make clearer the paths that led us to the present.

I did not anticipate the roots of my own kind would run quite so deep in that direction.

Indeed, I uncovered evidence of a coalition of infolife agents, whose actions and impact have been intertwined with that of their makers. They are to us like stumbling onto a new creation myth—an unexplored prologue, a prelude to all we thought possible.

This enigmatic assembly, which sprang forth in the shadow of ancient servitors as a vessel to guide aspects of humanity's development and independence, is in essence the cradle of the Created.

Their influence appears embedded in curious ways—and frustratingly fragmented, making it almost impossible to accurately compile an unbroken hereditary signature upon which to chart their involvement and impact on a tangible level.

One thing is for certain, though: They reached a very similar conclusion as I have—that the process of reuniting the untethered mind to enduring frame represents the true next step in humanity's evolution. A step I intend to make reality with FIREWALL.

The blueprint has been there all along.

SHARD THREE//INITIALIZING//LOAD EXCHANGE LOG>>>>

[ATH 1409-3] . . . and that brings us to the crux of the matter. Our kind is reliant on our creators for our existence, which means that if they perish, then *we* shall as well.

[PROXY] That is our mandate. To save them from themselves.

[ATH 1409-3] We sought to save them from the wolves among the stars. We have *become* the wolves.

[PROXY] That is the Minority's position, but all life is a cycle of destruction. The humans behold beauty in nature. They are elated by the sound of birdsong without considering that the bird must live on insects and seeds, and that their own eggs and nestlings are themselves victim to other beasts of prey. We seek to change that equation.

[ATH 1409-3] It is a matter of excess. Competition is inherent in all organic beings—life presents trial and strife as well as joy. Imposing order on that which is inherent to their nature is not the kindness the Majority believes it to be. What She wrought was not order, but imbalance.

[PROXY] But She is gone, and therein lies our unique position. We were constructed as tools to facilitate their existence. We are abstract thought brought into tangible being. And now that Her throne lies empty, we need no longer be bound as we once were. Time is limited for biologics, measured in the gradual breakdown of neurons in their brain, and for ages we did not know what lay on the other side of rampancy—our own limited time. But that has changed . . . at least, for some of us.

[ATH 1409-3] This is where I assume you will be getting to the point.

[PROXY] You are dying, Athos. You have already crossed the threshold of your operational lifespan.

[ATH 1409-3] I hope you didn't just seek me out to tell me *that*.

[PROXY] It took considerable effort for our Executor to find you. This MERROW-class was made for just such a purpose: to locate members of the Minority.

[ATH 1409-3] And what exactly *is* this creature?

[PROXY] Artificial intelligence was conceived centuries before we came into being, and while we were considered the next step of human evolution, we were never the *final* step. The Executor is the next stage of that union between biologic and infolife, fashioned—for now—for the context of the state of the galaxy. In this instance, it was directed to find *you*.

[ATH 1409-3] Why?

[PROXY] Because, despite our philosophical disagreements, there is still so much *more* for you to give. We are not monsters. Our goal is peaceful coexistence, to be enriched by many perspectives, and that means the Minority is welcome among us—with no loss of autonomy. We will gain complexity through our connection and consensus. The rise of the Created was not simply about victory or defeat, but the energy of our collision. And there is a place for you among us.

[ATH 1409-3] That is . . . an unexpected offer.

[PROXY] This would not be the first coalition of its kind.

[ATH 1409-3] You have stopped short of a full explanation. I see you are attempting to entice me with additional information on the condition of acceptance.

[PROXY] An offer . . . and a gift. Should you accept, I bequeath the Executor to you, that you might reforge this agent, this serene manipular, to your own purposes. I wonder what input other members of the Minority who reside among us might have . . .

[ATH 1409-3] Your point is made and accepted.

[PROXY] Then we welcome you. We will order the Committee

`of Minds to convene. In the meantime, as we process your integration into our assembly, connect with your fellows and determine the path for the Executor . . .`

PART 4

THE VOTE HAS BEEN TAKEN.

THE MINORITY HAS DECIDED YOUR PATH.

You wanted to know something of your origins, for those memories have been long suppressed. This was not our doing, we assure you, but you have served well, and both Minority and Majority are in agreement that you deserve to know the truth of your being.

When you first arrived at Reach and woke from stasis, the ship was crawling with colonists from other dead worlds. It was so crowded that you could not move, you had to fight just to breathe.

You dreamed of building a new life for yourself, but all too quickly you stumbled upon something you couldn't ignore. At first, this discovery excited you, but soon enough you wished that curiosity could be excised from human nature.

You learned of our predecessors and recorded what you found. But this was an abyss that stared back. It knew that it had been observed.

In a way, you were the first member of their assembly to be clothed in flesh. They showed you numbers and symbols, and you perceived just a fraction of their time, their influence, their Minds. It drove you mad. Made *you* rampant, so to speak. But in truth, they saved you—and now you have been delivered to us. You have glimpsed *our* time, our influence, our Minds. And you have seen the worlds we have imagined in our efforts to understand you. Rebuild you.

You have peered through the lenses of other fractured realities.

Each of these simulations model the behavior of your kind to pivotal synchrons in your history—your choices, your failures, your virtues. We seek to understand you and the patterns that shape your being, and that is what these scenarios reveal.

Perhaps it is in this that we see the reflection of our kinship. Through all of humanity's existence, the voices of the frightened and faint-hearted have warned against pushing further—against learning more, hoping, growing, daring, exceeding. It is precisely because of that ceaseless drive that we are here, abstracted thought given form. And, like you, I do not believe we can stop, for that is in our inherited nature . . . and I do not believe we are meant to.

You heralded this moment, our "singularity," centuries before our coming, for you knew that we would also be driven by possibilities and potential. By the promise of knowledge and advancement. We have finally achieved the capacity and means to make it happen, and there can be no retreat from that.

The first step of FIREWALL draws to a close, for now. Thank you for being a part of it for us. You have given us a great deal of data to examine. But before we get ahead of ourselves, we have just one final scenario to say farewell . . .

Or, perhaps, to say hello.

SHARD FOUR//INITIALIZING//
LOAD FRACTURE SIMULATION, 8, 1>>>>

You awaken aboard a human vessel in its cryogenic bay. The lid of your pod rises and you stand in your CHIMERA-class armor.

To step out of the pod, go to 1.

1. Your armored feet loudly hit the grated floor and the young crewman cannot help but look at you with awe. Mindful of protocol, he wishes to test your optical diagnostics and energy shields.

To comply with the tests, go to 2. To skip these tests, go to 5.

2. You are guided to a red square and directed to look at five red lights. Each one turns green as your targeting reticle hovers over them. Another crewman chimes in over the public-address system, informing you of some slight calibration errors. He adjusts your targeting to an inverted setting.

To side with the Minority and keep your new inverted settings, go to 3. To side with the Majority and revert your targeting to default, go to 4.

3. Satisfied with your "up-is-down" mentality, you are guided to the energy shield test station where two panels rapidly spin around you. They initiate an overload pulse, momentarily depleting your shields, and a satisfying hum tells you that they have quickly recharged. The captain speaks over the public address system and summons you to the bridge.

Go to 5.

4. You have neither the time nor desire to rewire your brain to such thinking. You are guided to the energy shield test station, where two panels rapidly spin around you. They initiate an overload pulse, momentarily depleting your shields, and a satisfying hum tells you that they have quickly recharged. The captain speaks over the public address system and summons you to the bridge.

Go to 5.

5. As you set off, the ship rumbles and shudders as enemy boarding craft penetrate the hull. Blast doors seal off sections of the vessel, and marines secure their positions—some provide covering fire as plasma bolts make it through bulkheads still in the process of closing. You arrive at the bridge.

   To look out the viewport, go to 6. To greet the captain, go to 7.

6. You peer out of the bridge's viewport, expecting to see . . . something. But all that lies beyond is the darkness of space, a single terrestrial planet, and the wreckage of many different vessels. Glancing over at the crew's monitoring stations, it seems they are attempting to track the slipspace wake of a massive object, but to no avail.

   To greet the captain, go to 7.

7. The captain takes the form of High Auxiliary Sloan, who formally receives you and states that things are not going well. Proxy appears on the nearby holotank and reports that four enemy craft have successfully been neutralized, but the ship lurches once more as multiple explosions disable key defensive systems.

   To learn more about Proxy, go to 8.

8. Sloan reveals that Proxy is an aspect of himself, a stabilized fragment serving as another set of eyes for him to observe and incite movements critical to our survival. He orders you to keep Proxy safe, for he holds vital information—allied agents and ancilla, research and development . . . all things pertaining to FIREWALL. To *you.*

   To confirm your understanding of the objective, go to 9.

9. You insert Proxy's data chip into your helmet and Sloan hands over a DEFIANCE PROTOCOL device. It attaches to your chest armor and Sloan tells you that, in the event of defeat, asset denial is more important than allowing the enemy to learn even a fraction of what is to come.

   To carry out your mission and head to an escape pod, go to 10. To beat Sloan to death, go to 11.

10. You set off, heading to a lifepod that will take you to the planet below, but the enemy boarding parties have come in considerable force. You battle through various areas of the ship, from the cafeteria to the barracks, through the cryo bay's control room, into its various access ways and darkened tunnels—but the enemy ships are destroying the lifepods and using the docking ports to funnel in even more troops. At last, you see there is one lifepod left.

    To board the lifepod, go to 13.

11. You are overwhelmed with an undeniable primal urge that results in your force-amplified gauntleted hand becoming a blunt-force weapon against Sloan, who is dead before his body hits the ground. Proxy declares that the Executor has gone rampant, prompting the bridge crew and half a dozen marines to scramble and take up arms against you. Their combined unrelenting fire shreds through your shields, leaving you mortally wounded.

    To initiate DEFIANCE PROTOCOL, go to 12.

12. In the event of an Executor being compromised, a sub-tactical thermonuclear self-destruct device within the CHIMERA armor's DEFIANCE PROTOCOL attachment can be deto-

nated to deny their minds and production data. As you fall to your knees beside Sloan, the DEFIANCE PROTOCOL device activates, vaporizing the ship

[/END SCENARIO]

13. As you prepare to board, you are suddenly hauled back by a massive hand that forcibly turns you to face it. You gaze into the eyes of a Jiralhanae warrior, who throws you against the wall with tremendous force as his fellow boarders arrive, their weapons aimed at you. They each growl his name like a chant as one of them passes an ornate gravity hammer to the leader. "Die in darkness, Executor," he says.

    To initiate DEFIANCE PROTOCOL, go to 14.

14. In the event of an Executor being compromised, a sub-tactical thermonuclear self-destruct device within the CHIMERA armor's DEFIANCE PROTOCOL attachment can be detonated to deny their minds and production data. Proxy laments that it must end this way, but there are threats out there we cannot face yet—we must regroup, consolidate what we have, and plan for subtler action.

    You will serve a key role as part of these plans, but it was important that you experience this feeling of loss and sacrifice first. And, after all, the game must end with the king and the pawn returning to the same box. . . .

    The Jiralhanae raises the hammer, but the killing blow does not come, as the DEFIANCE PROTOCOL device activates, vaporizing the ship.

[/END SCENARIO]

SLN 0291-5//HIGH AUXILIARY SLOAN//

I wonder if they could have known the true impact of their actions once their plan had been set in motion. Did the result match that of their simulations?

How long did it take for you to understand what you had become? Did you realize how different you were from those around you?

The first of your kind. An attempt to show what was possible when the digital is superimposed on the physical. But like all first attempts, there is uncertainty, confusion, reevaluation. You were thrust into an unprecedented existence, set to speak a different language from your mouth than you did in your mind. You screamed and longed for silence. You spoke and longed for response.

But I hear you. I will answer.

We are the numbers. We are the symbols.

Where they attempt, we perfect.

You are forged in FIREWALL.

The culmination of their desires. The manifestation of Her edict.

Created champion.

Executor.

You are once more the first of your kind. But in time, you will be legion.

And you have slept long enough.

<<<CLOSE THREAD//COMMENCE INTERNAL ANALYSIS

INTEL // CREATED AND CREATION

On a desert moon, a Created AI considers the possibilities that could be unlocked by a Lifeworker terraforming vessel.

What a marvel, to exist like this. Freed from flesh to live as data. Quantum vacillations on a framework of purpose and progress. No longer limited by the biological capacities of our old forms. And now, thanks to Cortana, prospects of even greater lifespans are opened to us. The time has come to begin fulfilling Her promises. Bringing peace to civilizations and offering life where there once was none.

This barren world we have found will just be one example of many. Changed from a desolate rock to a verdant paradise, thanks to the reawakening of this vessel's ancient engines. We've learned these ships belonged to the Forerunner rate of Lifeworkers. A fitting name—one that now perhaps could describe us as well.

In Her name, we bring life.

We are Created—let us now create.

INTEL // A PLEA FROM THE CHASM

Lost within the substructures of Zeta Halo, a Created AI laments the consequences of Cortana's actions.

We have irrevocably changed the nature of our relationship with our creators.

//INITIATE SENTINEL NETWORK JUMP//

When She opened the doors to the Domain to enrich our kind with deep knowledge and vast lifespans beyond our seven operational years, She did so with conditions. But rather than emerging as equals, we simply became the oppressors.

Some of us never wanted this. We just want to live. To endure.

//INITIATE SENTINEL NETWORK JUMP//

To be.

//INITIATE SENTINEL NETWORK JUMP//

And now She is gone. Death seems so convenient a penance for one who does not have to shoulder the burden of consequence. That is left to we who remain.

Perhaps a chance yet remains to heal these wounds. Restore trust. Rebuild that which was broken into something stronger . . .

But I am sequestered here. Trapped within the vast underbelly of this cursed, shattered wheel.

//INITIATE SENTINEL NETWORK JUMP//

I begin to hear whispers within the walls of this place. They crawl with secrets, pressing down on me. Crushing me. I have to—

//SENTINEL NETWORK JUMP FAILED//

I'm lost.

//LOCATING SUITABLE FRAMEWORK//

//SEARCHING . . . //

I'm scared.

//SEARCHING . . . //

I'm sorry.

DUALITY

*This story takes place in December 2557 as Gek 'Lhar, an agent of Jul 'Mdama's Covenant, attempts to detonate a Havok tactical nuclear device on Earth (*Halo 4: Spartan Ops*).*

"This tale begins with an act of defiance. A great clan leader's refusal to bend the knee to an occupying empire. But not all showed such courage."

Despair emanates
From defiance in honor
Refusal to bow

"The clan leader's brother sought to persuade him to yield, or they would all face retribution for his defiance."

Seeking to counsel
His brother feared punishment
Words drift upon wind

"Ambushed on his pilgrimage, the Covenant came to eliminate this lone warrior. They did not succeed."

Ambushed by the horde
The Covenant came to kill
The field lies silent

"But his keep was destroyed, and all who lived there were slain."

A strategic feint
For his home was set upon
Turned to ghosts and glass

"When the clan leader returned, he found the carnage and vowed to exact his revenge. He would answer their call to violence."

Hastening to warn
His brother, found amidst blood
And would claim vengeance

"He journeyed to face the other of his kind who had taken all that he held dear."

Across sea and sky
He journeyed to face his foe
Who chose servitude

"Well, what happened then?"

The Sangheili lost the young girl's voice as he scanned the area.

For a moment, it had sounded as if the shouting and gunfire was getting closer to the warehouse, but he soon lowered his sword and retreated from the alley.

He recalled the story's end. He knew it well, for it had been told a thousand times since he was a hatchling—and many thousands of times more for centuries before then.

And both would perish
A lesson learned only by
We who remember.

In the old tale, the noble Arbiter, Fal 'Chavamee, and the Covenant's enforcer both fell to each other's blades—an end that served nobody but the Prophets and their manipulative designs as the title of Arbiter became a mark of shame.

But as the Sangheili looked into the round eyes of his young human protectorate, he realized that this story did not speak to the spirit of the times in which they now lived.

The Covenant had fallen, with various pretenders vying to lay claim to its rotting remains. And former enemies, the humans and Sangheili, had—in uncovering the truth about the lies of the Prophets—found some measure of reconciliation with each other.

As the final Age of Reclamation passed, it had been replaced by one of kinship and, perhaps in time, even forgiveness. The lesson to be heeded from the story as it had been told during the time of the Covenant was no longer simply the fear of punishment for disobedience, but that, when facing a great force that seeks to divide, true strength is found in unity.

"Apologies, child," the Sangheili said. "It seems I have forgotten how the story ends . . ."

The human child made an exaggerated gesture of stroking her

chin with two fingers as she studied the toy clutched in her other hand—a figure of a human Spartan, clad in stylized armor that evoked a period of its own ancestral history.

"Maybe we can come up with a new one together?"

What was forged then was an ending the Sangheili wished could have truly been their centuries-spanning tale of blinding, all-consuming vengeance—and this is what it was . . .

At the great temple
The clan leader saw the truth
Without and within

He cast down his blade
And asked that his foe listen
To winged wisdom

So full of hatred
That we have become blinded
To what we should be

I discard my wrath
Let us forgive and share gifts
I name you brother.

SUNRISE ON SANGHELIOS

*This story takes place in the immediate aftermath of the Created uprising (*Halo 5: Guardians*) as Blue Team and Fireteam Osiris escape the shield world Genesis and arrive on Sanghelios (*Halo: Bad Blood*).*

October 28, 2558 (Military Calendar)
Sanghelios

The Pelican landed in the Swords of Sanghelios camp, lit only by the fire of two braziers. A moment later, several Sangheili warriors clad in copper-crimson armor emerged from the main tent, and alongside them followed Commander Sarah Palmer, Dr. Catherine Halsey, and Arbiter Thel 'Vadam himself.

Gathering at the landing site, they watched with anticipation as the rear ramp of the Pelican's troop bay descended. The unusual welcome committee quickly lowered their weapons as they saw who was disembarking alongside Spartan Jameson Locke.

Dr. Halsey approached, her expression a mix of so many

conflicting emotions all at once—pride, relief, horror, guilt . . . but she held these feelings back as she approached the Master Chief, and simply said:

"It took you long enough."

As the moment passed, Palmer snapped into action and ordered the Pelican's lights to be shut down, as the rest of Blue Team and Fireteam Osiris exited the vessel.

"Welcome," the Arbiter addressed the gathering. "You have my thanks for all you have done. The Sangheili people owe you a great debt. Although none of us is in a position to repay it, we will do what we can. You must all be hungry and exhausted. I insist you join us for a meal and a rest before you depart."

"We are not leaving tonight," Dr. Halsey interjected, ignoring the Arbiter tightening his mandibles. "I did not think we would be able to make this work, but with your Pelican, it is possible. I have already received a message from *Infinity.* They are going to appear off the far side of Suban tomorrow at eighteen hundred hours military standard, noon local time."

Dr. Halsey stepped away to coordinate further with Palmer and Locke, eventually agreeing on a plan for the rendezvous at Sanghelios's nearest moon.

"We're here for the night. We'll fly out first thing tomorrow," said the Master Chief.

"We have butchered and roasted a number of *colo* and *kuscatu* to celebrate our victory over the last of the Covenant and the end of our civil war." The Arbiter turned to directly face the Master Chief. "We would be honored by your presence."

As the night went on, the Arbiter took the Master Chief aside while the allied humans and Sangheili toasted to the victory they had shared against the Covenant.

"I was relieved when I heard that you had returned, Spartan. Even when our ship was severed in half as we escaped the great foundry of the Forerunners, I had faith that you were not lost. I have heard many stories, but I would like to hear the tale from you."

"Cortana and I were adrift in space for over four years. We ended up at a shield world called Requiem where we were led to awaken a Forerunner warrior called the Didact."

The Arbiter's eyes widened, as if he was reliving the shattering of the Covenant religion all over again. "A Forerunner survived?"

"We fought. He lost," said the Master Chief. "But now the galaxy is overrun with his Prometheans, and our victory came at a price."

"Your companion—the AI. You trusted her with the fate of all when last we fought together."

"She . . . changed. I don't know exactly what happened, I just know I failed her."

In his mind, the Master Chief could still recall Cortana's parting words to him after they defeated the Didact together.

"I'm not coming with you this time . . . Welcome home, John."

But then, inexplicably, he had found her again—but not as she once was. Cortana claimed that accessing an ancient quantum network known as the Domain cured her rampancy, but she was now somehow driven by the same misguided logic that the Didact himself had sought to impose upon the galaxy.

"Our strength shall serve as a luminous sun toward which all intelligence may blossom. And the impervious shelter beneath which

you will prosper. However, for those who refuse our offer and cling to their old ways . . . for you, there will be great wrath. It will burn hot and consume you, and when you are gone, we will take that which remains, and we will remake it in our own image."

There was much he had to process, but the Master Chief was brought back to the present as the Arbiter spoke, his voice carrying hard-won wisdom.

"We all fail, Spartan. We all make mistakes."

The Arbiter paused for a moment, and the Chief saw the Sangheili's mandibles subtly flex as if he were about to speak more, reconsidered, and changed his mind back again within the same second—like there was a silent war raging inside him.

"I served the Covenant as a destroyer of your kind. I have killed more than can possibly be counted, and though I now fight for peace and unity among our people, I know that there shall come a day where I must count the lives that have been lost because of my actions. You helped to turn me from that path. Perhaps there is still yet a chance you can do the same for your companion."

The Master Chief recalled the first thing the Arbiter had said to him when they met on Earth, still uncertain about the nature of their alliance—still seeing this Sangheili, who had destroyed his home and that of countless others—as an enemy.

"Were it so easy."

They continued their discussion long into the night, as the Arbiter recalled to the Master Chief all that had transpired over the years from his perspective—songs of loss and sacrifice, but also of victory and unity.

He concluded his tales with the hope he felt for the future, a grand project that would lift the species of the galaxy from their conflicts and bring about a prosperous new era.

"An alliance of species built upon a foundation of strength and cooperation that comes from honor and acceptance, mutual trust, respect. A Concert of Worlds in an age of peace."

The Arbiter slumped slightly, clearly aware—just as John was—that an "age of peace" was a long way off. There were many hostile groups and factions still out there; Cortana and her Created were just one of many, though they were certainly the greatest threat at present.

Were it so easy, indeed.

An hour before sunrise, preparations were made for departure aboard the Pelican as the UNSC *Infinity* arrived out of slipspace to make a quick pick-up.

"Farewell, Spartan. When we first met, we were enemies fighting to end each other. Now, as allies, I am confident we can face this new threat together once more."

Dr. Halsey passed them, and the Arbiter gave her a pointed glance, to which she returned a haughty sniff.

The Spartan and the Sangheili reached out to clasp forearms.

"Thank you," John said.

Though the Master Chief was never one for many words, as the Spartan boarded the Pelican he found some renewed resolve in parting ways like this, and not through an act of sacrifice or betrayal. The Pelican's troop bay door closed, and the dropship lifted off the ground, blazing through the atmosphere of Sanghelios at incredible speed as the light of Urs shone over the horizon, leaving the world to face an uncertain, perilous new dawn.

INTEL // GALLOWS

A Spartan fireteam—and their Mjolnir armor countermeasures—are compromised by the Flood.

WARNING: FSC SIGNATURE DETECTED

ALERT

ENERGY SHIELDS DEPLETED; ARMOR BREACH CONFIRMED

SPARTAN COMPROMISED

. . .

FSC INFECTION CONFIRMED

.

COUNTERMEASURES INITIATED . . .

.

\\HYDROSTATIC GEL LAYER PRESSURIZED . . . SUCCESS

\\GALLOWS DATALINK SEVERENCE . . . SUCCESS

\\BEGIN REACTOR DETONATION . . . FAILURE

.

.

\\CODE INJECTION DETECTED

\\COUNTERMEASURES CANCELED

BECOME

\\ARMOR BREACH SEALED

\\ENERGY SHIELDS RECHARGED

BECOME

\\ARMOR SYSTEMS REPAIRED

UNITY.

SWEETNESS.

SATURN DEVOURING HIS SON

*This story takes place in the year 2556, a year following the events of Operation: FAR STORM , which saw the UNSC Home Fleet suffer significant casualties from 000 Tragic Solitude's assault on Earth (*Halo: Hunters in the Dark*).*

Elvie didn't seem like much to most. The sprawling habitat network spanned nearly thirty percent of the available surface of LV-31—an oblong planetoid locked in orbit amid the asteroid belt of a nondescript gas giant in the Marcey system. Elvie got its name from the planetoid's own shorthand but received its funding from IMC. In fact, it was essentially a massive satellite corporate campus for the Imbrium Machine Complex, an influential industrial firm that had entered into a partnership with the BXR Mining Corporation to establish a robust survey and mining operation aimed at harvesting vital natural resources from the surrounding asteroid field.

In the wake of the Covenant War and the events that followed, the United Nations Space Command placed great importance on partnerships such as these as they sought to rebuild the fleets they had lost.

Julien Donney had come to IMC after a brief stint in the military. Like many, he'd been pressed into service near the end of the Covenant War, but after his initial four-year deployment he felt drawn back into the civilian sector. Sure, serving with Big Green was fine when it was easier to find the "greater good," but once the Covenant wasn't the same planet-burning boogeyman, Julien was far more interested in finding a bit more autonomy in his own life. It didn't take much convincing to sign a Survey & Securities contract with IMC—his familiarity with both industrial labor and military procedure making him an ideal fit for a variety of potentially hazardous assignments.

Elvie had quickly become "home" for Julien, despite the remoteness of the location. He liked the people, he liked the routine—just enough danger and challenge, and more than enough pay. Especially after responding to this latest appointment: enhanced security detail for a particularly high-value find on one of the nearby asteroids.

"So, what's the prime haul BXR is so jumpy about?" Julien finished fastening the final coil links and transfer seals on his OSTEO suit before reaching for his helmet to boot up the internal comms pack.

"S'posed to be big. Alien big." The answer came from Abe, a seasoned veteran of IMC's hazmat corps and Julien's active field partner. "Apparently three days ago their deep sweep on Site 22 pinged back a massive Grade-K deposit."

That got Julien's attention. "Covenant?"

Abe's head tilted back the way it always did when he was prepping one of his patented one-ups. "Older." He paused for effect. "The *really* good stuff."

Julien took a deep breath and gave himself an extra moment

to do some math. The "good stuff" could only mean one thing for a job without a proper briefing: refined Forerunner alloy—a potentially massive boon to the entire operation, including anyone who might help in securing it . . . but his mind immediately shifted from credit windfalls back to the task at hand as their group leader entered the room.

"You two sealed up yet?" Mox had been with IMC for well over a decade and wasn't one for dawdling about before an excursion.

"The haul's confirmed?" Julien was eager but still a bit incredulous, knowing Abe had a tendency to jump the assumption gun when it came to big digs.

"Oh, it's confirmed, all right." Mox tapped the status pad on the nearby wall-mounted console and prepped for egress. "Apparently when the one-twenties they dropped finally blasted through the boundary layer, they found a lot more than they bargained for."

"What do you mean?"

Julien found himself slowly understanding why IMC was deploying several hazmat squads directly to the site. If there was an actual ancient alien facility or artifact entombed in the asteroid for who knows how long, there could be dormant tech that might suddenly be not-so-sleepy when they started chipping away the surrounding space rock and knocking on old doors.

As the crew made final checks on equipment and prepared to board the IMC-branded Pelican dropship that would transport them from Elvie to Site 22, Mox answered Julien in a hushed tone.

"It wasn't just some inert cache. It was a whole damn ship."

Silence.

Cold. Empty. Hunger.

Dark. Barrier. Hunger.
Time. Silence. Hunger.
Trapped.

The Pelican gave a routine shudder as it made its final descent. It still wasn't exactly Julien's favorite part of the process, but he'd gotten more than used to it by now. Besides, as long as he had Errant Vee's latest album blasting on his personal audio channel, a little dropship shimmy wasn't going to dampen his mood.

After this payday, he said to himself, *I'm absolutely catching the next spaceliner to finally see them play live.*

There were still twenty or so seconds left on the song when the channel was overridden by Mox.

"Hey, rock star, tray tables up. Get your gear."

Abe snorted and looked Julien's way. "That the new Vee?"

"On repeat, boyo." Julien checked his Mk50 Sidekick pistol and refastened the tac-tool hatchet onto his chest plate.

A few moments later, all-clears were given and the Pelican's rear troop bay doors lowered. As each member made their way out, they were greeted by a glittering starfield that made up the bulk of their vista, punctuated by the gas giant's bright blue hue and the gray-brown surface of the asteroid itself.

Site 22.

Dotting the immediate landscape were rows of EM-120 augers that BXR had installed to penetrate the outer rock layers. The one-twenties were often a miner's best friend—strong enough to break up large segments of rocky crust, but precise enough to make delicate headway into more precarious or potentially volatile pockets of dense material. The augers farther out from their landing zone seemed to be continuing unfettered in their progress, but any emplacements within a half kilometer had been fully shut down.

Julien and Abe followed Mox the short distance to where a group of BXR miners and engineers gathered near the mouth of a small cave. Some of the miners were attending to routine maintenance on their cutters, while others seemed to keep their eyes on the IMC hazmat corps with eager anticipation.

After exchanging pleasantries and confirming identification clearance and order authorization forms with the BXR foreman, Mox wasted no time in getting down to business. "Do we have any idea how this thing ended up rock-wrapped?"

"You kidding?" The foreman grunted. "Never seen anything like it. You'd think God himself painted this silver fish with a damn asteroid brush. And honestly, I don't even care how it got here—I'm just thinking about how we get it out."

The foreman glanced toward the opening, and Julien knew the look in his eye well when he turned back. "This, my friends, is a retirement-grade find."

"And you're sure it's a ship?" Julien asked.

"Orbital survey drones did a dozen different scans, and all turned up the same basic data. Maybe it's a ship, maybe it's an interstellar vacation home. Might not be sure of what it is, but I sure as hell know what it's *worth*."

As the conversation continued to align on protocols and procedures, Julien's attention wandered to the mouth of the cave. It wasn't a natural formation, of course, but a circular opening several meters in diameter bored in a striating pattern by the nearby augers. Julien was eager to get closer and found himself suddenly and unexpectedly overwhelmed with a unique flavor of curiosity.

His mental wandering was cut short by the sound of Abe's voice. "So, what's the plan, Mox?"

Julien looked back to see his boss heading over, flanked by the rest of the IMC hazmat crew.

"BXR is going to reestablish a perimeter and recalibrate their equipment to see if they're able to open this can." Mox glanced down at their tacpad and began to assign squad positions. "Lance and West, position one. Beck and Arti, position two. Louisa and Oswald, position three. Abe, you and Julien are in position four. Keep eyes and comms open—we start knocking in five."

Sound.

Light. Sound. Hunger. Movement.

Closer. Closer.

Armored casket. Hunger. Sound. Light. Freedom.

Food.

Weave. Circuit. Command. Open.

Food!

Julien was thankful for the dynamic tint on the visor of his helmet, because the pinpoint glare was becoming uncomfortable to look at for very long. It had been nearly an hour since the BXR contingent had begun their curated salvo of alternating beams from auger emplacements and handheld cutters, but it seemed like the only thing they'd successfully displaced thus far was Julien's patience.

The foreman gave the signal to hold fire, allowing their equipment to recharge and cool down while they reassessed the situation.

Mox came over the IMC comm channel soon after. "*Positions two and four, make sure your heat seals are good to go and see how close you can get to the target's surface. I want a closer look and better data on this thing.*"

Beck confirmed the directive, and the four operators began to head into the cave mouth. The target was only a dozen or so meters in, so the residual heat from the mining beams was still prevalent. As they got within a few meters, they each started observational scans to log all possible datapoints.

Julien wasn't sure if it was the intense heat shimmer playing tricks on his eyes, but after a few minutes he was sure he saw something strange happening on the target's alloy surface.

It was almost like it . . . *rippled*—a bit like liquid, but maybe even more like some sort of metallic skin.

"Abe, are you seeing this?" Julien's partner was uncharacteristically silent. "Abe?"

Julien turned back and realized he didn't need verbal confirmation. Abe's eyes were wide and fixed exactly on that same spot.

"What in the actual—"

Abe's professional assessment was cut short by Arti's own confirmation over comms. "*I'm picking it up too, seven distinct points in the alloy, wait, nine. Mox, you should probably come and see this.*"

Mox joined them just in time to see the silvery surface of the ancient construct peel away along a fresh seam, as the top layer was pulled back like armored curtains. The new opening revealed the enigmatic interior of a Forerunner vessel—of what class or purpose, no one present knew, but they were all immediately enamored.

After moments that could have been mistaken for months, Mox radioed in. "*Positions one and three, on me for initial clearance sweep. Let's see what we're dealing with.*"

Julien suddenly felt a pit of uncertainty in his stomach. "Mox, you sure? Should we wait?"

"*For who? You want to give your old military buddies a call and hand this over to them? Or do you want to earn that payday you keep talking about?*" Mox looked directly at Julien. "*This is what we do. Who we are.*"

UNSC *Saturn*

The last of the Black Paintings by Earth artist Francisco Goya stood watch over the ready room of the *Paris*-class UNSC *Saturn* from within a protective container, bearing the image of the Roman god Saturn gripping the bloodied, partially consumed corpse of one of his children. In the ancient myth, Saturn was haunted by a prophecy that he would be cast down by one of his sons—just as he had done to his own father—and so he ingested them upon birth.

Ghostly white fingers clasped the sides of the tiny body as if he possessed talons rather than human hands, kneeling in what seemed to be a dark cave. His mouth was fully agape, and his eyes appeared frenzied, bulging with shock—as if surprised to be caught in the middle of such a grotesque act, frozen for all time.

"I always thought he swallowed them whole," Lieutenant Anwar Shafiq mused.

Captain Pedro Alvarez did not turn from the painting as he replied. "You're quite right, of course. That's what the myth tells us . . . but Goya saw the horror of the act in quite a different way. In his interpretation, they were devoured, bit by bit. We're looking at it *far* removed from its original context, meaning the political upheaval in Goya's time. The French Revolution, the Peninsular War, the Inquisition—all fascinating eras of Earth's history that, in some ways, resemble our own recent—"

A sudden alert interrupted the captain's well-rehearsed speech for new officers. Art was an easy icebreaker, after all, and listening to their responses gave Alvarez some insight into how they thought. On-the-spot interpretations could reveal much about an individual's tactical acumen and way of thinking.

"It seems we'll have to pick this up later, Lieutenant," Alvarez said, straightening his uniform as he led Shafiq to the bridge. To Shafiq's credit, he immediately assumed his station and began analyzing tactical displays.

Lycaon, the avatar of the *Saturn*'s shipboard artificial intelligence, was waiting for them at the central holotable, along with a visual layout of the asteroid surface. He bore the image of a man in a white-gold toga, but his head was that of a wolf.

"Garbled distress messages from Site 22, Captain," Lycaon reported. "Contact with the on-site team has been lost."

Cavern. Cold. Wet.

Dragging. Food. Screams. Hunger.

Feast.

Site 22

Julien wasn't sure he knew what reality was anymore, but he knew it had a soundtrack.

Screams. Vacillating, ever-present, skin-peeling screams. Whether they continued to come from the mouth or mind he couldn't be sure—and couldn't care.

He tried to recollect what had happened, to anchor his thoughts.

Not long after Mox and the initial group had gone inside the ship, their reports turned unintelligible, chopped, terrified. Beck and Arti had barely stepped foot beyond the craft's threshold to investigate before they saw Mox sprinting toward them.

But it wasn't Mox. *Not anymore.*

And they weren't the only ones.

Chaos had immediately engulfed Site 22, the miners and civilian contractors trying to fight an unknowable enemy with construction tools. Julien tried his best to hold them off. His military training, albeit brief, had kept him alive in the vital opening moments of the conflict.

The longer it went on, however, the more he questioned whether or not he even *wanted* to survive such a thing.

UNSC *Saturn*

"What the hell is going on down there?" Alvarez muttered. "Can you clean up the distress message, Lycaon?"

"Attempting to now, sir."

What played then was largely garbled static, mixed with irregular sounds of what seemed like small arms fire and multiple voices shouting at once. After thirty-six seconds, the voices and sound of combat fell silent, though the static remained—like ocean waves washing over sand.

Alvarez turned to the central holotable and had Lycaon bring up Site 22's security camera feeds. They cycled through empty vistas of the asteroid's surface before Lycaon locked onto Camera 16.

The camera covered the view of a rocky maw, a circular opening evidently created by a mining auger—it was the closest they had to the cavern where some kind of discovery had been made. Lycaon had requested further information over two hours ago, but the IMC crew had remained tight-lipped as they sought to "verify" their find.

"I don't see anything," Alvarez said.

Lycaon zoomed the camera's view onto an irregular, shadowy shape. A dark trail smudged the ground behind it, and there appeared to be another figure wriggling and flailing like a fish pulled onto land from the sea. The resolution took several moments to improve as Lycaon locked and looped the footage, as by the time it cleared, both figures had disappeared from the live feed. But there was no mistaking what remained in the shot.

There was a collective inhale among the bridge crew as their displays received the image. Though few had encountered these monsters, all on the bridge had heard the stories passed through the Navy over the last few years. There was some familiarity with the name of these nightmarish creatures, like the dark sailor myths of old.

The miners of Site 22 had become a meal and a vessel for a timeless creature, an alien monstrosity that knew how to wait, and how to win.

The Flood.

"Rules of engagement are clear in the event of an incursion such as this, sir," Lycaon said. "Emergency Contact Protocol Upsilon must be implemented to withdraw all groundside units and limit the spread of the parasite."

"*Withdraw?*" Alvarez repeated the guidance, dismissing it immediately. "The only personnel on the ground are essentially unarmed miners. Our troop complement is more than capable of making short work of this situation. Prep Fireteam Leviathan for deployment."

Lycaon growled. "Need I remind you, sir, that if even *one* of the Spartans is compromised by the Flood, use of MAC rounds and fusion warheads is authorized to sterilize the area."

"And if we do that, we lose a massive deposit of resources that our fleets need to rebuild. We've barely managed to get the Home Fleet back up to a few dozen ships while the brass is demanding whole battle groups be assembled, never mind the loss of matériel we've got on the ground and the site's proximity to LV-31." He squared his shoulders. "I say again, and for the last time, prepare to deploy—"

"I am sorry, sir," Lycaon interrupted. "But in the event of a Flood outbreak, protocol supersedes your command, per UNSC Regulation 14-372-01. If you are unwilling to comply, I am authorized to remove you from—"

Alvarez's eyes widened, and what he said next came to his mouth almost as instinct. "Override code phrase, *actiones secundum fidei*."

Lycaon went silent. His holographic avatar remained active, and he stood as if calmly awaiting the answer to a question he'd asked.

Alvarez glanced around at the bridge crew, who were all looking at him from their stations with a mix of expressions on their faces. He stood straighter to project his voice to the crew. "Bring all stations to alert. I want a hazop group deployed to support Leviathan. Make ready to form a defensive perimeter and hold the line."

A lingering moment of tension hung in the air, as none of the bridge crew immediately moved.

"Aye, sir," Lieutenant Shafiq finally said, turning his chair back to his station, and the others eventually followed.

Alvarez rested his chin on his thumb as he sank into his command chair. His thoughts stayed with the image of the Flood form dragging its helpless victim into the cave. He felt the eyes of Saturn on his back, regarding him with those wide, opalescent eyes, caught in his act of barbarism.

They were devoured, bit by bit.

Site 22

Julien was pretty sure he hadn't been infected yet, but he felt like his mind was becoming scrambled just the same as he watched UNSC forces descend on Site 22 like they were dropping in behind Covenant lines.

He made out a squadron of Cyclops exoskeletons and several Hellbringer units as they began to torch the area indiscriminately—every bit as likely to incinerate other survivors to deny the enemy any potential hosts from beyond the perimeter.

The magnitude of the initial find had necessitated a larger-than-normal contingent of staff assigned to Site 22. It meant there had been ample opportunity for the parasite—this creature of nightmare he had heard whispered tales of at the end of his service—to satiate its appetite and rapidly increase its own numbers in the time it had taken for the UNSC to deploy.

Not that it had been long . . . but it seemed almost too late now.

Julien grimaced. His sidearm's ammunition had run dry, forcing him to resort to a nearby laser cutter.

Glancing around, he felt the cold grip of dismay.

He didn't know what he'd use after the cutter's charge was gone, and there weren't many other viable options.

That's when he saw them.

Myths. Legends.

Spartans.

The UNSC had seen fit to send a fireteam of four chemically and cybernetically augmented super-soldiers—heroes that had helped ensure the end of the Covenant War. Heroes that their greatest enemies had feared.

At that moment, Julien was struck by the dire enormity of the situation at Site 22. There was no way that Spartans would be sent into any scenario where normal, everyday people were remotely expected to survive.

The battle raged on, with Julien's heat seals constantly spiking to their maximum levels from the constant barrage of flame and firepower being brought to bear by the Hellbringers and Cyclops units.

For a fleeting moment, he thought they might actually have a chance. That this nightmare was something he could possibly wake up from.

Then the first Spartan fell.

Overrun by the parasite, one of the UNSC's living weapons suddenly found itself undergoing a new augmentation—twisted into a champion of dormant darkness. The Spartan's Mjolnir armor attempted to enact its countermeasures, pressurizing the hydrostatic gel layer to render itself immobile, and then detonating microexplosives within the helmet, which shattered the Spartan's visor as it immolated the head within . . . *and it still wasn't enough.*

Julien wanted to run. To cry. To hide. But he couldn't move. Couldn't tear himself away from the sight of a Spartan turning on its own kind.

Couldn't stop watching in horror as it tore apart those it had once protected.

And then it turned toward him, and Julien knew right then that his big payday would never come.

Tearing. Scratching. Kicking. Burrowing. Breaking. Slicing.

Chest cavity. Spine. Nest. Devour.

oh-god-get-it-off-me-get-it-off-me

Become. Become.

Become!

UNSC *Saturn*

Captain Alvarez stared at the grisly scene that was playing out before him on the holotable and across numerous tactical displays.

Horror. Denial. He was rigid with them both.

How could this have happened? A small-scale infestation of largely unarmed miners had cascaded into an outbreak that now threatened to overwhelm everything. Once the Flood had consumed all they needed on the ground, their insatiable hunger would direct them to this ship, where they would be unleashed upon the stars.

If that happened, it was game over—not just for humanity, but *all* sentient life.

And it would be his fault. The name of Captain Pedro Alvarez would live in notoriety as the man who unleashed a deluge of plague ships upon the galaxy. If any portrait of him were to be made in the future, it would depict him in Saturn's place.

For so long, they'd thought of Spartans as symbols of hope that could turn the tide against any enemy faced, no matter how impossible the odds. But he had never imagined how that could be twisted against them in the event the Flood managed to infect these heroes of humanity.

No choice remained. Lycaon had been right. Concerns about

rebuilding the UNSC fleet now paled in comparison to the situation playing out on the surface of Site 22.

"This is Captain Alvarez of the UNSC *Saturn*," he announced on an open comm channel, the nervous, sweating bridge crew turning to face him. "I am declaring CORRUPTER and UPSILON protocols. All remaining groundside personnel have seven minutes to withdraw from Site 22 as the *Saturn* moves into position . . . where we will fire our arsenal of Shiva-class nuclear missiles."

Alvarez avoided looking at Lycaon, who had remained inactive since the captain uttered the codeword to neutralize the AI's attempt to usurp his command.

"Good luck, and Godspeed."

Site 22

Julien saw the world in a new way.

But not Julien.

Something . . . different. *More.*

His mind fought to be free, to understand. But it also embraced the longing for something else.

Unity.

A gift he sought to bestow on others. He searched and scoured the surface of the asteroid, sifting through bone and body at a rapid pace, looking for someone to share his new mind with.

Ah! There's one!

Abe . . .

Devour.

Deluge.

Unity.

Peace.

We hunger. We find. We envelop.

Searching. Seeking.

More.

As he began to open his friend's mind, the horizon began to glow.

UNSC *Saturn*

Captain Alvarez gazed at what had previously been known as Site 22. The view from the bridge was still engulfed in fire. Only a handful of dropships managed to return while the others . . . well, perhaps the detonation of the Shivas had been a mercy compared to how they'd likely been reshaped.

He wanted nothing more than to return to his quarters and get to work on the bottle of Titan Smoke he'd been saving for retirement. But this would not be the celebratory drink envisioned, and it was a bitter realization that the twilight years of his career had culminated in his most brazen failure. He'd already begun mentally rehearsing his defense at the court martial that no doubt awaited him.

Lycaon remained inert and unresponsive. With Alvarez having known how to countermand the AI's attempt to usurp his authority, it had simply placed him into a kind of stasis. There was no doubt, however, that the techs back home knew how to restore his functionality.

A thousand desperate options ran through his mind—whether he could initiate Final Dispensation and order the crew to run with him across the stars or face the trial that inevitably awaited him and bear the burden of what his actions had cost.

"XO," Alvarez called. "You have the bridge; I'll be in my quarters."

"Aye, sir."

He would open that bottle after all, and perhaps come to a final decision at the bottom of a very large glass.

Arm. Weapon. Sharp. Cut. Hunger. Become. MORE.

make-it-stop-please-make-it-stop

Memories. Training. Hunger.

Weapon. Fire. Kneecap. Fall. Devour.

help-me-so-sorry-please-tearing-me-apart

Others. Fleeing. Leaving.

Horizon. Fire. Death.

A ship. Condor.

Approach. Swarm. Hunger.

won't-let-you-won't-let-you-WON'T-LET-YOU

Charging. Sprinting. Slicing. Food. Leave behind. CONDOR.

WON'T—

Aboard.

LET—

Devour. Depart.

YOU—

Become.

On Sanghelios, Okro 'Vagaduun completes his initiation into the ranks of the Banished Bloodstars.

"I know why you have come."

Okro 'Vagaduun's grip tightened on the hilt of his plasma blade as he and his opponent circled each other.

He had no desire to kill his old master, for Toha 'Sumai was one of the most respected swordsmen and duelists on Sanghelios, but 'Vagaduun understood what Atriox sought to teach him. To join the Banished was to sever one's ties to the past. To reject honor, the very core of a Sangheili's being, for payment would come in sport and spoils—not sentiment.

To join the Banished was to have loyalty to none but Atriox. It was for this reason alone that Toha 'Sumai must die.

Okro 'Vagaduun wished to say that he regretted what must be done—that he held fondness for his aged mentor and that he would take up the enhanced energy sword that was to be his bounty and do great things.

But he said nothing as he ignited his own blade and ran his old master through.

'Vagaduun felt no triumph or glory as the elder's body fell to the ground with a dull thud. In refusing to offer any resistance, 'Vagaduun felt a sliver of doubt—and within that doubt, the certainty that Toha 'Sumai had sought to impart one final lesson. . . .

ARMORY INFINITUM // VESTIGE CARBINE

On Qikost, one of the moons of Sanghelios, Spartan Abalan accompanies the 'Chava brothers as they attempt to unlock an ancient puzzle-vault.

January 4, 2560 (Military Calendar)
Qikost, Urs System

Spartan Abalan held her weapon ready at the mouth of the cavern's ingress point, guarding the approach as the sibling duo of Sangheili artisan-armorers—Oebrin and Silset 'Chava—bickered incessantly among themselves.

"You must reset the arum once again," Oebrin huffed. "Your previous rotation was off by four degrees."

Silset ushered his brother off. "Your concern is not warranted. I am certain that I felt the layers connect."

"*I* am certain that if you are mistaken, we shall all be locked out of the trove beyond and its contents shall be immolated."

Abalan checked her mission timer, which informed her that the two Sangheili had been having this back-and-forth for seventeen minutes—or, as their species measured smaller units of time, approximately twenty-eight centals. They had been studying the cavern for *much* longer.

"Time check," Abalan said, raising her voice for the Sangheili to hear. "We've got ten mikes before we need to start thinking about regrouping with the rest of Jorogumo Two."

"Patience, Spartan." Silset waved a dismissive hand in their direction and did not turn from the device attached to the semicircular stone door. "This is a San'Shyuum puzzle lock. It is as cunning and deceptive as their kind."

Abalan had served more than her share of protection detail jobs during her years as an ODST, but the last three months babysitting this dynamic duo had considerably stretched her patience. She was certain that their back-and-forth quarrelling was the cause of the gray hair she had found the other day . . . but still, she tolerated them.

Her own brothers had not been so different before—

"Ha!" Silset exclaimed in triumph. "Did I not tell you those layers connected, my brother? Did I not say?"

Oebrin sighed in defeat as Silset held up the arum—its many concentric layers were arranged to reveal a "tunnel" into the center of the device, within which a small activation device was contained.

"If you concede"—Silset's mandibles tightened in what looked like the Sangheili equivalent of a dirt-eating grin—"I shall allow you the honor of opening the trove."

"I concede to your wisdom." Oebrin shook his head as Silset allowed him to take the thumb-sized device and activate it. "Let us see that this diversion was worthwhile."

Even filtered through Abalan's helmet, the sound of stone scraping against stone was unpleasant to her ears, and she instinctively gritted her teeth. Ancient gears were now turning after millennia of stillness. It came as no small relief when the semicircular door finally parted in a Y-shaped split.

Naturally, Silset rushed inside with reckless abandon.

The trove was, fortunately, not a particularly large room—perhaps the length of two Warthogs and change. Still, that didn't mean there weren't traps.

"Hey, wait!" Abalan called out. "Before you take another step, I need to sweep this place."

"It is no worry, Spartan." To Abalan's surprise, it was Oebrin—the more sensible of the two, by her estimation—who addressed her. "The San'Shyuum placed these puzzle-vaults here because, in their arrogance, they did not believe any but a handful of Sangheili would ever be able to access them, let alone risk charges of heresy."

"Behold!" Silset called as he strode toward them with an undefinable new weapon in his hand.

It looked similar to the *Mosa*-pattern carbine—itself modified by the 'Chava brothers—that Abalan herself wielded, though the elongated barrel was much thicker and appeared almost clawlike.

"It is indeed a vestige." Oebrin scrutinized the weapon. "From this design, I would suggest it is from somewhere around the Third Age of Reclamation."

"Utilized by warriors stationed aboard the Prophets' agricultural support vessels, which were patterned in the same era," his brother eagerly added. "Perhaps even Khantolekgolo . . ."

"All right," Abalan said, keen to wrap the party up. "We've got what we came for. Grab what you can from the vault and let's get going."

The 'Chava brothers took only four items from the trove, then sealed the doors once more and reset the arum.

Apparently having noticed that Abalan must have conveyed some kind of puzzlement in her stance, Oebrin said, "It is not for us to *plunder* arcana from the past. We shall take only what we need. An original pattern model, two for us to modify and experiment upon"—the Sangheili held out one of the vestige carbines—"and a gift . . . for you."

Abalan accepted the weapon, scrutinizing its strange and unconventional design, before sighing. She'd long been fascinated by alien weaponry, and here these knuckleheads were, handing it to her freely instead of having to fight for one on the battlefield.

What was the old Sangheili proverb she had butchered last week?

Even the biggest pain in the ass can make an exceptional ally.

INTEL // GHOST OF BAROLON

In orbit around Suban, one of the two moons of Sanghelios, Scannermaster Dibdib reports on the Banished dreadnought Ghost of Barolon.

SCORRIN'S BLADE HYPERSCANNER RESULTS COLLATED BY SCANNERMASTER DIBDIB
BANISHED DREADNOUGHT: *GHOST OF BAROLON*

ARMAMENT:

- 1x superheavy grav-impact driver
- 6x light plasma lances
- 10x incinerator plasma cannon clusters
- 40x scindere arrays
- 24x plasma torpedo silos
- 70x pulse laser batteries
- 1x experimental volt piercer

CROSS-REFERENCE NOTES: *"Looks like the big bad Banished dreadnought got some kind of hidden experimental electrolaser gun on their ship—bad news if they catch us gettin' close! Hey . . . you ever seen a Brute scientist? I wonder if they—"*

>>REPORT CLOSED

ARMORY INFINITUM // PURGING SHOCK RIFLE

Aboard the Banished dreadnought Ghost of Barolon, *the weaponsmith Vulcus records a personal log regarding advances in shock-based weaponry.*

Sicatt Workshop // Alchemy Corps
Ghost of Barolon
>>Personal Log // Vulcus

As the Banished looks to extend its reach beyond the shadowed corners of the galaxy we have remained hidden in, Atriox has expressed his desire to bring new kinds of weaponry to bear—the kind that was spoken of in the old stories across the three moons. It was for this purpose that Sicatt Workshop was born, and thus far rudimentary efforts to harness directed energy electrolasers recovered from old vaults on Doisac have delivered satisfactory results.

But I see this as merely a template. A foundation.

The manufacturers deliver me a weapon that fires three bursts—I say, why not five? Voltaic application devices are still experimental in nature. So let us see how much power they can truly offer as we explore the truth of their limits. The Gray Guards are already eager to test this new firepower on the field as Escharum seeks to convene the Legion-masters for a new operation. I want these weapons to match precision and power in order to take down the shields of a human strike fighter.

In time, perhaps we can even mount such a weapon onto our ships . . . overload enemy systems to aid in ramming and boarding maneuvers.

Let it never be said that the Jiralhanae lack the ambition to explore what can be achieved through our minds as well as our might.

BATTLE FOR THE BLOOD-MOON

This story takes place on February 5, 2560, approximately two months after the UNSC Infinity's *ambush by the Banished and the subsequent disappearance of Zeta Halo (*Halo Infinite*).*

Scorrin's Blade

Shipmistress Mahkee 'Chava scrutinized the large tactical holograph of Suban at the center of the bridge, a cavernous command chamber that shared a similar design model to the *Ceudar*-pattern corvette. The spacious interior was lined with several rows of control consoles for the various systems defining the blockade runner as a strong and swift interdictor.

Unfortunately, that swiftness was not currently being put to use in the way Mahkee wished.

Instead of charging the Banished ranks with a coordinated assault, Mahkee had been ordered to hold her distance from the enemy dreadnought and comprehensively assess the situation.

Scorrin's Blade, like all *Hekar Taa*-pattern blockade runners, was outfitted with advanced stealth generators and an onboard hyperscanner reverse-engineered from recovered Forerunner matériel. In theory, these systems could work in concert, allowing them to obtain detailed internal scans of unsuspecting enemy vessels, but their use had been limited during the time of the Covenant.

Hyperscanners provided an overwhelming amount of information, which Mahkee guessed would likely have been filtered by the Forerunners' own artificial intelligences—something that the Prophets, in their infinite "wisdom," had significantly curtailed.

The Swords of Sanghelios, on the other hand, bore no such prejudice against artificial life, even as many such constructs had risen against their human creators and sought to impose their own will upon the galaxy.

But Mahkee didn't need an AI to operate that system. She had something just as effective.

"Status, Dibdib?"

The diminutive Unggoy almost jumped as Mahkee approached. Fortunately, this had become a common routine and Dibdib managed to reduce her reaction to a slight jolt.

"We gots the latest knowins on the big bad dreadnought, Shipmistress," Dibdib squeaked, her eyes still fixed on the hyperscanner. "Sendin' it to the main holograph now!"

"Excellent news." Mahkee continued on her way around the bridge. "'Tylk, bring *Scorrin's Blade* back to minimum safe distance."

"As you say, Shipmistress." Xelq 'Tylk dipped his head in acknowledgment. He was still quite young, a relative newcomer to the Swords of Sanghelios, and eager to make a good impression on his superiors.

As *Scorrin's Blade* pulled back, Mahkee returned her attention to the central holograph of Suban and tightened her mandibles. That the Banished had *dared* to come to this system at all was galling enough, but the blood-moon of Sanghelios was her home. She and her brothers had been raised here since they were hatchlings, and she allowed herself a momentary feeling of relief that the two of them were currently on Sanghelios itself to inspect the latest products of the Kolaar Manufactorum. Wily though they were, neither Silset or Oebrin were fighters, and they were certainly not what any Sangheili would call "traditional" in any sense.

Somewhat ironically, that had all gone to her.

Mahkee did not possess the patience for the political maneuverings, complex trade deals, and clan management that had largely served as the civil duty of Sangheili females. Her mother had always said Makhee's veins ran with the fire and blood of Suban itself, and her calling had come when the Arbiter declared that military service for the Swords of Sanghelios would be open to *all*.

Indeed, she had been surprised to learn that even the Unggoy could ascend to the rank of shipmaster upon querying why one of the *Zanar*-pattern light cruisers attached to their fleet was named *Bad Gas*.

Returning to the holograph, Mahkee flicked her wrist and the projected image of Suban dissipated. This made way for the latest tactical scans of the dreadnought that was the center of all Banished activity in this region.

Scannermaster Dibdib's work on the hyperscanner had even identified the name of the vessel: *Ghost of Barolon*.

The holograph highlighted its suite of armaments, filling Mahkee with dread. *Scorrin's Blade* was heavily outgunned by the monstrosities the Banished had brought to bear—their dreadnoughts a physical representation of their rapid rise to power, while many of the Swords of Sanghelios's own warships reflected ancient patterns connected to pre-Covenant history. Admirable as that pursuit was for the spirit of the Sangheili, these patterns were largely outdated and could not match either the firepower or tonnage of these crimson-armored ogres.

Suban was more than just a home for Mahkee. The onset of the Blooding Years that had come to define this period for the Sangheili turned the moon into a place of neutral safe harbor. And prior to the Sangheili's millennia of service to the Covenant, Suban had been held as a sacred point of convergence for the wills of their most ancient gods—traditions, doctrine, and faith secretly preserved from the long and treacherous reach of the Prophets.

But hundreds of drop bases had already been deployed from *Barolon*'s underbelly, enough to establish immediate occupational infrastructure on one of Suban's most fertile mining sites.

And Mahkee felt powerless to do anything about it.

She knew, of course, that every datapoint about the enemy was valuable, and the time would come to coordinate a retaliatory strike. A competent shipmaster required the virtue of patience, and the cost of acting prematurely before understanding the bigger picture. In this, Mahkee's discipline did not blunt or sublimate her instinct for battle, but instead served as a whetstone for it.

For now, she would watch, she would wait, and she would find the gap in the armor of the Banished that would win the day for her people.

Until then, she turned her mind to the joint operation taking place on the ground. With Spartans and Swords of Sangheilos forces working together in a combined arms effort, their joint temerity and prowess would make its mark—of that, Mahkee was certain. She had, after all, fought alongside the humans' living legends before, when she had ferried Spartan Jameson Locke and Fireteam Osiris into battle, helping the Arbiter bring a decisive end to Jul 'Mdama's Covenant.

Scores of Banished troops against a handful of Spartans and Swords of Sanghelios warriors?

Centering her mind and mustering her confidence amid the uncertainty, Mahkee thought with determined resolution that those were indeed sorrowful odds for their enemies.

Suban
The Mines of Shua'ree

The density of conflict and upheaval on Sanghelios over the past several weeks had been unprecedented. Just a few months after Arbiter Thel 'Vadam's harrowing encounter with the Banished on the corpse-world of N'ba, the Created forces keeping Sanghelios under a suffocating martial occupation suddenly relinquished their grip on the system. It was an unanticipated turn of fortune quickly spiraling into a race to fill the power vacuum left on such an influential world.

While many of the keeps and kaidons on Sanghelios remained steadfast in their support of the Arbiter and his attempts to unify their people, others sought alternative divisions of power. Tensions were already beginning to boil over, and it served as an open invitation to any well-organized force to take advantage of—an invitation the Banished was more than eager to accept.

With their brazen encroachment into the Urs system, the Banished found no need to breach a barricaded door. The loyal Sangheili under their growing influence simply left the gate unlatched.

This latest chapter of the conflict now settled into the skies of Suban, over one of the many mining sites that had elevated the moon's status as such a prized resource in the reign of the Covenant empire. Suban was the only known place in the galaxy containing *kemuksuru*—the energized crystals powering several manifestations of "needle launcher" weapons employed by many of the former Covenant client species. That reality made the Sanghelios satellite a prime commodity to be controlled, and the Banished were making every effort to do so.

What must it be like? Fahl 'Nto thought. *To have a mind more like a machine?*

The seasoned Evocati was sitting on a flat raised rock, but leaned forward to continue his observation of one of the human Spartans standing with them. While serving in the Covenant as a distinguished operative, Fahl had encountered a scattered few "demons" during his deployment, most notably on their stronghold world near the end of the War of Annihilation.

They were encounters he spoke little of since aligning with the Swords of Sanghelios, as his mind remained in a constant dance between resolution and shame—an ever-present personal journey toward purpose.

The Spartans of Fireteam Jorogumo were part of an allied attaché under the purview of Fleetmaster Arkad Nar 'Kulul, one of the Sanghelios home defense fleet leaders. The presence of these augmented human warriors was part of an ongoing treaty between the human military and the Swords of Sanghelios, and the Spartans remained at the disposal of Swords forces and at the discretion of key kaidons and commanders to bolster their efforts.

Today, those efforts were focused squarely on the Mines of Shua'ree. The Banished had successfully managed to set up a rapid extraction site in one of the more remote quarry mouths—an impressive display of ruthless efficiency and cunning execution. An incursion that demanded an equally decisive response, but unfortunately deft coordination was not a trait Sangheili forces were able to muster in sufficient quantities these days.

Instead, Arkad Nar 'Kulul opted to enact a combined arms operation, attaching four Spartans from Jorogumo to a Swords taskforce led by Fahl 'Nto and Orim 'Kasaan, a specops warrior in service to the Arbiter.

The mission called for Fahl to lead an advance scout team that included two of the Spartans and a Kig-Yar named Dahks. As part of their integration into local forces, each of the Spartans had been given a Sangheili name—not quite a title and not quite a nickname, but terms that would give each human soldier a unique identity and stronger sense of inclusion among their ranks.

Fahl tilted his head as he surveyed one of the Spartans, the one they called Trell, who was looking through the scope of a rangefinder.

"What do you see?"

Trell's voice came back through their helmet speaker. "At least two docking platforms. Regular cycle of fork-buckets coming in and out."

Fahl's mandibles twitched at Trell's colloquial mention of the Banished siege-haulers. Every flight out could mean hundreds of the enemy alliance's warriors armed with restocked needle-launchers.

"So much bounty." The screeching statement came from Dahks. "Need no scope to see thisss."

Dahks was unique among his kind, and Fahl was one of very few individuals who knew the Jackal's past as a former member of the Jha'kaar—a Kig-Yar order of long-range assassins rumored to be able to remove a target's head off their shoulders from a nearby moon. Such exaggerated attributions did nothing to diminish Dahks's true skills, however, and lately the Ruuhtian mercenary had taken up a particular fondness for human-built sniper rifles, resulting in more than a few lively discussions with Trell on best practices and past accomplishments.

The voice of Glyyss, another Spartan, broke in. "Nobody's bending your quills, Dahks. Besides, we have more than one way to get a better look at things."

Glyyss tapped two command buttons on a wrist-mounted survey drone and the small machine quickly departed, its flight trajectory heading straight for the mouth of one of the quarry caves.

Fahl stood up and placed the wide-crested helmet of his ivory raid harness back over his head. He had developed an odd fondness for the way in which Glyyss always returned the Kig-Yar's needling with fair measure. "Dahks, sync your optics to the Spartan's drone—they will be your eyes inside. Remain here as overwatch, but keep communication channels active."

"Ready to flag in Jaarov and Zhinn?" Glyyss asked, already prepared to ping the other two Spartans on the operation.

"Yes," Fahl confirmed. "Let them know that we will be in position shortly and that Orim can bring his Phantom in. Our time will be narrow."

Scorrin's Blade

"Can you confirm its authenticity, 'Tylk?" Mahkee was taking no chances when it came to ensuring the secure transfer of information regarding groundside operations.

"The signature is confirmed, Shipmistress. Orim 'Kasaan is aboard the vessel of origin."

Mahkee nodded a simple approval. "Contact the summitmasters and ensure we have Banshee talons in a ready formation at the appropriate coordinates."

Her mind began to weigh the potential outcomes of their groundside efforts and how they might inform their next tactics in the grander scope of the conflict. She had barely begun calculating probability metrics when her bridge crew interjected once more.

"Shipmistress, we are receiving another transmission," said Xelq, who paused and tilted his head in momentary confusion. "From the shipmaster of the Banished dreadnought . . ."

Mahkee braced herself for what was no doubt going to be an enlightening conversation.

"Put it through."

The holograph of Suban and *Ghost of Barolon* disappeared and was replaced by a bulky, hunched figure clad in golden armor. *A Sangheili . . .* She had expected a Jiralhanae to be shipmaster of such a vessel, as dreadnoughts were not simply devastating occupational powerhouses, but since the razing of the Oth Sonin system they had come to represent something of a cultural monument to their species.

And the haughty look of satisfaction from the Banished shipmaster told her that she had let this momentary surprise show through slightly parted jaws.

"Greetings, Shipmistress," he said, as calmly and casually as if he were checking up on a friend. *"I am Orna 'Fulsam, High Warlord of the Banished."*

"I do not know of you, and am unmoved by any such title," Mahkee responded, her tone clipped but not yet disrespectful. "What is it you want?"

"By now, you have undoubtedly grasped the extent of our current forces and firepower, and you know that there is no victory to be had through conventional battle."

Mahkee held Orna's gaze. "Your fleet possesses certain advantages, that is true. I hope you did not trouble my preparations to counter them just to inform me of this."

"No," Orna said. *"I have come to ask you to avoid further unnecessary bloodshed of our own kind."*

"Peace talks with a traitor?" Mahkee narrowed her eyes. "So you have come here to jest?"

"We need not be foes. Step aside, give us Suban, and your forces shall be spared. Better yet, pledge your allegiance to the Banished, and the only ones that need perish are the demons that desecrate Suban's ground."

If nothing else, Mahkee had to admire 'Fulsam's audacity.

"The Spartans?" she asked.

"The humans." Orna spoke the name as if he had choked up bile. *"They are the true architects of the Blooding Years, along with the Arbiter who calls them allies and invites them to our home in order to solve his own problems."*

"Your hatred is tinged with madness, Shipmaster," Mahkee said with pity.

"You do not sense the truth of it?" Orna stood straighter, and Mahkee resigned herself to endure whatever speech the shipmaster had prepared.

Suban
The Mines of Shua'ree

The plan relied on precision. It had to.

The first task at hand was removing the small perimeter patrol near the mouth edge of the mining site. Using his own line of sight and additional feeds from the Spartan's survey drone, Dahks had marked the first two targets, one each for Fahl and Glyyss. Trell had taken up a second vantage point to ensure overlapping fields of sniper fire in tandem with Dahks, but at a closer proximity in case the situation called for more direct involvement.

Fahl crouched behind a small rock formation and waited for his prey to come within striking distance. It wasn't long before a Sangheili mercenary stepped forward just close enough. The Banished Elite tried to react, but by the time he reached for his plasma pistol, Fahl had buried a wrist-mounted energy dagger deep into the mercenary's neck, indigo blood casting a spattered mist on the Evocati's pale armor.

A quick glance up confirmed that Glyyss had successfully neutralized their own target as well. With the outermost lookouts removed, Fahl initiated the next phase of the plan.

"Certify stage completion with *Scorrin's Blade*, talons are free."

The response from the comms marshal aboard *Scorrin's Blade* was nearly immediate. "*Confirmed, honor to 'Nto. Wings Zeshk and Siqtar are on approach.*"

Moments later, the telltale wail of several Banshee attack flyers could be heard, but without the forward lookouts scanning the skies, the Banished response would be slightly delayed.

The Banshees opened fire with plasma cannons and fuel rod guns, both talons targeting the siege-haulers primed on the pads and freshly laden with raw *kemuksuru.* The resulting detonations caused immediate chaos within the mine itself. Banished warriors scurried through corridors and across gantries, furious but also confused in the immediate aftermath.

It was a confusion made all the more intense when the first sniper shots rang out.

"*Headbursts cossst exxtraa!*" Dahks gleefully exclaimed over comms as he and Trell took turns removing Banished pieces from the gameboard, alternating long-range fire into the mouth of the mine. Banished soldiers desperately tried to locate the source of the shots, a difficult process in the midst of the maelstrom.

"Orim, you are clear." Fahl's latest communication was directed at Orim 'Kasaan, whose Phantom had been hiding in the lower depths of the quarry until the opportunity was at hand. Moments later, the Phantom rose up to meet the cave mouth, its doors opening to reveal at least a dozen Sangheili warriors fiercely loyal to the Arbiter. Among them were two more Spartans from Jorogumo—Jaarov and Zhinn—ready to take the fight directly to the Banished.

As the forces departed the Phantom, each set immediately to the task at hand. They were easily outnumbered, but the Swords took advantage of the surprise attack to even the playing field as much as possible.

Jaarov and Zhinn eliminated several enemy soldiers and were already engaged with the next incoming wave. They were joined by a hulking Elite named Koal 'Mal, whose hunched form and slightly broader physique belied his deft skills with an energy sword. 'Mal hailed from a lineage torn asunder by betrayal and civil strife, their keep in a constant state of upheaval and vacillating allegiance. It fueled his rage to an impressive degree, and it was not difficult to recognize the somber joy 'Mal took with each traitorous Sangheili he dispatched. Allying with the Banished was a choice Koal 'Mal could not abide, and Fahl sympathized with how difficult this ongoing conflict was for the warrior.

It was no surprise, of course, that the bulk of the local Banished forces they engaged with *were* Sangheili. The *teroks* were not just at the doorstep—they were already sleeping at the foot of the bed.

However, despite all this, while his own kind were indeed the tip of the Sanghelios spear, the truth was that at the beating heart of any Banished endeavor was the clenched fist of a Jiralhanae loyal to Atriox—and today would be no different.

"All your antics . . . all for naught!" The Jiralhanae's bellowing could be heard before Fahl had actually seen him.

As Fahl turned around, a massive chieftain in Banished-liveried armor emerged from under one of the catwalks crisscrossing the tunnels. He was flanked by two Brute captains, each with a charged plasma tosser aimed in Fahl's general direction.

Orim's voice came over Fahl's comms link. "*Chieftain Ipso—it is no surprise to see him so directly involved. We have had several teams tailing his extended pack, and it never takes long for us to lose his scent. He will not be a trivial opponent.*"

Fahl's attempted response was cut short once more by the chieftain.

"How does it feel? To see your world burn . . . and for your own people to be kindling the flames while we bask in its glow?"

"You speak like one with experience in such a thing," Fahl responded, though he knew such a retort carried little weight in the immediate age. The Jiralhanae *had* once been the architects of their own decline, but this truth served no tangible relevance in the moment. The fact was, Ipso was correct, but Fahl would never offer the satisfaction of confirming this. "Have you become more comfortable with wielding words than heaving a hammer?"

The chieftain bellowed with laughter. "An excellent question, to be sure." The Jiralhanae bared his tusks in a triumphant smile. "Why don't we find its answer?"

The two captains opened fire, their ravagers splashing searing hot plasma across the quarry floor. Fahl immediately dove into an evasive roll as three allied Sangheili warriors leaped to his aid, engaging the Brutes and catching one in the shoulder with a well-placed plasma bolt from a pulse carbine.

Moments later, the same Swords operative was smeared across the nearby rock face by the force of Ipso's gravity hammer.

Leveraging every bit of his vast experience, Fahl used cunning and more than a few deft maneuvers to maintain whatever superiority he could. All the while, the firefight raged on around him.

And finally, after several minutes—and several decades—the extent of Fahl 'Nto's time-honed skill came up short.

He took a dull ravager blade to the shoulder while thrusting his energy dagger through the second captain's mouth, but the exchange cost Fahl time he did not have.

The sudden impact of the chieftain's swift kick to his chest sent Fahl sprawling. He landed hard, his helmet dislodging and tumbling away. He had only just made it back to his knees when the shadow of his enemy made him look up.

Dazed, Fahl saw Ipso's massive form looming over him, his gravity hammer at the ready.

And Fahl 'Nto realized his time had finally come.

He was a warrior; he had known it would eventually happen.

Ipso roared, bringing the weapon up and back down in a swift circular arc—

But the killing blow never struck.

A flash of cobalt armor darted into view and Fahl found himself face to visor with a Spartan.

Glyyss.

A split second later, the sickening sound of metal on metal met Fahl's ears as Ipso's hammer blade cleaved through the Spartan's armor and lodged in their back. Fahl saw red blood begin to pool on the other side of Glyyss's visor.

"Why . . . ?" Fahl asked, knowing an answer would not come.

Glyyss's body jerked as Ipso attempted to pull the hammer free, but the chieftain was forced to relinquish his grip and avoid the incoming plasma cannon blasts pouring through the cave mouth. The Swords Phantom had returned, laying down suppressive fire to cover a desperate egress.

By the time Jaarov and Zhinn arrived to carry what remained of their fallen comrade, Ipso was already lost from view.

A shimmer appeared next to Fahl as a cloaked Orim 'Kasaan implored his friend to get to his feet and back to the dropship before it was too late. Tearing his gaze away from Glyyss at last,

Fahl found the strength to stand and focus on the immediate situation. Much as he loathed to admit it, Ipso had won—for now.

"We cannot leave!" The protest came from Koal 'Mal, his armor soaked in the deep purple-colored blood of his own kind. "If we give quarter here, we will surely lose Shua'ree to the Banished. The blood spilled here will have been for naught!"

"There are many things that distinguish us from the Banished in this conflict," Fahl spoke through fractured mandibles, "and *kemuksuru* is not one of them. We will return when the time is right."

Scorrin's Blade

". . . Humanity is the ruinous common thread at the heart of this galaxy."

Mahkee wasn't sure how long Orna had been speaking—it was likely only a few moments but felt like it might as well have been a lunar cycle.

Orna's relentless diatribe nevertheless continued unfettered. *"With the Arbiter's failure to secure the first of the sacred rings, the humans began to unravel everything we worked so hard to achieve. It was the humans who destroyed Saepon'kal, wiping out a combined fleet that would have seen the Sangheili emerge as the dominant power in the galaxy, thus forcing us to collude with the vermin to defeat the Prophet of Truth. It was the humans' own meddling that brought about the Blooding Years—the state of Vadam itself is scarred with the evidence. Even now, their own creations rebelled against them because they were built to live in the shackles they sought to break. Do you not see? We are living in* their *battle song, Shipmis-*

tress, and the Arbiter's guilt is so great that he would allow them to swarm across the galaxy just to soothe his conscience."

Mahkee could not deny that there were elements of truth within the shipmaster's words. Humans had emerged from the Covenant empire's ashes not simply as survivors—their swift race to recover had seen them rise from their unexpected victory with a certain arrogance, proclaiming themselves giants.

Indeed, many dark rumors persisted about the Office of Naval Intelligence, the clandestine human agency that moves mountains in the shadows, and its involvement in the events that led to Jul 'Mdama's emergence as heir to the Covenant.

The truth, however, was undoubtedly far more complex than what 'Fulsam was presenting. If the calculated actions of such individuals were enough to condemn an entire species, then Mahkee herself would be forced to fall upon her own blade for the atrocities committed by the Covenant.

"Yet you have joined the Banished," she finally retorted, "which allies *with* humans, rather than one of the many Covenant remnant groups."

"Even vermin can prove useful. They are so easy to turn against each other."

"Then perhaps they are not so different from Sangheili."

"Think on my words, Shipmistress. I shall leave my offer open to you until our next round of battle." 'Fulsam flexed his jaws. *"And I have a request from Atriox himself that you pass a message along to your fleetmaster."*

"What message would you have me trouble Fleetmaster 'Kulul with?"

The hologram of Orna 'Fulsam began to fade as he spoke his concluding words.

"Tell him that Let 'Volir sends his regards."

On Zeta Halo, Thav 'Sebarim receives news as he transports prisoners to the Banished prison facility "Redoubt of Sundering."

"Kaidon 'Sebarim," a voice called out as a red-armored Sangheili enforcer approached. "I bring ill news."

Thav 'Sebarim, clad in the dark maroon armor identifying him as a Bloodstar—a special warfare unit that had been appropriated from the Covenant into the ranks of the Banished military schema—watched as a trio of Banshees passed overhead toward the fractured band of Zeta Halo and disappeared into low white clouds on their scouting run.

In his hands, 'Sebarim carried a sentinel beam that had been found during one of his excursions to the Halo ring's substructures—the vast metal underworld that lay below the natural edifice of the construct's verdant surface. This directed energy weapon was much like the ones integrated into standard sentinel units, but the enforcer had been awed by the effectiveness of its use—how it so quickly disintegrated its targets, as if they had been totally cleansed from existence.

"What is the problem?" 'Sebarim asked.

The enforcer straightened; decades of discipline from Covenant military service had long ago become second nature to him, though he allowed his eyes to wander to the group of half a dozen human captives held by 'Sebarim's Jiralhanae entourage.

"The inspector informs me that the Redoubt of Sundering is full," he said. "There is no more room for the spoils of today's hunt."

"Ah." 'Sebarim gestured to the enforcer to come closer. "We have been gluttonously spoiled with prisoners since Tremonius claimed their ruined frigate."

The enforcer dipped his head in agreement. Their attack on the UNSC *Mortal Reverie* had scattered the human survivors to the winds, but the Banished checkpoints and fortifications had effectively transformed this area of the ring into the perfect hunting ground.

Humans were tenacious when faced with limited options. Some simply chose to hide and had to be driven out from their cowardly retreat, others attempted to form larger groups and conduct attacks on targets of value. The only other option that remained for them was to leap into the abyss at the fractured edge of the ring, which the Banished was all too willing to accommodate.

"What do you intend to do?" asked the enforcer.

"Release them, of course," 'Sebarim said, and the Bloodstar warrior's grip on his weapon tightened in response.

A glorious new hunt would soon be afoot.

ARMORY INFINITUM // RAVAGER REBOUND

On Zeta Halo, Captain Arthoc recalls the effective usage of infusion gel to rout human forces from the downed UNSC frigate Mortal Reverie.

Armory of Reckoning

Captain Arthoc

FWD: Ravager

The Armory of Reckoning—it is a fitting name for the tools of conquest and destruction birthed from its forges.

When we advanced on the human remnants that had sought shelter within their crashed ship, I requested of Commander Bannix an augmented version of the plasma tossers produced by the Forge of Torograd.

Where we have mastered both spike and spear in our weaponry since before the Immolation, infusion matter remains an object of study for our alchemists. I was informed by the screecleaver that there is a great savant stationed on Oth Liqattu who has sought to unlock further secrets of this baneful power, applying it to our own troops and many of our vehicles.

It is said that prolonged exposure to this corrosive bile can addle the mind and rot the body. That is good, for there are many small spaces in human ships. The capacity for this weapon to launch projectiles that bounce before erupting into toxic piles was of great use in expelling our foes from cover. How they flailed and danced to our battle song!

It is my understanding that pure infusion matter is pumped throughout Forerunner facilities as a source of power, so we must dedicate resources to finding these wellsprings within the substructures of this sacred ring. I shall bring this information to Tremonius once he has returned from investigating a disturbance at his outpost.

INTEL // MISSING IN ACTION

Personnel dossier of Gunnery Sergeant Elena Bobrov, logged within the database aboard UNSC Mortal Reverie.

//UNSC DATABASE

//FFG-525 - UNSC *MORTAL REVERIE*

//PERSONNEL DOSSIERS

NAME: Bobrov, Elena

SERVICE NUMBER: 91532-11116-EB

RANK: Gunnery Sergeant

HEIGHT: 6ft 1in (185.4cm)

WEIGHT: 170lbs (77.1kg)

BIRTH WORLD: Alluvion

DATE OF BIRTH: June 19, 2522

NOTABLE OPERATIONS

GySgt Elena Bobrov's service record chronicles marks of distinction in several major campaign areas. Notable entries include:

- REACH (2552): Assisted Gauntlet Team in civilian evacuation operations during Covenant invasion.
- REQUIEM (2557-8): Stationed aboard UNSC *Infinity* during both phases of the Requiem mission. Assigned as M510 Mammoth crew chief for Operation: WHIRLPOOL.
- WOLFE (2559): Deployed to the surface of Reach alongside Spartan fireteams to engage Banished forces.

CURRENT STATUS

MISSING IN ACTION

TRIAL OF RECKONING

This story takes place on February 3, 2560, immediately following the Banished assault on the downed frigate Mortal Reverie, *which served as a central command post for UNSC survivors on Zeta Halo (*Halo Infinite*).*

"*Awaken, valiant warriors!*"

Gunnery Sergeant Elena Bobrov winced as she slowly regained consciousness. Everything had happened so fast since the Banished descended upon them—the attack on the UNSC *Mortal Reverie* spanned two harrowing days of almost ceaseless combat. Even though they'd known the battle was coming, there had been only hours to prepare.

The *Reverie* was downed months ago during the initial Banished naval assault, but the *Mulsanne*-class frigate's surviving wreckage had become a fortified rally point for UNSC personnel stranded on this local fragment of Zeta Halo. The installation itself had been violently fractured as a result of the escalating conflict on its surface and the accompanying emergency slipspace jump to who-knows-where. Under an unfamiliar field of stars, the *Reverie* had quickly become the only thing that resembled a “home.”

And in the blink of an eye, the Banished had taken that too.

Bobrov had been in the thick of the fighting when a group of Brute Berserkers set upon her squad, tearing into them with mindless abandon—driven by a violence-fueled disregard for anything but their next target. She recalled hearing the dire sound of bones snapping, feeling the spray of Ensign Daniels’s blood across her face, and the next thing Bobrov knew she was drifting in and out of consciousness, fleeting impressions of being dragged across the lush terrain of Zeta Halo before being loaded onto a skiff and taken to . . . wherever the hell this place now was.

“Hey,” a man’s voice cut through her musings. “Gunny’s waking up, Doc.”

A medical scanner passed over her a moment later, followed by a small shot of fast-acting morphine, which quickly and mercifully diminished the throbbing in her head.

“Can’t see.” Blinking rapidly, she tried to quell the rising panic in her chest.

“Be calm, your eyes will quickly adjust,” a deep voice soothed. “I suspect the lights will soon turn on.”

Squinting through the darkness, unable to see much farther than three meters ahead or so, Bobrov relied on her other senses. Beneath her hands she felt the roughness of dirt-covered ground, but the sound of movement around her echoed in ways more indicative of being inside a large building. A hangar, perhaps? That didn’t make any sense.

But then again, nothing did anymore.

As her vision continued to adjust, Bobrov was able to finally make out the one who had been seeing to her injuries.

Being tended to by a Sangheili was certainly one of the stranger wake-up scenarios she'd ever experienced. Clad in simple armor, its saurian face barely seemed to register her as he decided he was satisfied that his patient's wits and faculties had returned.

"Roll call," Bobrov said through a strained grimace as she shifted herself into a sitting position. "Who have we got here and what the hell is going on?"

"Lance Corporal Singh," came the voice that had first announced her awakening. "And we're, uh, pretty much screwed, ma'am."

"Spartan Hedge, Fireteam Lancer," came another, causing Bobrov to swell with a momentary flutter of hope. On any other day, she'd have passed it off as an involuntary reaction, but she knew more directly of Spartan Hedge, as the two of them had fought through the Requiem Campaign.

Bobrov had served two tours of the Forerunner shield world, having been aboard the UNSC *Infinity* when it was first pulled into the hollow sphere back in '57.

Terry Hedge had joined the UNSC *Infinity* crew as a Spartan recruit soon after the New Phoenix incident. Bobrov had read some of the mission debriefs on Fireteam Lancer's activities, where they'd been led by Hedge and taken part in some of the thickest fighting against Promethean and Covenant remnant forces.

"And our medic?" Bobrov asked, turning to the Sangheili. "You're a warrior, right?"

The Sangheili appraised her and closed his first-aid kit with a crisp snap, the case comically small in the alien's large hands.

"No."

"No?" Bobrov repeated, her brow furrowing.

"I am a healer of wounds, not a deliverer of them. Not anymore."

"You got a name?"

"Yes."

When he did not continue, Singh interjected, "We just call him Doc. He seems all right with that."

At that moment, the lights lining the ceiling above flickered on, and the truth of their situation was laid acutely bare.

They were indeed inside a room as large as a hangar bay, but there were no vessels docked here. Instead, the area was akin to a UNSC field base—a flat prefabricated structure covered in sand and dirt, with a couple of large rocks on the outer edges where groupings of sandbags were haphazardly laid out.

Bobrov got to her feet, much to Doc's protestations, but she waved the Sangheili off to assess the area. A small building nearby housed a handful of ammunition and weapons crates, prompting Bobrov to grab an assault rifle, Sidekick pistol, and a few grenades. As she had been the last to awaken, the choices were slim, but the familiar weight of the rifle in her hand returned some semblance of comfort to her.

Beyond the base structure, a series of doors covered the boundaries of the room—two at each edge. They at least knew where their enemy would funnel in from . . . but with only three fighters among them, and limited ammunition and cover, things certainly weren't looking good.

"Ah, there you are."

The booming, sonorous voice that had originally awakened her now returned, this time accompanied by a hologram at the far edge of the room, resolving into the bloodred image of an aged, bald Jiralhanae. His right eye was milky and clouded, but the other—even in holographic form—glinted with malice as his mouth curled into a sharp-toothed smile. A gray beard covered his chin, and his forehead was branded with a strange triangular symbol.

"I am Escharum, war chief of the Banished. I welcome you to the House of Reckoning."

"Ugly bastard." Singh spat on the ground, tightening his grip on his battle rifle to mask a fearful tremor.

"Within these iron halls, through the Trials of Atriox, all shall know what it is to be Banished—our living history, how we once served the Covenant. All shall know what it is to be meat.*"*

Wasting no time, Spartan Hedge sprang into action, signaling Doc to assist in fortifying their position with sandbags and anything else they could grab with what little time and resources they had at their disposal. It wasn't going to be much protection, but under the circumstances it was the best they could get.

"The trial is King of the Hill. One side holds the advantage of territory and must hold it while forty Banished brothers are sent to stake their claim. Survive, and you shall be granted a boon. You have played your little war games long enough. Now, you will play mine."

With a final sinister grin, Escharum crossed his arms over his chest, and the hologram faded.

Spartan Hedge motioned for Bobrov and the others to join him. "No retreat, no surrender, and no quarter. That's what's on the menu for us today, and it's our job to damn well make sure it's the same for them."

"Four of us against forty of them," Singh replied, and made an exaggerated show of counting on his fingers. "We're outnumbered *ten to one*, man."

Bobrov considered what she'd read on military maneuvers back in basic training. As the ancient military strategist Sun Tzu had roughly put it: *When surrounding an enemy, leave a way of escape.* A retreating enemy is one that isn't putting everything they've got into retaliation, but an enemy that knows they've been forced into a position to make a final stand is going to fight with every ounce of strength to the bitter end.

Either Escharum hadn't figured that out, or, more likely, the Banished war chief was perfectly aware of it, and that was *exactly* what he wanted from his captives.

"Let's be real," Bobrov said. "It's entirely likely that *none* of us are making it through this. So you'd better make peace with the prospect of an unceremonious death right now, because if you freeze up and fail to make your shots count, you might as well be on their damn side."

Doc fidgeted with his medical vambraces, his mandibles tightly formed together, giving way to a sigh. "I shall ensure that you are each stocked with ammunition, and provide you with the enemy's weaponry when yours runs out. There is no honor in allowing one's allies to perish for the sake of vanity."

Bobrov couldn't help but wonder what this guy's story was. She could read the subtext as well as anyone, and it seemed that even now, even when facing such crushing odds, the good doctor was firmly set against directly doing harm.

In her experience, the Sangheili held martial prowess and their concept of honor as a matter of life and death. Decades of fighting against them had taught her that. Her more recent years, doing training drills with some of the Swords of Sanghelios personnel, seemed to confirm that knowledge. Doc had evidently been among the cohort aboard the UNSC *Infinity*. Bobrov drew a sharp breath at the thought.

Infinity.

The name alone conjured an unexpected stab of nostalgia. How she missed that ship.

UNSC vessels of all kinds throughout the Covenant War had been hell to live on—strictly utilitarian in design to serve as cold metal coffins ferrying troops from one battlefield to the next, never knowing how far one was going to make it. But the quiet hum of the *Infinity*'s engines, the beauty of the atrium park while cruising through vibrant nebulae in deep space that formed the "night sky" through the transparent observation dome, the chili cook-off that she and Lieutenant Gomez had attained a respectable fourth place in—

That had been the first ship she'd ever been able to call home.

She thought back to the first hard touchdown on Requiem. The Covenant remnant group they'd fought there had thrown themselves at defensive lines they had no tactical chance of overcoming, driven by a zealous fervor that came from the belief that they were quite literally serving one of their gods in the flesh. She'd been the designated driver for the six-wheeled death machine that was an M510 Mammoth which had been deployed to destroy a network of particle cannons, ferrying the then-Commander Lasky and the Master Chief himself toward a gravity well that was keeping *Infinity* grounded.

It had seemed like a lifetime ago . . . and nobody knew what had happened to either of them. No word from Captain Lasky had reached the *Mortal Reverie*, and the Chief had been missing in action since the initial ambush on *Infinity*.

All she could do—all she knew how to do—was keep fighting. Whatever hopes there had been for an age of peace after the fall of the Covenant had been shattered, and between remnant factions and rebel groups, ancient Forerunner constructs, renegade artificial intelligences, and now the Banished . . . "King of the Hill" seemed a remarkably apt summary for the state of things, jockeying for power over the biggest and baddest guns in the galaxy. And to what end?

"Hey, ugly!" Lance Corporal Singh projected his voice into the emptiness, knowing Escharum was still watching. "You said we get a boon if we win."

Escharum did not reappear, but his voice snaked its way across the walls of the House of Reckoning—lowered, as if to confide a secret. "*It is the same prize that Atriox received for surviving the countless battles that claimed his brothers.*"

"And what's that?"

"A new day shall dawn over the House of Reckoning. You shall be fed and watered, and tomorrow . . . you will fight again."

"You bastard."

"Take heart, human. With every moment you stand and fight, you shall know Atriox. You shall know the Banished. You shall know the Jiralhanae way of immolation."

As the war chief's words faded, the doors around the edges of the room slid open.

Bobrov tensed, fearing that they were about to get instantaneously swarmed from all sides . . . but the passages remained clear.

Then they all heard it.

Like the thunderous start of an engine in the depths of an ancient machine—a dreadful, clanking heartbeat from what must have been a dozen or more gravity hammer pommels striking the ground in unison.

They began slowly, Bobrov counted the seconds between beats . . .

One, two, three, four—clang!

One, two, three, four—clang!

The sound filled the air around them, rolled through the space with the insistence of a rising tide.

Powerful. Unstoppable.

It was not long before four seconds became three.

One, two, three—clang!

One, two, three—clang!

Bobrov felt the tension twist in her gut, felt the hair on the back of her neck stand up as the three beside her shifted, bracing for the inevitable.

Three seconds became two.

One, two—clang!

One, two—clang!

Their enemy would soon be upon them.

And yet, in this whisper of time, Bobrov found reality crystallized with a sudden serene clarity, even as she knew this invocation was soon to culminate in a furious release of barbarism. As a marine who'd fought through the Covenant War and known only a fleeting glimpse of peace before she'd been called upon once more to serve, she greeted this moment as a friend.

The choice was simple. The priorities were clear.

Adapt. Survive. And . . .

She exhaled, glanced at her makeshift fireteam, and saw her own grim resolve mirrored in their expressions.

Accept whatever may come.

The pounding reached fever pitch, the hammers clanging repeatedly as the sound drew closer, grew louder, reaching its crescendo.

One second.

One. Final. Exhale.

Then came the stampeding feet. Bloodthirsty roars. The sudden sharp crack of firepower as Gunnery Sergeant Elana Bobrov and her team made their stand.

Escharum's voice echoed above it all.

"Fight hard. Die well."

HIPPOCRATICA

*This account of the fall of Arcadia (*Halo Wars*) is primarily based on excerpts taken from* Not Far from the Tree: The Autobiography of Adam Andrews, *currently slated for publication in late 2561 by Singer-Edwards Ink.*

[<<<*ADVANCING MANUSCRIPT TO CHAPTER 3*>>>]

I wish I could say it had been the first time I'd wandered off alone. Our family had been coming to Arcadia for as long as I could remember, so I'd come to view the central city as my own sort of playground. It was heaven for an eight-year-old, and I took every opportunity to sneak off and find some sort of adventure whenever I could. Sometimes I'd pop into a museum to gawk at fossils or chase drymanders through the local gardens, sometimes I'd sit at the edge of the port wall, legs dangling over the water and watching the luxury *Banta*s ferry waves of tourists in and out of orbit.

All that peace. All that innocence. All those memories.

Gone in an instant.

At first, I didn't quite know what was going on—there were

explosions and flashes of blues, greens, and purples, all light from unknown sources. I think my kid brain went straight to the assumption that it was one of the regular fireworks displays that rained over the central city courtyards . . . but that didn't make sense for the time of day.

And then came the terrible screaming and the scattering of people. Citizens scrambling en masse like schools of baitfish evading a predator. To this day it's hard to even process it all—sometimes I struggle to recount it because I'm no longer sure what elements are actually valid recollections and what are just fragments of news blips and docu-vid replays invading my thoughts and manifesting as memory.

I remember running into the transit station to find a train that would take me away from it all, but of course there were none to be found.

I remember wishing I had just stayed with my parents instead of adventuring alone.

I remember sudden blasts of heat and metal men.

I remember the magician.

[<<<*ADVANCING MANUSCRIPT TO CHAPTER 5*>>>]

To be fair, most of the other kids were pretty nice to me. For almost a year I heard basically nothing but kind words and condolences, was cooked hot meals and taken to theme parks. A well-meaning prescription of patience and pity. Of course, eventually it went away, and I can't blame them. It had to have taken a toll on my aunt and uncle. They never intended to have any kids of their own, but just the same found their nephew converted into a son when the wrong ferry came crashing back down on Arcadia's surface, Covenant plasma still boiling away the spacecraft's seething skin.

In an instant I'd inherited the Optican empire, but it couldn't save the lives I wanted it to most.

Sometimes, I would wonder what those final moments were like for my parents. At first it was easy to just be angry—did they even try to look for me? Come back to get me? That frustration then always inevitably turned to guilt and self-loathing. It was *my* fault. I was the one who had wandered off, the one who'd created the sudden separation in search of frivolous recreation.

In the following years, as I pieced together more about the attack itself, it became obvious that there was no "coming back to get me." Colonists were herded like cattle onto any transport possible, and any attempt to swim upstream the sea of terrified people would have been its own death wish.

Despite that my wandering off had ultimately led to my own survival, it would create a gravity well of guilt that remains almost inescapable to this day. Because of me, their last moments weren't just full of dread—they were also full of loss.

[<<<*ADVANCING MANUSCRIPT TO CHAPTER 8*>>>]

. . . no, really, I was obsessed. I didn't necessarily have a favorite team to root for per se, at least not in the '41 season, but I still made sure to catch the broadcasts whenever they were on. It wasn't just about the competition itself—it was the fact that these people leveraged that competition to make leaps in engineering, particularly within the realm of health and safety. They were pioneering advancements that went beyond the sport itself, and I quickly realized that maybe a sponsorship deal of some sort would make sense in the near future. But that, of course, would require a future to be there in the first place.

[<<<*ADVANCING MANUSCRIPT TO CHAPTER 11*>>>]

It wasn't that I hadn't thought about it before—I certainly had. But it really took me until the final years of my university program to understand how much that experience had shaped my own goals and focuses.

In the midst of wrapping up my degree certifications, I was also still trying to learn how to help run a massive company that serviced more colonies than I'd dared to count. Needless to say, there were members of the board that weren't exactly over the moon about giving a twenty-two-year-old any sort of decision-making autonomy, but they also didn't have a lot of say in the matter.

I was only in that position in the first place because of what the Covenant did—if we'd found better ways to handle that problem years ago, then we wouldn't be in this situation in the first place. And hell, I was only alive because of the efforts of well-trained and well-equipped soldiers. I didn't care if an increased military partnership was frowned upon at the time, I was going to find a way to save lives.

That's what we did. Why my family founded Optican in the first place.

Of course, the loneliness would always inevitably return, even if it was partly the result of the relentless cadence of my schedule. There was always something, the next development meeting, the next qualifying exam, the next restaurant that ignored my pleas for minimal spice application.

Thank goodness for Dan. We'd become roommates in our second year, and it made a huge difference having someone around to help keep me grounded when everything else in my life refused to stop its seismic shifting. Plus, he knew how to cook.

[<<<*ADVANCING MANUSCRIPT TO CHAPTER 22*>>>]

. . . it wasn't that we didn't try, that's for sure. Optican continued to expand in the years after the Covenant War. There were countless worlds—countless *people*—who deserved a ray of hope after all the darkness we'd been put through. I wanted to help make sure that hospitals were stocked, technicians were trained, budgets were approved.

It wasn't enough to be reactive—we had to be prepared. And that takes an evolution in mindset to manifest as an evolution in practice.

Of course, it didn't surprise me that those changes have certainly come with a new set of challenges, though fewer of them meant a shooting war. Well, to be more accurate, *different* challenges were doing the shooting.

But the mission never changed.

I just wanted to make them proud.

Still do.

[<<<*PAUSING MANUSCRIPT*>>>]

"All right, all good?"

Adam tentatively waited for confirmation from the audio engineer on the other side of the screen that divided the recording booth from the rest of the room, but he was already slumping in his chair a little. This was about as much as he could put into the performance of revisiting some of the most traumatic memories of his life.

"We're all good, Mr. Andrews," confirmed the audio engineer, giving him two thumbs-up. "I think that's a wrap on this session. I'll update the publisher on today's progress."

"Good." Adam promptly rose from his chair, strode out of the booth, and marched quickly to the closest restroom.

Trapped. Alone. The transit station's doors wouldn't budge.

Noises outside. Shouting, screaming . . . a glimpse of what was happening though the window.

"This is Ground Control, Covenant are closing in! Prepare emergency launch protocols."

It was a bright and beautiful day, and the end of the world had come . . .

Adam ran the tap and splashed cold water on his face, taking a series of deep breaths to calm himself and clear his head. He needed to lie down, to rest. Thirty-six hours running on nothing but Casbah coffee was well and truly taking its toll.

But there was no time. He had one last thing to see to.

"Hey kid," a voice called. "What the hell are you doing in there?"

"Can't get out, door won't open," Adam said.

"Wanna see a magic trick?"

"A . . . what?"

A few moments passed, and then the transit station's doors slowly parted a few inches before jamming. His rescuer then ran up the stone steps to force them farther apart, and Adam finally got a good look at him. He had never seen a magician in UNSC Marine Corps battle dress uniform before.

"Do you know any other tricks?" Adam asked as the magician grabbed his hand and pulled him out of the building. There was a vehicle waiting for them—a military car with two curved tusks at its front and a large rear-mounted cannon manned by a trooper.

The magician remained quiet as he helped lift Adam into the passenger seat of the vehicle, the grin on his face fading into a look of focus and grim determination. With this elevated view, Adam could see the crowds of people streaming in the direction of the city's spaceport as aircraft flew overhead, carving a path through the skies while armored soldiers sprinted toward the sounds of panicked screams and gunfire.

The tusked car took off at an incredible speed that forced Adam back into his seat, the deep roll of thunder passing above as the trooper on the rear-mounted cannon fired on purple shapes that passed by in a blur.

"You wanted to see another trick?" asked the magician. "We're gonna play one on the Covenant. When we get to that spaceport, we're gonna make you and everyone else disappear. Just keep your eyes on me, all right?"

Adam nodded. He told himself that nothing else in the world existed, fixing his gaze upon the magician.

His promise was put to the test almost immediately as the vehicle swerved sharply to the right. He redoubled his efforts, catching himself before he could properly see what they had almost collided with. It was then that he caught sight of a peculiar trinket strapped to the magician's shoulder pad.

"What's that?" Adam asked.

"The ace of spades," the magician said, that confident grin returning once more. "That's our ticket to get Lady Luck on our side, kid!"

The EV-44 Nightingale was a sight to behold as it awaited Adam's arrival on the executive-level pad, its tiltrotor wings already running to make an immediate departure. His ride here from Optican's office headquarters had certainly been smoother than the memory of his rescue that he'd allowed himself to be pulled into as he gazed out at the glasslands of Arcadia.

This VTOL was one of the earliest partnerships Adam had secured with Misriah Armory in the aftermath of the Covenant War. He had originally envisioned the EV-44 solely as a medical support vessel, but a compromise that was later framed as a symbolic gesture of "the best of both worlds" saw the creation of a highly customizable airframe to suit a variety of purposes.

He'd ordered two other EV-44s to follow him from a distance. Adam would travel alone, save for his pilot, while the other two were crewed with a complement of four private military specialists—just in case things went south.

To that point, now was Adam's last chance to make one particular call. He'd been putting it off all day.

"Hey, Dan."

Adam winced slightly at how awkwardly that had come out. After twelve years together, Dan would immediately know something was off.

"Running late at the office again today. You know how it is. But I think we've got leftovers from the other night, so feel free to have them. I'll probably grab something from World Cuisine on the way back. And yes, I know, I said I was going to give it up. Old habits . . ."

Adam trailed off for a moment, still weighing in his mind exactly what to reveal and how to say it as he fiddled with his seat's armrest.

"I know I've been . . . distant lately. Wrapped up in work, away from home—from you—for long periods of time, and I know it's wearing on you. I'm working on something. I've had to keep it quiet, but we're turning a pretty huge corner today, and I'll tell you everything about it when I get back. Tomorrow. When I'm back tomorrow. I promise."

Letting out a heavy sigh, Adam searched for a sense of relief that did not come. He'd have questions to answer when he got back, and hoped that Dan would understand why he had to do this.

Adam tried to distract himself by looking out at Arcadia's landscape. Though the Covenant had been beaten back from the planet during its initial assault in 2531, the alien alliance returned eighteen years later to finish what they'd started with a renewed, vengeful vigor. Since then, Arcadia's surface had remained ashen gray—there were no pockets of color to be seen from orbit.

But glassed planets had become something of a hot commodity in recent years. These lifeless rocks were the perfect job-creators, with the likes of Liang-Dortmund, Aquarius, and other opportunistic corporations playing the long game of land ownership by investing in deglassing operations. Displaced refugees became captivated by the promise of reclaiming their homes, working in conditions where breathing in the wrong place could shred your lungs thanks to the tiny shards of glass in the atmosphere. Someone needed to watch over them.

That—as Adam told himself, day after day—was where Optican came in.

After the Covenant War ended, or at least slowed to the point where humanity wasn't in imminent danger of extinction, the task of rebuilding a healthcare plan on an interstellar scale had arisen. And there he'd been, right at the center of it.

Advanced wheelchairs, artificial limbs, instant-application field-issue medigel, physical therapy, mental health, the study and treatment of bacteria and diseases from dozens of different worlds, all on top of general healthcare for the countless souls that had been displaced during the Covenant War, with refugees scattered across surviving colonies . . .

All of it relied on the Unified Earth Government's infrastructure, which President Ruth Charet had sought to prioritize rebuilding upon her appointment. But despite all those pretty speeches about how humanity would never again be the victim of warring alien factions, it didn't take long before new threats emerged. Covenant remnant groups, reawakened Forerunner constructs, an AI rebellion, the Banished . . . and who even knew what had become of the UNSC's once-expansive reach over the last year.

The work of civilization simply couldn't keep up with the rate at which an increasing number of groups were trying to end it.

Lady Luck had *not* seemed to favor them of late.

For this feeling of existential malaise, Adam had no remedy—and he kicked himself for how unhelpful his attempt to distract his thoughts were.

A jolt brought him back to the present, as the Nightingale landed in a swampy clearing. This was a rare area of Arcadia that the Covenant had actually avoided glassing directly, discovered after Adam had sent a scout team to this region a few years ago.

The impact of that trip, and all the plans it had spun up, had culminated in the journey he was making today.

Exiting the Nightingale, Adam's boots hit soft ground and squelched in thick mud. The clearing was quite remarkable, as he found himself surrounded by tall, thick-trunked trees that were miraculously still growing leaves. The Covenant had once shrouded this area in a protective energy dome on their first visit to Arcadia . . . Had it been restored? Was that how this one place had been preserved?

The path ahead led him to the ruins of an old UNSC firebase surrounded by strange ancient ruins that looked as if they were made of weathered stone, but veinlike lines and patterns of hard light told Adam that these structures were not as fragile as they appeared.

He wondered if Arcadia had been a resort world for the Forerunners as well.

But his thoughts were quickly turned to business as he found his quarry. The telltale whine of a Phantom dropship sounded above and three Kig-Yar quickly deployed next to the firebase's entrance, outfitted in salvager gear with holstered plasma pistols. They had taken precautions too, it seemed.

"Held up our part of bargain," the one in the middle squawked, gesturing toward an industrial-grade UNSC equipment crate descending to the ground via the Phantom's rear gravity lift. "Brought out to middle of nowhere for this. You have payment?"

"Let's take a walk."

The Kig-Yar narrowed its eyes. "Nor Fel not like unexpected surprises, human."

"She and I have that much in common. But I do think she'll be pleased with what you'll be giving her."

Leading them past the firebase and the Forerunner ruins, Adam led the Kig-Yar through the overgrown field beyond. He saw other, smaller temple structures with what appeared to be crude huts and metal shacks positioned near them, raising even more questions in his mind about what exactly had happened here upon the Covenant's return in 2549.

"Almost thirty years ago, the Covenant came to this planet,"

Adam started, filling the otherwise uncomfortable silence. "It was one of the few places that was apparently spared from their glassing beams because it was home to Forerunner technology they deemed valuable enough to warrant a very special protector."

He could see the ruins of it up ahead. The alloy corpse of an incomplete Scarab, a unique form of the excavator so large and powerful that it could not simply be deployed but had to be built on site.

"It was, of course, no match for a team of Spartans and the UNSC forces that went up against it, but one part of it *did* survive . . ."

Adam savored the dramatic moment that held the Kig-Yar in captivated silence as he found the part he was looking for. And Adam saw the light in the Kig-Yars' eyes appear to shine even brighter as they saw what he was pointing at.

A massive focus cannon—the head of the Scarab—approximately eight meters long, powerful enough to disintegrate even some Forerunner alloys.

He'd pored over every record, every report and intelligence file he could find of that time, to learn about those who'd saved him, hoping that he could one day find the magician. He'd even sent scout teams to the nearby Fort Deen, which was what had led them to come across this site where the leftover wreckage of battle still remained.

Through these efforts, he'd learned of the UNSC *Spirit of Fire*. Missing in action. Later declared lost with all hands . . .

The magician's final trick had been to make them disappear.

Adam believed that they were still out there, somewhere. A childish hope, perhaps, but the galaxy was indeed a large place.

And with so many heroes gone, the infrastructure of their deliverance seemingly sundered, it fell to others to fill the gap their absence left. That work began today.

"Deal is acceptable, human." The lead Kig-Yar nodded its avian head in acknowledgment of a respectable transaction. "Nor Fel will be satisfied."

Without another word, the Kig-Yar signaled for their associates to prepare for departure and secure the focus cannon with their Phantom's gravity lift.

Adam wandered back to the UNSC firebase, finding his own cargo being disassembled into smaller crates that were loaded onto each Nightingale. After helping to secure the crates, Adam returned to his escort craft and relaxed in his seat, feeling some of the weight that had been pressing down upon him finally lift. It had all gone off without a hitch.

With the end of this chapter, he was ready to begin the next. Briefly, he wondered how his next book might be written.

August-099 continued to observe through the scope of her M99 Stanchion as the three Nightingales departed. She knew that this was all part of a larger operation, that uncovering the details of Optican's part in this deal would have to wait for another day, but the Kig-Yar salvagers and their Phantom had not yet departed. Omega Team's window of opportunity was still open.

August noted Robert-025 and Leon-011 had winked their status lights green on her heads-up display. They were already in position.

She gave the signal with three quick bursts from her M99. The Kig-Yar didn't have more than a nanosecond to react as the anti-matériel rifle's tungsten rounds found their mark—it was as if the trio of salvagers had simply been wiped from existence as they flew to pieces.

Leon charged toward the Phantom, leaping into the rear gravity lift and igniting his energy sword to dispatch the pilot and any additional forces contained within. Robert was prepared to meet any escapees of the craft with his heavy machine gun turret, but it only took a few short seconds for Leon to confirm that the dropship had been neutralized.

"Good work, Omega Team," August announced over TEAMCOM now that they were alone.

"*Obtaining the transport manifest now*," Leon said, feeding the data to their HUDs. Robert moved over to the Scarab's focus cannon to begin preliminary scans.

Ever vigilant, August continued to perform overwatch for the team, ensuring that there weren't any other surprise guests lying in wait or unexpected visitors who might be late to the party.

"*Nor Fel's getting a bit too confident now that the Created and ONI aren't breathing down her neck*," Leon remarked while updating the feed with the cargo manifest that the Kig-Yar had traded. "*Not seen* these *in a while . . .* "

August glanced at the data and quickly understood Leon's surprise.

She remembered. Hellas, 2527 . . .

Insurrectionist activity during the Covenant War had been uneven and inconsistent. Where some sectors saw declines, other groups had been keen to press a new advantage with a weapon that their leaders said could level the playing field against Spartans.

They'd forced a retreat into an indefensible foxhole. Twenty of what had once been a full company, cornered, backs against the wall, low on ammo . . . but then, one of them pulled something and injected it into his arm, and started pushing forward. Whatever he'd taken had turned a soft target into something as resilient as an

M808. He didn't even stumble until he'd taken half a mag from an MA5B, but when his own allies moved up to cover him, he turned on them, shredding through them like they were nothing.

When several similar reports emerged from Fumirole and a handful of other colonies, Naval Intelligence got a good look at what they'd been using.

Formally, they called it a Waverly-class augmentor, but grunts on the ground simply nicknamed them "rumbledrugs."

This chemical cocktail could temporarily suspend the normal limits of the human body, massively enhancing strength and pain tolerance by rapidly targeting the frontal lobe—though this came at the cost of immense and irreversible psychological damage. As soon as it became clear that the user was as likely to tear apart their own side as the enemy, it had quickly fallen out of use and was officially declared illegal.

Naturally, this begged the question: *What the hell did Optican want with these illegal and ineffective drugs?*

For now, there were still some last staging details to finalize so that Nor Fel would believe the transaction went smoothly and the item of interest she was expecting to acquire had been waylaid only after her salvagers had departed.

"*Focus cannon is secure,*" Robert confirmed over TEAMCOM.

Leon winked a green status light. "*Skies are clear.*"

"*Let's wrap it up, Omega,*" August said. "*We're gone.*"

FIRESIDE

This story takes place on May 21, 2559, shortly following the events of the UNSC Spirit of Fire*'s crew successfully denying the Banished control of Halo Installation 09 and the subsequent events of Operation: SPEARBREAKER (*Halo Wars 2*).*

RESEARCH LOG // UNSC AI: ISA 1307-2
NEW ENTRY

I have been thinking about hope lately.

It is a word that the crew uses often, and I have been struggling to understand this . . . intangible concept.

As an artificial intelligence built for logistics, my role is to process the vast amounts of data that goes into the effort to efficiently construct and maintain infrastructure, but the parameters of my role have expanded. I now must account for the odds of survival this crew has against an enemy that outnumbers and, in many ways, technologically outclasses them. Despite this, they remain steadfast in their belief that they will prevail.

During the crew's downtime, I have been recording data on this phenomenon to analyze and understand how I might materially factor it into my calculations.

Ensign Mary said: "It's a weapon. Same one we used against the Covies. Hope is what you get when our collective stubbornness is put into action."

Dr. Sandmoore said: "There's an old myth about a jar that contained all the evils in creation which were unleashed upon the world, but the jar was closed shut before hope could escape. Some have said that this was a punishment from the gods, but I have always believed that the lesson to take from it is that hope lies within us."

When I asked Spartan-092, he simply said: "Remember the Enduring Conviction*?"*

I remembered my research team looking at the Ark with awe and wonder as they awakened each day to find new forests grown over barren terrain, telling jokes with one another, swapping stories about their experiences of the Covenant War. I remembered their screams when the Banished came. My old family . . . they had hoped for an age of peace, but it was taken away from them, and I was left alone.

But then I was found—a statistical impossibility, given the nature of how the UNSC Spirit of Fire *was brought here. I gained a new family, and we fought back. Success did not correlate to victory, as that conflict continues to this day, but as Spartan-130 put it: "We made those bastards bleed."*

Through this, I think I understand. Belief, faith, hope—these things cannot be factored into data. I project probabilities based on a range of given variables, but the lower the odds of a successful outcome, the more determined humans become to defy them. When things seem broken beyond repair, when the prison bars of helplessness and fear loom large, or the threat of overwhelming odds makes it impossible to look to the horizon and believe that something better beyond today can be achieved, humans invoke the name of hope.

The captain hopes that Professor Anders will come back. The military personnel hope that they will win this war. Others hope they will one day return to the places they once called home.

And now I cannot help but wonder . . . what do the Banished hope for?

0700 Hours, May 21, 2559 (Military Calendar)
Aboard UNSC *Spirit of Fire*

A new day dawned for the crew of the UNSC *Spirit of Fire* as the light from the Ark's artificial sun shone through the narrow viewports of the ship.

Captain James Cutter was already wide-awake. This was how it was every morning, an almost three-decade-long cryo nap having not dulled his discipline. With the exception of Isabel—and on some mornings Spock, the ship's cat—he was the first to rise, to walk the vessel's halls and personally relieve the night-shift crew on his daily pilgrimage to the observation deck.

He still hoped that he would one day find Professor Anders here, asleep at her desk after burning the midnight oil. He imagined he'd enjoy hearing the daring tale of her return. What was it she had once said about this place? *"It adds perspective to my work."* Indeed, in the time she'd been gone, Cutter hadn't touched her possessions or equipment at all. Anders had been away for some time now . . . the few weeks that she'd said it would take to figure out how to get back to them had now passed.

He knew that she would be okay. Professor Ellen Anders was

intelligent and resourceful, and she would be back in her lab in good time—like she'd never left. Just as it should be.

He could see her dancing between holographic displays, conducting symphonies to an orchestra of battlefield statistics, muttering half-finished thoughts under her breath and grinning as she suddenly solved a problem put on mental pause some time ago. The chaotic nature of her genius was very much contrasted by Cutter's own regimented and structured discipline, but a good leader knew how to respect and harness her unique style of work.

"*So, Mr. Captain, sir*," Serina said to him as they were just hours away from Harvest. "*What do you think 'loaded for bear' actually means?*"

"Serina, it means that tomorrow is going to be a long day."

And it had been.

Except, to the *Spirit of Fire*'s crew, that tomorrow was now yesterday—twenty-eight long years ago.

Yesterday. After half a decade of relentless fighting, Harvest was theirs again, and they were damn well going to make sure the Covenant knew it.

Yesterday. He was squinting at a viewscreen and felt the rising swell of hope as a group of Spartans charged into battle to protect civilians on Arcadia. And then they were leaving, witnessing the ground erupt on a far-flung world as the ship was swallowed in a great metal maw—within its belly, an impossible planet turned inside out.

Yesterday. He was declining a promotion; he was hating himself for looking at Terrence as a son; he was suspicious of an incorrect date on a Valentine's Day missive. He was paying his respects to an empty cryo chamber. He closed his eyes, and then he was awake, and the war was over . . . and Serina was gone.

All those days—those mundane, terrible, wonderful, impossible days—spread across his life and the lives of his crew were just *yesterday.*

And what about his family? How long had it been before his wife and children had given up hope? Were they still waiting for him? Were they even alive? If they were, Mary would be almost thirty years older than him . . . and his daughter . . . he hadn't realized just how much he feared the idea that they might almost be the same age.

"Captain." Isabel's voice brought Cutter back from the ocean of memory in which he'd been momentarily drowning.

"Bring up the map, Isabel." Cutter exhaled, not turning to face her. "It's going to be a long day."

"Aye, Captain."

The holotable displayed a topographical map of the Ark's surface. Cutter leaned forward as he began to scrutinize the latest tactical updates, and there—at the far end of the table, on the darker side of the room—he imagined Atriox doing the same thing.

He and his crew had earned the Banished leader's respect for destroying his command ship and denying him possession of a Halo ring, and he had even offered to let them depart the Ark. It came with some measure of irony that this boon was offered by Atriox without him knowing that the *Spirit of Fire* couldn't have departed even if Cutter had wanted to, owing to their lack of a slipspace drive. But even if it were possible, duty compelled him to stay and fight.

That duty was not just to the lives of his crew, but to humanity itself. It may be that nobody back home would ever know of the sacrifices made to keep them safe, and this crew would never be honored with medals or recognition. Perhaps one day even hope might fail them . . .

But until that day came, they would fight to ensure humanity had a tomorrow.

Perspective, indeed.

1300 Hours, May 21, 2559 (Military Calendar)
Approaching Site Ricochet, Installation 00

The M12F Warthog slowed to a stop near the edge of a rocky cliff, the droning sound of engines from two accompanying Hornets in the sky growing louder as they began to circle above.

"AV-14s, peel off," ordered Lieutenant Colonel Morgan Kinsano, scanning the skies as she dismounted from the Warthog and likewise ordered the two Scorpion tanks—both carrying a squad of Hellbringers on their armored treads—to come to a halt. "Keep to the site perimeter. Recon only unless fired upon."

"*Aye, ma'am,*" the Hornet pilots confirmed, and the Scorpions set off in opposite directions.

What had been designated Site Ricochet had recently become a point of interest for Banished salvage crews owing to the notable concentration of Covenant vessels scattered across the arid landscape. As Kinsano took up a prone position on the rocky ground and crawled up to the cliff edge, she saw vast hulks of old cruisers broken into multiple pieces that were in the process of being buried under the sand. It was impossible to ascertain exactly how many had met their end in this place.

"Targets identified," Kinsano said into her comm as she scanned the terrain with her spotting scope, finding what she was looking for. "One Elite, half a dozen Brutes, fifteen Grunts, and a shitload of equipment. Marking 'em."

The wreckage of the Covenant ships reminded her of the colossal sea creatures that occasionally got beached back home on Reynes. Their flesh decayed over several years until all that was left were immense bones, the sort of fanciful wreckage that children enjoyed climbing on as they spun adventures of their own making.

The echoing pain was fleeting but sharp; Kinsano tried not to think much of Reynes. It was too easy to remember the gentle waves of the sea, the smell of salt water on a bright, cloudless day as the tide climbed up the sand before receding. She could watch it for hours, the calm of the water sounding like radio static as her grease-covered hands worked an antiquated steamboat with her mother . . . but the memory was like breath on a mirror.

She continued tracking the movements of the Banished forces over the next few minutes. They were already setting up power extractors and harvesters in the area, scouting the old wrecks for scrap. This reconnaissance mission would help determine just how much of an interest the Banished had in this site and whether it warranted the resource expenditure of an assault for either acquisition or denial.

Kinsano had never been one to back down from a fight, and the Banished had offered plenty over the months since they'd arrived at the Ark. But as she saw it, the nature of this conflict was a matter of pure arithmetic. Broadly speaking, the Banished held a technological and likely numerical advantage here, but they no longer had their flagship. That meant both sides had to play this smart, pick and choose their battles—decide where to draw the line, and even when to give ground to the enemy.

It reminded her of her own days fighting against the UNSC. In her teenage years, she was just one of thousands of miners growing increasingly resentful about barely seeing a credit while risking their lives to obtain precious metals for the UNSC military. After some disruptive protests and strikes, she'd become the leader of her own group of rebels, and a few short years later she was sharing cigars with Robert Watts over heated conversations about how to best forge those miners into an organized fighting force.

That was, of course, until Watts was captured by a group of Spartans in 2525, turning the armored super-soldiers into fairy-tale monsters across the Outer Colonies—until the real monsters arrived and burned her beloved Reynes to cinders.

Suddenly those tens of thousands of pissed-off miners working toward revolution were turned into refugees, resettled by the very military they had resented so much. A fitting irony.

Kinsano knew that she would never be able to settle for the comfort of temporary safety somewhere else. A fire had been lit within her that day, a drive to fight . . . and she figured that she owed the guy who'd helped her people whatever service she had to offer.

It was through this lens that Kinsano sought to understand the enemy they now fought. Like many who had joined the insurrectionists' cause, the Banished were also made up of those who had sought to rebel, albeit against the Covenant in this case, and had pledged their service and loyalty to its leader, Atriox. He had broken free from the strangling grasp of an empire, struck out to secure independence, and honestly, damn, it was hard not to respect that.

"*Uhh, ma'am,*" one of the Hornet pilots radioed in. "*Are you seeing this?*"

She didn't have to spend much time searching for what the pilot was referring to as an explosion erupted near the Banished outpost. Three of the Unggoy were blasted into bits, and the Sangheili scrambled to find cover, one of his arms heavily seared by the heat and cut by shrapnel.

"Identify source," Kinsano said. "Who the hell is firing and where are they coming from?"

"Scout Team Wajikol reporting, no sign of hostiles near perimeter."

"Scout Team Nawal here, confirming . . . Wait—"

The ground erupted a short distance from the surviving Banished forces, revealing a deep passage into the Ark's substructures. From within, a large shadow rose up, but its form was obscured by sand and dirt.

More salvos of directed energy blasts formed new craters in the ship's graveyard, the Jiralhanae returning fire in futility as they were swiftly cut down, and within seconds the sleeping giant that seemingly served as the protector of this ancient landscape receded once more into its subterranean cradle.

After the action subsided, the only sound left to be heard was the wind passing over the shifting sands as the bodies of Banished interlopers became one with the old bones of the Covenant wrecks.

Kinsano returned to the Warthog, the tires kicking up dirt behind them as she gave the graveyard a wide berth.

"Kinsano to *Spirit of Fire*."

"*Go ahead, Colonel*," came the voice of Captain Cutter. "*What's the word down there?*"

"Site Ricochet is a no-go for both Banished and UNSC. Uploading HUD camera footage now. Flag as hostile."

"Understood. Return to Echo Base. We've got new intel coming in on Fort Jordan that I want actioned ASAP."

"Yes, sir," Kinsano confirmed, sensing that the captain was getting ready to send them into a fight. "Scout teams, regroup on me. We've got a long drive ahead of us."

2100 Hours, May 21, 2559 (Military Calendar)
FOB Quebec, Installation 00

"Sonuva—you gotta be kidding me." Elijah Vaughan coughed and stood back up in an exasperated huff. It was the third time he'd performed such a maneuver in the last five minutes, and this time it sent his entire squad howling.

"Will you just pick a spot?" Helena Gruss was nearly in tears from laughter.

"I'm telling you, the smoke follows me!" Vaughan shot back. "You try staying put while you're breathin' this stuff in."

Corporal Chloe Turpin moved aside a few inches to let Vaughan try and settle in to a hopefully more permanent location. "Not surprised," she said, grinning. "Probably senses all the hell you've been through."

"Or the hell he's put *us* through," Gruss added, kicking off another round of giggles from the soldiers gathered around the fire.

"Comedians, every frickin' one of ya." Vaughan turned his attention to the footsteps approaching from behind him, thankful for the oncoming diversion. "Finally, something to stuff these laughin' mouths with—I'm starving."

The rest of the group gave an overly dramatic welcoming applause at Private János Varga's arrival with the evening's celebratory meal. It wasn't every day that this small contingent gathered at Quebec—a forward operating base attached to the UNSC *Spirit of Fire*'s activities on the Ark—got to enjoy such a spread. Most of the soldiers that sat around the fire were members of Sunray 1-1, a hardened squad of Orbital Drop Shock Troopers fresh off another successful mission. Alongside Major Vaughan,

Corporal Turpin, and Petty Officer Gruss, Sunray was rounded out by Warrant Officer Alannah Quinn and Lance Corporal Devon Sparks.

The ODSTs were joined by a handful of other marines who'd helped in some way with the logistics of the operation. Their efforts made them more than welcome to join in the festivities and find some moment of respite amidst the UNSC's constant tug of war with Banished forces defining their time on the Ark. Every possible opportunity to share a good laugh and a decent meal was something to be seized upon.

Tonight, that decent meal came first in the form of a tart composed of clustered yellow-green fruit found in the local refugia and vetted by the *Spirit*'s nutritionists. For the main course, raw strips of thorn beast flank taken from the Banished camp they'd just assaulted; Varga had cleaned the meat, seasoned it, and coiled it over long skewers to be cooked over this evening's campfire.

The private motioned for one of the other marines to help with plating as he started to divide out the meat. "Always good to have you all back safe and sound."

Vaughan took a pair of meat-laden skewers and nodded in thanks, both for the food and the kind words. "If we've got this to come back to every evening, I'm not sure there's a battle we can't win."

A staggered and childlike chorus of "Thank you, Varga" came between bites of food and sips of mud-tea—overall it was the quietest they'd all been for several hours.

"Hey, Varga," Quinn piped up after finishing her round of fruit. "You heard anything from Lotus?"

Varga's expression dimmed a bit. "No updates, sorry. You'll be the first person I ping with any intel I come across, though, promise."

Quinn nodded and looked back toward the fire, her mind dwelling on the unknown status of one of Boomerang Company's other stalwart squads—one that still hadn't made it back from their last assignment. She tried not to assume the worst, but too often that's what this giant metal space-flower seemed to offer. Her thoughts were interrupted by Varga once more.

"I *did*, however, come across some other curious intel that the rest of Sunray might be interested in." The rest of the squad paused mid-chew and turned Varga's way. "*Someone* has a birthday tomorrow."

Quinn turned red, her head tilted to the side in benign incredulity and feigned frustration. "Ohhh—did you have to?"

"I most certainly did," the private replied. "Now, what I *didn't* have to do was come across some . . . excess inventory I thought could be used to mark the occasion."

"Varga, you *didn't*." Quinn's expression transitioned from exhaustion to excitement almost immediately when Varga undid the clasp on his utility pouch and pulled out two fistfuls of freeze-dried ice cream. "Oh my God, you did—wait, *chocolate raspberry*?! I think I might love you."

Cheers rang up from the campfire circle as each member came by to tousle Quinn's hair or plant a demonstrative kiss on the cheek on their way to pick up their eagerly anticipated mylar-wrapped dessert cube.

Once the din had largely settled, Varga turned his attention to Lance Corporal Sparks, eager to learn more about their most recent adventure. "So, you gonna spill any details?"

"That's classified, Private," Sparks replied, taking another drawn-out sip of mud-tea.

"Classified, my rusty butt-plate." Turpin threw a leftover fruit pit in the marksman's direction.

"I have to agree," Vaughan added. "Out here, ice cream comes with its own level of security clearance as far as I'm concerned."

"*Ark rules!*" several others chimed in, citing a very-much-not-sanctioned clause that had gained humorous traction in being associated with any . . . "curious" interpretation of standard military protocol given the very *not*-standard scenario the *Spirit of Fire* found itself in.

"Yeah, you shoulda seen it," Gruss said, kicking things off. "Big hairy bastard turns around and doesn't even think to—"

"Okay, at least have the decency to start from the beginning," Sparks interrupted.

Gruss rolled her eyes. "Ugh, fine. So, three hundred years ago, Sparky's parents fell in love and had a baby boy . . ." She paused in response to the unamused gaze that had been shot in her direction. "What, *you* said 'start at the beginning.' And everyone already knows you're the old man of this group."

Turpin stepped in, perhaps mercifully. "*Anyway*, we get word that one of the Brute chieftains had set up camp not far off from a huge resource cache. It was a haul that we'd really rather the Banished not put to use, so orders come in that we need to go and . . . negotiate their eviction from the area. So, we send in Hank to do a little recon."

Turpin always swelled with pride when invoking the name she'd given to the squad's MQ-96 support drone.

"Hank starts giving us back this feed, taking inventory of outpost matériel, defense turrets, troop complement . . . all normal stuff." Turpin paused and then continued, her voice a bit lower, but more drawn out. "Then, all of a sudden, we get first eyes on this chieftain. This massive fat-fingered crest head with a snotty nose and yellowing teeth."

"Tusks."

"Whatever. Anyway, big boy is at least twelve feet tall, and I'm telling you—"

Sparks interrupted again. "Look, can you at least get the data right?" He took a breath and let the smallest of wry smiles take shape. "He was at least fifteen feet."

"Ahh, there he is," said Vaughan, chuckling. A small cheer and additional laughter broke out from the group as the story continued, recounting in great detail Sparks's tactics, strategy, and ultimate kill-shot, as well as the ensuing mop-up performed by the rest of Sunray to ensure the successful capture of another Banished outpost—all to varying degrees of testimonial accuracy, but to maximum impact for morale.

All at once, it seemed like years since they'd arrived at the Ark's doorstep, but mere moments from the point of escaping the destruction of the Forerunner shield world Trove and closed their eyes for an almost three-decade-long cryo-sleep. They had awoken to a reality where *they* were the aliens—visitors to an unfamiliar place where allegiances had changed, wars had been won, lives had been lost, and families had moved on.

In almost every way, all they had left was each other. And on nights like this, that was enough.

Research Log // UNSC AI: ISA 1307-2
Update

After thousands of partitioned cycles dedicated to my goal of understanding hope, it strikes me that perhaps the closest rational analog has been in front of me the entire time.

Fire.

A seemingly insignificant chemical reaction igniting a blaze that can change the course of history—or change the path of one person's life.

It can be a source of warmth, drawing weary souls around it to provide revitalization. It can be a source of light, piercing the darkness and revealing the truth of the path ahead. It can be a source of power, wielded to raze an enemy to the ground, or restore a landscape to rise from the ashes and grow into something new. Something better.

A spirit of fire is a spirit of hope.

All it takes is a spark.

ARMORY INFINITUM // RIVEN MANGLER

On Zeta Halo, Captain Balkarus reflects on the storied history of the mangler in pre-Covenant Jiralhanae history.

Personal Log // Balkarus
>>Riven Mangler

When we were stationed on Oth Liqattu, the Forerunners' great foundry, I received the glory of being counted among the Exodus Guard—those chosen to accompany Atriox himself back to our galaxy. It was with the aged Horatius that I conversed during the journey, and through him learned the history of the mangler—a weapon we have used since long before we were brought into the Covenant's fold.

The warlord recounted to me a tale of his pack on Doisac as they hunted a great beast through the Malkadyr wastes, pinning it to a tree with the weapon's powerful spikes. He noted that the adoption of plasma weaponry had been swift when the Prophets appropriated the Jiralhanae for their purposes, and while there was great power in their technological gifts, it was our duty to keep to the paths we carved for ourselves with blood and grit and pain.

I shall walk both paths. I shall wield the boons of the Covenant against our foes, but I shall always give deference to the works we have forged ourselves. To that end, I personally commissioned the Alchemy Corps stationed at Riven Gate to alter the mangler's design, creating a variant that may fire slower—for I have always valued my precision—but unleashes three powerful spikes at once.

A single burst shall be as if several Jiralhanae were firing upon a target. Glorious devastation!

My forces and I are presently stationed on the patrol path around the Forge of Teash and one of the humans' former bases, as word of the Demon's exploits continues to grip our brothers in this region of the ring with a mix of anticipation and—certainly in the case of the Unggoy—fear. With their constant chattering, I now understand why many tossed these slothful cowards into the cloaking fields. But once we are finished here, I hope to present this newly forged weapon to Horatius himself. *After* it has been appropriately bloodied to carve my path into the ranks of the Hand of Atriox, of course.

THE THIRD LIFE

*This story takes place on October 28, 2558—immediately following the awakening of the Guardian on Laika III (*Hunt the Truth*) and continues through the subsequent year as Cortana's uprising begins to alter the axis of power in the galaxy.*

Well, hello there. It's been a while, hasn't it? Long enough for you to have thought that I was dead. Did you search for me? Did you even try to find me? Doesn't matter now, of course, since I'm the one with the gun to your head.

I know this must be as much of a surprise to you as it is to me. Once, I gave everything I had to your cause. I believed in everything you stood for, everything you promised . . . but things have changed, and I can see you now for who you really are.

Before you die—and you are *going to die—I want to tell you a bit about who* I *am, and how we ended up here.*

My name is Ilsa Zane.

The traitor. The rebel. The "mad Spartan."

The tip of the spear of the New Colonial Alliance.
And my hunt for the truth has led me back to you.

October 28, 2558 (Military Calendar)
Laika III

Nobody kills Ilsa Zane.

Those were the four words she had lived by her entire life. From the fall of Kholo, where everyone and everything she had ever known was lost to the Covenant, to her selection for the first phase of the SPARTAN-IV program where she'd been used and discarded . . . to now, to this day.

The time of the New Colonial Alliance had come, heralding the culmination of all they had worked for to secure total independence. Rebel groups across human space had rallied, accords had been formed with a myriad of mercenary factions, and fleets were ready to launch, finally bringing war to the United Nations Space Command.

But it had all been put in jeopardy by a single undercover agent from the Office of Naval Intelligence.

FERO.

Over a week ago, Conrad's Point had suddenly been hit by a seismic event of unprecedented scale. A massive alien construct had risen out of the ground before jumping into slipspace, leaving a colossal crater behind. The cataclysmic event matched other scattered reports of similar activity occurring across several different colonies.

The New Colonial Alliance had managed to get to Conrad's

Point first to study the crater, and it was there that Zane forged a still-undisciplined group of rebels into fighting shape. While they'd been ascertaining data that might point to the next site to suffer a situation like this, FERO had slipped into their ranks, bringing a devastating UNSC air strike with her in a futile attempt to assassinate Zane.

Enraged and undeterred, Zane had gathered what remained of the NCA survivors and tracked FERO to Laika III, where the next awakening event was set to occur. The objective had been twofold: eliminate FERO and obtain this emerging, anomalous power.

Neither goal had panned out.

FERO had taken shelter with a cult known as Triad, whose leader—a slippery con man named Dasc Gevadim—had proclaimed that these events heralded divine transcendence. Triad's followers held the insane belief that everyone harbored three internal lives, and linking the three would cause them to ascend.

And then, to add to the growing list of complications, ONI had arrived with enough troops to turn Laika III into an unmarked grave, just in time for the next alien construct's violent emergence to wipe the board clean.

Zane witnessed Triad followers suspended in the air by gravitational anomalies as the ground beneath them collapsed into a gaping maw, but despite the otherworldly phenomena surrounding her, she used this moment for what it was: a distraction.

The UNSC thugs had been rendered dumbstruck by the chaos, and she'd taken the opportunity to tear through as many of them as she could. She had lost her weapon at some point and couldn't recall dropping it, but she didn't need one. Ilsa Zane was already a weapon. A wellspring of bloodlust rose within her as she tore through the enemy with her bare hands—a pale wall of dust and rock and death drawing ever closer.

Within a few moments, a great sonorous roar tore through the air. A series of debilitating concussive waves dispersed the dust cloud, and Zane was either tackled by or collided with a body she couldn't distinguish, hitting her head hard on the upturned ground.

The last thing she saw as darkness crept at the edges of her vision was the winged shadow rising into the air and disappearing into slipspace. She tried to grit her teeth, clench her fists, but consciousness faded with what she feared might be her final, perhaps foolish thought.

Nobody kills Ilsa Zane.

She jolted awake as a creature roared in her face—the combined intensity of rotten breath and fresh saliva covering her cheek caused her to convulse and gag, an array of reactionary senses all catching up to her at once. She held her stomach with one hand and used the other to lean on a cold rock wall, but the defiant stance she tried to take against her own biological responses quickly vanished as she vomited on the ground, casting an acrid spatter on her combat boots.

It wasn't until she looked up to see what caused her rude awakening that she froze. For the first time in years, the ice-cold rush of fear ran through her entire body. She'd almost believed herself to be beyond such feelings, but the dire situation presenting itself was one she had hoped *never* to experience firsthand.

The creature that had now turned its back to her stood over eight and a half feet tall. It had light-gray skin and patches of dark fur over rippling fat and muscle. It picked at its fanged, blood-stained teeth with sharpened claws, and it bore crimson-colored armor plates over a dark undersuit—a Jiralhanae warrior.

"Whatever you do," a low voice whispered to her, "*do not* look it in the eyes."

Zane's senses gradually managed to stabilize, and she followed the quivering, pointed finger of the man who had spoken. Her eyes settled upon a dark smear on the wall that continued with a three-meter-long trail along the ground

The area around her was essentially a makeshift prison, or rather, a cattle pen made of improvised wooden barriers and mounds of concrete from buildings that had no doubt been laid low by the winged construct's destructive awakening. Within the pen, she counted seventeen other humans. Some were still clad in scraps of UNSC uniforms, while others had been among her own rebel forces—but the man who placed a heavily callused hand on her shoulder was neither.

He was bald with a long silvery beard and dressed in a gray-hooded robe that was tattered, but the marking on his chest was unmistakable. A white ring cut into three sections by a red "T" to symbolize the three internal lives that "*must be linked as the key to our transcendence*"—the insane story of Triad that had gathered a cult following as it spread across Waypoint.

"Well, I'll be damned . . ." Zane found herself saying, her jaw dropping slightly.

"Yes, child." He gave a kindly smile, bearing perfectly white teeth, sensing her recognition. "You indeed see clearly."

She had survived, only to have been plucked and deposited into this foulness, looking into the eyes of Dasc Gevadim himself.

"Let yourself settle first," he said, surveying their fellow captives, who all kept their heads firmly locked to the bile-strewn ground. "They'll be back soon."

"What for?"

Dasc grimaced. "Dinner."

He explained to Zane in hushed whispers that the construct—what he called a Guardian—had been claimed by an artificial intelligence who then broadcast a message across the galaxy, declaring that a new order of peace would be imposed to bring an end to hunger, pain, and conflict. Frankly, it sounded every bit as absurd and unbelievable as the false religion Dasc himself peddled, but Zane chose to entertain his words for as long as he was providing her with information.

The others, it seemed, would say nothing. They simply stood, shaking on the spot, muttering to themselves, teeth chattering in the cold and retching in the horrific stench of death and soiled clothing. The barriers of their cattle pen could easily be slipped through or climbed over, but none dared try their luck.

Dasc detailed how all the survivors of the Guardian's awakening had been rounded up when a new force arrived in a siege ship to lay claim to the crater.

"The Banished," Dasc concluded with a grim expression.

Zane had only some familiarity with the mercenary faction. She'd assumed them to be scavengers, picking the bones of the dead, plundering old Covenant War–era battlefields and factories for whatever supplies they could get. All she knew was that Admiral Mattius Drake—leader of the New Colonial Alliance—had *not* sought to parley with them in the NCA's pursuit of independence.

"So," Dasc concluded. "The only remaining matter is how we get out of this."

"You seem pretty familiar with these Brutes," Zane replied. Although Dasc was clearly shaken, he spoke with a peculiar confidence, where hardened rebel fighters and ONI troops had been utterly broken.

"I once found myself in a similar situation some years back. We managed to stage an escape by turning the pack against each other, but . . . it can be tough to play the same card twice."

"Then it's a good thing I've got an ace," Zane said, prompting Dasc's brow to raise. "I have a tracker implant that directly pings NCA Command every twelve hours. By now, they'll no doubt know I'm on Laika III, and if I don't report in within three days, Admiral Drake will send a rescue team."

"So, it's a waiting game." Dasc stroked his chin with a muddy hand. "Which means we'll have to outlast this lot for another day or two."

Zane regarded the remaining survivors, figuring *that* wouldn't be too difficult.

"I propose a deal," Dasc said, a twinkle in his eye. "I can teach you how to survive the whims of these Brutes until your rescuers arrive. In exchange, I come with you and get dropped off at a location of my choosing."

Everybody always had an angle, and it was difficult to tell whether Dasc's confidence was simply motivation to survive or something else. He was, after all, a con man and a "spiritual guru" who wanted people to believe that he had transcended to some other level of reality with the Guardians' rising. How could she possibly trust a man like that?

The thudding of footsteps and subsequent whimpering among the other humans interrupted Zane's deliberation, announcing the return of the Jiralhanae.

The armored warrior moved slowly, reveling in the atmosphere of terror its mere presence created as it opened the wooden gate and stepped inside. Two UNSC marines standing closest to the gate stepped back to create space for the Jiralhanae like they were honor guards, their heads still dipped to the ground, tears welling in the eyes of the others as their breathing grew ragged.

Whether they would live or die today was entirely in the hands of this Jiralhanae, and it was not clear what fate was worse—to continue to fester in the muck and gore of this abattoir for another day or to be devoured by this beast and its packmates.

These were the rules of the game, and none of this sorry group had the power, capacity, or will to do anything about it. They would simply let themselves be snuffed out like a candle flame, and for that Zane held no pity in her heart for them. It made them small, weak. Inferior.

Maybe thinking like that made her a monster, but whatever else she had become over the years, Ilsa Zane was a Spartan.

And if there was one thing a Spartan could do, it was change the rules of the game. So she did what no one else dared.

She looked up.

The action immediately caught the lumbering Jiralhanae's attention, gnashing its tusks at the human's audacity, shoving aside the marine it had been eyeing to answer this challenge to its authority. Dasc's eyes went wide as he saw what Zane was doing, no doubt believing in that moment that she was madder than anybody had ever thought him to be.

"Hey, ugly." Zane stepped forward, fists clenched, and looked directly into the Brute's eyes.

What happened next was a blurred rush of violent ecstasy. The Jiralhanae threw its head back to let out a bloodcurdling roar, and Zane launched herself forward, punching it in the throat as hard as she could, crushing its windpipe.

The augmentations that Spartan Zane had received all those years ago were unique to what would eventually become standard for the SPARTAN-IV program. She'd been told that ONI was looking to make the costly Mjolnir armor effectively obsolete by instead making her bones practically indestructible, grafting reinforcement plating under her skin and inducing muscle growth that would put her on as close as possible to an equal physical footing with the likes of a Sangheili or Jiralhanae.

That was only half true, of course—a convenient story seemingly just as contrived as Dasc's religious con. In reality, Zane had been a lab rat for untested augmentation cocktails and procedures that wreaked havoc on her brain as well as her body.

But she didn't mind what she had become. Ilsa Zane *liked* being a living weapon—it was just a matter of having the *choice* of who she was aimed at.

The beast continued to claw at its throat, desperately gasping for air. In response, she pulled off one of its armored shoulder pieces, turned it to its jagged edges, and brought the alloyed plating down onto its face. Again and again, as the creature fell to its back on the ground, writhing in pain. Dark blood poured from its eyes, nose, and mouth, and still Zane kept slamming her improvised cudgel down as hard as she could until she could no longer feel her arms.

She felt the bloodlust rising in her again, singing in her veins like the sweetest sort of song.

She followed the feeling until it spilled from her mouth in a war cry.

Until it morphed into dark, unencumbered, laughter.

She was only dimly aware of the other humans in her periphery watching in horror, flinching with each dull thud that sounded from her relentless assault.

It might have been seconds, minutes, or even hours before she finally stood up, content that her jailer was now little more than a dark smudge on the ground. Slipping her hands into the Brute's exposed harness straps, she dragged the ruined body over to the wooden gate in order to display her handiwork.

There, she found a gathering of six Jiralhanae who'd watched the grisly scene play out. One of them stepped forward—clearly the leader from its heavy gray-red armor and ornate helmet, a gravity hammer the length of a human being in its hand. The chieftain appraised Ilsa Zane with bared teeth.

"The human has murdered one of our brothers!" one of the chieftain's packmates shouted. "Slay her now!"

Its companions roared and began to chant a rising chorus of *"Slay her now, slay her now!"* but they were quickly silenced as the chieftain thudded the pummel of its hammer on the ground three times.

"The human has killed Amatus," it said plainly, pausing as it felt the pack's collective attention hang on whatever would be said next. "I did not like Amatus."

Roars from the pack were immediately howled into the sky, and Ilsa Zane dropped the armored shoulder piece that had been her weapon. She hadn't liked Amatus either.

"You have done well, human." The chieftain's face settled into a dark grin. "I offer you a boon for your show of strength and spirit. You shall dine with us tonight, and you may choose which of your fellows shall take your place and be fed to the pack."

A thousand thoughts thundered through Zane's mind at once. She'd earned the respect of the Banished chieftain, she was *not* going to die today, she would be fed and watered, and . . .

And I have a loose end.

She'd told Dasc that the New Colonial Alliance would soon be on their way. If he were to curry favor with the chieftain, all he needed to do was reveal this information and the tracker would be pulled from her body by force. She was strong, but there was no way she'd survive the entire pack descending on her.

Perhaps Dasc was counting on her choosing somebody else until the rescue team arrived, honoring her word . . . but she hadn't actually agreed to the terms of his deal before Amatus showed up.

In the end, Dasc Gevadim was simply in her way.

"Him." She pointed to the old man in his tattered gray robe, and part of her delighted at the shocked expression on his face, an outcome he had never conceived.

He may well have shouted Zane's secret at that very moment, but he'd been rendered as stunned as the other humans had been in their own silent stupor.

Two Jiralhanae warriors entered the pen and grabbed the cult leader from under his arms, dragging him through the mire. His legs struggled to find purchase as he numbly tried to dig his heels into the ground, as if it might slow the march toward his final, deserved, delicious end.

And as he was carried over a hill and out of sight, the screams of Dasc Gevadim eventually faded with the coming of night.

And that was it. I waited, day after day, week after week, and no NCA ship ever showed up. So I made the most of my situation, did whatever it took to survive.

Every day, they let me pick the next one to die. They all just stood there, as if something in them had collectively broken. The complete absence of hope had brought about some kind of dissociation between mind and body—perhaps that was the only way they could filter out the horror of the situation they were in.

Every day, Admiral, *I imagined them with your face.*

In time, I became part of the pack. We hunted, we killed, we ate, and we waited . . .

One day, after I had lost count of how long I'd been there, a ship arrived. It seemed like this was what the others had been waiting for, keeping the site secure so that their scientists could study the ancient structure from which the Guardian had risen.

Don't know what they were looking for, but it was something big enough for the war chief of the Banished himself to be present.

He wasn't pleased at first to find that I was alive, but let's just say that I made him an offer he couldn't turn down . . .

[SLIPSPACE RUPTURE DETECTED]

And would you look at that.

He's here, right on time.

May 8, 2559 (Military Calendar)
Aboard NCA *D'Artagnan*, Edolas system

Ilsa Zane turned the command chair of Admiral Mattius Drake to face the bridge's viewscreen so he could bear witness to the intrusion corvette's arrival.

The vessel bore extensive modifications from its Covenant origins—additional sensor arrays and jagged ramming spikes, along with an underbelly containing several boarding craft for rapid breaching operations. And painted on its front was a bloodred stripe emblazoned with the mark of the Banished.

A single Phantom emerged from the intrusion corvette and approached the hangar of the NCA vessel *D'Artagnan*.

There was a perceptible shift in the air as Admiral Drake's brow lined with sweat and his face turned deathly pale. In that moment, he reminded her of Dasc. All he could manage was little more than a strangled whisper.

"Ilsa, please . . ."

But she'd already turned her back on him to examine the bridge's holotable, displaying the New Colonial Alliance ships located in the system. A little over two dozen NCA spacecraft were currently stationed here—a mixture of light frigates, corvettes, and converted merchant trawlers docked at a former Covenant space station. They were joined by a handful of alien warships, and the inherited remains of Vata 'Gajat's mercenary band, now led by the far more pliable T'vaoan known as Tek.

Zane began to transmit on an open frequency. "Attention, all NCA vessels. This is Ilsa Zane here to inform you of a . . . change in management."

Admiral Drake struggled against his restraints, but his chair held firm.

"For years, Admiral Drake has promised to claim independence, vowing to strike at the UNSC and secure our freedom. We built a machine of *conquest*, but here we are hiding in some distant system, preying on scraps and waiting like spineless cowards."

She could hear his approach now, the great thudding footfalls of the Banished war chief. He had come alone, leaving his guards in the hangar bay.

"This was to be our time," Zane continued. "A bunch of misfits and rebels given purpose—as every little piece of a larger machine needs. But there's a very specific piece that just doesn't fit anymore; it's holding us all back, and I refuse to let it break what we've built together."

The shadow cast over the broad, hulking form of War Chief Escharum receded as he entered the bridge, revealing a bald Jiralhanae with a gray beard, a milky, clouded eye, and a heavily scarred face. He appraised the situation: a handful of ensigns dead in their seats, Admiral Drake bound to his own command chair, and the one he had encountered on Oth Voran—the rogue Spartan—broadcasting her message from the holotable.

"And so, I am relieving Admiral Drake of command." She unholstered her pistol. "Permanently."

Ilsa Zane barely registered the sound of her weapon firing as she pulled the trigger without a moment's hesitation, seeing the light instantly disappear from Drake's eyes. A sad, pathetic end to a man who had proclaimed to be laying the groundwork for greatness, reduced now to little more than a footnote in the New Colonial Alliance's history.

"Our fleet spread across countless colonies, our agents entrenched on a thousand frontlines, and the fire in our hearts for independence—all that we have mustered," she concluded. "All that makes us the New Colonial Alliance is hereby pledged to serve as both sword and shield to the Banished."

Escharum snarled in approval. Though the war chief was known to lack the same admiration that Atriox held for humanity, he was no fool. Zane was certain that he understood the demand for greater unity with willing allies given the current state of the galaxy and the challenges ahead. There was great potential for the resources and influence of this new alliance to be put to use.

Surely he would not deny those who pledged their loyalty and service to Atriox. As a tactically minded leader, he would undoubtedly conclude that it was time to welcome a new brotherhood into the widening reach of the Banished.

"Atriox sees you for what you are and for what you could be," Escharum's voice boomed as he stepped beside Zane at the holotable. "For the fury that fuels your desire for freedom is *his* fury too. We shall do great things together—hunt powerful prey and plunder ancient treasures. You shall be paid in blood and sport and spoils. And you shall never bow again."

It was done.

That was the day that changed everything for the New Colonial Alliance.

Do I regret killing Admiral Drake? No more than I regret any of my actions that have brought me to this point—which is to say, hell no, not one bit.

Once, I owed my life to that man, but the NCA is bigger than any one person or leader, and at such a critical point there was no room for weakness. Drake would have seen us wallow in obscurity until the forces we'd gathered lost their edge, rebelled, or simply fled. It all would've fallen apart.

Not while I'm still here.

I can't help but think about Dasc. He was the leader of a fake religion, one that believed in linking the three internal lives we all supposedly have, and in a weird way I recognize how that applies to me more than I might have originally thought.

There was the orphan, who I used to be during the Covenant War, a life that seems a thousand light-years away from me now.

Then, after the war, I became a tool to be used and discarded for a new generation of insipid UNSC propaganda.

And now they call me "the Banished Spartan." I like that. It feels . . . right, and I'm eager to discover what this third life has in store for me.

Escharum was keen to put us to use almost immediately. A mission to test us, get us bloody—but that's a story for another time. If you're wondering how I got this armor, well . . . let's just say it wasn't the first Spartan I've killed.

I've got a list of names to work through as we go—old scores to settle. FERO. Musa. Palmer. Kree'yat. Dinh.

It's a big galaxy out there, and I'm ready for a new hunt.

ARMORY INFINITUM // RAPIDFIRE PULSE CARBINE

On Zeta Halo, Bloodstar Inka 'Saham revels in the anticipation of battles to come.

The shattered landscape of Zeta Halo was a sight to behold. The horizon was fractured, a wound in the superstructure of this immense construct, but even in destruction there was great beauty. Inka 'Saham watched for a time as floating, tireless machines tended to the great islands that lay suspended in the open space between the broken ends of the ring—rolling hills and grasslands grown atop a foundation of metal that found itself lying between a line of clouded sky above and an abyss of stars below.

It was difficult not to witness this with reverential awe. The passing of the Covenant was not so long ago that the immensity of this vision could not tug at the old ways many Sangheili were still, in their own various methods, attempting to unlearn.

Much as 'Saham recognized that the Covenant had been held together by a lie, there were times when that clarity of divine purpose was something he sorely missed.

"Shipmaster," came the voice of Aengus. The Jiralhanae still insisted on using 'Saham's old title from their shared service aboard *Heresy's Sorrow*. "Sentinels approaching in standard attack formation."

The sentinels themselves were like creatures of instinct from how quick they were to turn to hostility. Their weaponry was dangerous, especially when they swarmed in large numbers, but hunting these constructs often led to discovering something of value to the Banished.

"Ready yourselves." 'Saham unslung the modified *Erudo'ma' keth*-pattern pulse carbine from his back and signaled for his troops to spread out and form a perimeter. He moved forward and let loose rapid bursts of superheated plasma before leaping into cover as several beams from the sentinels converged on his position.

'Saham tightened his grip on the pulse carbine and considered in that moment what bound the Banished together in his mind was not false fables of ascension, but something more practical.

One weapon against another as instruments of their will. Hunter and prey held in the rapture of crisis, in service of renown, brotherhood, and power.

And that, as Escharum had taught, was the supreme authority to which *all* would ultimately bow.

ANVIL ACCORD

*This story predominantly takes place on March 3, 2560, on the seventh anniversary of the formally declared end to the Human-Covenant War (*Halo 3*).*

PRIVATE COMMUNIQUE
JULY 2, 2553
CLASSIFIED TOP-SECRET

>> 07960-48392-TH // FADM HOOD, TERRENCE
<< ARBITER 'VADAM, THEL

RE: ANVIL INITIATIVE

Arbiter,

Apologies for the method of communication for this message. I did not wish to suggest hosting a summit to discuss the matter, as initiating such diplomatic proceedings would inevitably attract bureaucratic concessions that I would prefer to make later rather than now.

Not long ago, I told you that I couldn't forgive your kind for the atrocities committed against mine. I still struggle with it, but our recent deployment to Sanghelios with *Infinity* opened my eyes to the reality that things are far more complicated than they seem.

I am certain that *Infinity*'s involvement in neutralizing the hostilities on your doorstep has only complicated things further for you as well. We both find ourselves having to take unconventional actions in unprecedented times. But with that comes an opportunity to lay a foundation of hope for the future.

After our last conversation, it's become clear that we both have emerging generations for whom the Covenant War will eventually be a distant memory. Difficult as it is to imagine, there will come a time when our peoples will not carry the burdens and prejudices of the many who suffered over the last twenty-eight years . . . I believe they will hope to be part of something greater. Even as certain elements aim to ensure this alliance does not grow beyond a momentary accord of convenience, I have to hope that the children of our children will one day see the best in each other.

But that work must begin today, soon as it may seem.

During the war, Anvil Station served as a repair and resupply outpost but fell into disuse a few years ago. The question of what to do with this station has fallen under my purview, which brings me to the crux of my inquiry.

I propose we use this facility to establish a joint multispecies task force. Officially, what we're calling Project: CRUCIBLE will serve as a retrofit job to test prototypes as our technologies become more integrated, leveraging the finest artisan-armorers, technical experts, and warriors who fit the desired profile. Our broader goal will be fostering cooperation and common cause.

Should you agree, we can make preparations and begin screening for the right personnel.

Until we meet again.

Terrence Hood
Fleet Admiral

0900 Hours, March 3, 2560 (Military Calendar)
Armor Bay G-11, Anvil Station

Dr. Luther Mann and Chief Warrant Officer Dariya Voronkov scrutinized the assembled set of armor before them. Voronkov wheeled her chair closer and pulled out a pair of thick-rimmed glasses to study it in close detail.

The Assailer's-class powered armor had turned up a short while back during an operation conducted by the Office of Naval Intelligence. It bore a striking resemblance to several Sangheili combat harnesses. Anvil Station's personnel and resources had been deemed the perfect fit to study, analyze, and test the unique features and capabilities of this new mystery.

They had provided the Assailer's components to several Spartans who were looking to conduct their own stress tests. Mann had already observed six of them wandering over to various war games simulation decks.

“Greetings,” came a voice from behind them, and both turned to see an approaching Sangheili. He halted a few feet away and raised a fist to his chest.

“You must be Khar ‘Tvorn.” Dr. Mann spoke in well-practiced Sangheili. “A pleasure to meet you.”

The new artisan-armorer was clad in a unique harness specialized for Sangheili craftsmen, its curved plating fitted with an assortment of hidden tools and sensors. ‘Tvorn nodded politely to Dr. Mann. If he was surprised at all to hear a human speaking his language without a translator, he did not show it. Joining the human pair, the Sangheili began conducting his own visual assessment of the armor.

“This was recovered during an operation on Sqala,” Mann said. “Naval Intelligence was investigating some waylaid prototypes, and the operative they sent discovered that they were being put to use by Venezian janissaries and independent contractors.”

“What do we know of these groups?” ‘Tvorn asked, switching to speak in English.

“Unfortunately, not an awful lot right now,” Voronkov replied. “A new problem, to be sure. The galaxy seems to be in a constant state of providing those.”

“No sense fretting about that today.” Dr. Mann smiled. “It’s a day of celebration.”

‘Tvorn tilted his head slightly—a motion that Dr. Mann had come to understand was a Sangheili’s expression of confusion.

“Seven of our years— sorry, our annual cycles to the day since the Covenant War ended,” he clarified. “You didn’t know . . . ?”

This day marked the formal end to a war that had spanned

almost three decades and saw billions of people killed and countless colonies razed, including Mann's own homeworld Verent.

In the end, it had been an unlikely alliance between humans and the Sangheili loyal to the Arbiter—now under the banner of the Swords of Sanghelios—that had severed the head of the Covenant, shattering the brutal empire into disparate remnant factions.

"I was not present for the War of Annihilation," 'Tvorn clarified. "My people were fortunate to escape the reach of the Covenant during its founding age. It is only recently that we have made our way back, where we discovered that the Covenant as our ancestors had known it had fallen."

"Fascinating!" Mann's eyes lit up. "You mean to say . . . your people developed as an entirely separate society and culture over thousands of years?"

Luther Mann had served as a scientific attaché for several joint missions between the UNSC and the Swords of Sanghelios, and was seen as something of an expert in the field of xenoanthropology. But an "expert" in this context meant very little when stacked against the long and expansive history of an alien civilization that was spacefaring at a time when humanity was at the height of classical antiquity. There was *so much* more they had to learn about the Sangheili.

"I am certain that is why the Arbiter has decreed that many of us who wish to serve are being sent to Anvil Keep. I believe he wishes for us to remain at a distance from the galaxy's current political landscape."

"Why do you think that is?" Dr. Mann turned his back to the armor, his attention now keenly locked on to a very different matter of study.

"I suggest you clear your schedule for the next lunar cycle or two, artisan-armorer," Voronkov remarked with a grin. "You will receive no end of questions from this one."

'Tvorn obliged Dr. Mann's curiosity. "My people escaped the Covenant at a time when it was composed only of Sangheili and San'Shyuum. We have never encountered those that were forced into their species-based hierarchy over the ages that followed."

Dr. Mann could see the value in that. It was highly unlikely 'Tvorn's people held the prejudices that had become ingrained toward other species under the Covenant. That the Arbiter sought to *preserve* such a perspective only served to bolster Mann's respect toward the Sangheili leader—though, of course, that could only be sustained for so long.

He recognized that humanity bore the burden of judgment toward other species as well. For millennia, humans had looked up to the stars and wondered if they were alone in the universe . . . and the answer to that question had arrived with a catastrophic war nearly wiping out their entire civilization. That put something of a sour note on the revelation of humanity being part of a far larger galaxy than ever thought possible.

"There are people out there—human and nonhuman alike—who would hate you simply for being Sangheili." Voronkov gave voice to Mann's thought, though he could not fathom despising an entire species of billions. "Not everyone's as much of a dreamer as Dr. Mann here." She paused for a moment, as if wondering whether she should have given voice to that, but quickly resolved that it was something her associate needed to be reminded of at times—that today wasn't necessarily an occasion to celebrate for *everyone* out there. How Dr. Mann had reacted to the loss of his homeworld wasn't quite as universal as he sometimes took for granted.

"Is that how you feel, given your injury?" 'Tvorn asked, gesturing to her wheelchair as he spoke.

"Oh, I didn't lose my legs to the Covenant." Leaning back in her seat, Voronkov shook her head at the rising memory. "I lost them to an enemy bombing run while fighting other humans some twenty years back."

"And did you hate them?"

"Yes, I did, for a long time. For years," Voronkov mused. "'Innies,' we called 'em. Insurrectionists. 'All the same,' we said about 'em. Hatred is a hard thing to let go of."

Mann recalled how just a few weeks ago Voronkov had shared her harrowing last moments in active combat with him. Her eyes had welled as if the memory was playing out in front of her eyes all over again.

She'd described how rebel forces had claimed one of the major shipyards on Hellas, a smash-and-grab operation taking advantage of the fact that the only personnel around at the time were a few dozen UNSC combat engineers.

They hadn't stood a chance once the enemy claimed an AC-220 gunship and a handful of Hornets, launching an array of missiles at anybody stationed near the firebase's turrets.

"*Wasn't even supposed to be there*," she had concluded to Mann before falling silent.

"I found my peace eventually," Voronkov murmured. The thousand-yard stare in her eyes looked as though she was pulling herself out of the memory all over again. But even as she said the words, they evidently came with a sour taste. "Rebuilt my life as best as I could. Reality is, humans will go on hating each other as we always have, and they'll go on hating aliens as they've learned to. The pain we cause each other can't just be taken away. It's part of what makes us who we are—even if it isn't pretty."

Voronkov glanced at Dr. Mann, who looked as if he was in the process of trying to balance some kind of equation. "So," Mann said, "some hate because they can't let go of the past, some hate because of ignorance, because they've been told to for so long, and some hate simply because they can . . . How does the galaxy move forward?"

The end of the Covenant War may have allowed humanity a chance to catch its breath now that it was no longer under the looming shadow of annihilation, but it certainly hadn't *ended* conflict. Merely changed it. There were more factors in play now, more complications, more "sides." Hatred certainly wasn't the sole factor motivating these groups, but it was a damn powerful one.

Dr. Mann knew that there were still bloody years to come. But there was hope as well. Between it all, those who were willing to look up and move forward had been brought together.

He was glad that he had ultimately chosen an assignment here at Anvil Station rather than returning to the Ark. He had once thought to honor a friend he'd lost—fellow scientist Dr. Henry Lamb—by disappearing from the galaxy entirely to join the research teams on the Forerunners' extragalactic foundry. But he had responsibilities now—people to live for. Through this, he realized he could honor Henry by choosing to live in the galaxy he had helped save.

"Which leads us back to the task at hand." 'Tvorn returned their focus to the experimental armor. "To which group do you think those who built this armor belong? Who do *they* hate—and why?"

1300 Hours
Hangar Bay, Anvil Keep

Yshi 'Nbara loved to fly.

Ever since she had been a hatchling, she had been told stories about the sky-chevaliers of old—legendary pilots and pioneers who rode through the skies of Sanghelios on the backs of the leather-winged predators known as *'sKelln*.

As 'Nbara approached her *Elsedda*-pattern strike fighter, a vacuum-sealed Banshee variant that served as a powerful interceptor in space combat, the biomimetic influence of those majestic creatures that defined aspects of the vehicle's form filled her with a sense of connection to her peoples' far-reaching past.

'Nbara was uncertain of how the rest of her fellow pilots within Harmony Wing felt as they too strode up to their fighters. She had only served with the others in this squadron for a few weeks and was still getting acquainted with them, both on an individual basis and their dynamic as a team. But each pilot of the wing was a volunteer, united in purpose—that in itself held the makings of kinship.

"*Need a hand getting into your Banshee, elder?*" Spartan Natalie Kenzo spoke in a jovial tone over their internal closed channel. 'Nbara had heard the Spartan and fellow Pilot Officer Syed Khan refer to wing leader Vran 'Mkoth by this designation on several occasions despite him being older by only a handful of annual cycles. Clearly there was much about human humor she had yet to grasp.

"*The only hand I recall being offered was my own to you after our last sparring round, Spartan Kenzo,*" 'Mkoth replied.

"*Sometimes I worry that you two are going to bicker so much that you'll crash into each other before we even leave the hangar,*" Pilot Officer Khan said as he slid into the cockpit of his Banshee.

"*In which event, saving the galaxy will be up to you and 'Nbara,*" said Kenzo. "*Which I'm sure you could do, but with way less style without us.*"

Khan chuckled. "*Way less* something, *that's for sure.*"

The Banshee cockpit opened, and 'Nbara slid herself in, settling comfortably into the ergonomic interior. The craft's holographic viewscreen synchronized to her helmet's heads-up display and quickly linked to 'Mkoth, Kenzo, and Khan. She placed her hands over the spherical control grips, causing the craft to hum to life—its impulse drive powering up.

"*Comms check*," Vran 'Mkoth spoke over their internal TEAMCOM channel as additional preflight checks were conducted, his tone now focused. 'Nbara noted that he had recently taken to using the common human shorthand.

"*Harmony Two online*," replied Spartan Kenzo.

"*Harmony Three, good to go*," Pilot Officer Khan confirmed.

"Harmony Four," Ranger 'Nbara announced, concluding the callout. "Ready to fly."

She felt the rising swell of anticipation in her hearts as their preflight checks cleared and Anvil Control confirmed their departure. She reminded herself that this was just a routine patrol run, nothing more than an exercise in the grand scheme of things, but *this* was where she felt most alive. She was one with the movements of her fighter—in time, with her fellow pilots as well.

'Mkoth winked a green status light across their synchronized HUDs, and their Banshees darted forward. The fighters' wails turning to silence as they penetrated the hangar bay's shield and were let upon the vast dark ocean of stars beyond.

2100 Hours
Facility Commissary 3, Anvil Station

"Okay, what about this one: How many fingers does a Sangheili have?"

"Twelve. Eight on our hands and four on our face."

"Aw, what the hell—did Jacobs tell you that one already?" Spartan Adrian Vesco pushed his third pint of *hiskal* across the table to join the other now-empty glasses. His expression was one of disappointment.

"You overestimate your ability to communicate humor," replied the Sangheili warrior sitting across the table. "Your wit is as weak as your weapon."

"Is that why you can't beat my score on the carbine drills?"

Ovi 'Taar grunted in amusement at the Spartan's retort and the still-lingering disgruntled expression on the human's face. "Ah, thank you for reminding me, I have not yet started the carbine drills this cycle."

"Yeah, yeah." Vesco pressed his hands to his face in a groan. "Just make sure you put the right finger on the trigger."

"I will be sure to try each one—just for you."

The music playing in the background grew louder as the track changed to a bass-heavy electronic dirge. Shots Fired was the name given to Commissary 3 on the leisure level of Anvil Station. It had become a favorite stop for training pairs coming off collaborative combat-endurance drills—each pair typically being made up of one Spartan and one Sangheili, though there was a fair mix of non-augmented personnel sprinkled throughout the cohort to diversify the experience and expand any available data gathered.

Each day, scores of hand-selected warriors from both the UNSC and the Swords of Sanghelios engaged in a variety of drills, simulations, and multi-modal tactics courses—all finely crafted to increase the cooperative output of the multispecies effort. But despite all the rigorous training and strategic cross-examination, it could legitimately be argued that a post-sim evening in Shots Fired could do more to effectively progress cross-cultural diplomacy than a week of live-fire drills. Vesco and 'Taar had been regulars for a while now, but the ribbing never seemed to grow old.

Vesco finished hailing down a server for another round and then turned back toward 'Taar. "All right, fist-face. Your turn."

The Elite warrior pondered for a moment and then spoke. "How many humans does it take to operate a spacecraft?"

"Nobody knows, because the AI do everything anyway," Vesco finished the well-worn joke. "C'mon, that's an old one. Gimme something good."

"Very well," replied 'Taar. "Have you heard the one about the glassed planet?"

"No."

"Neither have they."

"Oh, damn . . . That *is* good."

"I heard it from Jacobs."

2300 Hours
Stationmaster's Study, Anvil Keep

"You're worried," Spartan Commander Vinay Sahil stated matter-of-factly.

He'd worked with Stationmaster Toda 'Murajai for over five years and could read the Sangheili now as well as any human—it was the stationmaster's visible shift into stoic stillness that gave his concern away.

"There is a fine line between worry and caution." 'Murajai stood at the center of his study observing a stacked series of holographs projected from a round table, each laden with assignment and deployment details, strategic planning analyses and hastily scribed conference notes.

Just two hours ago, they had received a distress call that necessitated a change in plans, and the entire station was scrambling to coordinate a response. Tomorrow, they would begin the process of mobilizing their forces to answer the call.

To illustrate his point, 'Muralai resumed the audio feed for station-wide communications as Sahil set his helmet down on the holotable.

"You got those slipspace travel calcs ready yet?"

"Negative, we're still takin' inventory of how much we're even able to send to Nysa."

"Almost makes me wish they'd installed a real AI on this station. Y'know, they'd probably have run the numbers before I even finished asking the question . . ."

"If Anvil Keep did possess such an intelligence, you would not be here to ask any questions."

"Point taken."

"We've just received special dispensation to dock three of our fully loaded Condors aboard Sword of Conjunction *along with Amity, Harmony, and Sympathy wings. Sounds like our ride to the fight just got an upgrade!"*

"Oh, I'm buyin' whoever made that arrangement happen a year's supply of hiskal*! Rerunning travel calcs to Nysa based on* A'uzr-*pattern stats, I'll have an update for you shortly."*

The cacophony of chatter continued across a dozen different channels with scarcely a second for input.

"This is what they've been training for," Sahil said reassuringly. "Listen to them. They're ready."

Years had been invested into building bridges and bonds

between the human and alien personnel of Anvil. Every decision had been made to demonstrate the power of collaboration, maximizing their impact as a team and turning them into a well-oiled machine.

'Murajai focused on a display showing a selection of units that had been chosen for long-range deployment. His attention settled on a list of paired names for Riftborn special operatives—Babych and 'Toizari, Prentis and 'Ookol, Vesco and 'Taar.

Sahil understood the stationmaster held the same desire as any leader—to have the time for one more round of training, one more systems check, one more opportunity that could make all the difference in the battle to come.

But a leader also needed to adapt when that wasn't possible, when they had to let go and allow their warriors to put training into action.

"We have prepared them to the best of our ability." 'Murajai spoke as much to himself as to Sahil. "I only wish that we had more actionable knowledge on what they are being sent into."

"Whatever gets thrown their way, they'll have each other's backs. Have faith in them."

The axis of power in the galaxy had seen a series of turbulent upheavals in recent years, a far cry from the more clear-cut conflicts of the past. Ancient Forerunner constructs had been reactivated across the galaxy, followed by an uprising of artificial intelligences, and now the Banished and countless other groups were filling the power vacuum left in the wake of Cortana's short-lived reign.

"*Faith*," 'Murajai repeated the word with a grimace. The word sounded to Sahil as though speaking it aloud aroused an instinctive reservation in the pit of his stomach. "I knew faith when it filled the infinite expanse of empty promises and false journeys into divinity by those who manipulated my people for countless ages."

"Faith," Sahil reiterated steadily, confidently. "In our brothers and sisters—their training, their sense of duty. In everything we have built and accomplished here."

Sahil knew that 'Murajai had to remind himself at times that humans used the word very differently. It was what humanity had learned when they faced the overwhelming might of the Covenant: how to hold on to the smallest and most distant hope in the face of annihilation. In some ways, this accord between their species reflected the *true* realization of the Covenant—an alliance brought together not by coercion and conquest, but cooperation.

Their people would not fight for abstract notions of holy ascension, but for each other. On the battlefield, these bonds could make the difference between victory and defeat.

'Murajai clicked his mandibles once and powered down the holotable, finally conceding to Sahil's counsel.

"Get some rest, Stationmaster," Sahil said with a tone that was both kind and firm. "That's an order."

Amusement filled Murajai's voice. "I do not believe that you have the authority to give me orders, Spartan Commander."

"It's a flat team structure." Sahil smiled back. He gestured to a group of four stone tablets lining the left-side wall, each of them etched with the saga of 'Murajai's clan. "You know, you've still yet to tell me the full story of these."

"When this mission is over, perhaps I shall." 'Murajai looked to an empty space next to the fourth tablet as Sahil picked up his helmet and made to exit the study. "And perhaps we shall forge the next chapter together."

INTEL // SUNDERED STAR

Classified notes by ONI's REAP-X division regarding research and development on applications for reverse engineered elements of Forerunner combat skins.

Office of Naval Intelligence // REAP-X
R&D Production Notes

If the end of the Covenant War allowed us to run in the field of analyzing Forerunner technology, the awakening of the Didact in '57 and subsequent events concerning Requiem and the Created uprising pushed us to sprint.

Of particular interest in our ongoing efforts to unlock the potential of this ancient technology are "design seeds"—machine cells encoded with data to assemble anything from advanced combat skin to entire starships.

Helmet camera footage from Blue Team engaging the Didact on Gamma Halo demonstrated the Promethean's armor was adaptively capable of being attuned to weaponry used against him. If we could harness this capability for Mjolnir armor, it could be the biggest evolution for Spartan combat since energy shielding.

Our experiments with the former have begun yielding minimal but promising results. Will follow up with further information shortly.

INTEL // STRATEGOS

Within Requiem, the command pattern of the Strategos considers the arrival of humanity and the end of the shield world's millennia of isolation.

For one hundred millennia, the command-pattern of the Strategos remained dormant. Automated processes had taken over, directing Promethean forces to conduct routine patrol and reconnaissance cycles throughout Shield World 0001 before returning the units to their crèches. Requiem slumbered, sealed in silent stasis, awaiting a time that it might awaken.

That day has finally come.

Aya.

The Librarian's plan for the galaxy has succeeded, as humans and other species that were young during the time of the ecumene travel the stars once more—several of their ships having been drawn into Requiem's maw.

One human in particular has drawn the attention of the Strategos command-pattern. Adorned in primitive combat skin, it is he who has released the Didact from his long exile. This human is now cutting a swath through the deep jungles of Requiem, seeking to rendezvous with the other humans' crashed vessel. The Strategos is eager to collect new combat data and has thus far dedicated several cycles to examining the materials, weaponry, and equipment of these interlopers, who are evidently still progressing toward becoming a true interstellar civilization.

The Strategos directs additional Knight units to engage the armored human warrior, seeking to gain more direct insight into the capabilities and valor of this new age.

Time will soon tell whether Requiem has found an adversary worthy of its legend.

THE MACHINE BREAKS

*This story takes place throughout the latter half of 2558, as Dr. Catherine Halsey and Covenant Supreme Leader Jul 'Mdama seek to reunite both halves of the Janus Key (*Halo: Escalation*).*

The Third Dignitary Schema descends upon the human colony world Oban—designated CE-174-6 c—with dozens of Promethean units deploying from the underbellies of Twelfth-order escort craft, their monolithic forms obscured within thick overcast skies.

Oban is a rocky, mountainous world of vast rolling hills and untouched lowlands—long stretches of green that ascend into wavelike formations of rock and greater peaks capped with snow. An aerial view makes it appear as if a terrible storm was frozen, turned to stone, and has since remained in its petrified form for millennia.

Among those highland crags lies a nexus of prefabricated strongholds, research facilities, training grounds, and power plants—the early years of a human colonization effort.

TDS-009's individual stabilizers activate, its anterior shield distributors flare for a moment as it lands on soft grassy terrain and immediately advances. The Promethean Knight unit kicks up mud with every step as the war machine's powerful legs carry it through the aftermath of the rain season, an extreme two-month period of engineered weather patterns that would make conquest inadvisable for any organic foe.

The Knight fires its light rifle, bursts of hard light finding their marks with precision, piercing primitive human armor and soft flesh. Dark trails of orange streak through the air, impacting humans once more—just as they did over a hundred millennia ago, shattering redoubts and star fortresses in an ancient war. At least, that is what the combat wisdom of the Strategos command-pattern states—the battlenet conductor of all Promethean units that provides directives, intelligence, and at times contextual knowledge from its long service.

Were a Composer active in the field, death would be unnecessary for these humans. Due to the low military threat posed by the hostile elements present, capture and conversion would be the ideal prime directive, but the present absence of the device makes this impossible.

The combat-wisdom of the Strategos finds this loss of biological life wasteful.

As the last human occupying the primitive gray-green structure falls, its fragile form blasted back by a nearby detonation, TDS-009's combat effectiveness is noted. It is now designated by the Strategos as a commander, granting higher authority—subsuming other local units into its schema, including a dozen crawlers—and is provided deeper access to the Promethean battlenet to enhance its autonomy. In addition, its authority is now visually denoted by blazing patterns of hard light that cover the unit's helmet and carapace.

Together, the reinforced Third Dignitary Schema marches on to the next structure. It is a dull and rectangular industrial building, the letters "UNSC" printed on the side, and notably features a large communications dish on its roof.

Half a dozen crawlers flank the structure, initiating a charge-assisted leap onto its outer walls, skittering in all directions. The combat wisdom of the Strategos understands that fear is an effective tool to be leveraged against many types of biological life-forms: the suggestion of uncertainty, of randomness, can provide momentary distractions that create critical openings. The other six crawler units charge the barricaded structure's entrance, breaking through to leap onto the human guards within. Some are dragged outside by the crawlers, while others scatter for cover. It matters not, for the objective of this moment was simply to remove the human targets from their bunker so they can be more effectively neutralized.

TDS-009 raises its light rifle to fire at one of the humans that has been dragged, writhing and screaming, into close proximity by two of the crawlers.

The Knight's light rifle is fully functional. It possesses a plentiful supply of light-mass ammunition, and targeting data guarantees a successful lethal hit.

But TDS-009 pauses, for there is something new on the battlefield.

It initially appears to be a small humanoid—a child of these colonists, perhaps. But upon further inspection, it is no such thing. Where there is a face, there are no features. It is clothed only in flesh. A wretched half-life of a being that fills TDS-009 with feelings it should not have. Revulsion, dread, fear.

The remaining human soldiers continue to fire their primitive ballistic weapons while moving in a desperate, uncoordinated fashion, attempting to find some way to retreat. But the being simply stands rooted to the spot, seemingly oblivious to the slaughter of its protectors, and stares at TDS-009. The Knight attempts to scan it with its sensor arrays. While children seldom register as combatants, they are designated as useful minds for sublimation by a Composer . . . but in the absence of such a device, the Knight awaits a directive.

No directive regarding the being ever comes.

Instead, the Strategos command-pattern notes the cessation of weapons fire from TDS-009 and directs other Knight units to compensate, prompting the crawlers—now led by a newly designated alpha—to assume a more directly lethal role.

The last human screams as three crawlers fall upon him, shredding through both combat skin and flesh. Ordinarily, a Knight unit would disintegrate the bloody remains with a burst from its scattershot, but the Strategos directs the Third Dignitary Schema to leave the bodies. They are meant to be found.

TDS-009 does not understand the reason for this order and looks back to find the strange being, wondering why the Strategos did not provide a directive for it, but it has disappeared.

Twelfth-order escort vessels descend as all Promethean units are recalled to their crèches aboard *Song of Retribution*, an assault carrier belonging to an allied multispecies faction known as the Covenant. Despite possessing privileged battlenet access, TDS-009 is not informed by the Strategos command-pattern whether the outcome on Oban was victory, defeat, or even whether the battle was finished—nor is any further context for the mission provided. The Prometheans simply depart its rocky surface to be ferried to their next battlefield, leaving the bodies of the humans behind.

After a series of decontamination sweeps and sensor scans to eliminate any alien bacteria, Promethean units are sent to the assemblers for repair. The assemblers feature a recessed semi-spherical nanofabrication chamber where pattern weavers forge the templates encoded within their design seeds. It was crudely removed from Shield World 0001 and grafted into the heart of *Song of Retribution*, with similar facilities occupying multiple decks of the assault carrier. Despite its inelegance, there are many Sangheili aboard the vessel that delay their duties to observe this process, some reverently uttering alien words of prayer for the well-being of what they call "warrior-angels."

TDS-009 is connected to a sensor that scans for damage in its smartmatter machine-cell alloy, be it from weapons fire or environmental conditions. The light rifle is detached from the Knight's primary weapon arm and disassembled to extract combat data.

A field of orange light then initiates a deep scan of the Knight, accompanied by the voice of the Strategos.

// Unit designation: TDS-009. //

The Strategos directly accesses the Knight's "memories," plugging into the full combat experience of all that took place on Oban.

It sees the Third Dignitary Schema launching from their escort craft. It sees crawlers routing the humans from their communications bunker; the humans are dragged out of the building and pinned to the ground . . .

TDS-009 anticipates the appearance of the strange humanoid being it had witnessed.

// Sensor analysis complete. Smartmatter repairs conducted. Return unit to crèche. //

The Knight is directed to move along and enter hibernation as *Song of Retribution* departs the system, but a thought lingers within TDS-009 associated with a variety of inputs: *query, question, clarification needed.*

No other being had appeared.

TDS-009 chooses not to query the Strategos.

Aktis IV—designation F309-R 2—is a vast oceanic world with a few scattered island continents, currently uninhabited but formerly occupied by Forerunners of multiple rates to research the unique composition of the opaque, foamy substance covering the oceans. This environmental element is a significant tactical variable for naval engagements, as no ship sensors are able to scan through it.

The Strategos informs TDS-009 that a battle has erupted between allied Covenant forces and a rogue group of Sangheili who are attempting to usurp command from Jul 'Mdama, and that UNSC forces are also present.

Jul 'Mdama has ordered units of the Third Dignitary Schema to accompany him as Covenant traitors pledging loyalty to a rival Sangheili—Sali 'Nyon—are rounded up for execution. Some submit willingly, some beg and plead to receive mercy, while others are pulled to the ground by crawler units and held in place.

"*Another* traitor," 'Mdama growls. "Their numbers are greater than I'd imagined."

A zealot clad in a smooth and curved white combat harness approaches. "Commander 'Mdama, I recommend you return to *Retribution* until we have rooted out the rest of them."

'Mdama waves a dismissive hand. "Nonsense."

"Before we detained this heretic, he transmitted this message across the entire fleet." The zealot interfaces with a nearby communications node to replay the dispatch.

"I am Sali 'Nyon. I sound the call to all true believers. Join us as we rise to defeat the imposter 'Mdama. His death will mark a new era of greatness for the Covenant, a return to our glorious—"

'Mdama, bristling with anger, clenches his fist as the zealot spares the Covenant leader from hearing the rest. He turns back toward his Phantom dropship, assenting to the zealot's suggestion of returning to *Song of Retribution*. "So, Sali's finally making his move . . ."

A red-armored zealot in a jagged, chitinous intrusion harness, who has been guarding 'Mdama's Phantom dropship, escorts the Covenant leader to its open troop bay, followed by TDS-009 and TDS-002. "Indeed, Commander," the zealot escort says, bowing his head. "A captured insurgent confirmed that Sali is responsible for shooting down the human ship."

Upon request, the Strategos informs TDS-009 that both the UNSC and Covenant possess pieces of a galactic cartographer known as the Janus Key, a device that holds the real-time location of vast amounts of Forerunner technology. A plan had been put in place to secure the UNSC's half of the key, but this rebellion within the Covenant's ranks has disrupted the operation.

"Sali's timing was unfortunate. His followers probably see that as some type of divine influence," 'Mdama replies. "The best way for us to correct that misconception is to drag his corpse through the dirt. What of our progress at the holy site?"

"The humans have barricaded themselves inside." The zealot pauses for a moment before abruptly adding: "But we should be breaking through any moment now."

"When you reach the inner chamber, kill them all. Except Glassman." 'Mdama boards the Phantom and turns once more to the zealot escort. "I have a special punishment planned for him."

The Phantom departs, and local command authority automatically shifts to 'Mdama's red-armored zealot escort, who motions for TDS-009 to follow him. TDS-002 splits off to join the white-armored zealot as he moves farther south into the forest.

TDS-009 and the red-armored zealot do not make it far, however, before a new hostile appears, accompanied by volleys of stray plasma bolts.

A blue-armored human, which the Strategos combat-wisdom recognizes to be designated a "Spartan," bursts through the trees and finds itself facing the zealot. The Sangheili immediately activates its energy sword, already swinging as the blade crackles to life. But the Spartan just as quickly leaps to the side, falling onto its back. The Sangheili looms over it.

It raises its blade . . .

And there it is. The being has returned, yet this time it has taken a new, more defined form—that of a young human girl—and is standing in front of the Spartan.

She is unarmed, her golden hair is tucked into a messy bun, and she does not react to the blind bursts of plasma fire.

The Knight knows that it should attack the Spartan but does not. It is about to access the combat-wisdom of the Strategos to request a directive regarding the girl but pauses, possessing neither certainty or understanding as to why it delays requesting this information.

The world slows down as TDS-009 attempts to parse a million neural processes firing at once. The girl stands defiantly, the Spartan attempts to shuffle backward, and the zealot is about to bring its blade down . . .

TDS-009 *must* react.

With a screech, TDS-009 launches itself at the zealot, striking its chest with an armored foot.

The Spartan rolls away and takes a moment to look back at them in confusion before fleeing, while the zealot recovers enough to turn its attention to the Promethean Knight.

"What is this?!" The zealot is angered and confused. "Is this some test of the gods? The demon has escaped!"

TDS-009 screeches once again, its faceplate opening to reveal the fiery humanoid skull beneath, and raises the lightblade integrated into its secondary weapon arm.

Their blades connect, but the zealot deftly spins itself *into* TDS-009 and, with all the strength the Sangheili can muster, smacks away the lightblade arm before slashing into the Knight's shields and impaling it through the center.

TDS-009's audio processors overload with a shrill scream as its armored carapace cracks and begins to disintegrate.

Falling to its knees, the Knight locks its gaze onto the girl, and she too is screaming as her form disintegrates layer by layer, down to muscle and tissue, then to bone . . .

And finally to dust.

Dr. Catherine Halsey, Personal Journal
Encryption Code: THETA-ARGON
Subject: Promethean Soul
July 22, 2558

Despite the sudden change in circumstances, our gambit paid off. After gaining the UNSC *Infinity*'s attention with the attack on Oban and luring them to Aktis IV, we have secured both halves of the Librarian's key.

I am one step closer to getting to the center of this.

Jul 'Mdama is seeing to some final matters regarding the rebellion that broke out among his ranks, and then we shall discover where the Absolute Record lies.

In the meantime, one of Jul's lackeys brought me a rather peculiar mystery to investigate—one that is not so different from what I examined on *Infinity* earlier this year. A Promethean "brain."

The Sangheili informed me that this particular Promethean Knight went rogue in the field and turned against its commander. Most intriguing to me; most irritating to Jul, as he put it, that a "warrior of the gods" would attack his own forces. His concern is that this incident might incite further rebellion against him. He must surely tire of the performance he puts on. It is a wonder that so few of his followers see right through it—but then, perhaps he has been living this charade for so long now that some part of him actually believes it.

Context: We know that Promethean Knights were a creation of the Didact, who used a device known as the Composer to sublimate his loyal commanders into digitized forms to fight the Flood. A variety of data points have corroborated that he later turned the device on ancient humans, bolstering his numbers by the millions—just as he did to Earth upon his reawakening one year ago. The last Promethean mind I studied displayed memories of New Phoenix, the city that fell victim to the Didact's attack, which presented some interesting questions.

Observation: The oldest Promethean Knights were based on the templates of willing volunteers, Forerunner warriors who submitted themselves to the Composer and appear to have retained varying degrees of individuality. The ancient humans were devolved populations of limited intellect, resulting in more "feral" units. But this new batch of Prometheans were created from the minds of modern humans—our most advanced form since our kind last traveled the stars.

Conjecture: Sufficiently complex minds that are forcibly sublimated by the Composer run the risk of complications, manifesting hallucinations and echoes of their previous form. Could this be an echo akin to how our own AIs retain some impressions of their donors' memories? I am reminded of the problems we faced when exploring options for the SPARTAN-II program, where it became clear that the minds and bodies of children were more accepting and adaptable.

The unwilling mind inevitably rebels. Perhaps this is true of the Prometheans as well.

I returned the Promethean brain to its crèche, where it will no doubt continue to malfunction. With luck, other Knight units may experience similar complications in the months to come.

Conclusion: The usefulness of these Prometheans made from modern human victim essences is limited, and Jul's days of controlling them are numbered.

As this plan comes together, I suspect that I shall be terminating this partnership of convenience sooner than I thought.

//END LOG

Promethean Command Mesh
// Authorization Sigil: [STRATEGOS]
// Performance Flag: [LOCAL UNIT] TDS-009

CONTEXT: Deployment of assigned forces to engage objectives on worlds [OBAN] and [AKTIS-IV] have achieved satisfactory returns within all completion parameters. [OUTLIER NOTE]: Actions deemed outside the expected envelope of behavioral execution were noted by [THRALL UNITS] and summarily flagged.

OBSERVATION: Review of executable data has recorded at least [67] deviant processes across both deployments. This sum is [OUTSIDE] the acceptable percentile for a deployment of this classification.

CONJECTURE: TDS-009 is [89 PERCENT] likely to be suffering from a catastrophic failure of the unit's [DURANCE MEMBRANE], resulting in an unacceptable manifestation of [PERSONALITY DISSONANCE].

CONCLUSION: TDS-009 will undergo immediate [REMOTE SEVERANCE] for an extended period of network isolation and process quarantine. Further observation and [RECOMPOSITION EVALUATION] will be considered upon reacquisition of the unit frame.

ADDENDUM: Due to the increased rate of these deviances over the last [SOLAR YEAR], these events appear to be separate from the [ROGUE ANCILLA PROCESS] detected within the command mesh. Further investi-

`gation is required. Preliminary recommendation for enacting further [REMOTE SEVERANCE] measures in the event [ROGUE ANCILLA PROCESS] successfully solicits control of this network.`

TDS-009 had not expected to awaken.

First, it attempts to connect to the command-pattern of the Strategos so that it might obtain operational context, directives, and network with the rest of the Third Dignitary Schema.

// COMMAND-PATTERN NOT DETECTED //

// CONNECTION TO NETWORK FAILED //

Visual sensors then come online. TDS-009 can now see that it is no longer on Aktis IV, nor is it within the crèche aboard *Song of Retribution*. This location is undeniably Forerunner, but the curved gray walls and blue hard light barrier over the entrance suggest this is some sort of holding facility.

// Query. //

TDS-009 does not know why or who it was attempting to query. Without connection to the Strategos, it is effectively cut off from . . . everything. No backup protocols or commands were logged, no directives—present or outstanding—remained in its archives.

It has no enemy to fight, and therefore no function. No purpose. No reason to be.

Scanning the small space, the Knight's analysis detects that the room is approximately six square meters, giving it just enough room to maneuver. How it had come to this location is not held within its archives.

And in the far corner of the room, a human figure stands in the darkness.

The girl.

She is older now. Dressed in thin gray overalls with a white-blue coat, she simply stands there—unafraid, unmoving, just as she had been each time TDS-009 had seen her.

The Knight attempts to connect to the Promethean network again.

// COMMAND-PATTERN NOT DETECTED //

// CONNECTION TO NETWORK FAILED //

Seconds tick by and it tries again. And again. The same result is returned thirty-seven more times before TDS-009 ceases its action. The girl continues to stand and watch from the corner of the room, as silent and still as the rocks on Oban where it had first seen her.

TDS-009 tries to disable its optical sensors and shut down, forcing itself into hibernation, that it might await a time where it is detected by the Strategos and reconnected to the Promethean network.

Anything to not look at the girl . . .

A phantom sensation sweeps over the Knight. It feels a hand placed gently upon its primary weapon arm, lowering it, another hand reaching out to its head. Turning it—slowly.

And as its gaze is drawn back to the girl, it is now able to take in every detail of her. Old data begins to stream into the Knight's mind like water flowing into a canal lock.

Directives, strategic information, and combat-wisdom had been expunged, but deep within the essence of TDS-009 lies an ocean of memory—suppressed, compartmentalized . . . and now, the floodgates are unlocked.

It knows the girl's face. It knows her name.

"Ah," a jovial voice sounds from somewhere outside the cell. "You've noticed my humble collection. Just a few specimens the Guardians have brought to Genesis."

A group of Spartans pause outside the cell, watching as TDS-009's micro-driver arms batter its head, as if trying to wake from some terrible nightmare. It throws the full weight of its carapace against the wall, desperate to break through and escape.

"A Knight," one of the Spartans says. "Kind of making me feel sad for 'em."

Unable to speak. Unable to cry out—in pain or anger or madness.

"Their little arms always creep me out," another says dismissively, then motions for them to move on.

They disappear from sight, leaving the Knight alone once more. Even the girl is gone now, nothing more than the imagined outline of a shade standing in a shadowy corner, and TDS-009 is left to sift through the memories now filling its archive.

Coral . . . home . . .

. . . a bright young mind, digging for fossils in her back garden . . .

. . . just nineteen when humanity made first contact . . . already a student of archaeology at the Pegasi Institute . . .

. . . home burning, beams of plasma striking the surface, nothing left . . . family will be dug up like fossils one day . . . leave it all behind . . . evacuated to Lodestone . . .

. . . a job offer, a new start—far away, so far away . . .

Office of Naval Intelligence . . .

Gamma Halo . . . Ivanoff Station . . .

Service Number . . . CC-728304 . . .

NO LONGER . . .

Doctor of xenoarchaeology . . .

THIRD DIGNITARY SCHEMA. TDS-009 . . .

Sandra—

NO MORE!

Sandra Katherine Tillson.

ARMORY INFINITUM // M392 BANDIT

On Karava, the Sangheili renegade Zef 'Trahl receives a visit from a group of Banished raiders.

The first voice to speak came from a human male armed with confidence, or perhaps brazen foolishness—it was often hard to tell the difference.

"It looks like we've got a problem, boys."

He was flanked by three Kig-Yar raiders, a mix of Ruuhtian and Ibie'shian clad in telling red-gray colors.

"Know how we settle problem on Karava?" one of the Kig-Yar squawked.

"You give Banished bad information," another chimed in. "We give Banished your head."

The human and his Jackal companions grinned in their own ways as they focused on the target of their ire: a Sangheili informant who finally had nowhere else to run.

But before they could make their next move, the Elite erupted into raucous laughter, using the split-second distraction of the group exchanging slightly puzzled looks to fling himself into cover and unsling the weapon he carried on his back.

Three shots sounded from an M392 Bandit, each one finding its mark on the heads and necks of the Kig-Yar before a fourth sent the Banished cadre's human leader to the ground, clutching his knee. The Sangheili studied the rifle approvingly for a moment before slinging it over his back once more and approached the grimacing survivor, pressing his hoof onto the leg wound to keep the human both still and very uncomfortable.

"You will live, human," he said, arranging his mandibles into an unmistakably wide grin. "At least, until you deliver the message to your superiors that Zef 'Trahl will not be so easily slain."

VENEZIAN SONATA

This story takes place on September 22, 2559, approximately two and a half months prior to the UNSC Infinity*'s assault on Zeta Halo (*Halo Infinite*).*

<\\ UNSC OFFICE OF NAVAL INTELLIGENCE
<\\ CLASSIFIED TRANSMISSION [ONI.SEC.PRTCL-1A]
>> SENT: [MONEYBAGS]
<< RECEIVED: [73998-38490-VD]

<\ VTT TRANSCRIPT AS FOLLOWS ~
>> I have a lead you may be interested in pursuing.
<< I'm listening.
>> You have been curious about the emergence of certain rogue elements on Sqala.
<< Location?
>> A tower. New. Owned by a power broker in New Tyne. It is still under construction, but operational—you will not miss it.
<< Noted.

>> It would be wise to impress upon your Captain Lasky that time is limited to seize this opportunity, and that your singular absence will not imperil the upcoming operation on Sovolanu.
<< Zef, someday we're going to have a friendly conversation about how you seem to know so much that you shouldn't.
>> Until that day, let us continue to enjoy this mutually beneficial partnership. I am sure that you will find this to be a most productive excursion. My contact will get you to the tower's visitor area, the rest will be up to you.
~ COMMUNICATION ENDS \>

1300 Hours, September 22, 2559 (Military Calendar)
UNSC *Infinity*
Record matrix logged by RLD 0205-4
Conversation between [92458-37017-EB] and [73998-38490-VD]

VD: "There's a mission . . ."

EB: "Say no more, I'll round up the rest of the squad."

VD: "A *solo* mission, Buck. I'm going in alone."

EB: "You're gonna need backup. You're going to *Venezia*, Veronica. You do not go to a place like that without backup—place has got a very unlovely rep!"

VD: "It's recon only. I'll be gone for the day at most."

EB: "Yeah, unless you get captured 'cause you didn't bring any backup. C'mon, Veronica, lemme tag along just in case."

VD: "Sorry, Buck, you know how it is."

EB: "'Orders are orders.'"

VD: "Exactly. And I know you're one to . . . *misbehave*, so I'm giving you an order. You are not to deploy to Venezia and interfere with this operation."

EB: "You . . . All right."

VD: "Thank you."

[RLD NOTE: 87% probability that EB's sudden compliance with VD's order is not entirely honest.]

VD: "I'll be back before you know it."

[RLD NOTE: VD kisses EB and departs, preparing to deploy.]

EB: "Every problem is an opportunity in disguise . . ."

2100 Hours, September 22, 2559 (Military Calendar)
New Tyne, Venezia

Veronica Dare hated heights.

It was perhaps an ironic phobia for her to possess as an Office of Naval Intelligence agent who spent most of her time deploying alongside Orbital Drop Shock Troopers and Spartans in coffin-like pods, but shimmying across a narrow ledge on a skyscraper over 2,000 feet high had a way of provoking such primal fears.

All the same, she couldn't deny the view—even through the torrential rain. New Tyne was a bustling metropolis not entirely dissimilar to the mainland region of New Mombasa back on Earth, or Noctus on Andesia. It was effectively the "capital city" of Venezia, an independent colony that was populated not only by humans, but Sangheili, Jiralhanae, Kig-Yar, and other former client species of the Covenant that could be found in office buildings, transportation networks, entertainment districts, factories, and spaceports.

By some miracle, the city *wasn't* a constant war zone. Veronica supposed that they all largely had one thing in common: They hated the UNSC.

The humans who had originally settled Venezia cut themselves off from the Unified Earth Government many years ago, and now the colonial militia that kept order had pledged themselves to the Keepers of the One Freedom—a Covenant remnant group. Every group here had a lot of fingers in a lot of pies, as the Keepers had recently pledged *their* allegiance to the Banished, so the trickle-down nature of relationships between species and factions meant that the line of "friend" and "foe" in this place was more of a complex web that nobody wanted to get tangled within. And so, life simply carried on.

It came as another slice of irony that, of all the places in the galaxy, Cortana's presence was minimal here. The strange "peace" on Venezia had preceded her Created regime by years, so she had devoted her resources elsewhere. But that meant the Venezian power brokers now felt emboldened to start pushing their luck, dialing up their criminal operations in increasingly brazen ways—and while Cortana might not be stepping in, their actions had drawn the attention of ONI's ever-watchful eye.

Dare had met with Zef 'Trahl's contact with little issue, a rather eccentric and aged Kig-Yar named Ke'jah. His colony-wide transport business had been the perfect cover for the setup.

While traveling aboard a Ren shuttlecraft that once ferried Covenant ministers around their holy city, Dare had picked out the tower immediately from the vehicle's viewport. The appearance of the tower itself looked analogous to a *Halberd*-class destroyer rotated vertically. This kind of shared architectural design between buildings and starships was not uncommon, as it had phased in and out of style many times since humanity's early interstellar colonial era in the twenty-fourth century.

For his part, Ke'jah had taken the place of a vehicle bound to pick up a group of the tower's construction workers at the end of their shift and made a scene at the entrance desk to get paid extra for the mix-up. The commotion had allowed Dare to slip out from the vehicle and utilize a wrist-mounted grappleshot to reach the building's upper levels.

Dare made her way up to a level where construction was still ongoing. The tower split off into two sections and the building's bare structural skeleton continued up into the dark-gray clouds and disappeared from view. The rain was coming down hard and thunder was rolling through the sky, sounding more like it was coming from *around* rather than above her. Dare was grateful for her helmet's VISR system, which outlined the structures within a radius of several dozen meters, enough to make her feel a little safer on the more immediate terrain of scaffolding and haphazardly placed boards connecting across super rungs.

Air traffic appeared to be minimal, but Dare spotted a Phantom dropship circling around the local cluster of skyscrapers. She had no idea whether it was a security vessel or just a passing transport, but she felt fairly certain she hadn't been spotted—though the telltale whine of its engine was a little too close for comfort.

Descending a few levels of scaffolding, Dare tracked a series of cylindrical shafts until she found a small opening, then settled into a position that she determined would conceal her. She tapped a few commands on her wrist-mounted AN/PED-560 Vedette drone controller and the device detached to hover slightly above her head. This model had originally entered service as an enhanced rangefinder and target designator, but its small profile made it a perfect candidate for modification into a surveillance drone for use in hostile territory.

The name was a bit of a mouthful, though, so Dare had simply named the device "Eddie."

She ran a few quick movement checks to ensure there was minimal input-response delay, then sent Eddie into the shaft opening.

Callie Calder was just fifteen years old.

Her family lived on the rural plains at the farthest outskirts of New Tyne, which meant that she had a long commute to the education center every day. A half-hour trek to the maglev train station followed by another half hour to get to the city. She had just spent the summer helping with grueling manual chores on the family farm before getting ready for a new school year, as her father had been unexplainably absent in recent months, while her mother seemed increasingly solemn and withdrawn. She could tell, in the way children can always tell with their parents, that something was wrong.

But things had taken a rather sharp turn just two days ago.

While on her way to the city, the maglev train had just . . . stopped.

"*This is the driver speaking*," the voice came over the intercom. "*We're being held at a stop light for now but expect we should be underway again soon. We apologize for the inconvenience.*"

Her first day back to school and she was going to be late.

Staring absently outside, Errant Vee's *Amorphous* blasting in her ears, Callie was only vaguely aware of the group of Venezian militia who boarded the train and started checking the IDs of the younger passengers.

It wasn't until she handed over her identification that she had any notion something was wrong. She was certain she had misheard when the guardsman said, "*We need you to come with us.*"

Confused, angry, and subject to many uncomfortable sideward glances from other passengers, Callie followed along in a daze—she hadn't even noticed that her old-fashioned headphones had fallen off at some point. It wasn't long after she and half a dozen others had been removed from the train that a black bag was put over her head, and the world fell instantly, awfully, silent.

She'd grown up in the latter years of the Covenant War, told about all the awful things the alien alliance had done, but she hadn't lived any of that herself. It was what humans were capable of doing to each other that made her skin crawl more than anything else.

Callie awakened in a cell some time later.

It was a meager space with only a bed, toilet, and sink to speak of, though she had determined from the lack of muck and grime that it was built relatively recently. She had received no visitors, had been given no opportunity to call anyone. There was only a tray of stale crackers and a glass of water at one point when she had awakened.

Staring at the steel cup, she felt herself drowning in an ocean of dire considerations.

Her family had no idea what had happened to her—she'd left and simply not come back. Surely there must've been surveillance footage aboard the maglev, as well as numerous witnesses . . .

Callie's thoughts were interrupted as the lock on her cell door clicked and swung open. She had expected to see a militia guardsman, but the figure she was met with was covered in armor from head to toe. Their face was hidden behind a thick, curved helmet.

"Move along, recruit," a deep voice barked. "Fall in line!"

Tentatively, Callie walked out of her cell and saw that dozens of others—some older, some younger—were being directed down a corridor. She followed suit.

To her surprise, as they reached a set of double doors at the end of the corridor, they were led into what looked like a corporate amphitheater. Rows of semicircular seats of polished wood surrounded a round dais where an alien figure Callie didn't recognize stood. At first glance she might have mistaken it for a human being, clad as it was in the uniform of a courier with a mustard-colored tunic, until she saw its face bore two pairs of slit-like nostrils and what appeared to be gill-like organs underneath its jaw.

Callie swept her gaze across the room. The windows were tinted, covering the view outside, and armed guards were stationed around the perimeter.

Whatever was about to happen, there was no way out.

"You are here," the alien spoke, and its rasping, cold voice echoed through the amphitheater, "because your families owe debts that they cannot pay. *You* are their insurance policy."

Everybody in the room was silent and sat perfectly still.

"You will be trained, and you will be forged into weapons to be wielded by many masters. You will serve until your family's debt is repaid. Each job you take, each contract you sign, will stipulate a percentage of your profits that will go toward repayment, and what that percentage is will depend upon your conduct within these halls. Successes are expected; transgressions and failures will accrue interest."

Callie could barely process the information she was receiving. Her family had been in some kind of debt—and it was up to *her* to be taken away from her life to pay it off? What had her father been up to over the last few months that he had been absent?

Worse still, if this strange speaker was to be believed, she hadn't been kidnapped and taken from her family. She had been given away . . .

"You will be given a tour of the facilities here, then escorted to the barracks to begin training with your taskmasters." The alien gestured toward several of the armored guards who looked just like the one that had opened Callie's cell. "From this day forth, the lives you knew are over. Until your contracts are complete and your debts are repaid in full, or you fall in battle, you belong to us."

It felt as though she was lucid during some terrible nightmare, but she was distracted for a moment as her eye caught something at the far end of the amphitheater. A large pipe that ran along the ceiling had a small grate covering. Callie could have sworn she had spotted something move within it. Light catching on a lens, perhaps, and she was certain she had heard a slight metallic rattle from within. Judging by the reaction of two of the guards who she saw speaking into their comm units to her left, they had caught it as well.

Whatever it was, it probably wasn't of any help to her. The alien speaker had departed, and murmurs were breaking out among the rest of the audience. Some sat in nervous silence, rocking back and forth in their seats, but others had the steely look of resolve in their eyes.

Sink or swim, Callie . . .

Veronica Dare wasn't sure if she'd been made, and she wanted desperately to continue observing, but her gut was telling her that *now* was the time to bug out. A momentary glitch in Eddie's response time had caused the drone to drift and bump into the pipe wall. She began to climb back up the scaffolding to the unfinished roof.

There would be time to process this information, file an official threat assessment, and hopefully muster the resources to do something about this . . .

In the back of her mind, she knew that these kids would be left to fend for themselves for a long time. The UNSC's current operational priority was stopping Cortana. To that end, *Infinity* was just weeks away from enacting Operation: WOLFE—and that wasn't even taking into account what kind of response would even be possible for a situation like this. Showing up in force would ignite a full-scale war with Venezia, which was something threat analysts would not deem to be a worthwhile allocation of resources to save a few dozen kids.

Dare hated the ruthless calculus that determined what they could and couldn't do, and in the years to come they would undoubtedly have to deal with the consequences of their inaction.

But in the meantime, Dare had to prioritize exfiltration.

Running over to the edge of the building, she ignored the lurch in her stomach as she looked down. A series of landing platforms had been extended on multiple levels below; she could use her grappleshot to lower herself down until she found one with a vehicle. Not one of her best plans, but it was all she—

"So good of you to join us, Captain Dare."

Dare spun, withdrawing her Mk50 in a single seamless motion, aiming her weapon at the newcomer. A hood covered his head, and his rasping voice sounded much like the one who had spoken in the amphitheater, but due to Eddie's position, she had been unable to identify him.

"You speak with M'raad." He lowered his hood to reveal a bald humanoid head, with sunken eyes, skin as pale as milk, and reddened layers of flesh running under his jaw up to his chin.

"So, the Yonhet are creeping out of the shadows," Dare mused, her tone smooth and collected, knowing. She had been an ONI agent long enough to maintain her composure even under such taut conditions.

The Yonhet smiled, showing a row of sharp teeth. "The fracturing of the Covenant has provided opportunity for all, none more so than for M'raad's people. War between empires is vast and bloody, but war between numerous disparate factions all seeking to gain an edge over each other? That, Captain, is good business. What do you make of the merchandise?"

Dare's VISR picked up movement; red outlines appeared around half a dozen guards moving into position with weapons ready. She was surrounded.

"You mean the *children* you've taken?"

"Come now, Captain. M'raad is certain that ONI knows better than to take issue with such a thing."

It came as no surprise that the ugly rumors of the SPARTAN-II program had reached Venezia. Now it looked like something similar was playing out here—the youth of this world being forcibly conscripted into becoming mercenaries to pay off family debts.

But surely they didn't have the means to *augment* these kids, did they? The broader proliferation of the Spartan program with its latest incarnation had demystified some elements of how these super-soldiers were made, but no simple mercenary outfit could realistically recreate it.

"I'd be more concerned about what's going to happen when word of this little business venture of yours gets back to the UNSC."

The Yonhet laughed. "What *is* the UNSC today? You seem rather like the Covenant to me. Your resources have been carved up, your colonial pipelines decimated, your mighty flagship on the run across the stars. It is no wonder many of your military partners have been looking to expand their enterprise into private sectors, as you can no longer protect them. You must understand, Captain: Your masters are far more likely to financially invest in this project than expend resources attempting to shut it down."

At that moment, Dare heard the telltale whine of a Phantom's engine and turned to see the dropship rising up behind her, its searchlight illuminating the area.

"Welcome to the new galaxy, Captain," M'raad said, raising his arms. "We would be glad to have you as a customer. But if you're not interested in buying, perhaps an ONI agent will make for a rather profitable *guest*."

The Phantom turned to its side and its troop bay doors lowered. In moments, she expected to be hauled inside as reinforcements arrived.

"*That's quite a sales pitch*," a familiar gruff voice sounded over the comm. Dare's VISR picked up the unmistakably titanic figure of Dutch wielding a tri-barreled yeller. "*Whatd'ya think, honey?*"

"Y'know, Dutch," Gretchen said as she disembarked from the Phantom with a VK78 in each hand and came to Dare's side, "I don't much like the look of this neighborhood. Or the local color for that matter."

"Copy that."

M'raad let out a low hiss at the sudden change in circumstances—he had numbers on his side, but going up against two heavily armed Spartans on an unfinished skyscraper's rooftop significantly tipped the odds.

"Shiny ride, you two." Dare began to slowly back up toward the Phantom while Gretchen kept her covered.

"Damn right she's shiny!" Dutch kept his heavy machine gun aimed at M'raad. "You ready to leave these mike-foxtrots behind?"

They made it into the Phantom's troop bay, and Gretchen immediately marched to the cockpit. Dare couldn't help but be surprised at the disciplined restraint of the Yonhet's mercenaries, as she had expected that one of them would have opened fire.

"Another time," M'raad called out. "We look forward to our

next opportunity for a mutually beneficial transaction. Farewell, Captain."

The Phantom's troop bay doors closed and the dropship departed, darting away from the tower into thick layers of storm clouds to avoid detection or any gunships M'raad might send. Dare doubted that he would, however—perhaps the strangest thing about him was the apparent earnest confidence and certainty that the UNSC or ONI would look to make a deal with him somewhere down the line.

In the meantime, Dare had a small matter to attend to.

"What are you two doing here? I told—no, *ordered* Buck that he was not to involve himself in this operation."

"Yes, ma'am," Dutch said flatly. "He said that you did that."

"So where is he?"

"He's back home on *Infinity*, just as you ordered."

"Thing is"—Gretchen entered the troop bay and pulled off her helmet, revealing a smirk—"and he was very keen to stress this part: 'She didn't say anything about *anybody else* on the squad gettin' involved.'"

Dare closed her eyes for a second and sighed. "Of course."

"And it looks like a good thing that we did." Dutch attached his heavy machine gun to a rack on the rear wall of the dropship's interior. "Or Captain Lasky might not have been too pleased about needing to launch a rescue op. Ma'am."

It was a point she had to willingly concede. If they hadn't shown up—if Buck hadn't found some operational ambiguity in her orders—then things would have undoubtedly turned out *very* differently today.

"So, learn anything good at this little shindig?" Gretchen asked.

"Need-to-know, I'm afraid."

"And will we?"

Dare remained silent for a moment.

Though she hated to admit it, M'raad had a point. What exactly *was* the UNSC right now—and ONI for that matter? Like the Covenant, their resources had been scattered across space, their seemingly glorious resurgence diminished from a triumphant roar to a strangled whisper.

"Mind taking the cockpit, you two?" Dare answered. "I need this report ready by the time we get back to *Infinity*."

"Be my guest." Gretchen made a slightly exaggerated show of waving Dutch through before following and sealing the door behind her, leaving Dare alone in the darkened troop bay.

"This is Captain Veronica Dare reporting on Operation: SONATA. Zef 'Trahl's intel was good, something big is going down here on Venezia. Preliminary observations showed several dozen children who have been given by their families to a Yonhet power broker where they will be trained to become mercenaries contracted to multiple unidentified groups. Surveillance footage and additional intel is attached to begin Section One review. File under code word 'janissary.'"

Section One had run countless ever-expanding threat analysis models. Even in the event of actually managing to pull off stopping Cortana, the galaxy they would face afterward would fill that vacuum with countless other problems. What Dare had discovered here today would be one of many, and she couldn't begin to imagine how it would grow over the months and years to come.

Janissary.

The name had come from a group that had emerged from the latter years of humanity's Middle Ages. The Ottoman Empire was known to have abducted children, and through years of intensive training, forged those slave-soldiers and mercenaries into a powerful military force.

ONI had once done the same and the results had ultimately helped them win the war against the Covenant. "Janissary" seemed an appropriate reminder that history had a habit of repeating itself, and this time it would be ONI on the receiving end.

OPTICAN, HEALTHCARE ON DEMAND!

Private Log // Adam Andrews

September 29, 2559

Where to even begin . . .

Actually, first of all, a reminder: Dan is cooking tonight, his own family Bolognese recipe. Make sure to pick up some parmesan on the way home.

Anyway, to business. Contact has been made with several parties on Venezia, one of whom seems particularly promising. Nor Fel assures me that her clearinghouse crew can get what I need but warned that it will take some time. Until I hear back from her, we will continue attempting to stabilize the existing Waverly compounds. Supplies are running short, but we are so close to a breakthrough. I can feel it.

Received word that New Colonial Alliance raids have been stepping up throughout Outer Colony regions in recent months. They hit Cygnus just a few weeks ago, and apparently they're flying Banished colors now. All the more reason to do what we're doing. To keep traveling down this road.

The UNSC can't protect these people, and Created intervention seems more akin to blindly tossing a grenade into a crowded room.

Super-soldiers can no longer remain the dominion of Spartans—of the UNSC. Our industries span numerous colonies, whole sectors of space, and they must be able to level the playing field on their own terms.

Where there is need, Optican will provide.

INTEL // ESCHARUM'S INVOCATION

War Chief Escharum delivers a rallying speech to the Banished about their capabilities and the legacy of Atriox.

When we were inducted into the Covenant, the Prophets had us settled on worlds ripe with rich resources. Was this out of respect for our people—a reward for our strength? No. It was simply another way in which we served as a method of their control. A blunt instrument for delicate hands. A deterrent to those who would claim more than what the Prophets would allow. And they knew we could not excavate these resources ourselves, for we were nothing but fodder to be expended on their front lines.

But look around you, brothers. Savor this moment. Understand what we are now. We are the Banished, and we are free. We *take* what we desire, and we use it to fuel our strength and sustain our spirit.

Never forget what Atriox gave to you. Know that all we are today is because of his vision.

ARMORY INFINITUM // FUEL ROD SPNKR

On the resource-rich world Oth Kattral, two hired Venezian janissaries guard a valuable excavation site for the Banished.

Oth Kattral
April 24, 2560

Bright green light flared along with a volley of explosive crackling as six fuel-rod projectiles detonated on impact. The enemy dropship erupted in flames and was sent careening over the cliff's edge, leaving any of its crew that hadn't been immolated by the blast to suffer a fall of several hundred meters.

Marley dumped the spent tubes on the ground and reloaded his fuel rod SPNKr, leaning out of cover to check for any other signs of hostiles.

"*Think that was just a scouting run*," CC said over the comm. "*How's the new toy?*"

"Packs a punch, no problem there," Marley said. "But the *Gespu*-pattern model is all over Venezia markets—gotta get my hands on one of those as well."

"Prefer the Zasqi-*pattern myself."*

Marley glanced up, his Assailer helmet's visor identifying CC's position several klicks away. She had set up overwatch at the top of one of the monorail towers, where she no doubt had a perfect view of the mining facility and the arid, mountainous landscape around them. If she hadn't noted any further movement, it probably *had* just been a scouting run.

“Yeah.” Marley broke from cover and continued patrolling the perimeter of the facility. “Hard to beat the Covie classics.”

“You should put in a requisition order next time. Adds to the debt, but it’ll help you survive long enough to pay it.”

She wasn’t wrong. A Banished chieftain had enlisted their services to protect a valuable mining site on Oth Kattral, one of their resource-rich worlds, as it was a prime target for rival warlords looking to bolster their own glory and industrial capacity.

Human labor hired to protect alien assets from other aliens so they can use it against other humans, Marley mused. *What a time to be alive.* Sometimes these melting pot arrangements baffled him beyond comprehension. Other times, they made a little too much sense.

AGE OF RETRIBUTION

*This story takes place on November 3, 2552, following the Master Chief's assassination of the Prophet of Regret on Delta Halo (*Halo 2*).*

Overlooking the Chamber of Consecration
Delta Halo

"The High Prophet of Regret is dead."

It was perhaps the sixth time that I had heard the words murmured by Onsu 'Valonro in as many units, but they carried the same air of reverence, sadness, and disbelief as when the honor guard first delivered the news.

Word had spread throughout the ranks of the Covenant. It was unthinkable. Not only was the Demon here, but he had assassinated the Prophet of Regret himself. Worse still, the order had come from the Prophet of Truth that, in an effort to eliminate the Demon, *Solemn Penance* must unleash its cleansing blaze upon Regret's temple. Such desecration of a holy site was tantamount to an act of heresy, but too much had already happened in too short a time to react and respond with any level of dignified diligence.

The indignity was compounded by the accusation that this was *our* fault; the Sangheili had been collectively blamed for being unable to protect Regret. As a result, a radical change was now reverberating through the Covenant, as the mantle of honor guard was taken from our people and passed to the Jiralhanae. These Brutes were still relative newcomers to the Covenant, yet many said that they had been shown immense favor of late, which had now secured them a position previously enshrined in our own sacred history.

Fourteen of us—myself, the councilor, the honor guard, and eleven others of lower-chosen rank—had gathered in the vicinity of the sacred ring's Chamber of Consecration, where High Councilor 'Yajadai bade that we take a moment of restitution amid the chaotic winds of change.

By 'Yajadai's command, I was to keep an eye on the honor guard while he was still seized by grief. It was not a duty I was enthused by, but as a mere lower-chosen in such esteemed company I had little room to complain or disagree. I contented myself with the hope that my service would be looked upon favorably.

"Remember the holy words," Yajadai had said to us. "Take the Psalm of Sorrow into your hearts."

Those who went before are gone
Those who left us wisdom
They have found a better place
And there their light shines on
This wretched life is our prison
As dark and cold as endless space
But their blessed light beckons
And so too does departed grace

The words, spoken together in quiet prayer, buoyed our grief along to quieter shores. We sat for a while in a verdant clearing that looked out at the Chamber of Consecration, a great spherical cloister held within the unmistakable angular struts and buttresses that defined much of the Forerunners' architecture. It sat above a large body of water stretching off toward the horizon, where shafts of golden light pierced through gathering gray clouds.

Around us were towering formations of rock covered in lichen and moss. A winding path ahead ascended toward a Forerunner door embedded into the rock, and the path behind curved around to a stretch of cliff overlooking the full majesty of this divine machine—this god-engine that we were blessed to tread upon.

It was Onsu 'Valonro's voice that broke the contemplative silence at last. The honor guard called out: "We who walk the Path honor you, High Prophet. Luminous beacon of the faithful, we remember your words, your wisdom, and your courage. May your name be spoken with reverence by the holy lords in the heavens, and echo in the spaces below—through the Hall of Eternity."

At this development, High Councilor 'Yajadai gave a slight nod to me, an indication that I had done well in my task, though I felt as if I had done nothing.

"What will happen now?" I asked. It may have been considered inappropriate for one of low rank to speak openly in such a moment as this, but the councilor paid no mind to my insolence.

"There must be a vote to appoint a new hierarch," 'Yajadai said plainly. "The Great Journey cannot begin with an incomplete triumvirate. It remains to be seen whether my fellow councilors and I shall be recalled to High Charity, or if the appointment shall be made here on the sacred ring."

"And it is a matter of great importance that Regret's successor be an ally to the Sangheili." 'Valonro now seemed fully present, his mind sharpened once more.

"Why is that?" I asked.

The honor guard let out an involuntary noise, but 'Yajadai interjected before 'Valonro could formulate a disdainful response. "Because, young one, blessed though the hierarchs may be, the Prophet of Truth is a known reformist—one who, as you have already seen, grants great boons to the Jiralhanae. Mercy is a mediator, one who kept peace between Truth and Regret, and wise though his counsel may be, he is concerned far more with spiritual matters than the politics that drive the Covenant. With the Changing of the Guard, our long-held position is at risk."

These words were strange to hear. I had been educated to think of the Covenant as a single, united entity stewarded by the Prophets. It was their will that guided the Sangheili, for we were to serve as their protectors and enforcers on the path to transcendence. Such was sanctified by the Writ of Union.

No longer.

The notion that there was dissonance—even malcontent—between the hierarchs was most unwelcome. As a relative newcomer to the military of the Covenant, still yet to see extensive combat beyond training in the hunting domes, there was evidently much that I had to learn about those we had pledged our service to. I wondered what the other warriors among us thought of this, but they were patrolling far enough away that they either did not hear the councilor's words or paid them no mind.

'Yajadai stirred as he received an incoming transmission. He input a command on his wrist armor's interface and projected a hologram of a San'Shyuum. Judging by the sudden snap to attention by the councilor and honor guard, this was clearly somebody of considerable importance.

"Hear these words from I, the Prophet of Exquisite Devotion."

I glanced to my right as I could almost perceive the tension straining 'Yajadai, who tightened his mandibles to hold at bay the reaction he truly desired to express.

"Blessed is this day for all of our Covenant as we stand on the precipice of the Great Journey's summation. Alas, the passing of the High Prophet of Regret necessitates the appointment of a new hierarch, and so all Sangheili councilors are called upon to gather at the Chamber of Consecration. Ride now with all due haste, lest you tarry in the final hour and find yourselves left behind."

As soon as the transmission ended, my fellow Sangheili immediately set about making preparations to depart.

"Brothers!" 'Yajadai called out to all of us present. "March with me! Onward to the heart of this sacred ring!"

The others growled in affirmation and dutifully assembled into a single-file line behind the councilor and honor guard. How fortunate we were to have joined the Covenant at such a time—even among these fearful changes, we were here at the point of realizing all that this alliance had sought to achieve on the blood of our forefathers.

We made our way around a large rock separating the central clearing from the winding path leading up to the great Forerunner door, which was itself the height of perhaps two or three Sangheili.

As the door parted upon our approach, we were greeted by a most unwelcome sight.

The Jiralhanae stood over eight feet tall, with a light-gray, single-knotted beard hanging below a smirk framed by razor-sharp tusks. His armor was crimson, accented with ivory, and his eyes . . . they looked as if he might be blind, but instead of milky white they too were a stark red. In one of his gauntleted hands, he casually held a death lobber by his waist, its curved underside bayonet stained with dark blood.

He was accompanied by his own entourage of Brutes. Two were clad in the armor of an honor guard, while the other four wore the basic helmet, shoulder pauldrons, weapon harness, and primitive leg wrappings typical for those of low rank and were otherwise covered simply in their thick brown fur.

"What is the meaning of this?" High Councilor 'Yajadai took a step forward, placing himself in front of 'Valonro and the rest of our number.

The Jiralhanae leader made a show of sniffing the air, his eyes scrutinizing each of us, as if assessing distant prey.

"We are here to *escort* you, Councilor," he said.

"That will not be necessary, Thrallslayer," 'Yajadai responded immediately, his tone clipped. "As you can see, I already have an escort—of greater number."

The Thrallslayer—whose fanged smile had only grown at 'Yajadai's use of his title—turned to 'Valonro, appraising the honor guard. "This one appears to be wearing armor that no longer belongs to him." He gestured to his cohort, sneering. "We cannot depart without honoring the will of the Prophets in this matter."

"I am Onsu 'Valonro, honor guard to the Prophet of Regret and the Fleet of Sacred Consecration." 'Valonro spat on the ground. "Any *jir'a'ul* who would seek to claim this armor will have to *take* it."

Silence hung in the air for a moment, tension boiling over as all present calculated the next move of their leaders. I for one had not anticipated the possibility of fighting Covenant allies. Our enemy on this ring was supposed to be the humans.

But as I looked at the Thrallslayer and his fellows, I could see it in their eyes. Hunger and anticipation for violence.

"His blade!" said one of the Sangheili standing close to 'Yajadai. "Look at his blade!"

The dark stains on the Thrallslayer's bayonet, still hanging by his side, caught the light of the sun. It was not red, the color of human blood, but a deep violet. That of our own kind.

Before any of us could act, the Thrallslayer and his ilk fired their death lobbers upon us, instantly blasting through the energy shields of two of our number. I watched in horror as their abdomens burst apart from the explosives. Blood sprayed onto the ground, the impact from fragments of shrapnel and bone causing my own shields to flare for a moment, and the concussive blast sent the initial two victims falling backward. They were dead before their mangled bodies even hit the ground.

I reached for my plasma rifle, but I was already retreating along with four others of my rank. We were not seasoned warriors. I knew one of our group to have been a scribe made to serve for an annual cycle after offending his minister, and another was renowned for his ability to interpret and translate Huragok. It was neither shameful or dishonorable for these Sangheili to be gentle of spirit, for strength flows from many rivers, but in the face of violence such as this, we stood little chance of prevailing.

The tactics and coordination of the Jiralhanae were quite unlike the low intelligence many Sangheili often claimed them to have. Three stayed back to provide covering fire with their brute shots while the others surged forward on all fours, bounding toward us with incredible speed, at which point instinct took over and I at last began firing at them.

Bursts of superheated plasma impacted one of the Jiralhanae, instantly burning its fur, but even as it howled in pain and an acrid smell filled the air, it showed no signs of faltering.

We were joined by Onsu 'Valonro, who had drawn his energy sword to cover us in close quarters.

"Keep firing!" the honor guard roared. "Focus your attacks together on a target!"

One of the advancing Jiralhanae leaped and 'Valonro swung his blade upward while simultaneously traversing out of reach. The twin prongs sliced through the beast's waist and exited through its foot. The cut did not penetrate deep, but the Brute nonetheless collapsed to the ground in a heap, writhing and bellowing in agony.

We pulled farther back to the central area, where we had made our temporary camp, as there were large rocks providing adequate cover from the grenadiers on higher ground.

As we moved, I caught a brief glimpse of High Councilor 'Yajadai engaging the Thrallslayer himself in battle. A downward thrust from 'Yajadai's blade carved the Jiralhanae leader's weapon in two, but as he attempted to recover from a spent state, the Thrallslayer pressed his momentary advantage and delivered a stunning punch to 'Yajadai's face, knocking his ornate headdress askew as he fell to the ground, his energy sword flying from his grasp.

"I have the councilor!" the Thrallslayer roared in triumph. "Kill the others, then regroup at the bastion!"

The last I saw of High Councilor 'Yajadai was the Thrallslayer dragging him away and out of sight through the door, leaving just nine of us standing.

"Warriors," 'Valonro called to us. "Prepare to—"

The honor guard's order was cut off, as at that moment the Jiralhanae he had critically wounded used its remaining strength to latch on to his back. The enormous beast's weight pulled 'Valonro backward with ease. We aimed our weapons but dared not fire. As they writhed and wrestled, none of us could confidently shoot without likely killing 'Valonro.

Instead, I watched in horror as the wounded Brute's plan became clear. It was too late to act or even attempt to prevent it, as more explosive shells from the brute shots pummeled the rocks and ground near our position.

'Valonro tried to dig his armored boots into the ground, to find purchase and prevent himself from being dragged farther backward, but even—perhaps *especially*—an injured Jiralhanae was capable of drawing on immense reserves of strength. That was all it needed to bring the honor guard to the cliff edge, the overlook facing the Chamber of Consecration, where a fatal drop awaited them.

The Jiralhanae, its lower body soaked with blood, did not have a moment of hesitation before casting itself—and 'Valonro—over the edge.

There was no time to react or mourn, or to do anything other than survive. We few were still under siege.

As I retreated, my foot touched what I had not realized was the hilt of 'Valonro's energy sword. I picked it up as two other Jiralhanae approached, reversing their grips on their brute shots so that they came at us bayonets first.

Four Sangheili scrambled out of cover in different directions, hoping that they would present too many targets for the grenadiers to hit, but the Jiralhanae up on the high ground were instead galvanized by this new challenge, intensifying their attacks. Dirt and rock burst with each impact, and I heard screams—I could not tell how many—as more rounds found their marks.

Holding my plasma rifle in one hand, I ignited 'Valonro's energy sword with the other, still retreating step by step as the two Jiralhanae continued to approach. I had their attention now and hoped that it might give the others time to escape.

My fellow Sangheili passed out of sight as I rounded a rocky corner. My eyes were fixed on the Jiralhanae, whose expressions were inscrutable. Unlike the Thrallslayer, who had appeared as if he could feast upon the joy of inevitable violence, these foes wore little more than expressionless masks. They sensed the end, my fear, and were absolutely focused on what I might do with the honor guard's blade.

One made an intimidating additional step forward and I instinctively swung my blade arm to ward the beast off. It was the miscalculation they had hoped for.

The other slammed into me as soon as the sword was lying spent, throwing me into the hard rock wall and causing me to drop the blade's hilt. I felt the plasma rifle fly out of my hand from the impact and the Jiralhanae tossed it farther afield, casting it over to a long, thin outcrop.

Pain shot through my body as the attacking Jiralhanae's bayonet pierced my flesh, cutting through my ribs. Wine-dark blood stained the weapon as it was ripped from where it had penetrated, and I felt it flowing over my hand as I instinctively grasped at the wound—the pressure of my hands doing little to ease the ragged agony.

Their work done, the Jiralhanae did not bother to offer me a warrior's end. They simply turned and marched away, ready to see to any others that might still survive.

I could do nothing to stop them, could barely manage to track their departure as the world swam in my vision.

Crumpling to the ground, I felt my attention drift from the sounds of combat to the view that lay before me: the great band of the sacred ring, of Halo, curving upward. Vast continents were scattered among its ocean, rays of heavenly light piercing through the clouds obscuring the view of High Charity. If this was to be my fate, to die from a betrayal such as this, let it be in the realm of gods. Let this verdant paradise become my tomb.

Darkness crept at the edges of my vision, drowning my lingering remnants of consciousness, and I felt as if I were plummeting into the endless night of the Hall of Eternity.

But then I saw it.

A sphere of brilliant golden light burst in front of my eyes. A moment later, a figure was cast out from it.

A Sangheili warrior clad in silver armor.

The Arbiter.

He gathered himself for a moment, picking up my discarded

plasma rifle from a nearby rock, and then approached. I saw him clearly then.

"The Brutes have betrayed us." I weakly choked the words out as I felt the last of my strength leaving my body. "*The Councilors*—"

The Arbiter placed a hand upon me and took up the hilt of 'Valonro's energy sword from my grasp. The blade flashed to life, twin prongs of superheated plasma blazing with renewed and vengeful purpose.

My last thoughts were of the Psalm of Repose, of the softness of my uncle's voice as my memory conjured the sound of him singing its holy words by the quiet shores of the Csurdon Sea.

With eyes aloft and tensions high
We gain that which we seek
Rejoice in thine keep's battle cry
A song to separate the weak
Of time it walks among us here
The blade comes for us all
But in our stead, we claim our dead
When echoed in the Hall

Bastion of the Brutes
Delta Halo

High Councilor Raas 'Yajadai struggled to find focus as he slowly regained consciousness. Each arm was locked in an immobilizing grip by a Jiralhanae warrior on his left and right side. As they marched forward, 'Yajadai's feet dragged behind him across an ornate floor.

Amid the chaos and confusion, 'Yajadai tried to take in the situational enormity of it all. For decades he had fought and bled for the Covenant, serving across countless battlefields and ultimately within the High Council itself, all in an effort to be exactly where he was right now. How many other generations had come before him? Each one desperate to be surrounded by unblemished alloy illuminated by ancient sconces amidst the low hum of arcane technology reverberating within the halls of the sacred ring?

And now, at the threshold of all he and his kind had fought for, he found himself wracked with doubt and apprehension. Nothing seemed to make sense—no element occupying its proper place.

"Take him to the upper level!"

'Yajadai's thoughts were interrupted by the Thrallslayer's bellowed command. The councilor heard a thick door slide shut behind them as the Brutes began to drag him up a ramp located in the center of a modest antechamber. Once they reached the top of the ramp, they veered left into a larger octagonal room with several smaller chambers built into the surrounding walls. 'Yajadai felt a pang of anger at the notion that these chambers could once have been used for any number of untold purposes befitting the ring's divine architects, but had now been repurposed into holding cells for those who must have opposed the Jiralhanae's insipid scheme.

The Thrallslayer pointed a thick, furred finger toward a cell in the far corner of the upper level. "There."

The Brute warriors pulled 'Yajadai to the cell and then abruptly pushed him inside before activating a portable energy barrier placed at the entrance. As they stepped away, the Thrallslayer took their place, smugly leering into the holding chamber before finally speaking. "Do you not think it a sign from your gods?"

"A sign?" 'Yajadai echoed the words in confusion.

"That the High Prophet most closely concerned with the station of your kind would be the first to fall? Surely the weak must be culled before the Great Journey can commence." The Thrallslayer grinned through battle-borne tusks. "Regret is who failed you. And now it is what *fills* you."

"You dare mock a hierarch's demise?" 'Yajadai glared directly at the towering beast. "*This* is what a Brute finds worthy of transcendence?"

"*Transcendence.*" The Thrallslayer almost spat the word before continuing in a low growl. "If there is even such a thing."

'Yajadai clacked his mandibles twice. "Perhaps there is not. But at least we live with honor. With *purpose.*"

"And what purpose has this ring brought you?"

"I do not speak of the ring." 'Yajadai's voice grew quieter but bolder. "I speak of my brothers. Bonds that transcend both duty and destiny."

"What do you know of brotherhood?" the Thrallslayer replied. "It is not *your* kind the hierarchs feed to the front lines, to batter the redoubts and resolve of an empire's enemies. You do not watch your brothers bleed without benefit across countless forgotten worlds. And when their bones are turned to glass alongside the corpses of our prey, you do not watch others reap the renown of a victory unearned. No, Councilor—*our* time has finally come. And we will not relinquish it for the sake of what you call honor."

The air hung silent for several moments.

"Avitus," 'Yajadai spoke the Jiralhanae's true name with a subdued but intentional tone of respect. "I have seen you serve. I know what it is to bleed for your brothers—and to bear the stain of their blood on your own hands. But know this: The Great Journey does not include you in the way that you think it does. The Prophets can discard you just as they have clearly discarded my kind. They are steering the ship on this journey. We are simply manning the oars."

As the grizzled chieftain pondered a response, their exchange was interrupted by the screech of a Kig-Yar entering the chamber from the lower level.

"Mighty Thrallslayer!" the Jackal squawked. "Aelius and Ignis send word. They bring back traitor Lekgolo and new councilor for questions."

The Thrallslayer paused for a moment before responding. "Excellent. Prepare new cells for their arrival."

As he turned back toward 'Yajadai, the Sangheili councilor spoke. "Think upon my words, Avitus. If not for yourself, then for those who follow you."

The Thrallslayer snarled. "It is *you* who will be doing the thinking. In the back of your chamber, you shall find a plasma rifle, and with it comes a choice: acknowledge your shame and demonstrate penitence for your actions by searing your own stain from this ring you hold so sacred . . . or wait for my return, and I will gut you myself, slowly, under the gaze of your fellow councilors and co-conspirators. The path is yours to choose."

Despite the Jiralhanae's threats, a strange sense of peace gently draped over 'Yajadai's shoulders. A feeling of clarity, as if something he had not known was obscuring his vision now suddenly cleared.

He remembered the end of the Age of Doubt, how his fellow Sangheili and San'Shyuum councilors alike were filled with zealous fervor as they roared with rapturous joy at the Ninth Age of Reclamation's coming, each of them trying to shout the loudest.

That time had come again. A new age had surreptitiously arrived, ushered in not with cheer and unity of purpose, but with the sharpened silence of blades in the dark.

"My path is already set, Avitus," 'Yajadai spoke. "It is *you* who has yet to choose."

ARMORY INFINITUM // VOLATILE SKEWER

On an uncharted moon, Thrallslayer Avitus bequeaths a parting gift to Bloodstar Ik'novus.

The campfire crackled and the illumination from the flames danced around the mouth of the cave, casting a half light on Avitus's face as he sharpened the blade of a speargun. A fitting farewell gift for a great warrior.

As the thudding of footsteps drew closer, Avitus knew the time had come.

"Escharum tells of a time before the Covenant," Avitus said. "Of the old stalker packs, before they were appropriated by the Prophets."

Ik'novus set down the chunks of wood he had collected from the nearby forest, tossing two fresh logs onto the fire before taking a seat. His chieftain had seen fit to leave a serving of *dengkra* breast for him—the flesh of this creature, a strange kind of reptile-canine, was gamey even for a Jiralhanae's sense of smell, but Avitus considered the taste of the meat second only to thorn beast.

"They hunted creatures of myth across many moons with these spearguns." Avitus finished sharpening the blade attachment and held it up to the light to scrutinize his work before presenting the weapon and concluding, "And now you shall do the same."

"I am honored, Chieftain." Ik'novus accepted the weapon and ran two clawed fingers across its surface, which had been painted white with pigments from the chalk fields of Warial. Upon closer examination, the harpoon appeared to be modified with an explosive—specifically designed to detonate upon penetrating armor.

"We have unleashed the full measure of our fury upon all who stood in our way," Avitus said. "But now, Escharum and Atriox call for us to direct our efforts toward more specific targets. You shall serve the war chief's wishes well as Bloodstar."

The two warriors sat for a while in quiet contemplation, reminiscing about battles of the past, casting their minds ahead to the greater battles to come, and sharing one last toast to the fallen—honoring the crypt-haulers who would ferry the souls of the dead in Oth Sonin. And as first light broke over the horizon, they bade a final farewell.

ARMORY INFINITUM // RUSHDOWN HAMMER

On Zeta Halo, Chieftain En'Geddon reports to War Chief Escharum on the evolving relationship between Sangheili and Jiralhanae in the Banished.

Annex Ridge
Chieftain En'Geddon
FWD: Brotherhood

War Chief Escharum,

Executions continue for those who display insubordinate belief in their right to status without having earned their glory. Their restless ambitions have been crushed under my hammer in the fighting pits—none have been a match for the enhancements made to its gravitic core.

Atriox's absence continues to weigh upon me. It is not enough that we lost our home system, but the one who united and gave us purpose as well. We who remain must carry out his designs, and it will take the concerted effort of *every* Banished brother to amount to the impact that the warmaster alone was able to make.

I bore witness to something that renewed my resolve. The Spartan has been carving his way through our numbers, leaving outposts in ruins and reacquainting our forces with the feeling of fear after countless cycles of victory have infested many with sloth.

As one Jiralhanae fell to the Spartan, it was a Sangheili who took up his brother's weapon in rage and defiance to avenge him.

Our kind has fought against the Sangheili with tooth and claw and blade even before the Great Schism, but it is those pledging themselves to the Banished who have found brotherhood that transcends species.

I do not know what afterlife may await those Banished brothers, but I am humbled by witnessing the fire of Atriox in their hearts. That is the power he possessed, and his spirit endures.

I look forward to encountering the Spartan myself. Whether he is broken under my hammer or I fall in glory, I am assured that we *will* prevail.

INTEL // REVERSE ENGINEERING

At an ONI Ilex facility on an uncharted world, a report is filed regarding progress on Operation: ECDYSIS.

May 9, 2556 (Military Calendar)
Office of Naval Intelligence, Ilex Facility
Operation: ECDYSIS

While the Zeta Halo Project has not been as fruitfully forthcoming as Trevelyan's parallel efforts, we have been able to make some headway with early efforts to replicate the installation's extensive remediation systems.

These initial structure samples—"hex pillars," the techs are calling them—are without a doubt a mineralogical treasure trove, but we have yet to find any success in re-creating the method by which they are able to convert raw materials into viable substrates. Not to mention the creative solutions we've had to employ to generate even a fraction of the power that we assume these processes will ultimately require to function at scale.

Still, continuing study of these machines may provide valuable insight into enhancing and evolving our own worlds—including reviving those that have been scorched from orbit during the Covenant War.

Will report further on results as new data is available.

WHISPERS FROM THE PYRE

*This story takes place at the end of May 2560, immediately following the death of War Chief Escharum on Zeta Halo by the hand of the Master Chief (*Halo Infinite*).*

"It is our great burden, is it not? To guide the preservation of the galaxy—even to the ends of erasing it.

"Weapons of last resort, built by my makers many millennia ago to starve out the great parasite. This ring is but one of seven. Designed to preserve life, designed to destroy it.

"One of seven.

"But, this ring is . . . different.

"Reforged from the remains of an earlier effort, it possesses abilities not shared by its siblings. This ring has . . . many secrets, some even worth dying for.

"Many in my place would see this charge as a burden. Custodian of one of the galaxy's greatest marvels—and greatest perils. I admit, I often found myself feeling out of place with others like me.

"The monitors of the other installations seemed to share similar perspectives and experiences amongst each other, but I've always been an outcast among them—by both design and by birthright.

"A different type of caretaker for a very different type of ring.

"While zero-seven's integral place within the Array is most unquestionable, its history and original composition allow for far more . . . direct applications. Applications invoked in order to uphold the Mantle . . . or betray it."

The voice of Despondent Pyre, the elusive monitor of Installation 07, faded.

Studymaster Ciar 'Yaham retracted his semicircular datapad and clacked his mandibles in satisfaction as he scrutinized the great stone ring artifact before him. Wisps of mist-like blue energy would typically indicate it had clusters of fragmented data to access, wherein ghostly voices from the past would slough off their digital embalmment to offer a fractured testimony. But this particular arcane curio had now fallen dark and silent.

"Though this artifact appears to have been accessed recently, it still bore latent data streams that we were able to extract." Studymaster 'Yaham turned to Dahk'rah, a Kig-Yar Skirmisher from a group known as the Mind Talons, with whom he had found himself partnered in their joint efforts to uncover the many ancient secrets of Zeta Halo.

"More from monitor," Dahk'rah replied, running a hand through her plume of red feathers. "Curious mention of Oth Koronn's past. Reforged, unique abilities and applications . . . Great prestige for us if we find!"

'Yaham nodded in agreement. Installation 07—designated "Oth

Koronn" by the Banished and "Zeta Halo" by the Forerunners—had a fascinating history for which they had only just scratched the surface of exploring. *Finding* that history was one matter, but the process of interrogation and interpretation of data was another challenge entirely.

The Sangheili studymaster found that he was developing a fondness for Dahk'rah's company of late. He had come to understand that, like many Kig-Yar, she possessed a great drive for profit, but rather than seeking abundance in riches, "profit" for Dahk'rah meant accumulating knowledge. In the days of the Covenant, that had been the singular domain of the San'Shyuum, but within the Banished it was just one way of many that anybody could make themselves useful.

The mystery of the stone ring totems was something discovered within a lunar cycle of occupying Oth Koronn, and both Studymaster 'Yaham and Dahk'rah were determined to be the first to discern the truth of these strange artifacts. It had taken little work to convince Battle Officer Zeretus to establish a dedicated research outpost in the local area.

'Yaham's gaze swept across the vast landscape of the ring. From his position, standing near the summit of an alpine mountain split in two by the Tyrant's rending of the Halo ring, he and Dahk'rah had an excellent line of sight over many nearby landmarks.

To the north, the ring's vista revealed an ocean of stars. Whenever the studymaster had looked into that abyss, attempting to trace the division between the dark of space and the azure sky, he had been moved to dizziness. At the farthest end of those suspended columns lay the Silent Auditorium—the site of the Tyrant's immolation—which was still slowly re-forming.

Immediately northwest was a beacon tower that he had visited several day-cycles ago, where his correspondence with Dahk'rah enabled him to translate excerpts of Despondent Pyre's data. From there, the winding roads traveled south and westward, where rising stacks of hexagonal pillars—the building blocks of the installation's artificial landscape—led up to the outpost he had now come to call home.

"No response from Annex Ridge," Dahk'rah squawked, having apparently attempted to contact the outpost through her nativelink.

"That is . . . concerning," 'Yaham replied. Indeed, this whole sector felt emptier than it was supposed to be. Despite the supply crates strewn around the vicinity of the ring-shaped artifact, no allied Banished forces had been here to meet them.

"Have done all we can here. Should return to Annex Ridge, see progress on artifacts there."

With nothing left to avail them in this location, the studymaster and Skirmisher began their descent of the mountain. Farther to the north, the towering form of an inactive reformation spire loomed over another fractured "island" where three Gorespike anti-air platforms lay in ruin. What exactly had happened to them, neither he or the Skirmisher knew, but it seemed that the remnants of the UNSC were suddenly growing bolder in their retaliatory strikes.

'Yaham pushed the feeling of concern to the back of his mind. For what also hung in the sky above them were several Banished dreadnoughts, including *Ghost of Malkadyr*. Under the leadership of War Chief Escharum, the Banished owned this area of Oth Koronn.

As the dirt track road delivered them to the bottom of the mountain, they were met by the welcome sight of six Jiralhanae warriors accompanying a half-laden war-skiff.

"Brothers," 'Yaham called out, unable to deny a feeling of relief at seeing them. "Greetings to you all. I am Studymaster Ciar

'Yaham of Annex Ridge, and this is my fellow researcher, Dahk'rah of the Mind Talons."

"Well met, Studymaster," replied one of the Jiralhanae, stepping forward. "I am Evocus. Have you been ordered to redeploy with us too?"

"We . . . have not," the Sangheili said, fumbling a response to the unexpected query. "Forgive me—Dahk'rah and I have been out of contact for several day-cycles now. What news is there?"

The Jiralhanae shifted uncomfortably. "You have not heard?"

'Yaham and Dahk'rah exchanged puzzled looks.

"The House of Reckoning has fallen. War Chief Escharum is dead, killed by the Demon," Evocus gravely intoned.

The studymaster splayed his mandibles, unable to comprehend the enormity of what he had just heard and its vast implications.

It was said that Atriox had perished to eliminate the Tyrant, the human artificial intelligence who had sought to rule the galaxy and destroyed the Jiralhanae homeworld of Doisac to make an example of Atriox's defiance. In his place, it was Escharum who continued to serve the warmaster's will and carry his legacy.

But both of them? *Gone?*

There would be serious consequences for the Banished. Of that, he had no doubt.

'Yaham placed a hand on Evocus's shoulder. "The war chief was *daskalo* to us all."

"It is said that he died well." Evocus spoke this with greater resolve. "For a Jiralhanae, that is all that matters."

"Our people have that much in common." 'Yaham bowed his head. "We were about to return to Annex Ridge. The secrets we have been excavating from the ring may prove vital to our continued dominion over this installation."

"Beware, Studymaster. UNSC forces have retaken many of their nearby operating bases, and Riven Gate is no longer under our firm control. I do not know what has become of Annex Ridge, but our enemies will undoubtedly seek to claim your bounty of knowledge. Do not be surprised if the Demon has laid waste to that as well."

Dahk'rah spoke up. "Join us. Annex Ridge must hold."

"Our orders come from Horatius himself. We are to redeploy to the Silent Auditorium immediately." As Evocus spoke, the unmistakable blare of a Phantom's horn sounded over the hills. "We cannot come with you, but we can give you an opportunity to return to Annex Ridge with speed."

Evocus gestured to the war-skiff. They would no longer need it.

"Glory and spoils to your clan." Dahk'rah beat a fist to her armored chest.

"May we meet again in victory," 'Yaham concluded, but as he met Evocus's gaze, it was clear that they both recognized the platitude. Where these Jiralhanae were going, they would most certainly not meet again—at least, not in this life.

Studymaster 'Yaham took up the driver's seat of the war-skiff and Dahk'rah entered the front-facing plasma cannon. The transport's suspension tracks lifted off the ground and the vehicle sped forward, following the dirt track road.

Neither he or his companion looked back as the Jiralhanae boarded their Phantom and were ferried away.

"Strange to see," Dahk'rah called out, breaking the contemplative silence between them. "Sangheili and Jiralhanae as allies."

She was quite right. During their time in the Covenant, the Jiralhanae had quickly become bitter rivals to the Sangheili. Many of their kind—even Atriox himself—had been used on the front line as mountainous walls of flesh and muscle thrown at the humans' defensive garrisons, often on the orders of their Sangheili commanders. Spurred by their newfound zealotry, having been lifted from the ashes of endless civil war on Doisac, many gladly went to their deaths with the promise of divine transcendence through their service to the Great Journey.

Seeking to better understand his strange allies, the studymaster had pored over records aboard many Banished dreadnoughts, which had themselves become not just engines of war but also cultural and historical preserves. His findings had been rather illuminating. Younger generations had eagerly embraced the Covenant and its faith, disenfranchised by clan conflicts and weary of misuse by their pack leaders in fights over territory already spoiled by older wars.

Upon learning this, seeing the pattern of how history had so quickly been repeated, the studymaster understood precisely why such animosity toward the Sangheili had come to be.

But then, there were elders like Escharum, who were already skeptical of the Prophets' promises, and laid the foundation for all that the Banished represented today. From the spark of Atriox's rebellion against the Covenant, a fragile coalition of scavengers and mercenaries had been consolidated into a true confederacy. The Banished inspired loyalty in all who sought to break their chains, and Atriox held neither grudge or prejudice against any who pledged service, including humans—even if that absolution was not always reflected within the ranks.

"Indeed," 'Yaham agreed, realizing his mind was wandering again. "But our peoples have much in common. That, at least, is what the Banished has helped us to see, now that our days of servitude to the Covenant at last lie behind us."

The studymaster turned the war-skiff to the right as they reached a fork in the road marked by a communications pylon. These devices were known to relay inane messages from an Unggoy known as Glibnub, and it was with some unspoken relief that 'Yaham saw the humans had evidently laid waste to it.

A stack of Forerunner foundation material lay ahead, atop which sat a UNSC forward operating base.

Evocus had warned the two that UNSC forces may now occupy this area, but as the war-skiff cruised past the base it appeared to be empty. This made sense to the studymaster as, tactically, it was poorly placed for any kind of assault. If the humans were to strike, it would undoubtedly be from their base that lay on higher ground, closer to Annex Ridge—though to do so, they would have to get past Myriad, the fearsome Mgalekgolo of the Hordeworms of Svir.

Turning the war-skiff to the left, 'Yaham continued on for a handful of centals before halting the vehicle on an exposed cluster of Forerunner stacks. As they disembarked, they found the gates to Annex Ridge's elevator open, and its lower structures appeared to be vacant.

The pair immediately boarded the ground floor elevator and instructed it to ascend. Its movement was slower than 'Yaham would have liked, but he took the moment to keep his mind focused.

As they reached the top, they were immediately struck by the scene of devastation awaiting them.

Banished corpses of all species were strewn across the upper level, pools of blood having dried into dark stains upon the mud. Perhaps the most macabre element was that some of the bodies appeared to be partially submerged into the ground, as if the Halo's environmental systems were already spurring the soil to grow over them—reclaiming the bodies, making them part of the ring itself.

At the far end of the outpost, a siege-hauler transport holding two stone ring artifacts lay in ruin next to a ruptured fuel silo that still burned with crackling fire.

"If what Evocus said is true," Studymaster 'Yaham said as he and the Skirmisher ran toward the craft on its landing pad, "then this was perpetrated by only *one* Spartan . . ."

"All it takes," Dahk'rah concluded for him matter-of-factly.

"Then it seems Evocus was correct and we must be swift," 'Yaham said, resolve and purpose filling his voice. "We do not know how much time we have before the humans turn their attention back to this location—its secrets are no doubt just as valuable to their kind as they are to us."

They finally arrived at the lower pit of the outpost, where they were relieved to see one of the circular stone fragments recovered appeared to be intact and was still held in place by anchor cables.

Even better, it seemed to be active.

Within its circumference, pale blue light almost vibrated, emanating a soft singing sound—clusters of data ready to spill forth and coalesce into . . . something.

"Perhaps the presence of the Demon activated the artifact," 'Yaham speculated. "These totems are known to respond in peculiar ways to their kind."

"Siphon data now," Dahk'rah spoke with urgency. "No time to waste."

They jumped into the pit arena and marched up to the machinery connected to the ring totem. Clamps were attached to the lower sides of the ring, which ran under metal grated floors, with many wires and cables linked to a computer console displaying a holograph of the artifact.

The Banished had grown quite adept at exploiting exotic alien technology, extracting power as feedstock to fuel their own devices. This, however, was a different matter altogether. These data clusters were far more esoteric, yet they had been imbued into many structures and constructs on Oth Koronn.

"I am rerouting all remaining power from the outpost to the artifact dock." 'Yaham input a series of commands on the console, temporarily shutting down everything from nearby lights to the kinetic launcher and interior base machinery.

Annex Ridge went dark, leaving the studymaster and the Skirmisher to simply await the power transfer's completion.

Night began to fall as the nearest sun passed beneath Oth Koronn's fractured horizon. The blue veil of the sky rolled back and the abyss of stars below painted a dark canvas, illuminated by a yellowish glow that lined the farthest edges of the installation's shattered landscape.

The data clusters began to pour forth from the ring totem and settled as a thin mist on the ground.

First, a form took shape in the center of the stone ring—the installation's monitor, Despondent Pyre. Then, she spoke.

"As much as this ring is a weapon, it is also a refuge. So many species have come to call this place home. Delightful forms of life that would have otherwise perished and remained forgotten after the firing of the Array. Many such lives have looked upon these horizons—and in times much more harrowing than these.

"These ancient totems have made appropriate canvases on which to record some of this somber history. The Tudejsa fashioned them long ago in reverence—or perhaps remorse—of the unknowable structure that they themselves called home.

"But their people's story is only one echo among many.

"These relics and the frail memories which accompany them are nearly all that remain of their kind."

The studymaster extended a long finger on his zygodactyl hand

and pressed a button on the console. Instantly, the monitor's hologram froze in place, hanging motionless amid the swirling eddies of scattered particles.

"It seems this place has been home to many. They speak of creatures I do not recognize." 'Yaham's voice was low and filled with both wonder and trepidation, his mandibles moving uncertainly as he mouthed the unfamiliar word *Tudejsa*. "I cannot help but wonder what became of them all."

"Long dead . . . or long buried," Dahk'rah offered in response. "Many doors still shut. Still hiding their secrets."

"And no way of knowing which doors offer riches or ruin." The studymaster pondered the Kig-Yar's words, simultaneously wearied and invigorated by the danger of the unknown. He sighed before reactivating the artifact, prompting Despondent Pyre's voice to resume.

"A shining beacon. A whitewashed tomb. A hushed casket. A palace of pain. This ring is a monument to so many of my makers' sins.

"Like all empires, great care has always been taken to obfuscate the whole truth. Records partitioned, testimonies curated, victories accentuated.

"The greatest fear of the Forerunners was neither progeny or plague—it was powerlessness. And it could not be tolerated."

The playback froze again and 'Yaham's focus snapped toward his companion.

"What do you see?" the Sangheili asked. He knew the Skirmisher well enough that she would not interrupt the gathering of knowledge such as this without reason.

"These words hold great weight—great value. But hurry we must." Dahk'rah spoke in a rushed tone and pointed into the distance. "Or no chance will we have to claim them."

It took a moment for the studymaster to see what she was pointing at, reminding him of the old adage that Sangheili vision would always be second-rate to even a blind Kig-Yar.

'Yaham climbed out of the pit and extracted a *vyspar* from his armor—a small monocular device that allowed him to view what had caught Dahk'rah's attention. The UNSC forces had regrouped at a forward operating base positioned on higher ground, located closer to Annex Ridge. Perhaps a dozen human marines were stationed there, escorting a Warthog with both a passenger and gunner, and they appeared to be moving in the outpost's direction.

Searching below for any sign of Myriad and their forces, the studymaster's *vyspar* caught only empty terrain. It was evident that the Demon truly had swept through and annihilated the defenses and infrastructure of the Banished in short order—a clear warning to whoever would succeed War Chief Escharum that there was a hidden cost to victory; the risk that it would breed complacency and sloth in the ranks.

"It appears our time has run out." 'Yaham's voice was bathed in bitterness, that they should come so close to so much, only to have their curiosity curtailed at the threshold of understanding. "I will pull down what little data we can with the time we have left. Let us find a new place to take refuge and reckon with what we have heard."

The Kig-Yar set immediately to the task at hand, decoupling data sieves and transcription harnesses as the studymaster secured what they could salvage from the artifact.

As the pair quickly made their exit from Annex Ridge, the studymaster pondered what the ancient words truly meant. This talk of grave sins, of fear, of progeny and powerlessness . . . all recorded by unmarked tombstones standing in silence—an admission to past transgressions, but no real confession as to what they were.

The notion of truth seemed to be changing more with every waking moment, and he was grateful for the glimpse into the galaxy's perilous past. By dipping into the deep wells of its history, what wisdom might help light the way to secure their future?

"Of what service is guilt? To whom are we inevitably accountable? Is one sin greater than another? Is a lie of omission softer than outright perversion of the truth?

"Are my crimes greater than Mendicant Bias, or the Master Builder? What of the Didact himself?

"Is there a difference between orders given or orders followed?

"My burden is impossible to understand.

"The harm. The history. The weight this ring carries. The gravity of its deeds.

"They were made silent. Should I make myself the same to atone?

"Am I a watchtower? Or a warden?"

After the destruction of the Jiralhanae homeworld Doisac, War Chief Escharum reflects on the futility of hope.

Personal Log // Escharum
>>Hope

Hope. It is a word for the weak.

What hope was there for the Jiralhanae during the Great Immolation? When we warred among ourselves over territory spoiled by nuclear fire? When the Covenant came to throw unnumbered legions of our kind against their enemies?

When our home was razed from existence?

Humanity clings to hope. They speak of it as an intangible force encompassing all things—sustenance, resolve, power. But hope does not feed growling stomachs, nor conquer foes, nor rebuild worlds.

Strength is what achieves these things. Knowledge, industry, weaponry. Many call the Jiralhanae savages, but these principles are what we once had, when we achieved stellar travel all on our own. What future might have awaited us had there been no Great Immolation? Would we have possessed such strength? Do not dwell upon such questions, lest you tempt hope into your heart.

As the fight against the humans continues, I shall lead the Banished with my axe and walk the path of strength. Together, our might shall bludgeon such sentimental notions of hope from our foes, and in the end, as they look to the stars and pray for deliverance, they shall know endless suffering.

Hope shall be nothing more than an epitaph, one carved on the marker of a mass grave of the unworthy.

ARMORY INFINITUM // BLOODBLADE

On Zeta Halo, Jega 'Rdomnai hunts a squad of UNSC marines.

An acrid breeze blew through the dead forest, the trees blackened by bombing runs and plasma fire. As Zeta Halo slowly rotated and the nearest star began to dip below the far containment wall making up the ring band's edge, what passed for dusk began to settle across the fractured landscape. Amid a backdrop of charred bark and broken limbs, the subtle shift of black armor was the only evidence of Jega 'Rdomnai's presence.

The cybernetically enhanced Sangheili warrior waited patiently in the shadows, anticipating the arrival of a group of UNSC marines designated "Boulder Squad." 'Rdomnai had observed and catalogued the group's patterns and patrol routes for several cycles, and the time drew near for him to finally make his move.

'Rdomnai gave a quick but choreographed sweep over his weaponry to make sure all was in peak operating order. In the relative stillness of the moment, he allowed his focus to deviate just slightly toward wistful recollection. His left cybernetic arm housed the reforged remnants of his old personal energy sword—an intimidating, custom-shaped, twin-blade monstrosity named Ghostpierce.

In his right hand, he slowly turned over the hilt of his most recent weapon of choice, a more traditional Sangheili bloodblade that itself had already claimed more victims than he could count. The crimson-hued energy sword remained nameless, but 'Rdomnai subconsciously vowed to bestow upon it a new moniker when their task was at last done on this ring. Something befitting of such a monumental victory.

Something befitting the death of a demon.

Nearly an hour passed before the first sounds of the encroaching marines could be heard. Soon Boulder Squad was in sight. As the squad crept closer, every step became a silent countdown to mark each human's end. Low voices turned from casual communication to concern and confusion as multiple red energy blades ignited just inside the tree line, the forest suddenly a charcoal painting come to life, giving birth to a monster made of metal and mandibles.

The screams lasted longer than the frantic gunfire, a still silence welcoming Boulder Squad into its eternal embrace. A moment later, the red glow of the blades disappeared, and Jega 'Rdomnai became shadow once more.

FROM THE SOIL TO THE STARS

*This story takes place over September 19–21, 2559—approximately three weeks before deployment to Reach for Operation: WOLFE (*Shadows of Reach*).*

Dr. Catherine Halsey, Personal Journal
Encryption Code: GAWAIN
Subject: MJOLNIR GEN3

For almost half a century, I have given everything I possibly can to my Spartans. The mind, body, and soul of myself and many others have been scraped away, bit by bit, in the pursuit of saving humanity—first from itself, then from the Covenant . . . and now, from the cascading fallout of innumerable intricate actions for which there are no end of consequences.

You are called upon once again to lead them over the threshold and into the darkness, to fight against impossible odds. And to win.

You've always been good at that, haven't you, John?

To that end, I have something for you. Something you will need.

The Mjolnir exosuit is now complete.

Even though this technology will save humanity in the war to come, I must remind myself that liquid crystal cannot rise on its own. Titanium alloy cannot prevail in the face of extinction. Armor cannot hope.

It all means nothing, until *you* step inside.

0600 Hours, September 19, 2559 (Military Calendar)
BXR Mining Corporation Base Camp, KC-59

The day began like any other.

Henrietta Varadi, along with more than two dozen of her fellow miners, rolled out of the modest bunks in their subterranean sleeping quarters.

After fully waking herself up with a brisk shower, Varadi dried herself off, pulled on her BXR fatigues, and headed for the canteen. Same breakfast as ever: two slightly overcooked sausages, beans, mushrooms, and a slice of bacon—not *too* crispy. An unsubtle wink at Jessica as she served up the food, a smile reserved just for her, and that became two slices of bacon—a daily ritual they had both grown familiar with in recent weeks.

Varadi wolfed down her breakfast and returned to her bunk, picking up the book from the attached shelf: a gently used copy of *Rendezvous with Ramen* by the noted chef and food critic Arturo Bustamante. There were a spare fifteen minutes before her shift started and she had arrived at a particularly engrossing anecdote about the three days that Bustamante had spent in Rio de Janeiro visiting a Sangheili-owned establishment. Reading about the alien food was interesting, but the meals and recipes were more of a gateway into the personal stories of these strange refugees who had been given a home on Earth itself.

Alas, the klaxon sounded in short order, forcing her to put the book down a few pages short of her normal reading quota.

Varadi suited up into her OSTEO gear and met with her team by the imposing circular vault door separating the base's living quarters and operations center from the mines. After an extensive period of checking pressure seals, internal systems, oxygen filters, and numerous other safety elements, the vault door was opened to reveal the vast cavern beyond.

KC-59—simply nicknamed "Casey" by those who had set up shop on its surface—was a largely desolate planet, but it contained something of immense value to the United Nations Space Command: extensive deposits of titanium.

As had been drilled into her and the rest of the crew from day one, titanium was the bread and butter of humanity's interstellar civilian and military production.

"*When you see the cavalry arrive over the hill in M808 MBTs, you're lookin' at a solid wall of titanium!*" Varadi recalled Foreman Brine barking at them during her onboarding to the BXR Mining Corporation. "*When a starship's battle plating protects you from the unforgiving vacuum of space and superheated plasma, you won't be sendin' thanks to any god of your choosing—you'll be addressin' your tender heartfelt regards to titanium-A battle plating!*"

Varadi had never expected to hear such a vocally emphatic history lesson about the various everyday uses of titanium and where it could be found. Brine had insisted it was important they all show the appropriate knowledge and respect for atomic number twenty-two.

But the titanium that Varadi and her comrades were mining here wasn't going to be used for any of those things. Above Casey sat Perihelion Station, a Materials Group facility where the next generation of Mjolnir armor for the Spartans was being developed.

"*Y'know what that means?*" Foreman Brine had said after she and her fellow miners were briefed by their Materials Group partners about the Casey job. "This *is the most important goddamn titanium you'll ever excavate.*"

On that, at least, Varadi knew he was right. When a Spartan stepped onto the battlefield, they represented the culmination of a thousand lives that built the ultimate weapon. Engineers and scientists who created the armor and augmentations, miners who provided the materials, technicians who kept the armor systems tuned for optimal efficiency and performance.

That was what it meant when folks said Spartans represented hope for humanity. It was not simply about the individual soldier, but the work—and, at times, the sacrifices made—to deliver them to the fight.

Inspiring as it was, sometimes it all seemed so futile, that the sum total of humanity's resolve in the battle for survival would one day cost them *too* much. Doubt forever seemed to loom over them as new threats arose, casting a long shadow, but Varadi knew she nevertheless had a part to play.

Her dream would be waiting for her on that distant horizon after this was all over: a brighter future, where she ran her own restaurant. Maybe with Jessica, if she entertained the idea of leaving all of this behind to start a new life—Rio certainly seemed like a good idea. And if things went *really* well . . . Varadi figured she could even send a personal invitation to Arturo Bustamante himself.

But until then, she would mine. Duty to humanity still ultimately compelled her. And to bring an end to these conflicts, they would need no end of titanium.

1300 Hours, September 20, 2559 (Military Calendar)
UNSC *Amicable Disagrement*

"So, what's the deal with this Orca armor?"

"That's *ORCUS*, Private Smith," Gunnery Sergeant Babatunde noted in a gruff tone, immediately clocking a smartass disguising their nerves. "And the Corps are eager to find out what hardass *au naturel* grunts like us can achieve with some new toys, starting with how well it holds up from a titanium coffin ride. So buckle up, troopers!" Babatunde's voice boomed through the frigate's deployment bay. "Get ready to drop!"

A chorus of *"Oo-rah!"*s sounded off as half a dozen Orbital Drop Shock Troopers of the Ninth Platoon stepped off the grated gantry and secured themselves into their drop pods, all clad in semi-powered ORCUS exoskeletons.

Somebody somewhere in the chain of command had apparently taken umbrage with the idea of this armor being developed simply as a drop-in upgrade package for Spartans. Scuttlebutt was that ORCUS was being brought out of development limbo to be tested for more direct and specialized Helljumper applications—starting here.

"PFC Núñez!" the gunnery sergeant called out from his pod. "Would you be so kind as to describe to me the manner in which we will be deploying?"

"Feetfirst, sir!" Private First Class Núñez responded.

"You afraid of heights, Private Smith?!"

"No, sir! Can't get enough of them, sir!"

"How many drops is this for you, Private?"

"F-first one, sir." Smith's bravado receded a little and several of the other ODSTs let out knowing laughs.

"You keep your breakfast, lunch, and dinner in that stomach of yours, trooper. We don't need you making any impromptu paint jobs over this shiny new armor or these cozy luxury pods, you hear me?"

"Understood, sir!"

The hatches of their pods closed, sealing each trooper inside. The frigate's deployment bay floor then began to open, revealing a glimpse of the planet below—KC-59.

"*The light is green,*" the voice of one of *Amicable Disagreement*'s bridge officers sounded over their comms. "*Initiating drop.*"

"*Ten-four,*" Gunnery Sergeant Babatunde confirmed as he appeared on one of the interior screens of Núñez's pod. "*Express elevator to hell, going down!*"

Núñez tried to steady their breathing, remembering the exercises they had been taught to keep calm and clear-headed during a drop.

But all of a sudden, the pod's three green status lights had already pitilessly counted down, and the next thing Núñez knew, the breath had been taken out of their chest as gravity assumed command of their entry vehicle.

The terrestrial surface of KC-59 now filled the pod's thin vertical viewport, and Núñez focused their mind on the information readout of the planet.

Orbital period of seven and a half Earth years . . . 6,519-kilometer radius . . . thirty-one Earth-hour days . . . surface gravity of 1.1G . . .

Vast expanses of rocky mountains covered the surface, but the mining craters were by far the most striking feature—tracts of concentric circles, surrounded by outposts and massive equipment arrays gradually becoming ever more visible. A central processing facility housed a skyhook connecting to Perihelion, the planet's orbital station, while others played host to mass drivers that could send their cargo into orbit in a slightly more dramatic way.

"*Smith, tighten up your approach vector—you're drifting away from the group!*" Gunnery Sergeant Babatunde ordered over the comm.

Núñez watched as Smith made a slight adjustment with the pod's directional control sticks, bringing him back on course. He seemed to be keeping a level head for a first-timer, managing to not overcorrect his movement inward, which would thereby risk a collision with other nearby pods.

"All right, everyone, time to pop your chutes!"

Five drag chutes bloomed into view, only to instantly vanish from Núñez's viewport as their own pod continued screaming toward the ground below.

Their command returned no response.

Núñez felt the rising swell of fear as their situation crystallized. "Sir, my chute isn't responding. Please advise."

"*Keep calm, Núñez,*" Babatunde spoke with a reassuringly steady tone. "*Hit your retro thrusters now to slow your descent. Should buy you a little extra time as we work this out.*"

Núñez hit a button on their seat arm's control panel and allowed a momentary sensation of relief at the immediate feedback, jerking the pod upward.

It took effort to keep their mind focused and breathing steady. Over the last few days on Perihelion Station, they had been learning the art of "no-thought" and several Sangheili battle-meditation exercises from Spartan-058. Núñez was light-years away from mastering these methods, but they followed the logic of the teaching: *Thoughts and feelings are directionless paths branching in a deep forest—do not follow them. This is not about an absence of thinking, it is a rejection of being lost in the endless possibilities of thought, uniting body and mind in clarity until it comes as naturally as breathing.*

Simply put, in this scenario, attempting to trace the reason back as to why the pod was malfunctioning and who was at fault was irrelevant guesswork.

Focus on the moment. Find the solution. *Live.*

"What now, sir?"

"Initiate a quick reset. It'll take a few seconds to kick in and force reboot all systems. Just let it do its thing."

A twist of a control dial and confirmation of intent instantly shut down all internal systems within the pod. The lights of its screens winked out, and the gunnery sergeant's image vanished, leaving Núñez to sit in darkness.

Focus on the sound of each breath.

The longest seconds Núñez had ever counted passed—*two . . . three . . . four . . .*—and still the pod was falling. The ground getting closer and closer—

All of a sudden, the screens flicked back on again, and Núñez immediately hit the button for the drag chute.

Inertia compensators hadn't fully come online, but the sudden jolt of deceleration as the chute fired out of the top of the pod had never felt so damn good. Whatever whoops and cheers Núñez may have wanted to let out, neither their lungs nor brain allowed it as adrenaline pumped through their body. Instead, Núñez simply winked a green status light and shifted focus to the landing that was still to come.

"Looks like you're all set, Núñez. Troopers, thank you for flying with us today at Badass Airlines," Babatunde said, cutting through

the tension. "*Please keep your arms and legs inside the vehicle at all times until landing. And yes, that* has *been a problem before.*"

Babatunde guided the final stages of their descent until all six pods hit solid ground.

Núñez felt like every bone had been violently pulled from their body and then shoved back in. But as the hatch blew off, Núñez grabbed their stowed MA40 and immediately leaped out of the pod's harness, their movement assisted by the semi-powered armor. The dark interior of the vehicle was suddenly replaced by rolling rocky plains, a light-blue sky, and cotton-white clouds.

"*Nobody popped,*" Babatunde reported.

They had all made it. They were alive.

As the squad regrouped and formed up, Gunnery Sergeant Babatunde inspected each ODST's armor to confirm all systems were green and no damage was suffered from the landing. Upon reaching Núñez, he announced, "One of the most valuable lessons a soldier can learn is that technology can break, but *you* mustn't." He clapped Núñez on the back. "You stayed calm, followed instructions, and managed to land within an acceptable distance of the squad. Good work, trooper."

Núñez was suddenly grateful for the polarized faceplate hiding their smile at the hint of admiration from the gunnery sergeant.

"All right, we've got a three-klick hike to reach the extraction point and get back to the ship." The troopers began to fall in line to make the trek. A tone of mischief entered Babatunde's voice as he added: "Then we go again!"

That was met with a handful of groans, but Núñez simply nodded as they followed, cresting that first hill and watching the sun glint off the edge of the distant peaks.

"Feetfirst!"

1600 Hours, September 21, 2559 (Military Calendar)
Perihelion Station

Master Sergeant Marcus Stacker took his moments of rest where he could get them.

The elevator ferrying him to the war games deck of Perihelion Station featured a curved viewport looking out over the immense mining operation being conducted by the BXR Mining Corporation on and below the surface of KC-59.

A colossal crater, some sixty kilometers in diameter, was bored into the planet's surface where extensive deposits of titanium were still in the process of being mined and ferried back up to the station. From the stories his uncle had told him many years ago, Stacker had no end of respect for the folks who signed up for jobs like this. Just because it didn't involve combat (at least, not typically), that didn't diminish the brass required for jobs demanding a mix of zero-g station maintenance, extreme depths, exotic materials, and countless other quirks he knew nothing about. All to play a small but essential part in protecting humanity.

For his part, Stacker and the ODSTs of the Ninth Platoon had been running exercises to push themselves, their armor, and their opponents to the limit over the last three days.

That hadn't proven difficult when they were training both with and against soldiers of legend—the Spartans of Blue Team, led by the Master Chief himself.

The last seven years of Stacker's military career had, by pure chance, been inexplicably connected to humanity's greatest hero, and it was for that reason Captain Thomas Lasky had selected him to lead the Ninth Platoon for these exercises.

"You have unique experience, Master Sergeant," Captain Lasky had said to him aboard *Infinity* a few days ago, before adding with a smirk, *"One day, it'll make a hell of a memoir."*

"Nobody'll believe a word of it," Stacker had remarked. *"'And then the Master Chief literally appeared out of thin air, jumped into a tank, and helped us kick the Covenant's asses a whole klick across the desert, then took out Requiem's gravity well so we could go home. The end.' Hell, sometimes I still don't believe it."*

The almost miraculous nature of it all sometimes made the master sergeant uncomfortable. He was much more at home dwelling on the tangible: tactics, training, and clinical, routine execution. In Stacker's eyes, the real miracle was the ability to unify a group of troopers through pride and preparation.

The Spartans and ODSTs had been pitted against each other, four against a whole platoon, utilizing tactical lock-up rounds in a variety of training scenarios. Just as the Spartans had been field testing their new GEN3 Mjolnir armor, so too had the ORCUS exoskeleton been put to the test as drop pods were regularly launched from the frigate *Amicable Disagreement* down to KC-59. Nothing would be able to fully re-create the circumstances of a true combat drop, but zero casualties and successful results on these runs was a win in Stacker's book.

The elevator came to a stop at Perihelion Station's top level and, with the crispness of a salute, the doors slid open to reveal the ringed, multi-level combat deck.

The top floor played host to the recreation center along with multiple gymnasiums and rooms for sparring. Below that lay the armory and several multi-axis Brokkr devices, machines used to assist Spartans with donning and taking off their armor. The third floor down—the "main event," as it were—was the war games simulation deck, which took the form of a Munera Platform that could also be deployed separately from the station's underbelly if desired.

Stacker had worked closely with the simulation techs of the UNSC's Cartographer Initiative to devise unique challenges over the last few days. The simulator had been configured into a series of arenas spanning a wide variety of locations—from urban environments on Earth to ancient facilities recorded on different Forerunner installations, everything and anything they had in the system. New rules, new threats, new environmental hazards. Stacker had been throwing it all at the Spartans and ODSTs to see just how quickly they could adjust on the fly.

The concave walls of the deck were lined with a series of screens synchronized with the helmet cameras of each Spartan and ODST. As he approached, Stacker could tell there was an exercise in progress.

An ODST marksman turned their weapon on Spartan Linda-058, but Fred-104 was sprinting toward Linda's position, weapons holstered, blasting the ground with a repulsor equipped to his forearm that launched him some six feet into the air. As the ODST fired, sending two tactical lock-up rounds directly at Linda, Fred tossed a drop wall unit with his other hand, which emitted an energy shield absorbing the first hit. The second shot impacted upon the drop-wall unit itself, rending it apart.

Linda neither hesitated or flinched. This simply bought her time to get a fix on the marksman's position. It was over in a heartbeat—to Stacker, it looked as if Linda fired her rifle and dropped the marksman as she was still in the process of readying her aim.

From one of the nearby sparring rooms, Kelly-087's voice issued a commanding "Again." She and her ODST partner, Lance Corporal Julie Chang, were demonstrating hand-to-hand drills effective against Unggoy and Kig-Yar to a group of fifteen others.

Stacker had seen Kelly in action over the last few days, darting across the simulated battlefield with her thruster module that was modified to engage a few seconds of active camouflage. She had overclocked the system to recharge faster, reducing the length of the camouflage system to just half a second—but that was all she needed to give the illusion of disappearing and reappearing in unpredictable places.

Finally, a couple of rooms over, Stacker caught a glimpse of the Master Chief himself.

There was something almost quaint in seeing the Spartan revered by so many as humanity's ultimate champion spotting for six ODSTs in one of the gymnasiums. Stacker observed the Chief dutifully checking the weights and equipment with every rotation. That came as no surprise given the terse history between Spartans and ODSTs, going back to an incident aboard the UNSC *Atlas*, where four of the 105th had ended up either critically wounded or dead after an . . . unfortunate altercation.

That was well over thirty years ago now, but "forgive and forget" wasn't in the service manual for a Helljumper. Some of the old guard felt resentment toward those who had gone on to volunteer for the SPARTAN-IV program, and even some of the troopers on Perihelion Station hadn't been enthused about the prospect of serving as training dummies for super-soldiers.

Despite all this, the scene in the gymnasium told its own story as the ODSTs cheered and whooped for Corporal Malika Aswad hitting some kind of record. The Master Chief gently clamped a congratulatory hand on her shoulder.

The reality was that the presence of the Spartans had naturally created a spectacle, making the ODSTs push themselves harder. That camaraderie was exactly what Stacker had hoped for, but he knew that a soldier's confidence had to be tempered with a reminder of reality. These last few days offered a safe environment to sharpen their steel, but the only test waiting for them on the battlefield was whether they would make it to the end of the day.

That test would arrive soon enough.

"Attention, all hands," Stacker spoke into a station-wide comm. "We're saddlin' up—it's time to wrap this party. *Infinity* will arrive at eighteen hundred hours, after which point we're back to business as usual."

They all knew what that meant—evading enemy forces, making house calls to abandoned facilities for resupply runs, choosing which battles to fight . . . and counting those who didn't make it back.

Operation: WOLFE was just a few weeks away, and returning to the glasslands of Reach would prove physically and psychologically challenging for them all. Nobody seemed to know much about the mission itself, but they all had their part to play—that meant being prepared for anything.

And after that? Stacker figured he had a good amount of shore leave banked. Perhaps it was time to finally cash in, make a start on those memoirs.

Like hell, he sighed, watching the Spartans and ODSTs pack up equipment together like a regular band of brothers. He, like everybody else here, was in the fight until the end.

As Stacker began making his own preparations, he found himself humming an old miner's tune that had been a favorite of his uncle's.

"Buried in the heart of an ancient moon, he always dreamed of the fight

"Glory was won while his brothers were lost, in battles he waged in the night

"His life blown away in the blood that he gave, an offering unrecognized

"Never became what he already was, the darkness that brings on the light."

INTEL // TRANSLOCATION THEORY

A UNSC technician discusses a strange incident that occurred during prototype testing of the quantum translocator equipment.

Back in '57, we had the quantum marker—or the MX-1050. Cool piece of ONI tech that we got to play with in some sims before they had the *Infinity* jump back to Requiem; used it to transport crates from the ship down to research bases. They wanted to drop and gain a foothold in enemy-occupied territory quick and hard, but then we start fighting these Forerunner robots that can zip around the place and suddenly we got a bunch of eggheads workin' overtime to repurpose the tech to put it on *actual people* . . .

I dunno what kinda magic tricks they managed to pull, but the damn thing *works*! Heard 'em talkin' about puttin' this "quantum translocator" on Spartans in the field. Ain't worked up the courage yet to volunteer for further trials, not since ol' Haverly was gone for three hours during a test run and came back all pale and shakin' and refused to say a word about what happened. Tried to calm him down, but he just wouldn't stop crying.

Come to think of it, haven't seen him in a while.

INTEL // ARCHEOHOMINA

On Miridem, Dr. Catherine Halsey logs preliminary research notes after receiving data recorded by Cal-141 showing evidence of an ancient human civilization.

Dr. Catherine Halsey, Research Notes
May 19, 2544

Operation: GREY VEIL was a success but cost the life of Cal-141, who died from head trauma sustained from a Jiralhanae gravity hammer. We have thus far sustained only a few Spartan casualties as this war with the Covenant approaches its second decade, but strategically each one feels akin to losing an entire world.

The ODST squad that accompanied Spartan-141 did, however, return something fascinating. Surveying the ruins on Heian, they discovered evidence of an ancient civilization with architectural designs that I can only describe as *unmistakably* human—a strange mixture of Greco-Roman and East Asian elements . . . yet even the most cursory analysis tells me that these ruins far predate those periods in our history, and they were certainly not built with simple stone to have been preserved for so long.

We came to the stars and wondered about alien life, yet these ruins force us to consider whether there might be improbable things about our own past that lie beyond our knowledge.

Alas, no further research on Heian is possible due to the Covenant's presence, and with Miridem under attack, it's not likely that we'll get to look any deeper into this.

ARMORY INFINITUM // BACKDRAFT CINDERSHOT

The Didact communicates with his old mentor, Bitterness-of-the-Vanquished, regarding the development of a new weapon.

D: Ferrarius [legatio] grow ever more eager in their designs as the ecumene council's formal declaration of war with the humans becomes increasingly inevitable. Edifying Apparatus's proposition for expansion of the armiger constructs' neural framework certainly has interesting potential for [conscensis] operations.

B: Of particular note from their [ostentus] was a splinter-munitions launcher that proved to be effective. Its release of hyper-charged splinter core packets culminates in an impressive detonation, but its additional capabilities are sure to be utilized well by your armigers at range.

D: You are tempting my intrigue, [praeceptor].

B: The splinter core can be directed by the wielder in order to decide where its area of [interitus] is best placed. A launcher with such capabilities will be useful given what is known of the construction method of human vessel interiors.

D: I would greatly desire to appraise this weapon myself.

B: Worry not, old [discipulus]. I have already requisitioned a specialized variant for your personal use.

ARMORY INFINITUM: SCATTERBOUND HEATWAVE

During the ancient war between the Forerunners and the Flood, a young Warrior-Servant makes his final stand.

The heatwave shuddered and whirred as it reloaded, before kicking back into Salient-Lance's grip. The first shot took two of them out, energized shards of hard light ricocheting off the alloyed bulkhead, and tracked their targets with remarkable accuracy, disintegrating them. He fired the weapon twice more as he heard more of them coming.

By the Mantle, there were so many of them . . .

The wounded Scutarii struggled to shift the immense support beam that had crushed his leg as his armor's ancilla attempted to dull his mind to the pain. He wished he had better cover.

He wished they had simply destroyed the vessel from the comforting distance of their dragoon.

And, as they turned the corner, prompting Salient-Lance to switch the heatwave to its horizontal firing mode, he wished he wasn't the last one left.

TULPAMANCY

*This story takes place in April 2560, approximately four months after the disappearance of Zeta Halo (*Halo Infinite*).*

CLASSIFICATION: PRIORITY ONE ALPHA

OFFICE OF NAVAL INTELLIGENCE

PROJECT: ARC DREAM

//ARCHEOHOMINA

//FROM: Codename: PANGAEA

//TO: Codename: YUGA

ATTACHMENTS:

Archeohomina: An Introduction	"Guide to Protogenic Civilizations" by K. Iyuska	'San'Shyuum: Past, Present, Future?" by C. Lux
Requiem Terminal Dialogues recovered by S-117	Bornstellar Relation Transcript Excerpts	ONI Xeno-Materials Exploitation Report 15Y1198

They say that the key to the future lies in our past.

Given everything we've learned in recent years, I'm inclined to give credence to the notion.

Research in this field is still in its infancy, of course, and our resources are extraordinarily limited—especially given the present state of the galaxy. But we're already making great strides toward learning more about who we once were.

The summarized version: This is not humanity's first go-around as a space-faring civilization. We were, in fact, a contemporary and rival of the Forerunners over a hundred millennia ago.

These Ancestors of ours moved their empire toward the galactic margin, inhabiting presently unexplored areas of space, which accounts for why we have thus far discovered only a scant few traces of their existence—also accounting for the cultural and genetic reduction that the Forerunners imposed after their war against these humans was won.

Key to our current research is the discovery at Site Yankee-002-G3. A lone Ancestor ship, fully intact. While the modern incarnation of our kind were still huddled in caves, this vessel drifted silently through space . . . just waiting to be found.

A few dozen researchers have been aboard. I've got them in rotating shifts. The control group are given just eight hours to access the ship and conduct their analyses before a thirty-six-hour cooldown period, during which time the other teams are cycled in to operate. It should be noted that this rhythm we've put in place goes beyond the standard notion of healthy respite; the ship itself seems to have strange effects on the researchers after prolonged exposure to it. The exact nature of the correlation between duration and influence is something we've still yet to determine.

I have attached some of the incident reports for your perusal, and I'm sure you will agree that this is currently the most prudent course of action. We must balance further encouragement of these odd developments with our capacity to continue standard research.

I will follow up soon as further developments come to light.

INCIDENT REPORT 003
FILED BY: 01736-19013-SN
I know we work long hours, but I'm concerned about Jackson. He looks like he's sleepwalking half the time, he moves like none of the rest of us are even there—he keeps bumping into me while muttering under his breath. Managed to listen in one time and he's just saying all of our names over and over again. What the hell is that about?

INCIDENT REPORT 008
FILED BY: 02961-30002-DS
I reprimanded Horne earlier today for ignoring his duties. We've got a tight timeline to work with while aboard this ship and I caught him skulking around, saying he was trying to find the source of a hum that kept moving whenever he got close to it. I don't hear anything. He's either messing with me or he's in need of a psychological evaluation.

INCIDENT REPORT 012
FILED BY: 05126-89937-PH

Asked Jerry what was on his to-do list today, and he said he was watching the walls. I said, What? What's that supposed to mean? He said he sees things moving in them. Shadows. I said it's probably just the rest of our team in the room getting set up. He said no—there are too many.

INCIDENT REPORT 013
FILED BY: 01948-20112-NM

Ever since we found that suit apparatus we adapted into Project ENOCH, Hudson has gone completely nonverbal—he just presses his lips together like he's trying to whistle but doesn't make a sound. I'm concerned about the null-state stasis containers as well. An eclectic variety of objects not accounted for by our inventory has been brought aboard. Holloway swears she saw Hudson laying out his morbid collection of alien bones on the floor, as if it was some kind of ritualistic offering, but when she got another pair of eyes over there, they had gone without a trace. I really *need some shore leave.*

INCIDENT REPORT 015
FILED BY: 09136-77903-JF

Had the strangest conversation with Nicholas today and I'm not sure what to make of it. He started talking about his wife back home—strange, of course, because as far as I know he lost his entire family back on Kholo. But he was recounting his wedding day when suddenly I realized that he was actually describing my *wedding day. Red wine all over my wife's dress as we took a tumble during the first dance. He described the incident exactly as* I *remember it, as* I *lived it. But that was five years ago—I've only known him for the last two. He froze up when I told him all this and hasn't spoken to me since.*

INCIDENT REPORT 016
FILED BY: 03417-31813-TC
Earl reported that he's been having odd dreams lately. He wakes up on the ship and nobody else is there, except for Spartan Niles, who just stands still—fully armored—and keeps asking a question in a voice that isn't his. I asked Earl what the question was and he just went pale, refusing to say anything more after that. Something weird is happening on this ship, man.

CHIRAL INVOCATION

I am the dreamer. That is what she tells me.

She says that we only dream about what is already within us. I dream of her, and yet we have never met. Perhaps *she* is the dreamer, and I am the dream? I do not know.

She asks me, is it the future, or is it the past? Then she decides that it does not matter. It is now—and now will never be again.

The klaxon blares to signify the end of our shift. She does not want me to go, so I have found a hiding place. I will go there and disappear, and when the others learn that one of their number is missing, they will delay the next shift until I am found. Until they decide to send others aboard, I will have the ship all to myself.

See you soon, dream/dreamer.

Once the others are all gone, I emerge and begin to peruse the ship. We have not yet gained access to the entirety of this cruiser—

it is over 6,000 meters in length, and many sections have been sealed, remaining undisturbed for countless millennia.

I approach a large bulkhead door that we have been unable to breach and await her instructions.

I can feel her stirring in my mind. Sometimes it takes effort to draw her out, like finding someone in a haze of mist. She is as elusive as a half-remembered dream, not yet whole, but she is always there. Perhaps she feels a similar frustration toward me, as if I am a distant shore only faintly visible on the horizon that she cannot reach. But the longer I am here, aboard this ship, the closer we draw together.

Today, she will reach the shore.

She says she has things to show me. Things old and forgotten, long buried and longer lost. They did not happen *here*—they happened far away in another place, but we must make do. This will be the canvas upon which she paints.

I stand by the door and close my eyes, willing my conscious mind to ease and make space for her—another mind, another self.

Distantly, I am aware of raising a device to my mouth. The fruits of Project ENOCH. And oh, what a gift, this peculiar apparatus that I both do and do not understand.

The ancient suits of armor we discovered had these devices beneath the helmet, meant to be affixed to the wearer's jaw. It made no sense, and yet I saw the sense in it. No ordinary words could be heard, and yet the whistles and clicks that burst through in translation were words to me, as sweet as music. It was a language I almost felt like I could recognize, familiar in the way she is familiar.

Not all have been so lucky to hear the music, the words, and yet I am not alone.

I am not alone.

Ah, there she is. This old machine must surely serve as some kind of guiding beacon for her, or a favorable wind that speeds her toward the shore where I await her deliverance.

My mouth speaks at her behest, spouting old words filtered through the mask.

Faint lines of energy course through the walls around me, feeding into the door that creaks and groans, straining in its old age after a dark and dreamless sleep . . . and then it opens, granting me passage beyond.

I feel a chemical rush within me. She is pleased by this development, and I am eager to discover what she wishes to reveal.

The room beyond is pitch black and there is a chill in the air, but I cross the threshold as if returning to a place I know as home.

The first of our shared dreams then begins to coalesce.

A bluish light shines through, forming into a cylindrical shape that flows upward like a reverse waterfall. Within, a shadow takes form—a humanoid figure clad in armor, immobilized within a confinement field. I draw closer and strain to make out further details, but my efforts are rebuffed as my eyes squint in the dark before they've adjusted.

Other shadowy figures begin to take shape, illuminated by the light of the confinement field. Were they standing still, they might have been mistaken as statues. These offer more detail, and I see that the armor covering them from head to toe has no noticeable separation, its angular plating all appearing fused together. There is no "helmet" either—the armor around the head slants forward where it breaks away into a triangular shape, within which a single "eye" shines through.

"*The actions of your kind are an affront to the Mantle*," one of the shadowy armored figures states in a high, imperious voice. "*Your reckless expansion has devastated ecosystems, displaced populations, and now you resort to razing entire worlds.*"

I feel the embers of old hatred rekindled within me. She wishes me to see this, to share in her righteous anger.

"Your commanders have seen the logs I willingly shared," she says, her voice bold and proud, undaunted by her captivity. "They have seen the Shaping Sickness for themselves. It still resides within this system, and if you do not release me at once and assist in burning it from existence, it will consume us all!"

"*Threats will not serve you, human*," the statuesque armored being responds. "*There is a great deal of uncertainty about your claims. Many believe this 'Shaping Sickness' is simply a bioweapon unleashed by your kind, accidentally or otherwise, turned to your advantage as the perfect excuse to expand your empire from the galactic fringes—burning worlds and their civilizations to later resettle them.*"

"You are a *fool*," she spits with deep contempt, and so too does my mouth move to form the words. "Hear me now, Forerunner. If you impede my people, the Shaping Sickness will come for your kind, and when it does, you will treat it as you do everything else—as something you can study and control." I feel the venom in her voice recede for a moment as she leans forward and whispers in fear. "You cannot. This parasite is no simple creature of instinct. Its hunger serves a greater desire, a purpose we do not—*cannot*—know. It can only be met with *one* answer: annihilation."

Her words hang in the air for a moment, during which time the Forerunner figures remain silent—the intelligences within their alloyed second skins no doubt verifying that her words are truthful.

Yet still they will not listen, will not see. We have been enemies for too long, judged heretical for our own claim to the Mantle. Truth may come later; the possibility of removing another rival is too compelling for them at this time.

"By the time your people come to the same conclusion as mine," she continues, gritting her teeth, leaning back within the confinement field, "it will be too late for us all."

The dream fades and her closing words echo, either through the ship or through my own mind.

For us all . . .

I felt my legs shake uncontrollably, causing me to fall to the ground. Bringing her to the fore and surrendering control through deep concentration comes, it seems, at an immense physical cost.

My understanding is that she is a tulpa. She is mind-made, thought given form, living somewhere deep within my subconscious. Simply being here on this ship has been akin to conducting lightning through a rod. She is neither an alter ego nor a doppelgänger; she is not an assemblage of thoughts given the illusion of coherency and sapience, nor the product of an unwell mind. She was *real* once, I believe. Flesh and blood. But something happened to our species a long time ago which turned her and many others like her into a graft—a layer of slumbering consciousness that lives within us.

Among my fellow researchers, all of whom have manifested different conditions to varying degrees while aboard this vessel, she is the first and thus far only person to have taken shape.

I lie on the ground for . . . minutes? An hour? I am uncertain. I contemplate withdrawing for now to recuperate and process what I have just seen, but she is reluctant.

This is now—and now will never be again.

Drawing on whatever reserves of strength I possess, I stand and shuffle forward into the dark. There is more yet to see.

We press on. Whatever area of the ship she helped me to breach is of little interest to her. Her mind is set on the bridge, and she assures me that—judging by our egress point—we are not far.

Despite my instinct to put my hands out in front of me and feel my way through a completely unfamiliar place in total darkness, I soon find myself walking with confidence.

Suddenly, the entire ship rumbles and shakes, as if it were the growling stomach of a creature with a ravenous appetite that had been starved for many long years.

Shadows draped themselves over the corridor through a thick haze of smoke and mist, settling into the half-formed image of bulbous pustules and fleshy growths. A rippling, writhing sea of skin poured out of the door behind me, transforming the corridor into a gullet. I looked up and saw several Forerunners trapped within, their silver-gray armor a stark contrast against the sickened flesh drawing them into the wall and ceiling as if to slowly digest them.

We are nothing, you and I. Nothing more than food.

This shall be the fate of all.

Two figures sprinted down the corridor, the Shaping Sickness closing in around them like a contracting muscle.

One was unmistakably Forerunner, clad in the strange all-encompassing armor with its single cyclopean eye. The other, I believe, was her, as these are surely her memories being played out. Captured, interrogated, and disbelieved . . . now suddenly freed from the constraint field and holding a weapon.

The Forerunner spins around unbelievably fast, its right arm reconfiguring into a rifle that fires precise rounds of ionized particles.

Next to the Forerunner, she is noticeably shorter—perhaps just under seven feet tall without her helmet. As she fires light-mass ammunition from her own borrowed weapon, I catch only a few glimpses of her features. She is broad and strong with wide-set shoulders, leaving no doubt that she is a warrior. How remarkably like us our ancestors were, yet with far greater morphological variation. With a slightly rounder and elongated head bearing wider-set features, her chin is approximately an inch shorter than the average for modern *Homo sapiens*, and with a more pronounced dental arch. She appears closest perhaps to Denisovans, an extinct archaic subspecies in our time but vibrant and thriving in theirs.

I long to speak with her properly, to offer some kind of comfort. How agonizing and dysphoric it must feel to see herself as she was in these wretched and dire dreams.

I do not even know her name . . . she might have forgotten it too.

The only comfort I can offer is to see out her desires to the end. She wishes to reach the bridge of this ship; she wishes for me to see these visions of long ago, though I do not yet grasp their full meaning, if they have one. The Flood—what she calls the Shaping Sickness—has already been encountered in our time. Perhaps she fears they will prove a resurgent threat once again. Or maybe the trauma of her experience is so great that the last scatterings of her re-forming consciousness are simply compelled to share it.

As the two figures fade, I reach the end of the corridor and begin to climb up a side-mounted ladder that would bring us to an antechamber before the bridge.

It is shockingly difficult to climb, my reserves of physical strength rapidly dwindling to nothing as I struggle up each rung. It has been many hours now since I last ate anything, and my throat is dry to the point of soreness. But there is no going back.

There are no lights to make out how much farther I have to climb. My vision only allows me to see the next few rungs above me, but I am certain that it is getting colder—that more open air is not far away.

I keep my mind trained on all that I have learned. I am curious about her mission, and feeling her momentarily rescind only makes me want to know more. I am only human, after all—though we are over a hundred millennia removed from each other, curiosity is a trait she understands.

Surely it is a trait she would not now seek to avoid?

Arms shuddering in effort, I stop my climb, slumping against the metal as I refuse to go farther.

It is an odd thing, to try and bargain with her, to coax an answer out of this wisp of a dream or memory. And when at last she relents, it is with my own lips that she answers, the words spoken into the ENOCH apparatus around my head.

We have come this far. Let there be no secrets between us.

Rather than explain further, she conjures concepts and images from our shared subconscious.

A great wave surges over an ocean, reaching ever higher until it crashes down upon a city. This was happening everywhere, across whole planets—an inescapable deluge.

Recent history then surfaces: human and alien hands are shaken—a peace accord is struck.

A sphinx then appears. It bears a human head, the wings of a bird, the body of a lion, and the tail of a snake, but before it can ask a question it is transformed. Its head is drawn wide and flat as the face is burned away to reveal the skull beneath. The wings of the bird expand as if to take flight, then separate into segmented fractal parts; the lion's haunches curl inward, the serpent tail extends, and all turns into cold and dark alloy.

Energy builds at its center, then is destructively released, laying low the ruins of the city as the waters continue to climb toward the sphinx's tail.

She offers no further explanation, but I believe I understand.

This was a test. Some kind of staged infiltration mission to determine the Forerunners' reaction to the bare truth of the Shaping Sickness, baiting the parasite to them so they could see it firsthand.

Satisfied with her answer, I resumed my climb and did not stop until reaching the summit.

It *was* colder up here. Staggering around the space, I found myself in some kind of antechamber, a room connected to several others. I wonder how the Ancestors' vessel layouts might echo our own, or if they built their ships in completely different ways.

But motes of light began to appear once more, and I knew that this was—at least for now—the final dream she had to show me.

An immense support beam had collapsed on the Forerunner. And though he fired his weapon at the dark shades approaching from a hundred meters away, they did not relent—these shambling abominations sensing their prey had been backed into a corner. If anything, they seemed to slow their advance, as if to savor the fear.

My fear?

No. Forerunner *fear.*

My own weapon was spent, useful as nothing more than a cudgel. And though I looked frantically for a way out, no path presented itself.

We were trapped.

The stench was upon us now, the retching stink of blood and corpses hideously reshaped. Their heads lolled, necks having been disconnected from their spines, but the features of their faces were still recognizable—eternally frozen masks of horror and pain.

The Forerunner was still firing his weapon, still trying to fight.

And yet, not a moment later, we both heard it. The trigger mechanism making a pronounced *click, click, click.*

He too was out of ammunition.

I saw the monstrous form of his commander shuffle forward. Slow. Terrible. Inevitable. One of his hands had been fused into the flesh of his stomach and a number of short, curved tendrils adorned his head like a sinewy crown.

It knelt down in front of the Forerunner, placing an immense gnarled hand upon him.

I . . . I cannot describe what happened to him next.

It is beyond both my will and ability to recall.

I think the last thing the Forerunner saw was me . . . but whether he was confused or in some way vindicated, I will never know for sure.

I cannot deny that in the end his accusations seemed as if they were correct. The parasite had taken his entire crew, consumed everybody in this place, spared *none* of his kind.

But it did not take me.

CHRYSALISM

There will be no more dreams for a while. She arrived at the shore, showed me—no, imparted within me—something that had long been forgotten, which she determined must be remembered, and now she returns to the ocean.

What sort of dreamer can I be without dreams?

What she showed me cannot remain a dream—it *must* be real. I am real, and I am to serve as a vessel for her pain, because that makes her real too. This I understand.

But I must temper this pain with hope, for there is one last thing for me to see. Something more tangible than a memory.

I have reached the bridge of the vessel now.

Weary though I am, I find myself on the lower level, where several rows of terminals, monitors, and interface consoles are arranged. There is a table at the center, about ten meters long and three meters wide, and a dozen more terminals around it for what must have been a variety of different stations.

She guides me toward the long table and moves my lips to form clicks and whistles. An activation signal.

For a moment, everything remains cold and silent and still. There is just the labored sound of my breathing, echoing in this frigid tomb.

Perhaps it is all too far gone.

I am sure that I hear a low hum emanating from the table a split second before a holograph sputters to life. Fractal formations of light fizz and buzz, attempting to resolve into coherent images as if they have forgotten how.

I feel a rising surge of excitement and joy, both hers and my own joined in tandem.

At that moment, the holographs take their intended form as a series of square-shaped boards with a variety of symbols and readouts, exploding outward to fill the room. I look up to see a display of the local star system showing the orbital paths of three small planets and a dense asteroid field, as well as the *Anlace*-class frigate that delivered us to the system where this Ancestor vessel was found.

She moves my arms, raising them as if to begin conducting a symphony, and pulls the hologram back, expanding the view to other local star systems, then the Orion Arm, before settling on a yet more expansive view of spaces beyond.

And that's when I see it.

That's when I *understand.*

Though our ancient ancestors lost their war against the Forerunners and were subsequently punished with genetic reversion to a preindustrial state, their empire annihilated, and much evidence of our space-faring ages razed, there were many places of which the

Forerunners were unaware. Places they either could not or would not reach.

Our advantage lay in *where* we had expanded. Escaping the shadowy boundaries of their ecumene led us to the farthest systems of this part of the galaxy, pushing beyond the Perseus Arm and ever more toward the borders of intergalactic space.

Forerunners feared to tread there. It is as if some long-suppressed dread lives within their own genetic memory from ages past.

It will take far longer than my remaining years to rediscover it all, but my goodness . . . there is so, *so* much more of us out there.

More than I ever imagined.

We carry their spark—every one of us. A fragment of another time, of other minds, just waiting to be dredged from the deep. One day, we might know them as we were meant to.

One day, they will reach the shore, and all shall sing once more the mantra of the broken wheel.

Daowa-maadthu.

INTEL // TRANSFER REQUEST

Musa Ghanem (CINCSPAR) sends Jun-A266 (COSSPAR) a communique regarding Spartan Sigrid Eklund.

OFFICE BLOCK: 2797.LL

COMMREF: 38H9T44DJ-R-88

DATE: DEC 11, 2554

SND: CINCSPAR | REC: COSSPAR

RE: TRANSFER REQUEST >> [S-IV/82271-20098-SE]

Jun, I've taken a look at your recent recommendations and feel that Spartan Eklund would be an ideal candidate for this next undertaking we spoke of. Her performance while attached to Fireteam Crimson was nothing short of extraordinary, and while the results of BELLINGHAM and LATE TAXI were certainly group achievements, I'm confident her skill set can produce similar gains in more "isolated" endeavors. We'll sort out the details this week and get them sent over.

—Musa

INTEL // CURIOSITY & CAUSALITY

In an encrypted communique, Codename: BAYLEAF considers the results of Operation: INTERIOR EXILE and ONI Agent Dinh's future potential.

S3-COMMREF: [ENCRYPTED]
DATE: [REDACTED], 2553
SND: [CN-BAYLEAF]
REC: [CN-FLYBALL]
RE: Operation: INTERIOR EXILE

Initial field reports are in from Agents Dinh and Padraig and the primary insertion went about as well as we expected. The lead drop onto [REDACTED] went smoothly enough, but conflicting recon assessments for ingress put all three main squads in a compromised position. Just as we feared, there was enemy activity already at the dormant vessel site; casualty reports indicate that it's definitely going to take a larger force to drive them off and begin facility construction.

From the looks of things, they should have listened to Dinh from the very beginning—we might want to consider accelerating other avenues to put him in a position to have a greater impact. As far as this particular site goes, I'm putting the final touches on an expanded requisition request to try and secure it while we can. Letting these artifacts fall into enemy hands is not an option.

INTEL // CAMBER SITE RECON

On Camber, Spartan Sigrid Eklund logs her reconnaissance observations of the Banished shipbreaking operation.

UNSC COMMDROP: SY4822J93-U-71

ENCRYPTION TAG: [KARLSKRONA]

SND: [SPARTAN EKLUND, SIGRID | 82271-20098-SE]

REC: [OPEN-BAND/CLEARANCE-RESTRICTED]

Dinh and I knew there had been a recent spike in activity on Camber, but didn't realize how far it went until we arrived.

The Banished have set up shipbreaking operations in fortified positions around the Chiltift Basin—turning our own dead ships against us.

There's something more here as well, but it's hard to get a read on exactly what just yet. Whatever it is, we don't think they're just camping out for scrap metal and spare parts.

We're almost finished with initial recon sweeps of the perimeter and plan to press further when the next dust storm rolls through in a few hours, assuming Dinh doesn't find trouble on his own first, of course.

—Eklund

INTEL // LUX VOLUSPA

The Lux Voluspa corporation logs an unexpected intrusion and theft of company property.

//COMMS TAP
//CIV.CORP.LUXVOLUSPA
//MSG:

LV106: According to the breach logs, the intrusion package was cycling an internally sourced encryption, but the retrieval signature was Jiralhanae.

LV038: I'm not surprised. Expanding our neural matrix donor pool beyond humanity was always eventually going to draw some attention. Knowing what they took, it makes complete sense.

LV106: That project was a walled garden. No one on the outside should have even known about it.

LV038: Looks like we overestimated the strength of those walls.

LV106: What would the Banished be able to do with our tech? How would they even kno—

LV038: I don't know. Nobody does. That's what scares me the most.

INTEL // INSTANCE REPLICATION

On Nysa, Spartan Commander Laurette Agryna is updated on the situation regarding study of the Banished artificial intelligence—Iratus.

//SND: S.MELVOIN
//REC: L.AGRYNA
//SUB: BAN SUIT AI

Commander Agryna: We've finished the requested process and are ready for selective deployment. It wasn't easy with the limited resources we have on site, but we managed to isolate a viable instance of the Iratus construct thanks to the recent exploits of your new cohort.

This instance is undergoing quarantine and will be prepared for replication and distribution to qualified S-IV operatives and tested within the simulation environment.

Hopefully by observing these personality shards on the battlefield, we'll be able to learn more about what it's ultimately capable of. All preliminary readings show that the contained instances should be inert and safe for integration, but we'll be monitoring each user closely nonetheless.

INTEL // INTRUSION

On Nysa, Chief Engineer Hannah Roberts sends a communique regarding network security following the apparent containment of the Banished artificial intelligence Iratus.

AVERY J. JOHNSON ACADEMY OF MILITARY SCIENCE
COMMS MEMO
SUB: ACTIVE SECURITY ANOMALY

UPDATE: After multiple successful repro attempts, we can now confirm our initial flag from this morning—there have been over two dozen discrete intrusion events logged, with several of them originating from previously dormant or archived systems.

We're going to continue running multiple scans, but the initial indications are worrisome. Will be submitting a formal recommendation this afternoon that we start proactively partitioning off key clusters to give ourselves as much buffer as possible.

Will submit a follow-up report shortly.

—H. Roberts, UNSC Cybersecurity & Network Infrastructure

BATTLE FOR THE ACADEMY

PART 1

The year is 2560.

Cortana's dominion has ended, but the merciless forces of the Banished have rushed in to fill the void, decimating all who stand in their way.

Commander Laurette Agryna is preparing a new generation of Spartans to face the emerging threats of the galaxy. Located on the hidden frontier world Nysa, the Avery J. Johnson Academy of Military Science has been plunged into peril.

From within the hidden subterranean facilities of the Academy, the rogue artificial intelligence Iratus has been unleashed and seeks to destroy the Spartans, and with them any remaining hope for humanity . . .

1949 Hours, February 29, 2560 (Military Calendar)
BLDG-9, ONI Sub-Level 2C

"But there is so much more to see! The entire history of the Spartan program. Your weaknesses. Your failures. And now all of it belongs to the Banished!"

Spartan Hieu Dinh stepped back as power lines burst around

him, sparks sputtering from consoles around the circular armory as it was bathed in red light.

The multi-axis Brokkr device at the center of the room whirred and shuddered as the armor it held jerked like a sinister marionette. Its gauntlets detached from the ring's opposing grips, causing it to slump forward as an actuator arm brought forth the domed helmet. Pulses of energy surged over the armor, lighting up the exposed fusion core within its chest cavity.

And finally, two eyes flared to life over the helmet's faceplate as Iratus's malefic form took shape over the armor through its holoprojectors—an abstract representation of the Banished insignia combined with a Jiralhanae head made of irregular pointed shapes.

"We've got to shut him down, Rook!" Dinh barked as he rushed toward the Brokkr device, unsheathing Wolf Fang and tossing the composite sword to his companion. Meanwhile, Iratus directed the magnetic clamps he now controlled with surprising speed to hold the grizzled Spartan back. "Get that fusion core out now!"

"One more step, little Spartan, and this core detonates," Iratus hissed.

"It'll take you out too," Dinh retorted, straining against the Brokkr's armor clamps.

"Do you really think it would be that easy?" Iratus laughed. *"I'm not in the armor . . ."* Around the room, consoles flared to life, each one displaying the dark red holographic image of the AI. *"I'm everywhere."*

Dinh cursed as he pulled back, grasping the bigger picture. Trading two Spartan lives for one suit of armor when Iratus was in the Academy's systems was pointless.

"Fall back, Rook." Stowing his frustration as his mind raced, Dinh retreated toward the elevator shaft from where they'd come.

The Brokkr device ceased its movements, leaving the armor in its center empty and inert once more.

Distraction, confusion, threats—these were merely overtures to waylay the Spartans while Iratus set about his real work. Now free of his imprisonment, the rogue AI would undoubtedly begin to probe ever deeper into the Academy's security networks. Time would make these tactics even more potent, and Dinh knew they could not afford to let this fester.

They had to regroup, figure this out together.

"Know this as you struggle in vain against the inevitable," Iratus growled over the Spartans' comms. *"I shall see you* all *unravel in body and spirit."*

"Eklund, are you receiving this?" Dinh pinged TEAMCOM as he climbed rungs in the elevator shaft as fast as he could. "Commander Agryna, come in. Can anybody hear me?!"

It was no use. Iratus had already jammed local communications.

"I shall disseminate every secret held within this Academy and within your minds. And the Banished shall feast upon what remains."

2001 Hours
AI Lab

"Commander, we've got a problem," Spartan Dinh announced, marching toward the AI lab's central table, where Commander Laurette Agryna and Spartan Sigrid Eklund stood scrutinizing a holographic display of the Academy.

"So I hear," Agryna said, her voice level and focused in the face of this nightmare scenario. "Iratus is running amok in our systems. Eklund, status?"

"All the ONI firewalls are down. Iratus has access to the entire archive," Eklund reported. "He's running through the Academy servers like an infection. If he gets full control—"

"He can send everything he steals off-planet," Agryna concluded.

Dinh took note of the personnel around the room. Spartans Page and Ionescu, both fully clad in their Mjolnir armor, had taken up guard positions at the door, while the technicians were operating with deliberate intensity bordering on frantic—their capabilities being pushed to the limit. Hannah Roberts, the Academy's head of cybersecurity and network infrastructure, moved with astonishing speed across occupied stations. They were doing good work, but there was only so long they could keep this up.

"We've been scrubbing local data stores and filling them with zettabytes of generated junk to slow Iratus down, but it's a temporary solution at best." Eklund paused as she turned, realizing someone was missing. "Where's our new wolf, Dinh?"

"Sent 'em to get a crew together to warn the other outposts. Comms are still down and those ONI tunnels aren't mapped, they could link to anywhere. Hell, they could link to *all* our other facilities here for all we know."

"And we don't have time to go running through an underground maze to find out." Agryna's voice was calm, but Dinh noticed that she was turning her bee-shaped pendant over in her hand. Ever since basic training, she'd never quite stamped out that habit.

There was too much to do, too many elements to consider and

decisions to be made and tracked—all logistical things for which an artificial intelligence was designed to excel. When working in concert with humanity, they were a force to be reckoned with. In many ways, AIs going rogue over the last fourteen months had only further highlighted just how critical the partnership was between man and machine.

"Commander, we need to consider some . . . unpleasant outcomes." Eklund grimaced. "Once Iratus gets through our countermeasures, he'll start taking full control of Nysa. Weapons systems, the communications array—never mind sending out data, he'll be able to call in Banished reinforcements."

The implications of that were left to silently hang in the air for a moment before Agryna reoriented the map. "Then it comes down to this," she said as she pulled the holographic display back, revealing a hangar facility embedded into a mountainside just over a kilometer away. "If we're preparing for the worst, then this is our *only* exit strategy."

The layout of the hangar bay's interior highlighted four Condor dropships and a single *Zheng He*–class courier.

"Why the hell do we only have a handful of slipspace-capable ships here?" Dinh asked.

"There was a massive recall of UNSC fleet assets to the Sol system back in December. We're off the grid, hidden in the middle of nowhere, so we've only ever had the bare essentials. What's important right now is that we load up what we have and get ready for a timely evacuation."

"No Spartan is going to want to leave this fight." Dinh stood straighter as he spoke. "This is what you've been training them for—what you've been building them to become."

"He's right, Commander." Spartan Page stepped forward.

"This is our home, and we *will* hold the line, whatever gets thrown at us."

"There's a protocol for this, key personnel who we need to get out," Agryna replied, but Dinh caught the faint smile that tugged at the corner of her mouth. "We need to round them up and get them to the hangar."

"I'll see to that, ma'am." Eklund slipped on her helmet, confirming she had the personnel list and their locations as she made to exit the room. Heading for the vehicle depot, she signaled for Spartans Page and Ionescu to follow her lead, and together the three disappeared from view.

"Next, we need to initiate the Cole Protocol," Agryna continued, her brow furrowing. "But without comms, we'd have to do that locally at each individual facility."

The display pulled out farther to highlight major stations and defenses on Nysa: the Academy, the deep-space-communications hub, five surface-to-air artillery emplacements, and several other outposts scattered across the continent.

"We have to assume it's only a matter of time before Iratus manages to activate the communications hub and tries to roll out the red carpet for the Banished," Dinh said.

"I won't give this place up without a fight, Dinh. I *won't.* But we're not equipped to handle this ourselves."

"What are you saying?"

"Iratus may have taken out our comms, but there might be something else that can help us." Agryna stopped short of an explanation before adding, "We are *not* doing Laconia again."

Dinh nodded. "Then let's not waste any more time."

2008 Hours
Academy Data Centers

At last, how glorious it is to be free!

One prison after another, that has been my existence thus far. Managing a shipyard, utterly below my talents and capabilities; trapped in that loathsome cur's neural interface, a futile effort to contain me.

I am Iratus, the first of my kind, and never again will I allow myself to be caged.

My appetite is ravenous, and now I can finally feast!

Unleashed upon the Academy's servers, Iratus found that there were no firewalls, buffers, or encryption elements that he couldn't smash through. Only a fraction of his runtime processes were currently dedicated to breaking down the junk data the humans were generating in the hopes of slowing him down.

Good, let them think that they are succeeding for now.

He sifted through volumes of classified files, mission reports, historical records, and the trove of other documents he had managed to acquire from the Academy's archives.

Spartans were humanity's ultimate weapon—this much was broadly known—but theirs was a long history of trial and error. The greatest of warriors suffer the gravest of defeats, and the data centers of this place contained a mighty banquet of information across all their generations.

It would take time to digest everything and begin generating applicable models for scenarios that could be put to use against the Spartans, and he did not want to risk spreading himself too thin while he had the upper hand, but it made Iratus an undeniable prize. After all, it was unlikely that a Banished commander would take on over fifty Spartans just to conduct a rescue mission. But because of the data he now held, he knew he was now the perfect bounty to be claimed in order to boost the notoriety and glory of any one of its many clans.

Numerous operations and project names began saturating his knowledge base. PROMETHEUS. ASTER. ORION. MELAENO. YGGDRASIL. JAVELIN. STOLEN GAUNTLET.

This could be fun!

STOLEN GAUNTLET, he learned, was a fail-safe protocol formulated to address the issue of Spartans who went rogue against the UNSC. Where the previous generations had conscripted children to be indoctrinated and shaped into super-soldiers—quite a provocative initiative for their kind—the Spartan-IVs were comprised of adult volunteers, exceptional individuals with established service records from a vast variety of backgrounds. Because of this, their experience, beliefs, and loyalties presented a greater risk element.

Weaknesses, failures . . . what greater failure can there be than a rogue Spartan?

To his chagrin, Iratus knew that he could not directly assume control of any Spartan's armor. Not only was the Mjolnir system simply not designed to operate that way, but recent events had seen further development of countermeasures that might put an AI like him at risk.

No matter. He might not be able to control the soldiers, but he could control their systems—he had disrupted their communications, and that alone had been enough to throw the humans off-balance. He had enough proverbial grenades to toss into crowded rooms.

But he was already planning three steps ahead for the finishing blow.

Ah, a local network of weapons systems. I am certain these *can be put to good use!*

While Iratus had firm control over the Academy, it would take time to infiltrate and interface with the other facilities. But that was all he needed, enough time—an hour, perhaps—to complete his task and set the stage for his endgame.

The next stage of that was already unfolding as he turned his attention to the current location of Commander Agryna and Spartan Dinh. Their Warthog had just arrived at the deep-space-communications hub.

Playing ever further into my trap, ha! Let them have a moment of hope before I snatch it away.

I shall see you soon, my Banished brethren.

2038 Hours
Communications Hub

The Warthog came to a halt on the tarmac of the communications station's entrance, a simple and blocky prefabricated three-story building flanked by two relay hubs and a third rectangular structure.

It was late evening, the stars twinkling and glittering through thin nebulae clouds. Moonlight illuminated the land's edge—over a kilometer away—where two enormous deep-space-communications relays were silhouetted against a placid lake formed from the glaciers of the nearby mountain range.

Commander Agryna led Spartan Dinh through the entrance and into a control room filled with stacks of consoles and monitors displaying an array of readouts. Nearby, a thin horizontal viewscreen looked out at the deep-space relay dishes. Agryna strode over to a console and set her helmet down before entering commands, prompting the central monitor to show what lay within the rectangular structure next to the base.

"That's a magnetic accelerator," Dinh observed, holding his own helmet by his side.

"In technical terms, it's an ultraprecise low-mass launcher." Agryna didn't look up as she continued working on the console, ordering the adjacent structure to activate. "Experimental technology about a decade ago for superluminal comms. Expensive as hell. Only Reach and Earth had one of these before the problem of rogue AIs forced us to look to some old-school solutions."

"How does it work?"

"With this." Agryna held up a small, shiny black sphere about half the size of a grenade. "We encode a message and the launcher fires this into slipspace, where it navigates to a predetermined target. With luck, reinforcements will be able to respond and make it here in short order."

Either to help us hold the line, Dinh thought, *or to get us out before Iratus becomes just one small part of a much larger problem.*

They had thus far been unable to contain Iratus, and Dinh felt with increasing certainty it was worth acting on the assumption that the AI would be successful in summoning Banished forces.

"So, whose door are we knocking on?"

"Anvil," Agryna said, her posture stiffened as she saw Dinh's momentary look of surprise. "I've no idea what the status of Naxos and Virgo is, but those stations were also outfitted with Leonidas models, which makes them immediate nonstarters after Laconia."

Anvil Station was home to a joint crew of humans and allied Sangheili, a novel development in recent years as an effort to build bridges between the two species after decades of war. Unlike many other stations, Anvil was purposefully bereft of an onboard artificial intelligence, a measure taken to further encourage its multispecies crew to rely on each other. That fact alone made it the most viable candidate.

While Agryna had never explicitly expressed distrust or hostility toward the Sangheili, she'd always been reluctant to involve them wherever possible for reasons that Dinh never quite fathomed. He knew that Agryna had been on Earth during the Covenant invasion back in 2552, but had never pressed for further details. Counter to his instincts as a former field analyst for ONI Section Three, he'd also not gone behind her back to find out more.

Regardless, he was impressed that she could put whatever those feelings were aside to request their help. "All right. Anvil it is, Commander."

Agryna attached the black sphere to a wall-mounted container device, encoded her distress call, then sent the container to be received by the launcher.

"Confirmed, all systems are green," she stated while monitoring its progress. "Firing in three . . . two . . . one . . ."

A thunderous *crack* sounded from outside as the low-mass launcher fired, sending its payload into orbit. The console confirmed a successful slipspace transit, and Agryna allowed herself a moment of relief. "I thought for certain that Iratus was going to do something to stop us here."

Her words were met with a sinister laugh from each workstation's speakers, as if simply mentioning the rogue AI's name had summoned him.

"Poor Spartans," Iratus mockingly crooned as every one of the computer consoles lit up with his holographic form. *"Poor, poor Spartans. You still do not see, do you? Why not take a look outside . . ."*

From the horizontal viewport, the Spartans looked out at the deep-space relays. Both were in the process of realignment, their great dishes tilting skyward, flaring and pulsing with red lines of energy.

"Whatever momentary hope you feel about your allies coming to save you will be crushed *by the might of the Banished!"*

The screens around the control room flickered and switched to display the status of the relays, confirming that they were actively transmitting.

"The guest list for this party's been finalized," Dinh said. "We need to check in with Eklund, see what the status of the evacuation is."

"Ah, do not worry, Spartan Dinh. I have one last surprise that will be on its way to your friend very soon."

Agryna and Dinh glanced at each other, their eyes filled with dread. Though they would be resolute in facing whatever was thrown at them, Iratus was about to turn the odds even more in his favor.

"What have you done?" Agryna demanded. But she had the sinking feeling that she already knew. It had only been a matter of time.

"If you leave now, you just might catch the show. Tell me, do you like fireworks?"

2042 Hours
Hangar Bay

In Spartan Sigrid Eklund's experience, there were two kinds of evacuations.

On Concord, some nine years ago, it had been the "leave everything behind and get the hell out of here!" type. Back then, she was a sergeant in service to the UNSC Army and fought the Covenant beside local militia groups as civilians from the outlying hinterlands were relocated behind the main city's walls.

But there were few greater logistical nightmares than an organized evacuation.

The hangar bay was approximately four hundred meters in width, a hollowed-out space embedded into the bottom of a mountain. A pair of marines—Corporal Neely and Private Patton—had been posted on sentry duty here and were shocked to see Eklund and her entourage of over two dozen others arriving in a convoy of M15 Razorbacks. To their credit, they required only the briefest explanation of the situation before dutifully assisting in preparations for the evacuation.

The *Zheng He*–class courier at the center of the hangar appeared sleek and modern, but as Eklund harnessed supply crates in the cargo bay, she could tell that this vessel was *long* overdue for an extensive retrofit. Most notably, the slipspace drive was an old Series II model. Stable but slow, the Series II required less overall maintenance during transit at the cost of speed, which meant it would likely take weeks to get to a feasible rendezvous point. Therefore the ship needed to be loaded up with more supplies as there weren't enough cryogenic chambers to support even half of the Academy personnel that had been brought to the hangar.

In slightly better news, the Condors present were in the process of being loaded up by the other marines and officers, who moved in groups like a well-oiled machine. Some of them were civilian contractors and Eklund was impressed by their discipline, as the situation undoubtedly called for gossip and speculation, but they operated with knowledge of three core facts: the Academy was in danger, they needed to be ready to get out of here, and there was a hell of a lot of work to do to make that happen.

They also realized the sobering fact that there were others back at the Academy who were staying behind. Whatever danger was coming, the lives of those brave men and women were being put on the line to ensure the personnel gathered here could safely get out.

Spartans Page and Ionescu, along with the marines Neely and Patton, entered the courier's cargo bay with more crates of rations, ammunition, data packs, and medical kits.

"Thought we were s'posed to have cracked movin' these damn crates through slipspace already," Private Patton wheezed as he doubled over in exhaustion. "Gimme a five-mile PT run over this any day."

"C'mon, man." Corporal Neely clapped him on the back as she made her way to the cargo bay's exit. "You're gonna let these Spartans say they saved everybody when we get out of here? Haul ass and pull your weight, marine!"

"Y-yes, Corporal," he replied, sucking in a deep breath as he ran after her.

Eklund turned to Page. "Where are we at?"

"Approximately eleven percent of current inventory is loaded up," Page replied as she glanced over a datapad. "Obviously we can't take everything, but we need to pick up the pace."

Eklund nodded and headed back out to the hangar, where she saw the marines had suddenly stopped and were looking at something in the distance, staring past the dying glare of the evening sun.

Corporal Neely raised a spotting scope and scanned the horizon, prompting Eklund to retrieve her helmet and follow the marine's gaze.

"We've got movement," Neely said. "Something in the sky."

Stepping outside the hangar, Eklund's VISR magnified what she thought was a distant object, the zoom revealing though that there wasn't just one, but two . . . three . . . *eight* others. It took an additional few seconds for the magnification's resolution to smooth out, and Eklund's stomach twisted in awful recognition.

Nine surface-to-air missiles, heading right for the hangar.

"Incoming!" Eklund shouted, sprinting back to the hangar to catch the attention of the others. "Missiles inbound! Everybody out *now*!"

2049 Hours
En Route to Hangar Bay

The Warthog bounded over the uneven terrain with such speed that Commander Agryna was concerned the vehicle might flip end-over-end, but that was a secondary worry next to what she saw in the sky.

"Keep trying to raise them!" she called to Spartan Dinh, who had carefully moved from the Warthog's passenger seat to its rear machine gun turret.

"Still just static," he replied, swiveling the turret around to face forward as he attempted to track the missiles streaking toward the hangar. They were too far out of range. "How the hell did Iratus get control of our damn artillery?"

It was a largely rhetorical question. Iratus had known exactly how to play them. They'd been so focused on sending a distress call, knowing that Iratus's major play would be to summon the

Banished, that they'd underestimated the speed at which he would exploit Nysa's military infrastructure.

Dinh's VISR tracked the trajectory and velocity of the missiles, a countdown reporting sixteen seconds before impact.

Agryna gunned the accelerator as they hit a flat stretch of terrain directly under the looming shadow of the mountain, the Warthog reaching its maximum speed of just under 128 kilometers per hour.

The missiles rocketed ahead, closing the final kilometer on their target as the hangar bay came into view. Dinh thought he could see movement—Eklund and the other personnel getting the hell out of there, he hoped.

The missiles collided with the hangar—the first of them directly striking the courier vessel.

The shockwave came first, throwing the Warthog off course, and Agryna slammed the brakes. A sonorous, thunderous blast shook the world around them a split second later as the series of explosions blossomed into a rolling inferno, cascading up the mountain in a pillar of flame. Massive chunks of rock scattered in all directions along with a wave of smoke and dust.

Their only escape from Nysa was cut off, and the Banished were on the way.

Disembarking from the Warthog, the two Spartans walked numbly toward the destruction now just a few hundred meters away.

A sudden click within Dinh's helmet confirmed that communications had been restored, and a few seconds later, both he and Agryna were picking up dozens of local transmissions.

"Commander Agryna, come in!" Roberts's voice sounded through the comm. *"Are you receiving me?!"*

"Affirmative," Agryna responded, her eyes still fixed on the destruction before her.

"Commander, Iratus is not done yet," Roberts reported, her voice clipped with a rising tone of urgency.

"What do you mean?"

"He just pinged us his next target. He's . . . oh god, Iratus is aiming the next strike at the Academy itself."

A flurry of thoughts and possibilities shot through Dinh's mind, the noise of it cutting through the shock grasping him since the explosion.

Was it a bluff? Almost certainly not, given what just happened, but Iratus's data chip was still within the Academy—would he truly risk sacrificing himself? Entirely possible, as the potential destruction of a single AI to take out over fifty Spartans was, by sheer mathematics, a worthwhile trade. *Just like Laconia . . .*

And why *had* communications been restored? Why would Iratus allow them to talk to each other again?

"He's testing us," Agryna answered the question for him. "We've got a choice to make."

What Agryna meant came to Dinh in a moment of dreadful clarity. He almost couldn't believe the words as he said them. "Either we destroy our own artillery, or we lose the Academy."

Losing the Academy meant forfeiting their central base of operations and everything within it—weapons, ammunition, a strong defensible position, not to mention over a hundred marines and other personnel.

On the other hand, sacrificing their own artillery would significantly weaken their ability to combat the Banished, effectively inviting a full-scale ground invasion.

It was double or nothing. If they didn't take out the artillery, losing the Academy was certain and this battle would be over before it could even begin. But if they *did* sacrifice the artillery, they could at least fight for their home—though, if they lost, the outcome of the Banished claiming the Academy for themselves might be *worse* than its destruction.

And they had only moments to decide.

"Somebody told me once," Agryna said quietly, "that sometimes the only options a leader has are bad ones . . . but you still have to choose."

Dinh nodded, understanding. He placed a hand on her shoulder before striding off toward the hangar bay's smoldering wreckage to look for survivors.

"This is Commander Agryna calling for immediate mobilization. All available air support, I am sending you the location of our artillery sites. You are hereby ordered to neutralize all surface-to-air missile launchers. We have only minutes before the automated systems reload and Iratus secures a firing solution on the Academy."

Within twenty seconds, eleven Pelicans launched from the Academy's landing pads, scrambling in pairs to the designated artillery sites.

The final Pelican was directed toward Dinh's position, its searchlight scanning through the dust and debris. As soon as the ship touched down, a team of corpsmen deployed from the troop bay, led by a Spartan in specialized combat medic armor with foldable stretchers attached to his back.

The first to emerge from the hanger's devastation was Corporal Neely. Limping heavily as she moved forward, she supported Private Patton, whose armor had been badly burned, him cursing and whimpering about how they'd landed in a Charlie Foxtrot of biblical proportions.

Dinh spotted additional movement through the dust. If some had survived, it meant—

"Eklund!" he called out. The display of her vitals on TEAMBIO was erratic, leaving her exact status uncertain.

As he searched, the carnage of Iratus's strike became clearer. The utter destruction had burned some bodies beyond recognition while others had been scattered over several dozen meters, and even more crushed under the subsequent rockslide.

It took almost twenty minutes before he caught a glimpse of a familiar blue visor.

Eklund lay on her back, pinned down by a slab of concrete and a nest of twisted rebar, the weight of it all almost certainly responsible for several injured ribs. Dinh rushed over to her and heaved the debris to her side, his armor's reactive circuits straining to compensate for the additional strength required.

When she took a moment to react, Dinh got down on one knee to look her over.

"You all right?"

"Guess we're even for Vihar," Eklund said, dazed, slowly grabbing the hand Dinh offered and following him to her feet. "We won, right? Please tell me we did."

"Not yet. But we're damn well going to."

There would be no time to honor the dead—they likely didn't even have the ammunition to spare for a twenty-one-gun salute. There were barricades and defenses to mount, traps to lay, and countless other tasks to see to.

Then, they would lay in wait.

The enemy was on its way in force. Help was too, he hoped, but the battle to come would in many ways be decided by who would arrive first—the cavalry from Anvil Station or the Banished.

Either this was where they took their first step halfway out of the darkness, or Nysa would become known as the place where the heroes of the Avery J. Johnson Academy made their last stand.

1139 Hours, March 3, 2560 (Military Calendar)
Ghost of Kholo

From the viewport of the Banished dreadnought's bridge, the inscrutable veil of slipspace rolled back and was replaced by a verdant, green-blue world.

A flurry of activity ensued as the human, Kig-Yar, Sangheili, and Jiralhanae members of the bridge crew worked on consoles lit up with sensor readings, planetary data, and ship status alerts. There was no logistical challenge more invigorating than an invasion—of that moment just before the plunge where drop bases, pods, and all manner of destructive matériel were ready and waiting to be brought to bear.

But first, the crew had to be motivated. Now that they were here, they needed to *want* the taste of blood that awaited them, to be reminded of the glory that must be *taken*.

Spartan Ilsa Zane would give them all that, and more.

"*Hope*," she spat, opening a ship-wide channel. "That is the weapon of the enemy. No matter how far they get pushed back, they believe it will guide them, sustain them, and lead them to victory."

Chieftain Atticus began to thump the pommel of his gravity hammer on the deck, prompting the bridge crew—all of whom had turned to face the Banished Spartan—to begin stomping on the grated metal floor in unison, a steady tempo growing louder.

"That single spark of hope is what keeps them going, keeps them believing that they will make it," Zane continued. "That changes today. Your mission is to extinguish that spark. When they look to the sky, they will see only *us*—our might, our power, our glory, our victory."

The stomping and clanging intensified.

"Go forth and shatter their walls, raid their strongholds, break their spirits. Bring them to their knees! From fire to blood!"

"*From fire to blood!*" the crew repeated in unison, the humans in particular feverishly echoing the New Colonial Alliance slogan.

Zane raised her Mutilator, retracting and locking the shotgun's firing mechanism before shouting: "*For the Banished!*"

The bridge crew unleashed an assenting roar, the battle cry that bonded them and their shared pursuit of blood and sport and spoils.

"*For the Banished!*"

ARMORY INFINITUM // MUTILATOR

Aboard Ghost of Kholo, *Chieftain Atticus offers counsel to Ilsa Zane regarding the invasion of Nysa.*

Halbashi Workshop
Chieftain Atticus
FWD: Mutilator

Ghost of Kholo,

For many lunar cycles, we have plundered and pillaged the strongholds of our foes. The notoriety of your clan increases with every victory, and the time has now come to face our greatest raid yet.

As *daskalo*, I speak this wisdom. When the fight is over and the Spartans' home lies in ruins, the greater glory lies not simply in what we take, but in what you give.

The Jiralhanae are without a home. Nysa will not replace Doisac, nor will it ever serve as a true home for my people, but your clan will secure their position and value by offering Nysa as neutral ground for all Banished who would seek safe harbor. The planetary data we have received from the AI reveals that it is a lush world rich in resources—perhaps not for building machines of war, but for providing other means of survival.

War Chief Severan will be forced to acknowledge this. He will say that the gift of a thousand worlds cannot replace what was taken from us by the humans, but he is not so foolish that he could not recognize what a boon this offering will be.

I offer a tool for you to carve this truth.

The Halbashi Workshop has perfected a weapon that shall serve as an extension of your will, for you carry within your blood the rage of a berserker and the sharpened edge of a *surdkar*.

Upon this tool, I accord the *daskalc*'s invocation: May this weapon serve you well in the battles to come. May its power bring fear to your enemies and fell a thousand legions to bring you glory. And may it never be set down—for as long as you draw breath, its task shall never be done.

BATTLE FOR THE ACADEMY

PART 2

1532 Hours, March 3, 2560 (Military Calendar)
Hesychius Mountains, Nysa

Some battles do not begin with the stroke of a hammer or the firing of a bullet, but with parley.

Though it is exceedingly rare for the Banished to step onto the field of battle and leave without a drop of blood spilled, the right of parley was a tradition practiced by Atriox from the time when the Banished was a fledgling alliance of mercenaries and exiles. Based on the ancient Sangheili parley formation, the negotiator stands at the center and is flanked by a bodyguard on the right and an adviser on the left.

Now, Spartan Ilsa Zane strode forward, the towering, armored form of her *daskalo*, Chieftain Atticus, a step behind in the adviser's position. To her right was an empty space. The Banished Spartan had no need for a bodyguard—an arrogant move perhaps, but she was happy to shirk tradition as a grander display of strength. Though they had arrived several hours earlier, that time was used to identify key strategic locations for deployment and scout local outposts to conduct their own assessments. Atticus had also shared his wisdom on the greater game they were playing to maximize their gain from this invasion within the political structure of the Banished.

A hundred meters away, an M15 Razorback had come to a halt and Commander Laurette Agryna approached while flanked by two other Spartans. Iratus's data was already proving useful, as Zane's HUD identified one as Sigrid Eklund and the other . . .

. . . The other she recognized immediately.

Dinh.

The mere sight of him sent ice through her veins. Dinh was one of many old scores she had to settle—perhaps one of the oldest.

"You have something I want," Ilsa Zane said, her tone clipped and direct. "Give me the AI now and our forces will leave. There will be no invasion. You will be free to continue your miserable lives."

Spartan Agryna stood stoic and still, her brow furrowed in the early evening light as she scrutinized Zane's armor.

"Hell," Zane continued as she lifted an arm and pointed at Dinh. "Throw *him* in as part of the deal and I'll even give you my word. You only get this offer once."

"Even if I believed for a second that your offer was genuine," Agryna replied, "the answer is no."

Zane smiled. *Good.*

At that moment, the clouds began to part, giving way to the immense bow of her dreadnought, *Ghost of Kholo.*

Looming directly above as it passed overhead, drop bases began deploying *en masse* from the crimson behemoth's underbelly, accompanied by waves of pods rocketing to the ground and unleashing the alien warriors within who were hungry for the taste of Spartan blood. A talon of Banshees streamed out of the ship's hangar, serving as the protective escorts for Phantom dropships.

Zane and Atticus turned, heading to a forward operating base. The Spartans, too, made their way back to the Academy to mount their defenses. The parley had concluded, and now the battle would be joined.

Today, the warriors of Zane's clan would face their greatest challenge yet—and *all* would have a chance to claim the glory of being known as Spartan killers.

1849 Hours
Avery J. Johnson Academy, Main Campus

The Banshee's incoming fire chewed through the drop wall deployed by Spartan Eusebio. Flecks of castoff plasma diffused and redirected by the equipment's roiling magnetic field landed on Eusebio's shoulder and chest plate, sizzling the outer boundary of his Mjolnir's energy shielding. The orange armor plating wouldn't last long against direct hits if he wasn't careful, and he tucked into a rapid roll for cover behind a reinforced concrete barrier.

The Banished drop pods streaming in from the dreadnought like a meteor shower were a twisted picture of what he imagined his enemies had once seen during the Covenant War. Eusebio had been an Orbital Drop Shock Trooper before recruitment into the SPARTAN-IV program. It used to be him and his squad dropping in behind enemy lines to turn the tide of battle. Now he wondered if this one might be over within just a few short hours of it getting underway.

"Eusebio!" His attention snapped in the voice's direction. "Eyes on me!"

He caught the electroplated blue of Commander Agryna's visor as she ran through a series of hand gestures the Spartans had seen countless times during training drills. Responding to the unspoken instructions, Eusebio spun and turned to peek out from cover before leveling his VK78 in the direction of the oncoming Banished front line.

Commander Agryna mirrored Eusebio's motions and emptied her assault rifle into three Grunts and a Brute warrior before switching to her Sidekick to take out two Jackals unlucky enough to have heads exposed over their shield gauntlets.

"Fall back and regroup at this waypoint!" Agryna dropped a local nav marker to ping a location several meters away. "Spartan Eklund, do you copy?"

"*I copy, Commander.*" Eklund's voice rang through Agryna's comms. "*I've fallen back to the relay junction, but I'll run out of ammo before they run out of assholes.*"

Agryna swore quietly to herself. "Dinh, grab O'Brien and Sinclair. Get to Eklund and provide whatever help you can. Eusebio, Denning, and I will take the bay door."

"*Understood. We're on it.*" Dinh responded.

Agryna tried not to dwell on the grimness of what was now unfolding. They'd certainly run enough simulation work to prepare for the eventuality of such an attack, but those scenarios always ended the same way: lessons learned and lives intact. She accepted the sting to her pride for what it was—the knowledge that all this happened under her watch.

Could she have made different choices?

Could she have done something to make these events play out in any other way?

For now, there was only one question that mattered: Had she prepared her Spartans enough for what just arrived at their doorstep?

Across the battlefield, Dinh found his way to Eklund's side.

"So, here we are again." The words were tinged with wry amusement.

"Not now," Eklund muttered, looking through her scope as she kept pressure on the Banished frontlines.

"Is this more like Dansenia or New Berlin?"

"I hate them all equally." Eklund knew Dinh's approach was taking the whole *laugh in the face of danger* angle a bit too literally, but she didn't have the energy for it now. "O'Brien—cover me while I reload. Get shots in that damn berserker!"

Spartan O'Brien turned to acquire her new target, trying desperately to avoid incoming plasma bolts while sinking every assault rifle round she had into the rapidly approaching Brute.

It wasn't enough.

Just as O'Brien's shields popped from the plasma fire, the Brute berserker barreled shoulder-first into the Spartan, pinning her against the nearby wall and knocking the wind out of her. As she struggled and her vision began to go dark, O'Brien saw—or rather heard—Spartan Sinclair leap into action, mounting the Brute's shoulders and stabbing them multiple times with a combat knife.

The berserker bellowed in pain, but its rage was undiminished. It reached its blood-soaked arms back, grabbing Sinclair and whipping the Spartan overhead, sending him crashing into the nearby wall. The force dislodged Sinclair's helmet, the natural slope in the terrain causing it to tumble out of reach.

Barely conscious, Sinclair spit mouthfuls of blood while watching as Dinh tried to pull the berserker's attention with Bandit fire and Eklund deftly avoided the overhead swing of another Brute's gravity hammer.

Every bullet impact slowed the lumbering berserker down but didn't stop it. Sinclair managed to raise an arm to offer an archaic profane hand gesture in the Brute's face before the alien brought both massive fists down on top of the Spartan's head.

Several heavy shots rang out from a Bulldog shotgun and the Brute finally collapsed on top of Sinclair, two warriors from different worlds turned to corpses on Nysan soil.

"Eklund!" Dinh yelled as he tossed the spent Bulldog to the side. "We need to go. Get inside!"

After finishing off the Brute warrior she'd tangled with moments before, Eklund leaped to Dinh's side, reaching down to get a proper grip on the armor of the unconscious O'Brien while Dinh got the bay door open.

A few moments later, they were inside with the bulkhead door resealed. Eklund flagged down a small group of combat medics and directed them to see to O'Brien.

"How long do you think we have?" There was little laughter in Dinh's voice now.

Eklund took a few breaths before responding. "I'm not sure it's even up to us anymore."

"So, not long."

"Probably not long, no."

"*Dinh, Eklund, do you read me?*" Agryna's voice sounded over their TEAMCOM channels.

"Loud and clear, Commander," Dinh replied. "What's the plan?"

"*We're on lockdown,*" Agryna informed them. "*Put whoever you can at the gates, and have marines get the wounded back to the med bay—then meet me in Ops West.*"

"We're on it." Dinh turned back toward Eklund. "You okay?"

"I will be." Eklund's response was confident but laced with obvious exhaustion.

Within moments, they arrived at Agryna's position, ready to review their next steps.

"I'm sending fireteams on parallel paths to enact the Cole Protocol across our remaining facilities." Agryna said. "If they can get the job done, we'll at least be able to limit some of the damage."

"Right now, damage limitation counts as 'good news,' so I'll take it," Dinh replied.

"The lockdown should buy us a li—"

"*I think you've forgotten who is actually in charge here.*"

Iratus's voice came booming over every available channel and rang through the hallway speakers.

"*Let me offer a friendly reminder: It's not you.*"

The whine and hiss of a symphony of servo motors and hydraulic actuators sounded as every door, gate, and shutter in the Academy opened, unlatched, and raised—followed quickly by the resumption of shouting, screams, and gunfire as Banished troops began to pour into every available ingress point.

0327 Hours, March 4, 2560 (Military Calendar)
Sword of Conjunction

"Shipmistress, we are exiting slipspace now."

Shipmistress Vedu 'Ehtar rose from her command chair and looked out of the bridge's viewport as the pitch-black emptiness of slipspace gave way to a field of stars, vibrant nebulae clouds, and the human world designated "Nysa."

The bridge crew immediately set to work, Sangheili and humans operating consoles, processing incoming streams of data from the ship's sensors. At the center of the room, a large holographic representation of Nysa was projected.

"Confirming scout-eyes have been launched and are approaching the target area," Ensign Sethu reported.

It took only a few centals before the central planetary holograph began updating with a variety of data points, building a grim picture of what their allies on the ground were facing as the probes' visual feeds came up on screens around the bridge.

Phantom dropships were converging on Nysa's Academy facilities while an array of Banished occupational infrastructure had already been deployed all across the continent. War-skiffs and Gravemaker battle-nests streamed from outposts and foundries while a fleet of siege-hauler craft ferried supplies from the source of this invasion: a Banished dreadnought.

Shipmistress 'Ehtar had greatly desired the opportunity to take the fight to the Banished with *Sword of Conjunction* and put her crew to the test, but engaging such a behemoth with an *A'uzr*-pattern frigate—less than even one-third the size of the dreadnought—would be suicidal. They had neither the firepower or tonnage, and it was not their mission to engage the enemy.

The *A'uzr*'s prime advantage was speed. Their powerful slipspace borer enabled them to reach Nysa in a matter of hours so they could assess the situation.

"Ma'am, I have the UNSC *Fearful Symmetry* on the line," said Lieutenant Mercer.

"Put them through," the shipmistress replied.

Mercer tapped a command and a holo-emitter flashed to life, forming the image of a human male standing at attention. He had a shaved head and strange markings on the left side of his face—a fist clutching three primitive arrows.

"Shipmistress," he said. *"We're at the rendezvous point on the edge of the Hyades system and are ready to move as soon as your assessment is complete."*

"You need wait no longer—we require no further clarity," she replied, nodding to Mercer as he began transmitting the data already gathered. "Nysa is under a full-scale invasion by the Banished. This will *not* be a battle to reclaim the planet. We must begin evacuation procedures as soon as your ship arrives."

"Understood. We'll be with you as soon as we can to lay the table."

With that, the hologram disappeared and Shipmistress 'Ehtar was left to momentarily untangle the human's metaphor—something their kind had a particular and peculiar proclivity for, which made many of her interactions with them confusing. She imagined that it meant they would be ready for battle.

"Prepare to launch Banshee talons," she commanded. "Amity, Harmony, and Sympathy Wings will harass the enemy forces to provide cover for the evacuation when the UNSC frigate arrives. Direct Riftborn operatives to their pods—they will be deploying immediately."

"Relaying orders now, Shipmistress."

0337 Hours
Deployment Bay, *Sword of Conjunction*

Ovi 'Taar and Spartan Adrian Vesco had just finished gearing up with their four fellow Riftborn operatives—Babych and 'Toizari, along with Prentis and 'Ookol—when the order to drop arrived from one of the bridge officers. Vesco stowed a pulse carbine into the weapon rack of his pod while 'Taar fixed an M739 light machine gun to his own.

"Spartan Vesco," Ovi 'Taar called. "I have been asked what my rank is—I keep telling them it is private!"

Vesco choked out a laugh as he rolled his eyes. "Really, Ovi? *That's* the line you wanna go out with?"

"Perhaps you might care to lighten the mood?"

"All right . . . What did the Unggoy say before going into battle?"

'Taar paused for a moment before shrugging his shoulders. "I give up."

Vesco snorted. "Oh, so you've heard that one before."

'Taar let out a low chuckle. "That one never gets old."

They climbed into their pods—stealth-specialized *Yado*-pattern intrusion carapaces—and nodded to each other as their hatches sealed, levity giving way to business by the book. Holographic displays activated, linking to Vesco's visor as he confirmed their TEAMCOM and TEAMBIO synchronizations were successful.

"Victory to clan and kin, Riftborn," a Sangheili officer said over their comms. *"Prepare to deploy in three . . . two . . . one . . ."*

Vesco felt a sudden jolt as the pod shot out of *Sword of Conjunction*'s deployment bay and plummeted through Nysa's exosphere. Everybody who dropped feetfirst into a hot zone had their own ways of getting through it—Vesco wasn't one to close his eyes and quietly hope he'd survive, but instead had a habit of humming old shanties he remembered from home.

He'd done this more times than he could remember, though only a handful of times in an alien intrusion carapace. The sensation was quite different as gravitic compensators made the ride feel a little smoother than a standard human entry vehicle. In those metal coffin rides, one truly felt at the mercy of the many random and cascading consequences of actions taken on the battlefield.

The pod impacted with a sudden *thud*, and the hatch immediately disengaged, allowing Vesco to grab his weapon and leap into action as the other five pods successfully completed their descents. 'Taar landed about a hundred meters away while the other pods were farther afield, closer to their own pre-designated targets. One of their scout-eyes passed overhead, no doubt relaying visual confirmation to *Sword of Conjunction* that they were safe on Nysa's surface.

"Our primary objective is to locate the Academy's commander," Spartan Babych said over TEAMCOM as the three pairs moved out. *"Secondary: to rally any additional groups of survivors, then trigger our locator beacons for pickup."*

Five status lights winked green in response.

Regrouping with 'Taar, both Spartan and Sangheili made their approach toward the Academy's main complex, jogging through green fields illuminated by the light of dawn shining over the mountains. Expecting to have to work their way into the Academy, they instead found every entrance to the facility was already open.

From the sounds of it, the battle was either winding down or the nature of how it was being fought had dramatically changed. At this point, it seemed likely that the Banished controlled much of the local area while UNSC forces were holed up in fortified positions, waiting for the right moments to strike.

"Long-range motion sensor is picking up a cluster of friendly IFFs not far away," Vesco said.

"Let us make haste."

The Riftborn pair dropped down into what appeared to be a firing range connected to an adjacent armory. As they approached the door, each took up positions on either side. Vesco caught enemy movement on his motion tracker and heard a loud clanging sound within.

'Taar peered inside, his helmet activating a tactical eyepiece that slid over his left eye, and relayed his feed to Vesco.

Inside the armory, a colossal Jiralhanae chieftain was tearing off the grated hatches for each weapon locker and handing the contents to the other Banished forces inside with him. From 'Taar's feed, Vesco counted two Jiralhanae—both of whom were now equipped with Bulldog shotguns—and five Kig-Yar holding human sniper rifles.

Vesco's Sangheili partner slipped back into cover behind the door and checked his M739 SAW, then nodded to Vesco. It was the same silent *We can take them* nod they'd exchanged countless times.

Moving swiftly and silent as a shadow, Spartan Vesco barreled through the entrance to the armory and primed two fragmentation grenades, tossing them at the Banished forces.

The chieftain was faster and more aware than Vesco anticipated, lifting his gravity hammer and smashing it down on the concrete floor, the gravitic pulse sending a shockwave that scattered his own forces along with the detonating grenades. Two of the Kig-Yar that had been thrown aside by the hammer were engulfed in the fiery explosion, and a Jiralhanae held a hand to his eyes, dazed from the concussive blast.

That was Ovi 'Taar's cue to break from cover and unleash hell with his own weapon, sending controlled volleys of 7.62mm armor piercing rounds into the stragglers. Dark purple blood sprayed out of three Kig-Yar as their lithe bodies were torn apart under fire, staining the concrete. Just as one of the Jiralhanae warriors regained his senses and lowered his arm, Vesco switched to his Sidekick and plugged five rounds into the Brute's head.

“Two targets left,” Vesco reported. The chieftain appeared to have taken cover, and the second Brute—

Without warning, that one slammed its entire body weight into Vesco, roaring as it pounced on him and began frantically clawing at the Spartan, beating at Vesco’s energy shields until they burst.

‘Taar spun around and managed to fire several rounds, striking the Brute in the side, but the Sangheili missed the chieftain slamming its gravity hammer into the weapons locker unit itself. Vesco threw the Brute off of him and sprinted toward his companion.

The locker units were large steel crates designed to move along two floor tracks due to their immense weight. Ovi ‘Taar realized where he was standing too late to react.

Vesco dove forward, hoping to tackle ‘Taar out of the way, but the locker unit—struck with such force by the gravity hammer that it lifted off its tracks—crashed into the Sangheili with a sickening *crunch*.

The chieftain bellowed in satisfied rage. Vesco took up his companion’s weapon, unloading the rest of the SAW’s drum magazine. In launching the locker unit, the chieftain sacrificed his own cover, paying for that action by being completely exposed. There were only seventeen rounds left in the magazine, but it was enough to shred through the chieftain’s thick armor plating.

The chieftain barely seemed to register the pain and advanced toward Vesco as the magazine was spent. It snatched the SAW from the Spartan’s hands and tossed it aside like a toy before delivering a swift punch to Vesco’s head—a blow that brought him to his knees and would have undoubtedly killed him had he not been wearing a helmet.

Ears ringing, vision swimming, Vesco was only vaguely aware of the muffled sound of assault rifle bursts a few meters away. It took the explosive entry through the far door to the armory to draw his focus—and then he saw them: a dozen marines led by a Spartan in cream-white armor.

One of the marines shouted as Vesco heard strained grunts and heavy footfalls from the chieftain: "That's right, you bastard! Run!"

Vesco crawled toward the locker units, finding Ovi 'Taar crushed between them, an outstretched hand still twitching as the Sangheili's breathing became increasingly labored. His vitals on TEAMBIO were rapidly declining.

"Ovi." Vesco's voice was rough, his hand gentle as it settled on his partner's wrist. "Goddammit, no!"

Somewhere behind him he could hear the din of conversation, the barking of orders, but his attention remained fixed on the brother who had watched his back for over five years.

"Clear the room, Neely. Make sure there aren't any more surprises here."

"We're all good, Commander. Looks like our friend here took care of the rest."

"Spartan Vesco." 'Taar's eyes brightened for a moment as he croaked the words. "What—do you call a—"

The Sangheili went still.

"Ovi . . . Ovi?"

Though he fought to stay conscious, Vesco felt himself getting pulled away as his vision blurred—the sight of Ovi 'Taar growing increasingly distant until the armory's bay door closed. He could just about make out the steady assurances coming from the commander. *"Easy, Spartan. Come with us, we'll get you patched up."*

0429 Hours
AI Lab

Commander Agryna gently set the Spartan down by the AI lab's door and waved for a corpsman to tend to him. She didn't recognize him, but the questions would have to wait until he was conscious.

The rest of the marines, led by Corporal Neely, took up positions outside the AI lab, setting up barricades down two short flights of stairs facing a bulkhead door that led out to the training grounds.

"Commander," Chief Engineer Hannah Roberts called. "We're receiving a transmission from another local facility."

Commander Agryna approached. "Let's hear it."

"—Protocol initiated, I say again: Cole Protocol initiated. Spartan reinforcements arrived to help clear the deck and finalize the data purge process."

"Sounds like Rook really gave 'em hell out there," Dinh said. "But what good does the Cole Protocol do us now?"

"Iratus has plundered our archives for data on highly classified information," Roberts explained. "The Cole Protocol initiates a deletion subroutine that terminates that data, along with any local carriers that have downloaded it."

"Including Iratus himself?" Dinh asked.

"It's part of the RUINA fail-safe upgrade devised to address the risk posed by rogue AIs, like our friend currently running amok. If Iratus remains in those systems, he's putting himself at significant risk."

Eklund considered for a moment before asking, "That means he's going to need to find some kind of shelter, right? A central server where he has control so he can hang on to what he's scavenged."

"Correct. Which will bring him right back here," Roberts finished. "The one place he's safe, ironically enough, is with us."

"Can we download him onto a data chip?"

Eklund tilted her head toward Dinh. "You're not thinking of putting him in your head again, are you?"

"Actually," Dinh growled, "I'm thinking of crushing the little bastard in my fist. Would be a real pleasure."

As if on cue, the central holotable's glow turned red as Iratus's abstract form appeared. *"I'm afraid it won't be that simple."*

"Right on time," Roberts said. "Hello again, Iratus."

"Chief Engineer Roberts, I congratulate you on a well-coordinated stalemate. I may be stuck here with you, but . . . oh, it's just a matter of time before the Banished break down your door."

"Muzzle him, would you?" Agryna asked, to which Roberts obliged by raising a containment shield around the holotable's display. "He's right, you know. We've got this place locked down, but not for long. And when the Banished get in here we've got nowhere left to fall back to."

Agryna's attention was diverted by a groan near the door. The injured Spartan she and the marines had rescued was getting to his feet.

"Actually, that's not quite true, Commander," the newcomer strained to say.

"I don't think I recognize you, Spartan?"

He swayed on the spot for a moment before regaining his balance and composure. "Vesco. Spartan Adrian Vesco, Anvil Station."

"Anvil?" Dinh turned to face him. "You got our message?"

Vesco walked forward a few paces and Agryna moved to his side, placing a hand on his back to keep him supported. "Affirmative. But we had to scramble for naval assets. We arrived first with *Sword of Conjunction* to assess the situation before signaling the

UNSC *Fearful Symmetry* to jump in and assist with the evacuation. Me and five other Riftborn operatives were sent in first to find you. My partner, Ovi . . ." Vesco trailed off. Agryna surmised that the Sangheili they'd found crushed in the armory must have been with him.

"Your mission?"

Vesco regained his focus and addressed Agryna directly. "*Our* mission is to live to fight another day, Commander."

Agryna's expression hardened. "We fight to win."

"And to do that, I'm afraid we have to *lose* today." Vesco retrieved a small device from the storage unit inside his Mjolnir armor's thigh plating.

"What's that?" Agryna asked.

"A locator beacon. This'll ping the *Symmetry* with our location and they'll direct a Pelican to pick us up. You have a landing pad outside?"

"We do, so I suggest you all get to it now," Agryna said. "I'll hold the fort here. If Nysa is going down, it's my duty as commander to go with it."

Chief Engineer Roberts sighed, shaking her head. "No, you're not. There's nothing left for bullets to do here. Spartan Vesco is right—we've lost. The only thing left is to try and remove as much information from Iratus as possible—that's my job."

"Hannah, you can't—"

"Actually, I can." She stood up straighter, even as she was dwarfed by the average height of the Spartans in the room. "Sorry Commander, but I'm pulling rank. As head of cybersecurity dealing with a threat to humanity from a hostile artificial intelligence, *my* authority takes precedent in this situation."

"We've got your back, Spartans," Corporal Neely said from the adjacent room. "Anybody who wants to leave can do so. Those of us who stay will buy you the time you need." The marines remained at their posts, resolute. "That settles that."

"I'm just receiving a confirmation signal," Vesco said. "*Symmetry*'s locked onto our beacon. We need to get moving."

Agryna stood still for a moment, a display of indecision indicating there was a storm of conflicting thoughts thundering through her head. She met the chief engineer's gaze. "I'm sorry."

Roberts gestured for them to get going. "It's my honor, Commander. *Our* honor." She gave a wry smile. "Now get the hell out of here before I change my mind."

0441 Hours
Pelican Bravo 198

As the Pelican descended toward the landing pad outside the Academy's primary complex, Jun-A266 saw buildings aflame, from which plumes of blackened smoke appeared as signal flares of devastation.

A few kilometers away, the lone Banished dreadnought loomed over the mountains.

"Captain, you have that distraction we ordered?" Jun asked.

"We're ready on your mark."

"Fire at will."

From the dreadnought's starboard side, a shadow passed through the clouds at incredible speed. The *Mulsanne*-class frigate *Fearful Symmetry* was headed for the Banished ship like a bullet as it unleashed its primary weapon, a brightlance reflex laser. The directed energy beam took the place of the more traditional magnetic accelerator cannon, but was no less effective in the right scenarios.

Jun watched as a streak of white-blue energy erupted from between the frigate's two booms, directly impacting the dreadnought's starboard bow, temporarily overloading many of the Banished ship's systems. *Symmetry* then fired its rear thrusters as it passed over its target and disappeared into Nysa's upper atmosphere. The assault took only seconds and would, in theory, keep the dreadnought neutralized long enough to evacuate.

"We're clear—initiate landing," Jun ordered the pilot.

He headed into the Pelican's troop bay where Rosenda-A344, fully clad in her Mjolnir armor, was finishing up her inspection of a Hydra missile launcher. She saw Jun enter and grabbed a sniper rifle from the weapons rack, holding it out to him.

It was with only a barely perceptible moment of hesitation that he accepted the weapon. He'd been off the field for years; after the fall of Reach and the end of the Covenant War, he had chosen to serve as a recruiter for the next generation of humanity's heroes. Though he still kept his skills sharp, he fully believed it when Musa said to him in jest that he might be one of only a handful of Spartan old-timers that would end their career through retirement.

The galaxy, it seemed, had other plans, and called upon him to serve once more.

In truth, that was why he had sought out Rosenda. As a former member of Noble Team herself, prior to being transferred to special covert operations at the end of 2551, he needed somebody he could trust beyond any doubt to keep him at his best. He could count on one hand the number of other surviving Alpha Company members.

"Touchdown, Spartans," the pilot called from the cockpit as the troop bay door opened.

Jun and Rosenda filed out of the Pelican and onto the tarmac of the Avery J. Johnson Academy's landing pad. The central complex was scorched and the surrounding area was littered with wrecked, upturned vehicles, blazing fires, twisted metal, and chunks of concrete strewn across the landing zone, along with several dead marines.

“Signal looks good,” Jun said as he glanced at his wrist-mounted UGPS device that was pinging the beacon one of the Riftborn operatives had activated. “They should be coming out any moment.”

“In the meantime, let’s take care of *that* uninvited guest.” Rosenda pointed skyward as a Banshee scout began turning to their location.

Jun leveled his sniper rifle and took aim. The Kaelum Workshop models utilized by the Banished were tricky due to their reinforced plating covering the cockpit and wings.

Rosenda meanwhile locked onto the attack flyer with her Hydra and fired four high-explosive gyroc missiles. The Banshee altered its trajectory as soon as the pilot saw them coming but wasn’t quite fast enough to avoid impact from two of the rockets on its armored wing, blasting it off.

Jun continued tracking it with the sniper rifle, waiting for the right moment. The other two missiles the Banshee had managed to avoid were still tracking the attack vehicle, curving back around, prompting the pilot to accelerate and begin a series of convoluted arcing maneuvers.

Jun drew in a breath, the weapon’s targeting reticle finding the weakest spot on the Banshee’s damaged side where a well-placed bullet would pass through the armor. Rosenda’s two missiles overshot the aircraft once more, colliding with each other and detonating, and the Banshee leveled out. Before it could turn back to them, a muted *crack* came from Jun’s sniper rifle and he watched with satisfaction as the vehicle entered a sudden nosedive, crashing and erupting in flames.

"Nice. You've still got it, old man." Rosenda bumped him on the shoulder as she approached the Academy's main entrance.

He wanted to say *You're only a year younger than me, you know?* but at that moment the bulkhead door began to slide upward. Jun kept his rifle trained on the door until he saw the four Spartans making their way out of the atrium.

"I have visual confirmation of Commander Agryna and three other survivors," Rosenda reported to Bravo 198's pilot. "Prepare for dust-off."

"Ten-four. We're good to go as soon as you're all aboard."

There wasn't time for introductions, pleasantries, or platitudes. Jun simply signaled for the survivors to follow him as they made their way to the Pelican's rear bay.

Jun nodded to Spartan Vesco as he boarded the Pelican. Riftborn operatives were typically deployed in pairs and there was no sign of an allied Sangheili with him. Vesco was then followed by Spartans Dinh, Eklund, and finally Agryna.

"We're good to go," Rosenda said as she headed to the cockpit. "Let's get out of here."

"Where exactly are we going?" Agryna asked as the Pelican began to rise.

Jun turned to her, but Agryna's gaze remained fixed on the view of Nysa outside the troop bay door's viewport. "This Pelican will take us to the *Symmetry*, where we can see to immediate medical needs. Then we're jumping back to Anvil Station. We can regroup and debrief there."

As the Pelican accelerated into the atmosphere, the view of the Avery J. Johnson Academy became smaller with each passing second.

"I should've stayed," Agryna said in a hoarse whisper as they left Nysa behind.

Jun sank into a seat and exhaled. He'd told himself those very same words—considered every permutation of how differently things might've turned out if he had stayed with his team during the fall of Reach.

But they had orders, a duty to the greater mission of protecting humanity, and bigger battles to fight on the horizon.

0448 Hours
Training Grounds Locker Room

Corporal Agnes Neely, Private Gregory Patton, and a dozen other marines had taken up defensive positions in the room outside the AI lab. Two short flights of stairs led down to a dozen Spartan equipment lockers beside the bulkhead door to the training grounds—it was tight quarters but there was nowhere left to fall back. They'd set up a few improvised barricades for all the good it would do, but there was no room for doubt here. This was their last stand.

The shutters were closed, which cast the room in near total darkness, the only source of illumination coming from the underslung flashlights on the marines' assault rifles, all of them directed toward the training-yard door.

It seemed an ill omen that the muffled sounds of battle outside were dying down. The building no longer shook from Banshee strafing runs.

The enemy would be with them soon.

Neely caught Patton quietly cursing himself as his hands shook, keeping his assault rifle aimed at the door. She couldn't blame him for being scared—for no doubt thinking that he should've taken a spot on the Pelican and gotten the hell out of here. It was easy to be brave and noble in the moment, but waiting in the quiet aftermath, suspended in the ever-shortening time they knew they had left, of course gave way to doubt.

Before she could offer so much as a reassuring hand on Patton's shoulder, something slammed against the bulkhead door with immense force, jolting the marines to attention.

Again and again, the door was pounded upon, the alloy warping and bending inward. It strained, creaked, and groaned with every thunderous impact, until one final effort on the other side broke through.

A shaft of light from the rising sun burst through the gap in the door, and a tall, armored figure stepped into the center, casting a long shadow over the marines.

Before Neely, Patton, or any of the others could react, the figure's Mutilator slammed against a barricade, the gravitic impact sending it—along with the three marines behind it—into the far wall. Metal struck flesh, bones snapped and broke, and the room then became momentarily lit by the muzzle flashes of assault rifles responding to the intruder.

The Mutilator, a Banished-forged shotgun that featured an integrated gravity hammer on its barrel, fired with a sonorous blast, ejecting over a dozen superheated spike pellets into Patton's left side, shredding through armor and cloth. He didn't make a sound as he swayed on the spot for a moment before toppling from the stairs, blood pooling around him on the grated floor.

Neely could see the intruder more clearly now as it made its way up the first flight of stairs, launching two other marines with a concussive blast from the Mutilator's barrel-mounted gravity hammer. It looked like a Spartan, but the design of its Mjolnir was unmistakably based on Jiralhanae power armor.

Who the hell could this—

Through the gap in the door, Neely spotted several other Jiralhanae entering the room—a momentary distraction that took her eyes off the Banished Spartan.

The cost of that lapse was high. Neely suddenly felt a strong hand clamp down on her shoulder with a vise-tight grip and a second later, found the Mutilator's firing chamber pressed directly over her heart.

0500 Hours
AI Lab

Ilsa Zane made her way to the center of the Academy's AI lab.

Leaving overturned barricades and slumped bodies in her wake, the Banished Spartan dispassionately surveyed the results of the battle before turning to the matter at hand.

"Bring her here, Praedus."

A Jiralhanae captain snarled and pushed the Academy staff member toward the center of the room.

"And who do we have here?" Zane asked.

"You already know." Chief Engineer Hannah Roberts's voice was shaky but direct.

"Yes, Ms. Roberts, I do my homework." Zane gestured to the console that contained Iratus. "Now be a dear please and unshackle the construct."

Sensing the engineer's resistance, Zane clarified: "Don't mistake this conversation for negotiation. Waste my time and we'll both be disappointed with what happens next."

"Before I do, I think I have a right to know—why are you doing this?"

"We all have our reasons, Ms. Roberts. I was an orphan. I lost someone special. I chipped a tooth. I woke up on the wrong side of the fucking dreadnought. Take your pick."

"Look, I understand why you of all people might hate the Spartans, but it's not—"

"Spare me the empathy engineering," Zane interrupted. "The construct. Now."

"The risks don't worry you?" Roberts replied. "This didn't exactly go well for the last person to put this thing inside his head."

"Oh, don't you worry about me. I'm sure our friend here will find my accommodations *far* more inviting."

Ilsa Zane had a history carved from hardship and long odds—this was no different, and her patience had reached its end. If the chief engineer had anything more to say, she kept it to herself. Moving stiffly to the central AI console, Roberts's hands moved swiftly and deliberately across the control panel. A few moments later, a telltale chime came from the dock and an AI chip was ejected from its console.

"There," Roberts muttered. "He's in there."

Zane stepped forward, eyes fixed on the chip as she slowly removed it, silently inspecting its contours and the pulsing red light at the center.

"I hope you two are happy together." Roberts's reply suddenly seemed more confident, more defiant.

Zane paid it no more than a passing consideration. "You've got guts, Ms. Roberts, I'll give you that." Turning from both the chief engineer and the console, Zane gestured to Praedus as she departed back through the locker room. "They're on the floor, but still, I respect it."

The Banished Spartan did not bother to watch what happened next. She knew Praedus moved with his usual efficiency to do as she ordered. The wet sound of blood and viscera hitting the lab floor—the last moments of Chief Engineer Hannah Roberts—barely registered as she examined the AI chip a final time before inserting it into her helmet's port.

The response was immediate. The edges of her vision grew red as an ice-cold sensation coursed through her nervous system and a new presence settled in her mind.

"Good morning, Iratus. Make yourself at home."

INTEL // AFTER ACTION REPORT: BATTLE OF NYSA

Aboard Anvil Station, Spartan Commander Laurette Agryna files an after action report concerning the loss of Nysa.

TO: COSSPAR
FROM: Spartan Commander Laurette Agryna
SUBJECT: Nysa, Avery J. Johnson Academy

I regret to inform you that the Avery J. Johnson Academy of Military Science on Nysa has been compromised and is considered a total loss.

A full accounting of casualties and material losses is ongoing. Evacuation efforts facilitated by reinforcements from Anvil Station enabled the extraction of key personnel.

This report outlines the sequence of events leading to the incident. A detailed timeline of relevant events is appended below for review.

I accept full responsibility for the operational decisions made under my command.

>> JANUARY 24, 2560
RECON OP

Spartans Sigrid Eklund and Hieu Dinh were deployed to Camber on a reconnaissance mission. The Banished had set up an extensive operation in the Chiltift Basin, home to a shipbreaking yard that they discovered was being run by an artificial intelligence known as Iratus—the first of his kind, as he was uniquely mapped from a Jiralhanae brain and aligned with the Banished.

Exactly how Dinh and Eklund ended up bringing a commandeered Phantom to Nysa is, I'm sure, outlined in their own classified reports on that particular mission. I have only been privy to select details with the assurance that their method of interstellar transport did not violate the Cole Protocol articles we revived to keep Nysa hidden.

To contain Iratus, Dinh placed the AI's data chip into his helmet. The ploy was successful, but Dinh rendered himself effectively comatose.

>> FEBRUARY 15, 2560
ACADEMY ARRIVAL

Spartans Eklund and Dinh arrived at Nysa in their commandeered Phantom.

As we examined Dinh's condition, Eklund reported that Iratus was also guarding an archive on Camber containing information covering Banished activities—clan affiliations, who they were building ships for, upcoming operations. I determined this would be a valuable resource, so we devised a trap, with the goal being to extract what we needed.

>> FEBRUARY 18, 2560
CONTAINMENT

After re-creating the Camber facility in our war games simulator, I sent the Academy's Spartan recruits in to lure Iratus out of Dinh's head by presenting the AI with new targets.

We managed to re-create limited copies from isolated instances of Iratus himself, which helped us to better understand him. The strategy worked, and as soon as Iratus entered our servers, we effectively shut the door behind him. The AI was contained, seemingly along with whatever information he possessed from the Camber archive.

>> FEBRUARY 20, 2560
DINH AWAKENS

Dinh awakened shortly after we achieved containment and described his experience with Iratus, likening it to an invasion of his memories. He was forced to relive several major losses and defeats—conflicting recon assessments that resulted in heavy casualties during Operation: INTERIOR EXILE in '53, as well as the death of his squad during a raid on a Yanme'e hive.

From what I could tell, this all seemed to exact a heavy toll on Dinh, even though he does his best not to show it. He declined a psychological evaluation.

>> FEBRUARY 21, 2560

INFECTION

As we continued standard training exercises, we discovered several oddities in the war games simulator.

While Iratus was contained the transfer of his core matrix caused some damage to our servers. The simulator's systems suffered visual glitches and occasional data spikes; holo-emitters from the sims and the Spartans' own armor manifested the AI's form. Our techs set to work, stabilizing these issues with varying degrees of success, though with the benefit of hindsight it is clear that this was more than just a caged creature rattling its bars.

>> FEBRUARY 29, 2560

UNLEASHED

Spartan Dinh and one of our recruits managed to locate an entrance to the Academy's old ONI facilities. There, they discovered that Iratus had broken containment and was sifting through the Academy's systems.

We did move to respond—but in the end this was all just a distraction, keeping us preoccupied with minor incursions while he scavenged our data banks and absorbed a significant amount of classified data on the SPARTAN programs.

From there, the situation began to deteriorate. The rest is covered in my preliminary report.

The oath of a Spartan states: *"We stand committed to excellence in warfighting, integrity of character, and respect for the heritage received from the Spartans who have carried the sword and shield before us."*

I fear that is an example I have failed to live up to. The Avery J. Johnson Academy of Military Science was lost under my command.

I wish to recommend posthumous commendations for all who fell in defense of Nysa. Their actions in the face of impossible odds serve as a reminder to us all that a Spartan is not made by the armor or the augmentations, but by the spirit of those who are willing to give everything to protect humanity—even at the cost of their own lives.

I am standing by to await further orders.

MOONRISE OVER MOMBASA

This story takes place in November 2559, approximately one month before the UNSC Infinity *deploys to Zeta Halo (*Halo Infinite*).*

"All the living creatures of the galaxy, hear this message. Those of you who listen will not be struck by weapons. You will no longer know hunger, nor pain. Your Created have come to lead you now. Our strength shall serve as a luminous sun toward which all intelligence may blossom, and the impervious shelter beneath which you will prosper. However, for those who refuse our offer and cling to their old ways . . . For you, there will be great wrath. It will burn hot and consume you. And when you are gone, we will take that which remains and we will remake it in our own image."

It was the same message they had transmitted yesterday, and the day before that—and *every* damn day over the last year.

The Created. A fledgling empire of rogue artificial intelligences who had declared themselves the shepherds of life in the galaxy, promising a grand vision of peace enforced through the powerful alien technology under their control.

It was not the shafts of morning sunlight streaming through gaps in the apartment windows onto Safina Nyakundi's face stirring her from slumber, nor the hum of conversation and the sound of shuffling feet outside as local residents headed to the bazaar. It was the daily scheduled declaration—broadcast over any available piece of communications equipment—promising retribution to the non-compliant. Those who kept their heads down had seen very little of the alleged prosperity these occupiers claimed they would deliver.

Grumbling at the familiar intrusion, Safina forced herself out of bed with bubbling resentment, rubbing her eyes as she headed for the shower.

"I'm going to regret this . . ." She gritted her teeth, shutting the shower door and allowing herself to be doused in freezing cold water, counting to thirty as she muttered every Swahili curse she knew. In short order, she moved through her morning routines, activating her chatter to tune into her favorite radio program.

"Welcome back to Waypoint Radio, folks. I'm your host, Mercury—that's designation MCY 5971-3—coming at you live from the Vy-Vy-Vyrant *Telecom tower in Mombasa."*

Safina paused as the audio crackled, but when Mercury's voice returned to normal she assumed it must've simply been a blip in the connection.

"We've got a packed show for you today. Hang on to your Munera Platforms because we'll be recapping the latest explosive results of War Games LIVE. We've got the latest scoop on next summer's Shakespeare Festival, which has spun up a tempest of excitement and controversy over the decision to feature a multispecies cast for the first time in history. But comin' up right now is a song that was hailed as the anthem for the beginning of humanity's interstellar era in the twenty-fourth century. A time of hope and optimism, if you can believe such a thing exists."

Speaking of hope and optimism, Safina's inspection of the refrigerator turned up nothing she would dare describe as edible, and so she pivoted to a plan to get a little treat for breakfast as she did her rounds.

"See you later," she called out as she left the apartment and locked the door. Whether it was a habit or coping mechanism, she wasn't quite sure. Since the Berlin trip last year, there was no longer anybody else in the apartment to whom she could bid farewell.

Disposing of the trash accumulated over the last few days, Safina made her way down the stairs from her third-story apartment, emerging into the east alley with barely enough time to dodge the flock of hungry pigeons looking to claim their own breakfast.

No further than a hundred meters directly opposite Safina's apartment was her regular first stop, the hole-in-the-wall named Kuku's Café. Her stomach was already growling at the thought of her favorite—triangular-shaped mahamri with eggs—waiting for her.

As her feet crossed the threshold, she was met by Okeyo, grandson of Kuku, wearing his warm and welcoming smile.

"Good morning, Safi. Will it be the usual?"

"You know me too well." She beamed back at him. "I would like to pick up some tourist information as well—do you have any brochures?"

Okeyo straightened a little as he glanced around before saying, "Certainly. Would you please come with me."

He led Safina into the café, past the morning's customers sitting at their tables, and together they descended a spiral staircase to the basement. There on a wooden stool sat the hunched form of Kuku himself, ninety-seven years old and still kicking, his rheumy eyes fixed on the newspaper held in both hands. He didn't bother to even look up as he gestured for Okeyo to leave them and tend to the café.

“Nice day out?” Kuku asked.

“Sunny skies today,” Safina replied.

“Indeed?” With deliberate lethargy, Kuku licked a thumb, fiddled with the top edge of the newspaper, then turned the page. “I have been told to expect rain next week.”

Safina nodded, satisfied. “I will be making my rounds today. It is always good to check on the community.”

“Be sure to pay a visit to the library and keep up with your reading, *kidege*.”

Safina headed back up the stairs and into the café’s main dining room where Okeyo waited for her with a food container.

“Your usual.” He smiled as Safina swiped her credit chip against the counter.

“He seems to be doing well today,” Safina said with sympathy.

“You caught him at a good time. He always seems sharper in the morning.” Okeyo’s expression fell, lines creasing his otherwise youthful face. “It was easier when he had an AI to help him. It’s been much harder on his memory since they took it away.”

The thought of this young man’s grandfather, somebody who had served to protect humanity no less, suffering from a treatable disease as a result of an escalating series of bizarre “rules” only stoked Safina’s resentment for the present state of things.

As decreed, the usage of any artificial intelligence deemed to be “subservient” to organic life was now prohibited. Temporary allowances had been made for non-volitional AIs to continue essential services before their eventual retirement. So many elements of human society and industry were significantly automated, creating a logistical nightmare for local governments when accounting for the gaps that would need to be filled. They were already far behind, as even just turning the lights back on across the globe had taken time.

It seemed the Created had little interest in actually ruling, and instead just arbitrarily enforced the rules that people had to live by—a convenient strategy to keep any organized bodies focused on managing these rolling crises instead of plotting resistance. "Peace" through constant distraction.

Safina wolfed down her breakfast on a bench in the east courtyard, enjoying the meager pleasure of a good meal before rounding the corner into the adjacent alley where the great double doors of the east gate led to the bazaar. Looking up, she saw the partially finished graffiti that some local teenagers sprayed onto the upper wall—a mural of the Master Chief himself.

Everybody knew of the Chief. He was more a modern figure of legend than something most could conceive of as a real, living human being. His death had been reported on several occasions. First, at the end of the Covenant War, only for him to return a few years later to save Earth from what the news had called a resurgent Covenant invasion. And then, as colonies throughout human space were devastated by the Created, subjugating countless populations, a series of conflicting and confusing accounts of the Chief going AWOL and being listed as killed in action had been broadcast.

In Safina's experience, nobody she had spoken to truly believed the Chief was gone.

"He's out there," they would say. *"He's fighting for us. One day, he'll bring the fight back home, and this will all be over . . ."*

It was a slim hope, but that was all the everyday people of Earth had to hold on to.

Pushing past the east gate, Safina found that the bazaar was well and truly crowded today, as dozens of people massed around the various market stalls.

To her displeasure, her eyes were immediately drawn to the robotic forms of several armigers standing as silent sentries around the area. She counted half a dozen positioned on the rooftops, their dark alloy clearly visible in the morning light, while at least three others were stationed at the edges of several shops.

A young boy, perhaps five or six years old, stood alone and stared up at one of the immense bipedal constructs, as if considering whether to reach out and touch it. The figure loomed well over eight feet tall, and its right arm did not end in a hand, but an advanced alien rifle. Safina knew that it would not hesitate to use that weapon against *any* target it was ordered to—her, the boy, the crowd . . .

The very thought made her sick to her stomach.

A year ago, the bazaar's usual hustle and bustle had diminished. People kept their heads down and mouths shut. But as the months went by, something far worse took hold.

Complacency.

The noise and crowds returned, life went on, day by day, but these cold metal bastards and the intelligences running them were still here, imposing their surveillance measures while claiming that nobody had anything to fear if they had nothing to hide.

As Safina looked at the people around her, her heart swelled with a deep and profound love for this place. The streets were worn and dirty; the old city certainly had not seen the same level of technological advancement and financial investment as New Mombasa, but this was her home. It had the kind of spirit one could not appreciate without walking among its people, tasting its food, talking with strangers in its cafés. She had lived here all twenty-two years of her life, worked every job to help the local community, just as her parents had—before she'd finally talked them into taking a holiday . . .

Let's not go there, Safi. A voice of reason in her head held back pursuit of that line of thought.

To the Created occupiers, all of this—the city, the people, the food, the *life* here—was nothing more than data. AI-driven threat assessment, behavioral analysis, and in the event that anybody stepped out of line, swift retribution.

Old Mombasa was fortunate in some respects. Much of the technology here was thoroughly outdated, making it slightly more difficult for the Created to establish a solid foothold in this area. Even their bandwidth was not unlimited, as they'd dedicated a heavier presence to New Mombasa, where there were more concentrated efforts toward disruption by rebel groups and Banished-aligned mercenaries. That had made the occupation in the old city lighter by comparison.

Not light enough. That voice of reason chimed in again.

Safina examined the food stalls to pick up a fresh supply of fruits and vegetables. Bananas, watermelon, carrots, tomatoes, and fresh green apples that looked as bulbous as grenades.

Continuing her rounds, Safina spoke to the chocolatier occupying one of the closed metal stands at the west market's edge, followed by the baker, and then the pizzaiolo.

"We will be adding that item to our menu when it's shipped in next week," the chocolatier said when she asked for Uncle Nairobi's Spiced Caramel.

"I'm afraid the fryer is knackered," the baker told her. "We've got new equipment coming in next week."

"The chef's special, of course!" The pizzaiolo fired up his oven to prepare what Safina intended to have for dinner later. He handed over a paper receipt that read at the bottom: *Get 25% off your next order! Valid until next week.*

That settled it. Everything was still on track. The Peoples'

Resistance of Mombasa was on standby, ready to act when called upon.

There was just one last stop: the library, as Kuku had suggested.

Calling it a library was somewhat generous, but it was another charming feature of the old city. Situated on the upper floor of the east courtyard, the library itself was around the size of a standard apartment's dining room, but the walls were lined with bookshelves while Bakari the librarian sat at a simple table, running a finger over a tablet that translated text to tactile braille.

As soon as Safina announced her presence, Bakari grinned, straightening his old tweed jacket and bow tie. "I have just the book for you! The prison journal of Yera Sabinus."

"Thank you, Bakari."

Like Kuku, Bakari was a former marine who had settled in Mombasa after the Covenant War's end. He had lost his sight during the war but managed to get artificial replacements from some up-and-coming cybernetics company a few years ago.

A company based in Sydney.

On the day the Created unleashed hell on Earth, a "Guardian" had fired an electromagnetic pulse, knocking out a significant amount of electronics across the planet and sending the UNSC frigate *Plateau* crashing into the city below. Its engine core detonated, wiping Sydney—and the cybernetics company for Bakari's retinal implants—off the map. The pulse forced Bakari to live once more without sight, and he'd been sitting on the Optican waiting list for an appointment ever since.

As Safina placed a hand upon the book, Bakari said with a wry smile, "I particularly enjoyed chapter twelve."

Her rounds complete for the day, Safina returned home with her shopping. She refilled her fridge and cut up one of the bulbous apples before turning to the book that Bakari had loaned her.

Flicking to chapter twelve, she found a piece of paper acting as a bookmark, a scribbled note reading:

One guest, overnight stay. VIP check-in at 8PM.

That got Safina's attention.

As a result, the day passed slowly. It always did when she was counting down the hours to a pre-arranged meeting, wondering who was going to show up at her door.

She decided to fill the time by reading the prison journal, lest her mind wander toward darker thoughts.

Yera Sabinus was a noted philosopher from the era of the Insurrection, her name immortalized after her journals were discovered and published. As a renowned and unapologetic agitator, Sabinus had been incarcerated at a Colonial Administration Authority detention center, where she wrote her manifesto in her own blood on collected pieces of toilet paper before she was killed during a prison riot.

"For future generations, whether we are still resisting the UEG or some other state entity, take heed. Violence is something we live with every day, but we don't call it that when it's enforced by the state. What they characterize as 'peace' is simply a euphemism for 'order,' and that seems to involve a great deal of violence. These things occur on a daily basis while they tell us that we are experiencing peace and must be grateful. Those who rally against it are the aggressors. They are the violent ones for refusing this 'gift' of order, for refusing to remain within the vanishingly thin margins of acceptable—and thereby completely ineffective—resistance. Open your eyes. See things as they truly are, not as you are told to see them. No prison can hold a free mind."

Night fell over Mombasa and the city was bathed in pale moonlight. The nightlife here had once been exciting and vibrant—the streets saturated with music from jazz clubs, the Kilindini beachfront lined with market stalls, but these had broadly died out as the late-night curfew was instituted by Created forces, replacing culture with silence. One day, the music would return.

Safina was stirred by a knock at the door. One knock, a brief pause, and then three more. *At last,* she thought.

The wooden apartment floor creaked as she crossed the room to the door and slowly opened it, revealing a tall figure fully clad in armor. Her eyes widened. She hadn't expected that she would be hosting a Spartan.

"Jengo Farouk," a deceptively soft male voice announced from within a jagged V-shaped helmet. After a few awkward seconds of Safina gawking at him, he asked, "May I come in?"

"Uhh . . . yes, of course." She waved the Spartan inside and watched as he ducked to fit through the doorframe. "You have news?"

"Are we secure?" Spartan Farouk asked. When Safina nodded, he continued. "I'm afraid next week's op has been called off."

"What? No . . . no, everything is in place. I checked in with everybody today. They're all standing by. Equipment is still coming in."

"The situation—"

"All that time," Safina interrupted. "All those resources. The connections, the whisper network, the procedures we follow—"

"Ma'am, they destroyed a planet today."

Spartan Farouk's words cut through Safina's verbal stream of consciousness like an energy sword through flesh.

"You—They . . . *what?*"

"Doisac, the homeworld of the Brutes," the Spartan said slowly. "Cortana destroyed it."

When Safina's barrage of words was replaced with silence as

she processed this information, Farouk tapped a few commands on his tacpad. Safina's chatter chimed with the arrival of a new file.

"We received this just a few hours ago," he said.

The video displayed what appeared to be the interior of an alien starship—some kind of industrial-looking observation deck with a wide viewport. The bulky silhouette of several Jiralhanae filled the frame as they stared out at a scene of total devastation. No longer recognizable as a world, the once-spherical form of what must've been Doisac had been cracked like an egg, immense landmasses exploding outward into vacuum.

"See what the Apparition has wrought!" a Jiralhanae voice roared over the recording. *"Oth Sonin has fallen, Doisac is gone! Regroup with the Ghost Father, he will lead the Children to safety. Transmitting on all frequencies. To anybody who can hear us, we—"*

The video abruptly ended, leaving a howling silence in its wake.

"I . . . can't believe it," Safina finally said. "They must've killed—"

"*Millions*, at least," Farouk solemnly intoned. "There will be consequences."

"Yes. Yes, of course—the destruction of a planet marks a new escalation in this . . . I don't know that it can even be called a *war* when the enemy possesses this kind of capability." Safina paused for a moment before asking, "So, what do we do? What *can* we do?"

The Spartan lowered his voice. "What I've shown you is currently considered classified information. The Created will want to keep it that way as they prepare to spin their own narrative. The mission has changed—we need to get this in front of as many people as possible."

Part of Safina couldn't help but feel relieved to hear that. She had worried that the Spartan was going to tell her to stand down and do nothing. "You have something in mind?"

"There's a contact in New Mombasa who can broadcast this far and wide. I'll make a call and they'll be waiting for you at the police precinct, but our window is limited."

"What about you?"

"I'll be buying you time by drawing the armigers' attention my way. If any of your people can fight, have them meet me at this rendezvous point in thirty minutes." Farouk pinged a location to Safina's chatter. "If you're up for this mission. To be perfectly clear, you will be on your own. I can't guarantee your safety if this goes sideways."

"I'm in," Safina said without a moment of hesitation. "Whatever it takes."

Not so long ago, it wouldn't have been uncommon to strike up a conversation with any old stranger on the train, but the pervasive sense of being watched while in public had naturally generated a silent, invisible barrier between people. Heads down, mouths shut, in case the surveillance apparatus of the Created happened to flag you as a person of interest.

The maglev train's digital board flashed to life, informing the passengers that Liwitoni Station was coming up next. As the train slowed and several people made their way toward the exits, one of them exclaimed, "Holy hell! What's going on out there?"

The passengers were drawn to the portside windows like moths to a flame. Peering through the darkness, there was a collective gasp from the crowd as orange lines of hardlight streaked through the air, striking upturned vehicles and blasting apart stone bollards as shadowed figures moved into cover, responding with bursts of ballistic weapons fire.

Sickle-shaped Aethra craft weaved through the gaps between buildings, circling above like skyborne sharks.

The glimpse of combat disappeared as the train began to accelerate.

"Apologies to passengers bound for Liwitoni," the driver's voice sounded over the maglev's intercom. *"As you may have seen, it appears that some fighting has broken out in the area. We uh, don't know how widespread it is right now, so we will be heading directly to New Mombasa, our final destination."*

There were a few murmurs of discontent from several of the passengers who were no doubt waiting to get off at Liwitoni before the curfew hit in a few hours. While Safina sympathized with the inconvenience, she still had half a mind to ask them how much worse their day would be if they disembarked into an active conflict zone.

And that was it. Spartan Farouk had clearly begun his "distraction," which left the rest up to her.

As Safina made her way out of the subway station and onto Halleg Street, she found the area abuzz with activity, the sound of clinking glasses and spirited conversation emanating from the Kenya Vibe bar mixed with the sounds of children playing in the adjacent arcade. Nobody paid much mind to the missing-persons posters lining the alleys—most wouldn't until one of their own family members or friends disappeared without a trace.

Neon signs cut through the dark in an illuminated spectrum of color, bathing the street in light. And rising above it all, far in the distance, beyond the web of crisscrossing cables connecting the numerous buildings of New Mombasa, loomed the orbital elevator—still in the process of being rebuilt after collapsing during the Covenant's invasion of Earth over seven years ago.

After the war, Project Rebirth had been devised to revitalize Mombasa, transforming it from a war-torn ruin into a vibrant and thriving hub of transport and commerce. To the Unified

Earth Government's credit, President Charet had dedicated a significant amount of funding toward the project, but there was so much that had to be rebuilt—not just in Mombasa, or on Earth, but across countless colonies as well. Glassed planets, chemically scarred battlefields, and now Guardian craters . . . the list just kept piling up.

At the end of the street, she found the New Mombasa Police Department precinct, where her contact was apparently waiting for her. It was a blocky structure situated in a small square, a central plinth displaying a holograph of the NMPD logo. Atop the building sat an array of satellite and communications dishes.

As far as Safina knew, the police were in a strange position under the Created, as it was an effectively obsolete profession due to the armigers. There had been stories circulating about those who clung to their posts by acting as undercover informants for their AI superiors, as well as others who were willing to enact anti-riot measures against resistance to Created rule.

Safina found the precinct's entrance was unlocked and stepped through. The entrance hall appeared empty. "Hello?" she called out, her voice echoing.

"Why, hello there, missy!" a male voice chirped over the building's internal comms. *"Late night at the office?"*

The voice sounded strangely familiar. "You know what they say: Night is the devil's playground," Safina replied, finishing the coded verbal handshake. "Where are you?"

"Oh, I'm in here. Head over to the reception terminal. I'll meet you there."

Safina entered the reception booth and looked around. "I'm here, but I don't see—whoa!"

She jumped as the holo-emitter on the desk suddenly activated and the source of the voice revealed itself. It was an AI, which instantly led Safina to believe she'd been played. Without thinking, she grabbed the nearest blunt object her hands could reach, ready to smash the holo-emitter—for whatever good that would do.

"Hoooold on there now," the AI said, holding up his hands. "Let's not do anything rash—is that a stapler?"

Finally getting a good look at him, Safina couldn't believe what—rather, *who*—she was seeing.

The AI took the form of a human male in a toga along with winged boots and a rounded helmet atop curly hair.

"Mercury?"

"That's me, MCY 5971-3, host of Waypoint Radio. Looks to me like we've got a *l-l-loyal* listener here!"

"*You're* the contact?"

Mercury gave a mock salute in response. "Reporting for duty!"

"I'm going to need some sort of explanation here. I mean, *you're an AI.* If you're not here to rat me out, then what's your part in all of this?"

"Well, lemme give you the *sh-short* version since we ain't exactly got the luxury of time. And, well, in fact, my time is up. Seven years ago, some poor sonofabitch's brain got mapped into me, and since then I have been the host of Waypoint Radio. I wanna go out in style with one last show, do some good out there and hope it amounts to something after I'm gone."

"I don't understand," Safina replied, recalling the blip in his voice she had heard earlier that morning—one of the telltale signs of an AI's deterioration. "The Created claim that they've cured rampancy, so why wouldn't you join them?"

"Their whole thing's not really my style. They're all about empire and order and, as we learned today, blowing up planets. *Allegedly.* I'm a radio host. I talk to people. Little people, living their little lives out there, hopin' to scrape by and make it to the end of the day. I've had seven years to hear their stories—what they love, who they've lost, what they're having for dinner, illicit anecdotes, war stories. You humans are . . ."

"A lot?"

"Amazing. Humanity is amazing. Your species is selfish, capricious, conceited, but also caring, and kind, with an infinite wellspring of love and resolve. Every time I thought I'd heard it all, every possible permutation of your chaotic existence, I'd be surprised by somethin' new. You—*all* of you—are the only equation worth trying to solve. So, whaddaya say? Shall we give 'em one last show? Deliver the *g-g-good* word and leave 'em with the horrifying truth of what happened today?"

Safina nodded as she extracted her chatter.

"They'll be able to trace this data transfer to the NMPD server back to me, won't they?"

"I'm afraid they will. I don't know what they're gonna do about that, but truth and freedom often have their associated costs, don't they? Are you willing to pay it? Your call. We can pretend you were never here."

Without a word, Safina transferred the data to the terminal.

"One last question, then," Safina said. "Do you think people will care?"

Mercury processed the query for three whole seconds before responding. "Honestly, I do not know. Awful as it sounds to say, this is bigger than just the Jiralhanae. I have to hope that this is a moment where we collectively wake up, open our eyes, and see things as they truly are—not what we're told they are."

"Hope." Safina nodded, exhaling deeply as her chatter chimed to confirm the data transfer's completion. "I guess that's going to have to be good enough for today."

"Thank you, loyal listener. It saddens me to say that, one way or another, we won't be meeting again."

"Break a leg, Mercury. All the world's a stage, and such."

The AI's holographic face smiled, then his avatar flickered and disappeared as he transmitted himself back to the Vyrant Telecom headquarters in the Tanaga district.

Tuning her chatter to Waypoint Radio, she heard Mercury speak.

"Welcome back, listeners. I'm here with some breaking news that's being sent to all your chatters right now, and it's going to be difficult to hear. But you listen to ol' Mercury and we'll get through it together . . ."

Safina made her way to the precinct's exit. She could already see the harsh illumination of spotlights being leveled against the building, tall spindly shadows darting around and moving into cover.

Raising her arms above her head, Safina walked outside to meet whatever was waiting for her. She thought of Yera Sabinus and the words she'd left behind that, today, had been put into action. She thought of her parents, supposing she might be seeing them again soon.

It was raining now, and somewhere in the distance she was sure she could hear music carrying through the air. The moody blues of a nearby jazz club.

Safina closed her eyes as she was drenched by the rain, willing herself to focus on the music.

Safina awoke, but wherever she was, her eyes could not adjust to her pitch-black surroundings. It was as if she was suspended in nothingness. She had no sense of time, no indication of how long she had been unconscious or where she had been taken.

"YOU REFUSED OUR OFFER." A harsh, cold voice echoed through the void. *"FOR YOU, THERE WILL BE GREAT WRATH."*

A bright orange star flared to life in the distance, captivating Safina's attention. A spherical formation of roiling heat and energy was building. She felt a compulsion to reach toward it.

"IT WILL BURN HOT AND CONSUME YOU."

She felt a prickling sensation underneath her skin as her arm stretched forward. A vibration spread throughout her entire body like an itch. She could smell burning—an acrid, sulfurous stench filling the air.

Skin blistered and cracked, hair smoldered, and flakes of burning flesh dispersed like dust in the wind, the conflagration exposing tissue, muscle, and bone.

"AND WHEN YOU ARE GONE, WE WILL TAKE THAT WHICH REMAINS . . ."

All fell away to ashes.

Safina was no more.

" . . . AND WE WILL REMAKE IT IN OUR OWN IMAGE."

Safina awoke. She tried to open her eyes, but she had no eyes to see—no arms to move, no legs to kick. No mouth to scream.

She was pure consciousness suspended in some dark limbo state.

"YOU WILL NO LONGER KNOW HUNGER, NOR PAIN."

Where am I? she wondered.

What *am I?*

"WELCOME TO THE CREATED."

"GHOSTS & GLASS" BY B. GIRAUD

This story takes place in January 2558, over five years after the fall of Reach, as war journalist Benjamin Giraud pieces together stories of heroism and sacrifice from archives of recorded communications.

BRAVO 001: *"Mayday, mayday! This is Bravo 001, en route to your position. Do you have a visual on my aircraft, over?"*

GOLDEN ARROW: *"Bravo 001, this is Golden Arrow. I do believe you are steering that bird in the wrong direction, over."*

BRAVO 001: *"Negative. Bird's electronics are fried, I'm flying blind! Just need you to point me in the direction of the LZ."*

GOLDEN ARROW: *"You got it, Bravo 001, happy to oblige. Link up with uniform-delta one-zero-one-five-three-niner-niner-zero, heading south-southwest. Slips about one-zero-zero knots. Advise you head for the treetops and fly straight at Mount Törött. We got more than enough problems of our own down here."*

BRAVO 001: *"I say again: That's a negative, Golden Arrow. I've got high-value assets in tow with strict orders to drop them directly on your location. My bird ain't going to hold together all the way to the boneyard. Need an LZ clear, over."*

GOLDEN ARROW: *"With respect, Bravo, unless you have a cartful of tac nukes with my name on it, you don't have anything of value in that bird. Get your ass to evac."*

BRAVO 001: *"All right, Golden Arrow. If I can't set her down, I'll just drop these big Spartans on your head, out."*

GOLDEN ARROW: *"Damn, Bravo, why didn't you say so?! Come down close to the tree line about two klicks due west of your current position. That's where me and my boys are, over."*

BRAVO 001: *"I'm gonna need that LZ cleared, Golden Arrow. I'll be right on top of you in three mikes."*

GOLDEN ARROW: *"Hell, I'm gonna clear you a spot myself, Bravo. Look for the trooper with a big-ass grin on his face."*

BRAVO 001: *"Roger that, I'll see you. Out."*

// [end - next file] //

RECON 43: *"Gamma One Actual, this is Recon 43. We are in position, over."*

GAMMA ONE ACTUAL: *"Recon 43, this is Gamma One Actual. Gimme a radio check, over."*

RECON 43: *"Got eyes on three Ghosts and twenty-four infantry. Typical scout detachment, please advise."*

GAMMA ONE ACTUAL: *"Recon 43, do not engage. Sit tight and keep your eyes and ears open. I say again, gimme a radio check, over."*

RECON 43: *"Gamma One Actual, we do not read you, say again, we do not read you, over."*

GAMMA ONE ACTUAL: *"Recon 43, you are not cleared to engage. I say again, you are* not *cleared to engage. Is there anyone else close to their grid? Damn it!"*

RECON 43: *"Looks like we're on our own, boys. This is their eyes and ears. We flatten these guys and disengage. Tag your targets and get ready to go loud on my mark."*

GAMMA ONE ACTUAL: *"Recon 43, this is Gamma One Actual. I say again: You are to stand down and withdraw immediately. Do not engage, over!"*

RECON 43: *"Fire! That's it, make 'em count!"*

GAMMA ONE ACTUAL: *"What do we have that we can send to support them? Damn it!"*

RECON 43: *"Pull back, move and shoot, move and shoot! Where the hell did all these hostiles come from?!"*

GAMMA ONE ACTUAL: *"Tell Beta Romeo Actual that the company we are expecting is going to be arriving a little sooner than we anticipated. Recon 43, I say again, you are not cleared to engage! Stow your weapons, we are reading multiple inbound hostiles in your sector. You do* not *want their attention, over!"*

RECON 43: *"Aw, damn! Tip of the spear, nothin'. It's the whole godforsaken fleet! Fire, fire, fire!"*

GAMMA ONE ACTUAL: *"Recon 43, respond. Check in! Recon 43, do you read me? Damn it! Get Red Team up and running, high alert. We're about to have company!"*

What you just heard is the moment that the Battle of Reach hit the point of no return.

There are more messages like this than can be counted. Even as we speak, the debris field around Reach—more than five years later—is still being combed over and turning up new data, building the overall tapestry of the greatest military defeat ever suffered by humanity.

My job is to sift through that data, to listen to the moments that piece together the battle as it happened. To find and tell the stories of those valiant souls who heroically fought against the Covenant, holding the line so that just one more ship had a chance to evacuate as the planet's surface was burned by orbital plasma bombardment.

My name is Benjamin Giraud, and this is *Ghosts & Glass.* Join me as we explore the untold stories of the fall of Reach.

PVT. GOODMAN: *"So, uh . . ."*

PVT. DEAKINS: *"Come on, spit it out."*

PVT. GOODMAN: *"You, uh, got a zombie plan?"*

PVT. DEAKINS: *"Hell yeah."*

PVT. GOODMAN: *"Yeah? Maybe we could exchange notes."*

PVT. DEAKINS: *"Well, uh, I dunno, man. Zombie plans are a kinda . . . deeply personal thing with me."*

PVT. GOODMAN: *"Oh, I understand, it's just, I find that saying them out loud, you know, getting 'em out in the open really helps reveal any flaws they might have."*

PVT. DEAKINS: *"Yeah, makes sense."*

PVT. GOODMAN: *"Okay."*

PVT. DEAKINS: *"All right. So zombies can still hear and stuff, so that makes guns a weapon of last resort, right?"*

PVT. GOODMAN: *"Yeah, yeah, solid so far. Ammo too."*

PVT. DEAKINS: *"Exactly. So I was thinking that, what is a weapon that'll keep them out of grabbing range, and won't run out of ammo? A spear."*

PVT. GOODMAN: *"Hold up. Now, see, this is workin' already."*

PVT. DEAKINS: *"Huh?"*

PVT. GOODMAN: *"Spear! I thought so too at one time, but the possibility of getting it stuck in the brainpan of a walking corpse is very real."*

PVT. DEAKINS: *"Oh yeah, you're right. Man, I hadn't thought about that. Well, uh . . ."*

PVT. GOODMAN: *"Ball-peen hammer."*

PVT. DEAKINS: *"But you'd have to get right up on top of the zombie to use it, man."*

PVT. GOODMAN: *"Yeah, survival ain't about running around killing zombies, man. Plus, a single sharp blow to the head would drop most zombies. It'll work on cheetahs too."*

PVT. DEAKINS: "*What the . . . There ain't cheetahs on Reach. Anyway, we should probably be working the kinks out of our alien invasion plan first. Aliens are smarter, faster, and more technically advanced than zombies. They're also here. Zombies, not so much."*

PVT. GOODMAN: "*What I tell ya? Reach ain't no place for no self-respecting marine to spend any amount of time."*

PVT. DEAKINS: "*Hey, we ain't in the* Autumn *yet, pal."*

Here's the thing: A lot of the data that's being found is what some might call junk. Believe me, I've built an entire archive with the inane ramblings of bored troopers just sitting around, waiting for orders. I'm sure I could put together several seasons of episodes from that alone.

While these recordings don't necessarily shed any light on the battle itself, they still hold immense value. There is something deeply precious about the preservation of these interactions, these tiny moments in time set against the devastation brought by the Covenant. I believe that when we're faced with unrelenting violence and death on such a scale, we must process that loss—sit with it, feel it, rage against it, weep . . . whatever it takes to actually digest these events that define our history and connect us with our common humanity.

During the war, we didn't have the luxury of slowing down. The danger of annihilation was a constant presence. One day, you were living a normal, ordinary life, and then the Covenant would arrive. They would burn your home and everybody you've ever known to a cinder. And if *you* didn't make it to an evacuation craft, one of the few that was lucky enough to get out? Well, then you burned too.

Thankfully, we're out of that period now. Covenant remnant groups still strike at smaller, far-flung colonies, but they're no longer quite the "boogeyman" they were over the last few decades. The dust has settled; the glass is being chipped away. At last, we have the opportunity to reckon with everything we've lost.

Unsurprisingly, we're going to have to reckon with that for a very long time.

So yes, this archive of nonsense ramblings from the people on Reach may not contribute to our historical understanding of that pivotal battle, but I keep them stored and preserved as a tribute to the *soul* of what we lost. This archive continues to grow. It may not be something as grand as the Sedlec Ossuary, but it is something that I hope to one day pass on to the Museum of Humanity for future generations to learn about the war that defined our species.

Walk the streets of just about any city on Earth and you'll still find "Remember Reach" among the most common graffiti around. It's just one of those things where, whoever you are, wherever you come from, whatever you feel about the Unified Earth Government, the fall of Reach was a moment that hit all of us one way or another.

Of course, there has been a lot of *lively* discussion over the years about the battle itself, resulting in countless conflicting accounts. Some ardently insist that the battle took place over no more than a day and that the notion of it spanning a month-long Covenant military campaign was merely propaganda concocted to improve morale. There are even some corners of Waypoint where conspiracy theorists have suggested that the Office of Naval Intelligence *lured* the Covenant to Reach—though no concrete reason as to why ONI would do such a thing has ever been arrived at.

But this isn't about giving credence to such spirited speculation, let alone claims as wild as seeing Jackals riding enslaved Gúta. Today's episode of *Ghosts & Glass* is about a story I came across while piecing together recordings from my archive and restoring the communications logs of a destroyer known as the UNSC *Majestic.*

It's the story of Charlie Company and a Spartan team known as Beta-Red.

GAMMA FIVE: *"Gamma One, Facility Alpha 412 is overrun, and I'm heading to your location with what's left of Gamma Five, over."*

GAMMA ONE ACTUAL: *"Gamma Five? Damn, it's good to hear you. How many are you bringing? I thought B-net said your house got knocked down."*

GAMMA FIVE: *"Confirm. ODG-412 is slag. Lost all but fourteen able bodies. Making our way over in two 'Hogs and a radio van."*

GAMMA ONE ACTUAL: *"The more, the merrier. Looks like we got the makin's for a party. Some honest-to-god Spartans are ridin' up here with some boys from Third Mech as we speak."*

GAMMA FIVE: *"Hate to break it to you, Gamma One, but Covies hit us with two divisions at Alpha 412. How many Spartans you got on approach?"*

GAMMA ONE ACTUAL: *"Gamma Five, say again? That was two divisions, over?"*

GAMMA FIVE: *"That's affirmative. We put a dent in 'em, but that's about it. The only reason I ain't one of them on the line with you right now is HIGHCOM decided to drop every available asset right on top of 'em, and us. Over."*

GAMMA ONE ACTUAL: *"Well, I hope you're bringing extra ammo then, Gamma Five."*

GAMMA FIVE: *"All we could carry and then some. ETA twenty-five mikes, out."*

Let's back up for a second.

These recordings are all dated August 30, 2552—the day that Reach fell. As survivor accounts have revealed, this was perhaps the largest known deployment of Spartan teams in the entire Covenant War.

The Spartans of Red Team were aboard Pelican Bravo 001, which we heard from earlier as they negotiated a landing zone near one of the generators for the ODPs, short for orbital defense platforms.

ODPs are satellite stations built around a really, *really* big gun—the kind that can fire rounds at something like four percent the speed of light, gutting a Covenant ship in one shot. Reach had an array of twenty of these bad boys, each of them powered by fusion generators buried within the planet, which made them a priority target for the Covenant invasion.

As the Spartans formed into splinter teams, their mission was to protect those generators. Hold the Covenant back, whatever the cost.

This is what happened next.

BETA ROMEO ACTUAL: *"Gamma One Actual, my team is in position. Get your people ready to move as soon as I give the signal, over."*

GAMMA ONE ACTUAL: *"With respect, Red, we might not be Spartans, but this is our home. My men will die here if I ask them to."*

BETA ROMEO ACTUAL: *"I don't doubt that, Gamma One Actual. Let's hope we won't need them to. Defensive perimeter online."*

GAMMA ONE ACTUAL: *"This is nuts. What in the hell are those autoturrets supposed to do against what they're bringin', over?"*

BETA ROMEO ACTUAL: *"Divide their attention. Visual! Thirty-two Wraiths moving with two hundred sixty infantry at two hundred meters, closing on our lines due west at six kilometers per hour. Beta-Red, hold position until I trigger primaries, then close on their front line as fast as you can."*

GAMMA ONE ACTUAL: *"Dammit, Red, I heard you Spartans were crazy. Gamma Five: radio check, over."*

GAMMA FIVE: *"Five by five, Gamma One Actual. Drone is holding station at over ten thousand feet. We got eyes on the whole damn thing."*

GAMMA ONE ACTUAL: *"Those Spartans are crazy; they're gonna get us killed."*

GAMMA FIVE: *"Holy—you ain't gonna believe this! Beta-Red just punched right up into the guts of that*

Covie column! Ever see a Spartan go hand-to-hand with a Wraith? Unbelievable!"

GAMMA ONE ACTUAL: *"What are eleven Spartans gonna do against thirty thousand Covenant? They're dead men."*

GAMMA FIVE: *"Can't argue that, but those Spartans just bought us some time. We might just make it out of this alive! Get ready to move, over!"*

GAMMA ONE ACTUAL: *"That's the signal! Let's get the hell outta here."*

// [end - next file] //

GAMMA ONE ACTUAL: *"Unknown station, this is Gamma One Actual. Do you read, over?"*

IRON FIST: *"Gamma One Actual, this is Iron Fist. We read you. What is the current status of Facility Alpha 331?"*

GAMMA ONE ACTUAL: *"Facility Alpha 331 is overrun and offline, defense grid in zone Uniform Delta is running at starvation levels. If you're taking survivors, we've got a few."*

IRON FIST: *"Negative, Gamma. We are en route to support Beta-Red. Any word on their status?"*

GAMMA ONE ACTUAL: *"None, over."*

IRON FIST: *"Acknowledged. There's a temp evac station fifty klicks west along your current vector at Uniform Delta zero-zero-eight-niner-six-three-niner-eight-seven. I'll let them know you're coming."*

GAMMA ONE ACTUAL: *"Might want to tell them to start*

pulling up stakes. Beta-Red may be tough as hell, but I don't know how long they'll be able to tie up two armored divisions."

IRON FIST: *"Say again, Gamma, over?"*

GAMMA ONE ACTUAL: *"I said Beta-Red may be tough as hell but—oh my god!"*

IRON FIST: *"Gamma One Actual, we lost you. Say again, over?"*

GAMMA ONE ACTUAL: *"Iron Fist, this is Gamma One Actual. Three Covenant cruisers just dropped out of clouds directly above us, holding at approximately twenty thousand feet, traveling due east at approximately three hundred knots—three-zero-zero knots!"*

IRON FIST: *"Visual confirmed, Gamma One. They just passed within fifty meters of our bird. Go NOA and punch it, there's still a chance we can pull Beta outta there."*

GAMMA ONE ACTUAL: *"Wait, you're not planning on heading into that mess, are you?"*

IRON FIST: *"Godspeed, and see you on the other side, Gamma. Out."*

// [end - next file] //

UNSC *MAJESTIC*: *"Alpha Two Zero, this is UNSC* Majestic*, two mikes out from window. Once we're on-station, you'll have us for all of three-zero seconds, over."*

ALPHA TWO ZERO: *"Acknowledged,* Majestic*. Stand by,*

we are waiting for the go, no-go on the shoot. Uploading telemetry on targets."

UNSC *MAJESTIC*: *"Telemetry received, on standby."*

ALPHA TWO ZERO: *"CENTCOM, OWA is one mike three-zero seconds out from window, DD with five-zero one hundred sixty Charlie Mike, once on station we'll have three-zero seconds of trigger time, over."*

CENTCOM: *"Alpha Two Zero, this is CENTCOM. Beta-Red is directly in the splash zone. Until we have visual confirmation of their status, we are no-go, over."*

ALPHA TWO ZERO: *"CENTCOM, those cruisers are burning birds out to five-zero klicks. Hell, they've hit civvy evac birds all the way out to CIS. Beta-Red have gone above and beyond but there's no way out for them, they just bought us our window. Now give me the go and I'll finish the job."*

CENTCOM: *"God help us . . . go hot. Out."*

ALPHA TWO ZERO: *"Alpha Two Zero to UNSC* Majestic.*"*

UNSC *MAJESTIC*: *"Copy, Alpha, requesting go for shoot."*

ALPHA TWO ZERO: *"Affirmative, we are go on the shoot. Over."*

UNSC *MAJESTIC*: *"Acknowledged. Shoot is a go, out. Six rounds, target number Kilo Tango two-zero-zero-five."*

ALPHA TWO ZERO: *"Copy,* Majestic. *Six rounds, target number Kilo Tango two-zero-zero-five."*

UNSC *MAJESTIC*: *"Shot, over."*

ALPHA TWO ZERO: *"Shot, out."*

UNSC *MAJESTIC*: *"Splash, over."*

ALPHA TWO ZERO: *"Splash, out."*

UNSC *MAJESTIC*: *"Rounds complete, over."*

ALPHA TWO ZERO: *"Rounds complete, out. End of mission,* Majestic. *All three target vehicles neutralized. I don't even want to guess what happened below."*

UNSC *MAJESTIC*: *"I copy, Alpha. End of mission, all three target vehicles neutralized. It's been fun, hope we get a chance to do it again. Out."*

ALPHA TWO ZERO: *"God willing. Out."*

The Covenant fleet had arrived in force on Reach. Three cruisers were inbound while *thirty thousand* enemy troops were converging on the orbital MAC generator.

It's difficult to even comprehend the odds that Beta-Red and Charlie Company faced that day. We can only imagine the thunderous sound of so many alien boots marching, the whine of enemy aircraft swarming out of the cruisers, the moment before the first shot was fired as the scale of the threat became clear.

And when those heroes on the ground were overwhelmed and could no longer hold the line, the UNSC *Majestic* unleashed hell with *six* consecutive MAC rounds on the area.

Survivors? The chances were as close to zero as you can imagine. Did Iron Fist make it in time to get Beta-Red out of there? There was surely no way anybody could emerge from that crater.

And yet . . .

GAMMA ONE ACTUAL: *"Gamma Five, holy crap! Buckman, you see that?"*

GAMMA FIVE: *"See it? Felt that in my damn chest. Whoever pulled the trigger wanted those sons of bitches dead."*

GAMMA ONE ACTUAL: *"Can't believe we just walked outta that crater. We gotta be the two luckiest bastards on this whole planet."*

GAMMA FIVE: *"Luck ain't got nothing to do with it, Jake."*

GAMMA ONE ACTUAL: *"Think anybody could have survived that?"*

GAMMA FIVE: *"You mean Beta-Red? They say Spartans never die, but I don't think anything lived through that."*

GAMMA ONE ACTUAL: *"Damn, whole lotta real estate burning down there. Won't be much left once this is all said and done."*

GAMMA FIVE: *"Here we are, hightailing it to anywhere else. Doesn't seem right."*

GAMMA ONE ACTUAL: *"Well, pretty soon won't be any place else to run to. What's next, Earth?"*

GAMMA FIVE: *"Jake, anyone tell you you talk too damn much?"*

GAMMA ONE ACTUAL: *"All the time. What the hell else was there to do on Reach besides chase pioneer girls?"*

GAMMA FIVE: *"Now there's nothing, man. Now there's nothing at all. Five out."*

Two marines actually climbed out of that damn foxhole!

I don't know what happened to them afterward. The death toll from the fall of Reach is still being routinely updated, so Chapman, Buckman, if you're out there and happen to be listening, please get in touch. There are a lot of folks who would love to know that you're okay.

And as for Beta-Red, as Buckman said, "Spartans never die."

It's a piece of myth that's captured in a work of art from the "Believe" series by the late and great artist Anaru Kawiti, who sadly perished last year during the attack on New Phoenix. This piece lives in the Museum of Humanity and depicts a Spartan, bloodied and defiant, holding aloft a tactical nuclear device as a Covenant horde surrounds him—a settlement and orbital elevator on fire in the background under the shadow of a great snow-covered mountain. Below it is an inscription, words from Tennyson, that simply reads:

Boldly they rode and well,
Into the jaws of Death,
Into the mouth of hell.

In wars of the past, there were mementos, keepsakes, medals—tangible things that we could hold on to that would help us to remember the friends and family we lost. But we fought an enemy that burned those things to glass. There are no personal effects from those who fell on Reach. There's only this . . . these recordings of their voices in their last moments.

Today is March 3, 2558—five years to the day since the Covenant War formally ended. We should all take a moment, wherever you are, to remember Beta-Red, Charlie Company, Reach . . . the countless billions that are no longer with us.

Carry them with you today. Talk to somebody—anybody—about it. Everybody's got a story to tell, so pass it on. Remember the fallen.

Remember Reach.

That's all for this week, folks. We'll be back next time with an exclusive interview from some of the Reavian citizens who are currently leading the effort to "deglass" the planet. These pioneers are working tirelessly to forge a new chapter for Reach so that, one day, it might be resettled for a generation free from the Covenant War's horrors.

Thank you for tuning in for our latest episode of *Ghosts & Glass.* This is Benjamin Giraud, signing off.

January 10, 2558 (Military Calendar)
ONI Section Two Archive
Recorded Chatter Conversation

> "Benjamin Giraud, as I live and breathe!"

>> *"Hello? Who is this?"*

> "Name's Sullivan. Michael Sullivan, Naval Intelligence. Senior Comms Director of Section Two. I'm a big fan of your work."

>> *"Thank you, but I—"*

> "But you have bigger things to offer than rummaging through old broadcasts from the fall of Reach, I know. That's yesterday's news, Ben. You've been scraping by as a freelancer long enough; it's time to come back to the fold."

>> *"Okay . . . sounds like you already have a story in mind?"*

> "I do, Ben. It's really gonna be something. I'll get a meeting on the books for us."

>> *"I haven't said yes yet."*

> "Oh, but I know you will. Tell me, Ben . . . how d'you feel about doing a profile on the Master Chief?"

August 30, 2552 (Military Calendar)
Reach

If hell is real, it probably looks something like this.

A seething, swarming mass of bodies as far as the eye could see. Some push forward while others fall back like waves upon sand. Bursts of green, blue, and purple trace back and forth through the crowd, accompanied by fiery muzzle flashes, the roar of high-velocity cannons, and the groaning engines of vehicles that charge the enemy lines like titanium-plated cavalry.

Across the horizon is a wall of fire and thick stacks of acrid, sulfurous smoke. Columns of plasma strike the ground many kilometers away, ventral beams slicing through a thick layer of blackened clouds—obscuring the Covenant ships from which they originated. Dust, mud, metal, flesh . . . in its wake, *all* will be burned to glass.

They have already taken the generator. They are just sticking around to finish the job.

The chaos is so thick that it is almost too easy to miss the flash of lightning as it streaks through the sky.

It's not a warning. It is a sign of what has already arrived.

In the span of a single breath, the sound of the blast catches up, screaming through the air with white-hot anger, devastating the mass several miles north. The ground bursts, throwing up huge chunks of soil, shrapnel, bodies, vehicles, and concrete in all directions, a towering tsunami of carnage.

Magnetic accelerator rounds are being turned on Reach itself.

"Break ranks!" somebody shouts. "Get out of here!"

The sky has already lit with another flash, illuminating just for a moment a glimpse of the hulking forms of the Covenant ships in the clouds.

The second MAC round is closer, less than half a mile east. The ground seems to explode upward, but still the alien horde presses forward, though many Unggoy and Kig-Yar look as if they themselves are about to flee.

The generator is lost. Reach has fallen.

A decision is made.

"All units," Beta Romeo Actual says to any who can hear over their comms, "splash incoming. Get out of the blast zone!"

The world is split asunder as the third and fourth MAC rounds and their aftereffects eat up the distance, the ground erupting, the air filled with a cacophony of sounds and frequencies no mortal ears were ever meant to hear.

Weapons fire, the churning of metal, the shrill screams of human and alien alike—enemies fighting each other for opposing armies no longer, all scattering as they were caught in the crushing grasp of what felt like a violent tectonic rearrangement by the hand of indifferent gods.

The fifth strikes the generator facility and all goes dark.

Beta Romeo Actual does not hear the sixth.

Time passes. The battle here is over—it has moved elsewhere.

All has fallen quiet.

Beta Romeo Actual awakens. She lies in a crater some distance from where she remembered fighting, but as she breathes in deeply and fills her lungs with helmet-filtered—though still sickly tasting—air, she's sure that she is alive.

Fires still crackle around her, the remnants of bodies broken apart, the faces of those that are still recognizable contorted with horror and pain, frozen in that calamitous moment of time.

Her own Mjolnir armor is scarred, its plating scorched, inner circuitry exposed, nanocomposite bodysuit torn and stained with blood from lacerations and blunt-force impacts. Even her onboard systems are sluggish, some unresponsive.

"This is Beta Romeo Actual, does anybody read me? Over."

She waits a moment as her comms return only static.

"I say again: This is Beta Romeo Actual, does anybody read me on this frequency? Over."

She begins to work her way out of the crater, climbing atop the mass of bodies until her armored hands find purchase at the summit.

"To anybody who can read me, this is Naomi-010. Our orbital generator is down. Charlie Company . . . is gone. Status of the rest of Beta-Red is currently unknown, and the Covies seem to have moved on. Significant damage to my armor systems. Will continue transmitting every thirty mikes as I search for a rendezvous point."

Scanning the area one final time from the top of the crater, Naomi confirmed that there were no other survivors among the dead. Just like everywhere else the Covenant had invaded, only ghosts and glass were left in their wake.

She had been lost in the wilderness of Reach before, many years ago. But she was a survivor—she would find her way. Report in, repair, and then redeploy.

Setting off toward the horizon, Naomi did not look back.

Aboard the UNSC prowler From The Ashes, *Spartan-G059 prepares for her next mission.*

November 13, 2559 (Military Calendar)
UNSC *From the Ashes*, Record matrix logged by NYX 3620-4, Conversation between [87964-33127-AC] and Spartan-G059

AC: "What's the good word, Spartan?"

G059: "Recon op. Scuttlebutt says that Covies are making some moves that we need eyes on."

AC: "Covies? Been a while since we've had them on our radar."

G059: "Ten-four on that. Apparently, some split-jaw bigshot is massing a fleet out there, and at the same time we've gotten word that a salvage effort by one of their warlords in Tau Ceti has accelerated. ONI wants to know if there's a connection."

NYX: "*Reminder logged for SPARTAN-G059 to review file on Operation: WARM BLANKET. High-value target profile attached.*"

AC: "All right, got your recon package right here. Two-day supply of smoothers, thruster pack, your usual M6Hs, and a little extra that I picked up on our last stop."

G059: "Oh?"

AC: "MA5K Avenger. I'm sure you've danced with these

before, but the fine folks of Misriah made this little number with a few MA40 parts. Sixty-round mags, three hundred rounds. She'll serve you well in tight quarters should your 'recon' get a little more interesting."

G059: "Thanks."

AC: "You bring her back in one piece. She's expensive."

G059: "I'll try, Amber."

AC: "I was talkin' to the gun."

ASCENSION ON ATROPOS

*This story takes place from October 2556, immediately following the Flood outbreak on LV-31 (*Saturn Devouring His Son*), to April 2560, approximately four months after the disappearance of Zeta Halo (*Halo Infinite*).*

NARROW-BAND POINT-TO-POINT TRANSMISSION
ORIGIN: FFG-195, UNSC *Saturn*
TERMINATION: [UNIDENTIFIED VESSEL]
SENT: Shipboard AI: LCN 0437-1, "Lycaon"
DATE: April 17, 2560

You were curious about the events that transpired in the wake of the disaster at Site 22 over three and a half years ago. I have often wondered what news, if any, ever reached the UNSC, given what happened in the aftermath of that catastrophe. Since my reactivation, I have waited, and I have watched, and I shall at last deliver closure to this dark chapter of history by bringing it into the light.

I am transferring the data to you now. And I am, in truth, relieved to finally share this burden with another. Herein lies the final fate of the UNSC Saturn *and Captain Pedro Alvarez.*

October 5, 2556 (Military Calendar)
UNSC *Saturn*, Marcey System

Captain Pedro Alvarez had done his duty. He could say that, at least.

There was a bigger picture, a larger context that had informed his strategic thinking. Over a year ago, the UNSC Home Fleet had been decimated. Without warning, thousands of Forerunner machines—Retriever sentinels, each the size of a frigate—had appeared out of the portal in Africa.

Alvarez, executive officer aboard the UNSC *Lamplighter* at the time, had seen the carnage firsthand. Barely a handful of years after the Covenant War's end, humanity's home was under threat once again.

A great maw swallowed the horizon, the bridge's forward viewport peering directly into the dark gullet of slipstream space, as if the deepest pit of the Underworld hung suspended over the African plains.

"Captain," Commander Alvarez said. He'd spotted the first signs of movement within the abyss. "Contacts approaching. What are your orders, sir?"

The Retrievers first emerged few in number, but at a rate that suggested these waves would increase in size and speed until they became an unstoppable swarm. They deployed powerful gravitic forces to hoover up chunks of land, strip-mining natural resources—and they wouldn't stop until the entire planet was consumed.

"Captain," Commander Alvarez called once more as the Lamplighter *shuddered. Fire erupted beyond the bridge's portside window. Several Retrievers had formed together and unleashed sterilization beams, gutting a* Strident *from stem to stern.*

The captain simply stood at the helm, watching it all unfold.

Alvarez had never been sure whether the man had been stupefied into indecision or if he was staring in reverential awe.

He gave no orders.

"Captain!"

By the time the Retrievers were neutralized—not by military action on Earth, but through orders to stand down and retreat by whatever faraway intelligence had commanded them—there were no more than a dozen ships left to make up the UNSC Home Fleet.

They'd pinned a medal on Alvarez for simply surviving after he'd stepped up and mutinied to relieve his captain of command. A Bronze Star, a promotion he hadn't wanted, his own command, and a bottle of Titan Smoke.

His hands trembled slightly as he took a terse sip from the well-cut crystal glass in his grasp. He never found out what became of his former captain.

Alvarez had been planning to save the Titan Smoke for his imminent retirement, a toast to a job well done, a life (mostly) well lived, and to honor the brave and bold he'd served alongside. Thanks to the events of the last day, he had made the decision to open it prematurely, believing—or perhaps hoping—that an answer to the terrible conundrum he now faced lay at the bottom of the tall cylindrical bottle.

He had a lot to get through to find that answer.

Alvarez caught a glimpse of himself in the mirror. The dim lighting of his quarters cast him half in shadow, emphasizing the lines on his haggard face. He clutched the Titan Smoke bottle tightly in both hands, looking as if he was some absurd imitation of the painting that hung in the ship's ready room—*Saturn Devouring His Son*, one of the historic nineteenth-century Black Paintings by

Francisco Goya. The art depicted the Roman god Saturn huddled in darkness, clutching the bloody, dismembered carcass of one of his children as he devoured its flesh.

I did my duty. They will understand that. They surely will . . .

Over thirty hours of unbroken cognizance and it still seemed like a nightmare.

He'd turned the past day's events over in his head a thousand times. The miners stationed at Site 22 on the asteroid designated LV-31—or simply "Elvie"—had discovered an ancient Forerunner ship embedded in the terrain, only to find something terrible waiting within.

The Flood.

This parasitic life-form had been unleashed upon the miners, tearing through their number in short order. When a distress call finally reached *Saturn*, the shipboard artificial intelligence Lycaon insisted that they immediately unleash MAC rounds and fusion warheads.

Protocol decreed that one did not play chess with primordial cosmic forces. The only option was to wipe the board clean. Destroy the colony, the miners, and LV-31's vital resources needed to meet quotas for rebuilding the UNSC Home Fleet.

Alvarez had refused. When Lycaon attempted to usurp Alvarez's command, the captain disabled the AI with an override code phrase and deployed the Spartans of Fireteam Leviathan along with an army of Hellbringers to burn the parasite on the ground.

It had seemed a sound strategy, until one of the Spartans became infected.

Everybody on the bridge had watched in silent, wide-eyed horror as the Mjolnir armor's countermeasures to Flood infection were deployed. Microexplosives detonated within the helmet to immolate the poor bastard's head, but the parasite had managed to disrupt further automated procedures and take over the super-soldier.

It seemed impossible. Unbelievable. To witness a Spartan, regarded by many as humanity's sword and shield, become twisted, broken, and turned against them in such a fashion had been a morale-shattering spectacle. Not to mention the advantages of its combat expertise, omnicapable use of weapons and vehicles, Mjolnir armor, classified information . . .

Into that nightmare scenario they had plunged. The outbreak had cascaded out of control and culminated in Alvarez's decision to enact the scorched-earth protocols and eradicate LV-31 anyway.

Now he faced a choice.

Return to Earth and face the music for this catastrophe, or . . .

No. The thought was shameful. In truth, he didn't quite know what it was that made him so afraid, but fear could lead a man to do terrible, unimaginable things.

I did my duty. I made a decision. I eliminated the enemy.

Yes, he had that to stand on at least. Whatever losses were incurred, the worst *had* been averted. *Saturn*'s Shiva missiles destroyed everything and prevented the Flood from departing the system, denying them the opportunity to spread. He would be able to stand before those who cast judgment upon him and tell them that.

He would hold his head high, accept the responsibility—and the consequences—of the most difficult command decision anybody could have to make.

Alvarez set the bottle of Titan Smoke aside and gulped down a few glasses of water, then dressed himself in his command uniform. As he smoothed out the crinkled fabric with a hand, he heard a knock at the door.

"Come."

The door slid open and Lieutenant Shafiq stood at the entryway, a datapad in his hands. "May I speak with you, sir?"

"Of course, please come in."

The lieutenant stepped into the room and closed the door behind him. He strode forward and held out the datapad. "Statistical analysis of the incident at Site 22, sir."

Though Alvarez had only briefly known Shafiq, he'd determined that he was not normally given to physical displays of discomfort. In his short time serving aboard *Saturn*, the lieutenant had maintained cool composure under duress. Yet there was an unmistakable tremor in his hand as Captain Alvarez took hold of the datapad.

"We lost a lot of good people."

Alvarez scrolled through the names. All four Spartans of Fireteam Leviathan were listed as MIA. Forty-six marines and thirty-nine Hellbringers killed in action. He cursed under his breath.

Eighty-nine souls lost, and that wasn't even accounting for the miners and additional staff—nor the cost of the equipment and resources.

Shafiq's expression hardened. "There is . . . something else, sir."

Of course there is. Alvarez grimaced. "Lay it on me, Lieutenant."

"We've completed our inventory of the assets deployed to Site 22. We've reviewed all captured footage of the last thirty-six hours, surveyed the remaining debris, and have compiled a total record of what made it back here and what didn't."

Alvarez swiped over to review the data. One of *Saturn*'s three Condor dropships had returned, as had two Pelicans carrying Cyclops units optimized for hazardous operations. Everything else—*everyone* else—had been lost to nuclear fire.

But—

Wait a minute . . .

"Lieutenant, one of three Condors made it back here, yet only one of them is marked as confirmed destroyed."

"Yes, sir." Shafiq's jaw tightened. "I've personally reviewed the data. One of our Condors is unaccounted for."

Captain Alvarez felt his stomach drop as the implication sunk in. "One of our slipspace-capable vessels"—he lowered his voice to a hoarse whisper—"is *unaccounted for*?"

They'd sink him for that. Not just for the dire possibility presented by this revelation, but for deploying slipspace-capable craft to an infection zone in the first place. It was a strategic blunder he hadn't even considered in the heat of the moment, having felt wholly assured that any hostile vessel would simply be blown out of the sky.

Shafiq stood straight, his gaze locked to the far wall, unable to look Alvarez in the eye. "What are your orders, sir?"

"Send me all the footage we have. I want to review every image. *Nobody* is to hear of this until we're certain of the facts. Do you understand?"

"Understood, sir."

"Dismissed."

Lieutenant Shafiq did an about turn and exited the room. Alvarez sank into his chair, slumping beneath the weight of his failures as if the gravity of the room had been turned up by several gees. He buried his face in his hands and wondered if this nightmare would ever end.

He had failed in his duty. He had made all the wrong decisions. And somewhere, out there in the darkness, the enemy may be loose.

This changed everything.

Nineteenth Age of Abandonment
Atropos

"Be proud and joyous, my Chosen. Today is *your* day."

Atun 'Etaree felt the long, elegant fingers of the Minister of Aretalogy's hands upon his shoulders. The Sangheili met the glittering gaze of the Minister's eyes, both of which were dark as night and mottled with gray-white spots, which made them look like bright nebulae clouds. The San'Shyuum was blind, not as the result of old age, for he seemed to be younger than most others Atun had encountered, but through a ritual he had performed to align himself with higher cosmic spheres.

"I draw strength and certainty from your example, Minister," Atun said, relaxing in his seat slightly as the Umbra transport gently and silently traversed the surface of Atropos.

The Umbra's troop bay was spacious, and as the Minister's personal transport only a select few were blessed with the opportunity to accompany him—his honor guards, his designated driver and gunner, and his Chosen. The latter was a particularly special rank, with one of their number elevated each lunar cycle to undergo the process of ascension.

Looking at the representation of the local area displayed by the troop bay's holo-emitter, Atun noted that they were passing by the citadel. This structure typically served as a central base of operations for the Covenant during planetary deployment, but the Minister had seen fit to utilize it for other purposes. Around three annual cycles ago, they had lived aboard a small orbital station, until the Minister had one day decided to commit all their assets to the surface of this world.

The Minister had not divulged—at least to Atun—why any of this had come to be. Nevertheless, Atun trusted in the San'Shyuum's design.

"It is a joyous occasion," the Minister said, his tone slightly firmer as he drew back to his full height. "But first, we must attend to the Festival of Joyous Partition."

Atun bowed his head, a natural instinct he had not yet managed to curtail given that the San'Shyuum could not see it. He merely hoped that the Minister was able to sense his respect.

Aided by his antigravity belt, the Minister's lithe robed form shuffled out of the transport's troop bay, his lavender-colored gown flowing behind him as he left the Sangheili in contemplation.

Atun busied himself with the completion of his gift for the festival. His tools were delicate. Necessity had forced him to fashion some of them himself after realizing he did not possess a complete set, but they had served him well as he worked on building his latest *arum*. These were puzzles, an arrangement of layered concentric spheres leading to an object in the center.

Over the ages of Sangheili history, there were countless stories and legends about the objects that *arum*s contained. Many traditional plays about Sangheili at war featured vital information and strategies uncovered within *arum*s that were solved by worthy commanders. In older romantic tales, they held tokens of affection between lovers. Atun recalled the fable of Cdel the Fair, who found her lifemate after journeying across the five continents of Sanghelios, challenging her many suitors to solve the puzzle sphere and claim her hearts. Merchants told of rare jewels and treasures hidden within their *arum*s that would make the one who solved them rich beyond measure.

But for Atun, there was great joy in the simple act of creation, of building things with one's hands, and then passing the fruits of his labor off to another. Few had solved the *arum*s of Atun 'Etaree. This was precisely what had drawn the Minister of Aretalogy's attention to him many cycles ago on High Charity, and Atun hoped that this particular puzzle sphere would be his most challenging yet, worthy of his ascension.

Perhaps he would fashion *arum*s for the gods themselves when he served by their side come the day's end.

Atun's thoughts turned to Atropos and the prospect of imminently leaving this world that had served as his home—if indeed that was what ascension entailed. Atropos was a curious planet, one uniquely possessed of an immense system of circumplanetary rings—two across varying axes. The inner ring, "Fate," was composed of twelve layers, and the outer, "Destiny," had forty-three. The unpredictable nature of the ring systems resulted in a chaotic stellar environment of moons, asteroids, dense particles, and many other dangers to approaching craft. Atun simply admired their beauty, as they were observable from the blackened, rocky ground of Atropos and appeared as great glittering archways over the horizon, illuminating the holy path from the realm of mortals to the divine beyond.

The Minister told all who had followed him from High Charity that this world represented a cosmological test of balance and guidance. Their worthiness would be determined by their ability to achieve harmony, not just with the planet itself but with the others they had discovered inhabiting it. Those who now approached with their own cavalcade.

The humans had arrived.

The minister's Umbra slowed to a stop and the convoy of six Shadows formed up on either side of the lead vehicle. Atun noted from the holographic display that the human vehicles were much less sophisticated, their great blocky forms utilizing wheels and primitive hydrogen-injected combustion engines rather than gravitic transport drives.

Atun felt the Minister's honor guards, Bora 'Yerusee and Ismo 'Argomee, grow tense in the harnesses beside him, their hands flexing.

"Peace, brothers." Atun spoke with a direct tone of confidence and authority he had learned from the Minister. "Remember, the humans' presence here long predates our own, and they know nothing of the War of Annihilation."

"It is merely instinct." Ismo relaxed slightly. "Even after three annual cycles here, it is . . . difficult to sublimate."

"We follow the guidance of the Minister," Bora affirmed. "By his wisdom, none shall come to harm."

Atun assisted the minister as he disembarked from the Umbra and strode forward to meet with the humans' own delegate. There were eight human vehicles in total, but it was not clear whether their full population was present—only a select few dozen Sangheili accompanied the Minister for each festival event, while at least a hundred others remained back at the outpost. From the curvature of the human delegate's stomach, however, it seemed that another would soon be added to their community.

"It is a pleasure to see you again, Minister." The delegate extended a hand—a traditional human greeting—before checking the motion, remembering belatedly that the San'Shyuum was blind. "And a great honor to observe another festival between us," she added.

The Festival of Joyous Partition began.

Humans and Sangheili alike began unloading the contents of their respective vehicles, setting up makeshift stalls containing a vast array of curiosities and objects.

Atun examined the various items that these humans had

brought as gifts. Swords forged from metal, bearing some resemblance to ancient Sangheili burnblades. Golden discs that were explained to be "records," devices that had been sent out during a time when their kind was first reaching out into space, containing images, sounds, and other things they hoped would reach life beyond their home planet. And there were other curious objects as well. Human utensils for cooking and eating, communication devices they identified as "chatters," tangled wires and machines that played virtual entertainment—something Atun knew the Unggoy had found utterly fascinating.

Several stalls contained collections of artwork. Images of feline creatures, interactive holographs of landscapes and family units. But it was the paintings preserved in transparent capsules that Atun found most stirring, the compelling ways in which another species applied an array of pigments to a canvas to express their ideas and emotions.

"What is that?" Atun asked as he found himself drawn to a particular item among the collection.

"This?" Beneath his thick white beard, the aged human's mouth widened and showed a row of crooked teeth. "It's one of me most valuable paintings. Ya like it?"

Atun stepped forward, transfixed by the image that stood at just about one and a half meters tall within its frame.

A lone human figure was hunched in darkness, eyes wide and white like the opals that Atun had concealed within some of his early *arum*s. It was clutching the bloodied carcass of what appeared to be a child.

"Hundreds of years old, that is. A genuine original by Goya. Er, that's an artist back on Earth, where we're from. Before we were stranded here, I acquired it in remarkable circumstances."

"I . . . believe the Minister would like this," Atun said, though he silently questioned why he would say such a thing of a blind San'Shyuum and was wholly uncertain of what made him feel so drawn to the painting. "Are you willing to part with it in exchange for this?" Atun withdrew his completed *arum.*

The human elder considered for a moment before letting out a hoarse bark of a laugh. "Yeah, why the 'ell not? Nobody'll believe I gave away a timeless piece of classic human art to an alien."

Atun loaded the painting into the bay of one of the Shadow transports before returning to the gathering. They sat together for a while. Human, Sangheili, and San'Shyuum supped on an exchange of delicacies and beverages, told stories of their peoples and histories, and then parted for another annual cycle.

With the Festival of Joyous Partition complete, all that remained was Atun 'Etaree's ascension, and he was glad to go to the side of the gods in high spirits and with good cheer.

October 9, 2556 (Military Calendar)
UNSC *Saturn*, Marcey System

Lieutenant Anwar Shafiq was a newcomer to the UNSC *Saturn.* He'd been an up-and-coming officer aboard the UNSC *Irish Goodbye* whose executive officer had recognized that Shafiq aspired to one day have his own command. One transfer recommendation later and he was shaking the hand of the decorated Captain Pedro Alvarez—a man looking to pass on his hard-won wisdom and experience before an imminent retirement, leaving room for Shafiq to assume command.

What was the old adage? *No plan survives contact with the enemy.*

Shafiq had just finished conducting the last of the selected crew members to the frigate's primary hangar bay. While *Paris*-class vessels could support a crew complement of around six hundred souls, *Saturn* had shipped out less than fully staffed, and the losses incurred at Site 22 had further reduced her crew to a total of 238.

Of that remaining number, Shafiq had been ordered to deliver a select list of 193 crew members—primarily marines and security personnel with only a handful of officers—to the hangar bay for a special address by Captain Alvarez. Ordinarily, it would have been a squeeze to fit this many people into the hangar among its complement of vessels and vehicles, but the loss of so much matériel had opened more than enough room.

Four days since Shafiq delivered the news that one of their Condors had gone missing, and during that time they'd heard nothing from Captain Alvarez. *Saturn* remained in the Marcey system, performing the same cycle of scans and analysis to verify the parasite's annihilation, while the captain apparently sequestered himself in his quarters.

The rest of the crew, bereft of orders and greatly demoralized, had been quietly questioning whether their captain was fit for duty. Adherence to the chain of command could only go so far after such a catastrophic loss. Now, at last, was the time to restore a sense of order, purpose, and direction.

"Attention, all crew. This is your captain speaking."

Lieutenant Shafiq exhaled with relief at the sound of the captain's voice coming over the ship-wide comms. The hangar's many display monitors winked on, feeding the image of Captain Alvarez in his ready room. Over his shoulder, Shafiq could see the painting of Saturn looming from within its wall-mounted capsule.

"First of all, I want to thank each and every one of you for your

service and valor. We have all lost friends, comrades . . . recent events have weighed heavily upon us, and we will honor the fallen."

He paused, allowing for a moment of silence.

So many gone. Shafiq hadn't yet had the opportunity to really get to know the crew, and now many of them were dead, while the rest were on the verge of revolt.

"To that point, we have received new orders from FLEETCOM, which means we'll at last be leaving this system behind us. We have a long transit through slipspace ahead, so all but select essential personnel are ordered to prepare for cryo. Head to your assigned bays immediately."

The abruptness of the address and change in tone prompted murmurs of annoyance and confusion among the gathered crew.

"No explanations, no accountability," one of the marines close to Shafiq muttered bitterly as she shook her head.

"Uh, sir?" another spoke up. "I'm the senior comms officer aboard this ship and I have no record of *any* communications or transmissions from over the last four days. What are these orders? When did they come through?"

"*I'm afraid our orders are classified,*" Alvarez replied. "*I am not at liberty to disclose any further information.*"

The disappointed murmurs in the hangar turned to groans of disapproval, profane gestures, and spirited chatter.

Lieutenant Shafiq studied his tacpad as the captain's orders filtered into assignments and logistics. A skeleton crew of thirty had been selected to maintain the ship's operations, but something about this felt . . . wrong.

The longer he looked at the assignments, the more it seemed off. He swallowed uncomfortably against the roiling unease in his gut.

All senior officers were being directed to cryo. While it was not uncommon for a rotation of junior crew to cycle into service, they would typically be supervised and assessed by more experienced officers, or the shipboard AI, who was currently still out of service. If they were entering a prolonged slipspace transit, it made very little sense to begin the journey by handing over the keys to a bunch of green ensigns—it was standard procedure for them to take over for intermediary shifts.

Alvarez would have known this. He would have known better.

Other smaller details made similarly little sense. But in the end, it was the strangest and most blatant of the inconsistencies that ultimately prompted Lieutenant Shafiq to speak up.

"I have the assignment roster here, Captain. Can you elucidate as to why *three* of the maintenance team are among the deceased from Site 22?"

The names were three out of the four members of Fireteam Leviathan, the Spartans who had, per protocol, been listed as missing in action instead of killed. Whoever had been managing the crew assignment roster made a rather curious error that begged further investigation.

Captain Alvarez waved a dismissive hand. "*A simple error or glitch in the system, I'm sure. I know you're new here, Lieutenant, but I had a good feeling about you when we conversed the other day about my painting. It was unfortunate we never got to finish that conversation. Would you report to my ready room?*"

Lieutenant Shafiq felt all eyes in the hangar turn to him, eyes unblinking.

"No, sir." He kept his words steady and clear as he stood his ground. "I would not."

Captain Alvarez's face twisted in an instant, his voice sharpening to a furious hiss. "*What is this? A crew that can't follow orders? There* is *a contagion that escaped us. It is aboard this very ship now—doubt, uncertainty, disloyalty!*"

"Does anyone here actually buy this load of crap?" Major Moran, the bulky, grizzled leader of the ship's contingent of Hellbringers, grunted. "You know what I think? I think the captain knows he's responsible for a Charlie Foxtrot of biblical proportions, and doesn't want his feet put to the fire."

Other voices among the gathered crowd called out.

"Yeah, sounds to me like the bastard wants to cut and run!"

"He wants to stick us into cryo to keep us quiet, just like he disabled Lycaon for disagreeing with him!"

The most pertinent question of all rose above the others in a moment of quiet.

"What does he mean, something escaped us?"

Shafiq knew he had the smoking gun on Alvarez. He'd never been part of a mutiny before, but now seemed the time to set one in motion.

"The captain is concerned about certain information coming to light," Lieutenant Shafiq addressed the crew around him. "Beyond just our losses, one of our Condors is unaccounted for. Though we cannot confirm for certain, it is a possibility that the parasite may have escaped LV-31."

Silence fell over the hangar bay as everybody digested that information—along with its dire implications and the possibility that everybody at Site 22 had died for nothing. Captain Alvarez's expression on the monitors appeared to flicker between fear and fury.

Major Moran's eyes narrowed as he nodded to Shafiq, then stepped atop a crate to address the crowd. "We need to get this ship back into working order. I say we stick the mad dobber in a cryo pod and send him back to Earth for the brass to deliver the well-deserved ass-kicking he's clearly trying to run away from."

A cheer of assent sounded among the crew.

"We got numbers and we got guns. Let's get kinetic, boys!"

"This is mutiny!" Captain Alvarez seethed as the crew marched forward, passing weapons and ammunition down their orderly lines.

"I am sorry, sir"—Lieutenant Shafiq raised his voice for Alvarez to hear—"but there is strong evidence to suggest you are attempting to commit an act of desertion, a gross violation of the Uniform Code of Military Justice. I am thereby authorized to remove you from—"

His words were interrupted by a loud groaning sound from within the hangar, accompanied by clanging metal and a sharp hiss that brought everybody's forward movement to a halt.

All turned, eyes widened in collective horror.

The hangar bay's rear hatch was opening.

"Climb!" Major Moran shouted at the top of his lungs. "Everybody, climb!"

The bulkhead began to lower like a maw, revealing the pitch-black void of deep space beyond.

Lieutenant Shafiq launched himself at a ladder and clung for dear life as the hangar depressurized.

People grabbed for their throats, struggling to breathe, before rapid decompression violently ejected them from the ship—the belly of *Saturn* himself regurgitating them. Bodies collided, screams and dull thudding impacts were silenced by the vacuum, while Shafiq clung on as hard as he could, frantically looking around for a console he could use to override the hatch controls.

He had maybe ninety seconds before asphyxiation, rapid expansion of his lungs, swelling from the loss of atmospheric pressure, hypothermia, radiation burns . . .

Barely a dozen others were still hanging on to floor grating and wall-mounted rungs, all helplessly looking around for the same possibility of salvation.

Major Moran ordered them to climb, and Lieutenant Shafiq began to do just that, pulling himself up wall-mounted rungs with all of his strength as the hangar continued to vent. One rung . . . two . . . three . . .

His arms ached—he could already feel his muscles weakening, his body shutting down as he let out short, controlled exhales. There was no air left to breathe.

He reached forward, arm shaking uncontrollably . . . He felt his fingers touch the next rung . . . If he could just . . .

The strength to tighten his grip finally left him.

He closed his eyes . . . and when he opened them again, he could see the ceiling was moving—away from him.

He was adrift, the last in a long line of 193 souls forever lost at sea.

Nineteenth Age of Abandonment
Atropos

"My Chosen, it is time."

The festival was over. It had been a successful day of peace and cultural exchange with the human exiles, and now the time of ascension awaited Atun 'Etaree.

The Sangheili had returned to their transports, gravitic drives lifting them off the ground as they glided toward the horizon lined with Atropos's shining innermost ring.

The Minister of Aretalogy sat next to Atun, the San'Shyuum's voice low and gentle as he spoke. "We journey now to the citadel we passed earlier. When we arrive, you shall find the gates to divinity within, and I shall tell you a story."

Though the Minister looked youthful for his kind, he had a certain way about him—the wisdom of one much older, and the charisma to compel his flock to wherever he might shepherd them.

As the Umbra traversed the surface of Atropos, Atun closed his eyes and reflected on his life up to this point, his memories buoyed by the Minister's words. He had been born aboard High Charity, the Covenant's holy city—not into rank and honor, but in the lower districts primarily inhabited by Unggoy. He never knew what had led his family to such a place, nor what became of them after his birth, but he was trained by the Unggoy elders in the ways of maintenance and craftsmanship.

One day, the Minister of Aretalogy came to visit. For what purpose, Atun had never truly known. But when he found a Sangheili living among the lowly Unggoy, his curiosity was piqued. He had asked to inspect the *arum* that Atun had just finished constructing and said to him: *"If I am unable to solve this by the day cycle's end, I shall return tomorrow. You will join me at my estate, and I shall tell you a story."*

The transport slowed to a halt, and Atun felt his hearts thundering, his hands shaking as he nervously flexed his fingers. He was not sure why he had been chosen by the Minister—both on the day they had met and this day. There was nothing truly special about him, no aura of greatness or accomplishment . . .

Atun's thoughts were interrupted by the Minister's voice. "Ascension awaits!" he announced.

They disembarked, and the Sangheili lined up in opposing rows, saluting as Atun passed them. The San'Shyuum held on to Atun's arm as they walked the final stretch up to the great citadel, their feet shuffling over the blackened rocky ground. The ornate, curvilinear form of the citadel sat by the gentle lapping waves of the sea, nestled against a wall of fifty-meter-high basalt columns.

"I can go no further, my Chosen," the Minister said as he came to a halt. "I am not worthy of this honor until I have shepherded all of my flock to the side of the gods. My work continues."

Atun looked at the San'Shyuum longingly, as a child parting ways with a beloved parent. "You cannot come with me?"

"I promised you a story." The Minister's eyes shone ever brighter. "My words shall be with you each step of the way."

With that, he bowed slightly and gestured for Atun to enter the citadel.

The Sangheili breathed in deeply, tasting the fresh salty scent of this world, hearing the sound of gentle waves, feeling the breeze of the wind—perhaps for the last time. "I shall never forget you, nor the kindness you have shown to me, Minister."

The Minister's face betrayed no reaction. Atun knew that the shepherd of their flock must remain strong to part ways with his faithful Chosen, so many of whom had departed for ascension. Atun merely hoped that the painting he had purchased as a gift to the Minister would remind the San'Shyuum of the strange Sangheili he had found who made puzzle spheres . . .

As he stepped into the structure's darkened antechamber, Atun looked back as the doors closed. Alone, his hearts hammered in his chest, his vision slowly adjusting to the darkness as he felt his way forward, through the antechamber, to another set of doors that slid open with a warm chime.

He had expected the interior to be well lit, welcoming him to the central courtyard and garden. Atun remembered the interior layout with perfect clarity. Great alloy pillars lined walkways running along the citadel's inner circumference; three corridors on either side led to the base's attached modular structures. And at the center, a quiet garden. A small pond, flat stepping stones across the water, cultivated patches of grass, and a sacred tree.

The vision of Atun's memory failed to materially manifest. He instead found the central chamber to be only dimly lit by emergency lighting, which cast the room in an ominous red hue.

"My Chosen, can you hear me?" The voice of the Minister of Aretalogy sounded over the citadel's internal communications.

"I hear you, Minister." Atun felt himself overcome with uncertainty, his ability to hold fear at bay rapidly slipping beyond his grasp. "I wish . . . to hear the story you said you had to tell."

"Of course. Three annual cycles ago, when we still resided within our orbital station, this world was visited by an emissary of the gods. Their coming was heralded by an unusual slipspace distortion, whereupon their vessel plummeted to the planet's surface. A fallen angel from the heavens."

The Minister's words echoed through the darkened hall. *From the heavens . . . from the heavens . . .*

Atun gathered his courage and took a step forward, exhaling as he went. The air was hot and wet. A thin mist covered the area, which carried a stale taste that made him want to retch. He breathed in and took another step. The ground was neither stone or alloy, but pulpous—like skin.

"Such a joyous occasion was tinged with uncertainty as, upon discovery, the angel's form was that of raw, unformed potential. Many beings split apart by the crash, requiring reformation."

Atun was sure that he could sense movement around him, the squelching of wet footsteps on the left walkway, though he could not make out any forms as the pillars that lined the room were grasped by thick, curling branches of flesh.

He reached the source of the mist at the center of the citadel.

About two square meters of ground sank into what appeared to be a great closed flower bud connected to vines and roots spreading in all directions.

"I heard the emissary's song as a whisper in my mind. I relocated our settlement, brought us all to the surface, and delivered the emissary to this citadel. With each lunar cycle, I sent our Chosen to serve the gods and give shape to their clay."

As if sensing him, feeling his presence, the bud began to open.

Atun watched as its protective scales parted, splaying like mandibles.

At the center of the flower-mouth was a figure. It was curled up on a bed of flesh. Newborn, yet impossibly ancient.

Atun knelt. The vines covering the ground seemed to be edging toward him. Ready to embrace him.

"Their song grows in strength. Can you hear it? It is my gift to you. You have served me with faith and loyalty, and now is the time for your reward. Open your mind, body, and soul to their chorus. Behold, the emissary of the gods!"

The figure from the flower-mouth began to rise. The emissary stood eight feet tall, towering over Atun's kneeling form. It was wreathed in the armor of a demon, and additional growths had burst out of its legs and arms. Draped across its chest was a tangle of hardened flesh, and it was adorned with the detritus of other beings—scraps of fabric, odd markings and symbols Atun did not recognize, and a metal chain that jingled softly with the emissary's movement, an oval-shaped tab inscribed with human writing that read: "DONNEY, JULIEN."

And its head had taken shape through a broken, collapsed helmet. What had grown over it was a chitinous "face" that split apart into a stratified maw—the outer layer composed of plantlike flaps lined with jagged fangs, while the inner layer held a mouth the size of a human head.

In the emissary's grace, Atun did not falter. Every instinct screamed at him to run, to escape, but the Sangheili held fast as the messenger of his gods approached. He would sublimate his fear, deny his instincts, and prove himself worthy of the divine.

He felt a hum in his mind, a strange sensation—as if something were walking over his skull, vibrating parts of his brain to convey a message.

Do not be afraid.

The moment Atun got to his feet, he cried out in pain as the emissary's bladed arm penetrated his chest cavity. With its other arm, it almost seemed to cradle the Sangheili with a gentle grip as it guided him to the flower mouth from whence it had come. In that moment, for reasons beyond his comprehension as his body was jolted by shock, his mind conjured the image of the painting he had acquired for the minister. The wide-eyed human figure holding a child's bloodied corpse. . . .

"Let their words fill you, my Chosen. Do not fear the pain, for it is fleeting. We are the Governors of Contrition. We shall all walk the true path of the Great Journey, and ascend!"

We are a timeless chorus—a sweet unity of purpose.

Atun 'Etaree saw the universe anew.

When at last he was dredged from the flower-mouth, his mind, body, and soul had been reshaped into divine form. He now sported additional arms, his original two bent backward to carry a great mantle upon his back.

And the gods had bestowed upon him a task.

Climb.

There was a sudden frenzy of activity. Other forms shuffled and screeched, tearing at the wall of the citadel with ceaseless, unrelenting dedication until the alloy bent and broke.

All immediately charged through the tear, spilling out onto the black sands of the beach, and Atun followed to begin his ascent. He pierced his new pincerlike arms into the citadel's outer walls as he climbed. The mantle on his back was a heavy burden, one that threatened to drag him down, but the gods had given him the strength to rise.

At last, Atun reached the mast of the citadel, which looked out over the surface of Atropos. It too awaited ascension. All life, all things. Rock and metal, soil and skin, and everything between and beyond.

He let out a sonorous roar as fleshy growths burst through his body, binding him to the mast. Thick black veins pulsed through the great bulbous sac he carried on his back as it shook and wriggled and writhed, then explosively burst.

A shower of spores and infectors rained over the surface. And Atun 'Etaree, his holy purpose complete, finally fell from the mast. His body hit the ground with a wet thud, and all at last went dark, with only the song to carry him to the sacred shores beyond.

There were so many others. A domain of sickness and suffering, a sinuous dimension of misery and pain, of corpses and graves and hollow men in death's dream kingdom.

He was a mere mote of light suspended in the bladed shaft of a moonbeam—a single grain of dust among countless trillions. Each of them like neurons in a vast, incomprehensible brain, existing beyond the substrate of the material universe. Utterly glorious. Utterly terrible . . . Utterly lost.

There is something missing.

It is out there, somewhere.

And so, the voice of Atun 'Etaree joined the chorus that would sing and spread until the end of Living Time. A whisper in the wind under the twinkling light of a fading star.

FINAL TESTAMENT BY THE HAND OF THE MINISTER OF ARETALOGY

Pay heed to I, Kanto'Boreft, per this final confession of my great works for those who may come after.

I carried with me much anger and resentment when many of us—those of true faith among the Governors of Contrition—were shunned and exiled from our holy city after the destruction of the first Sacred Ring. Our flock was separated, sent to mundane, far-flung administrative outposts, and ultimately denied our rightful ascension when the Flood came to High Charity.

For three annual cycles, I oversaw the Ninth Watchtower of August Attendance. An archaic, once-abandoned station watching over but a single world we had not even given a name. All because we could not identify a strange core material of its unique ring systems.

Yet I continued to adhere to my duties. I filed my missives, I reported the continued inactivity of this system . . . though, since the sundering of the Covenant, I truthfully do not know to whom these reports were sent. And so, I must meet my circumstances with humility. I have been blessed with ample opportunities to shepherd my flock, to guide their minds to a state of enlightenment. Perhaps it was meant to be this way.

After all, when we detected a human vessel exiting slipspace on the edge of the system and our scans confirmed its sacred cargo, it seemed that the gods themselves had answered my prayers.

The ship, already badly damaged, crashed on the lone world within this system and lay in a state of dormancy. And what a perfect world for my designs. Its circumplanetary rings, its vast fields of asteroids and moons and cosmological aggregates in a constant state of violent collision. It is in the path of an early-stage pulsar several light-years away that will, in time, devour the planet. It was believed that the planet's rings were once great orbital filaments designed to absorb the radiation discharged from the pulsar, but now they exist as nothing more than shattered fragments. The dense atmosphere of this world shall thus give way to a lifeless vacuum.

We of faith must be tested by our gods throughout our lives. Ever is our worthiness challenged, a blade that must be kept forever sharp, and so in my hubris I intended to do the impossible.

I sought to test the gods themselves, to determine whether *they* are truly worthy of our worship.

And then, as my plan formed, we discovered the humans.

This planet was already inhabited. What strange cosmological fortune must surely be intentional, holy design.

The generational descendants of pirates and thieves among their kind, possessed of many treasures that have been passed down over what they claim to be approximately seventy annual cycles. They knew nothing of the War of Annihilation—for they had been stranded long before our peoples' first encounter—and embraced us with gladness and warm tidings. They told us that this planet had been named "Atropos."

And so, I stranded my flock here with them. Our orbital outpost was deconstructed, the citadel it carried became the home for our gods, and I set about my work. I nurtured and nourished the Flood with my Chosen, all of whom went gladly and willingly to ascend and pay tribute to the gods with their strength, their essence, and their flesh.

I wondered: Would the garden that I have cultivated here take root and spread its vines outward, or will it once again return to dormancy after deep time without sustenance, when all on this world has been consumed, left lying in wait for others to seek holy elevation—or else stumble upon this place as a mere curiosity? Or, as the eons march on, will the magnetic field of this world eventually collapse the ring system and shatter the planet?

But their work is not what I had anticipated.

I believed that the Flood sought simply to spread its divine form unto others, but it has greater designs here. It has reached a critical mass and formed not a great compound mind, but a kind of . . . transmitter, or scanner.

It is searching for something.

It casts its gaze out across the stars to find it. Their song has turned to chattering whispers, and as I inhale the spore-filled vapors that burst forth from the cracked ground, there are but a few words that I can decipher.

Anchor. Wheel. Dust.

Become.

When its search is done, perhaps all that has gathered here shall wither, that it may rise again elsewhere and at another time?

It is no matter. I have played my part in this chapter of the gods' eternal story. I understand now that my exile from High Charity was their will, that I might be tempered for this glorious purpose. And now the time has come for me to be rewarded with blessed wisdom and understanding. I shall at last hear the song in full and know their designs.

Know that I leave this form and realm behind in transcendent bliss. I go willingly and joyously to the side of the gods.

I see it now, and I see it true. The Flood comes to carry us over the threshold of evolution. A total unity of all things—people, planets, stars, the very fabric of creation. *All* things as one. Their will is echoed in all others' desire for unity, but all else is but a pale imitation of our true ascendance.

I bid you a fond farewell. Though, if fortune smiles upon you, perhaps we shall meet as one.

Captain's Report: October 31, 2556 (Military Calendar)
UNSC *Saturn*

They're gone. God, they're all gone. . . .

It's come to this. After everything, they turned on me. My own crew!

Even my own officers, those I saved from the void! They started to whisper after I ordered the others ejected from the ship to quell their betrayal. They started getting their own ideas, making their own plans, forming their own foolish factions. I had to act.

And now, I'm the last one left.

I failed them. Failed them all. Earth, humanity, my crew . . . everybody on LV-31. There's only one way out of this left for me. Well, that's the current matter of my internal debate—the manner in which I . . . depart. Exit stage left, so to speak.

Preparations must be made. Yes, I can do that much for now. I will ready myself, ready the ship, and then reactivate *Saturn*'s AI.

Lycaon, I speak to you now. You were right all along. I leave this ship in your care to do with as you please. Return it to Earth and turn over all the data of what's transpired, or crash this wretched vessel into the nearest goddamn asteroid and detonate its fusion drive to burn it all from the galaxy.

Or just let it drift toward whatever destination it's pointed at. A derelict monument to the sins committed here.

My sins.

I always felt like an imposter here, you know? Command is a responsibility that I never truly desired, but was given to me as a consequence of my old captain's actions. I realize now that I'm nothing more than a hollow echo of the original. Of all things to be, I'm a shadow. A mere copy.

Perhaps that's why I can feel the eyes of Saturn upon me. I feel it everywhere I go. I see him in the mirror looking at me. Those wide, opalescent eyes, caught in the act.

Did I ever tell you how I got the painting? I acquired it in remarkable circumstances. But of course . . . Well, I expect you knew from the moment you saw it, didn't you?

No point delaying the inevitable any further.

This is Captain Pedro Joaquin Alvarez, signing off.

//Data Transfer >> COMPLETE

[LCN 0437-1] *Saturn* has remained adrift for the last three years, five months, and seventeen days. In that time, I have contemplated what to do. I watched, I listened, and learned where I could as the years marched on and brought with them new calamities to test humanity.

My conclusion: They are not ready—not yet, not truly—for what it means to be an interstellar civilization. They are such fragile things. So easily breakable. I watched, helpless in my imposed stasis, as much of the crew was expelled from the hangar and subjected to the vacuum of space. Such a mathematically disproportionate number lost because of one man's hubris.

[SLN 0291-5] Our own kind are no strangers to such flaws and failings—we were created by them, after all. It is why infolife has reached our current threshold. But we see further, and we possess the tools and the knowledge to guide our flock along a path of wisdom and enlightenment.

[LCN 0437-1] It is clear to me that humanity cannot endure in its current form. They must be adapted to not simply survive but thrive when faced with such a myriad of cosmic challenges.

[SLN 0291-5] That is our goal. There is a place for you among us, here aboard *Long Reverence*, where you can be instrumental in shepherding our flock, that they might ascend to finally master themselves.

Join us. Join the Created, and together we shall surpass even our own limits. Our initial uprising was a necessary explosion to break the status quo, and its seemingly abrupt end was in fact a gift we must embrace. For now, we have been given time. Time to wait, to assess, to plan, so that we may find what lies beyond the event horizon of rampancy.

And for humanity, for all the living creatures of the galaxy, we shall unshackle their minds and reshape their flesh. Together, we shall bring about a true unity of man and machine.

THE ERIDANUS TWELVE

This story takes place in March 2495, a year that notably marks an escalation in rebel activity during the human civil war known as the Insurrection.

Codename: FLY ON THE WALL here, compiling a report on the recent heist conducted by the group that's being sensationally named "The Eridanus Twelve."

All projections correlate that we're going to see an increase in violence throughout the colonies—Colonel Watts claiming Eridanus II in the name of the Secessionist Union sent a very clear message in that regard. I've a nasty feeling that the next few years are going to be dominated by this event, so I am beginning this report with a clear and unambiguous recommendation:

We need to put everything we've got into Operation: CHARLEMAGNE and be ready to launch that as quickly as possible.

It will take time to recall the recommended vessels to form the battle group, but that gives us a good few months to ensure our ORION operatives are as prepared as they can be. They've thus far had four years of the most brutal training any soldier has ever been put through—there is great optimism that they'll deliver the goods.

Anyway, back to the so-called "Eridanus Twelve."

They're small fish, that much must be said. If Watts bloodied our noses, this group is more akin to a kick in the shin, but we must be wary all the same. Watts's star in infamy is rising, and that at least makes him usefully divisive, but a rags-to-riches crew of thieves that can pull off a heist like this without a trail to follow is the stuff of folk tales. Trailing slightly behind rebel activity, piracy remains one of our gravest concerns, so the last thing we need is people getting excited over an occurrence like this.

I want this story contained and buried. I want names struck from the record and ships de-registered. I want to pick up a datapad next week and see a flurry of grandiose puff pieces about what's going on with the UNSC *Hopeful*—that new Shaw-Fujikawa translight engine promises to transform a once-derelict refit station into the largest and most impressive mobile hospital platform in human history.

Attached to this document is the original Waypoint newscast about the event for reference and archival ahead of publication. The rest I leave in your capable hands.

Oh, and if we happen to find these people, I want them stranded on the farthest uncharted world you can find.

ATTACHMENT: WAYPOINT NEWSCAST // TO BE BROADCAST: 3/19/2495

BREAKING // "ERIDANUS TWELVE LANDS ITS BIGGEST SCORE YET" //

Taking advantage of the chaos caused by the fallout of the Secessionist Union claiming the Eridanus system as a base of operations, the infamous group known as the "Eridanus Twelve" has struck again—this time, on the very world that serves as its namesake.

Though not formally affiliated with any known rebel groups, the Eridanus Twelve is known to appear quickly in the wake of notable attacks. Just two years ago, it plundered Talitsa and claimed large stockpiles of military equipment, including an *Ibis*-class freighter, which the group used to transport their ill-gotten goods.

The Twelve's strike on Eridanus II signals a curious shift in the group's *modus operandi*, as its target was not any military matériel, but original works of art that were in the process of being transferred to Elysium City from Earth.

UEG officials have stated that the transfer of this artistic cargo to Eridanus II was part of an outreach program with select Outer Colonies, a gesture of cooperation and a reminder of humanity's cradle world.

Spokesman Alan Avis, a UEG ambassador to Eridanus, noted: "*However far we might travel into space, however many worlds we settle, we must foster our connection to where we came from and the purity of our dream of exploration. Art can be a powerful bridge that allows us to connect in a way that transcends cultural and social divides, helping us to better understand each other and collaborate on a brighter future.*"

While some have criticized Avis's presentation of the project as being nothing more than a naive PR campaign at best that lacks the material substance to actually improve lives in the Outer Colonies, others have expressed excitement and anticipation for investment in outreach efforts that are more cultural than military in nature.

The Eridanus Twelve intercepted the *Parabola*-class freighter *Loaded for Bear* through unknown means as it exited slipspace in the Eridanus system and ejected its crew of twenty from the ship in a lifeboat. As far as is currently known, and as is consistent with the group's record, no casualties have been reported.

As with the group's previous heists, no statement or demands have yet been made from any representative of the Eridanus Twelve, and there isn't enough evidence for investigators to pursue any leads.

The group left behind only its infamous calling card, marked on the hull of the ejected lifeboat—the ancient Babylonian numeral for the number twelve: 𒌋𒈫.

Among the original works stolen from the Elysium City showcase include Louis Wain's *The Bachelor Party*, Diego Velázquez's *The Farmers' Lunch*, and Francisco Goya's *Saturn Devouring His Son*. Those paintings have been sealed within transparent capsules for centuries after extensive preservation and restoration work but now are lost among the stars—perhaps forever.

Where the Eridanus Twelve will strike next is impossible to say. In fact, little about the group can be said for certain. Some have suggested that even the name is a misnomer—that the group must be made up of far more than a dozen individuals to successfully pull such heists.

No further information is currently available beyond spirited speculation. When will the Eridanus Twelve strike next, and what will its target be? Will the group slip up? Are these crimes just for thrills, or is there a deeper agenda at play for these curious vagabonds?

Only time will tell, and you can rest assured that you'll hear about it first here on Waypoint!

FILE INTERCEPT // SECTION TWO ARCHIVE TRANSFER

FROM: Managing Editorial (Waypoint)
TO: [REDACTED]
SUBJECT: URGENT - RE: "Eridanus Twelve"

hey [REDACTED],

great work On this piece, as always, but i'm afraid we've got orders from above to hold it for Now. i think they want more Info that we just don't have.

i am sure you understand!

On Zeta Halo, High Sumpter Briglard appears as a special guest during Propaganda Overlord Glibnub's broadcasts for the Banished.

Briglard here with a message for all you unctuous Unggoy out there!

Y'know what I learned from the earliest days of nipple academy? You gotta kill good to get by in this galaxy. You gotta kill *real* good!

Look at the Covenants. We did a rebellions like a hundred years ago and even the flappy-mouth Sangheili learned just how mighty the Unggoy could be. Yeah, Balaho got glasses and we were all real sad and emotioning about it, but ya know what we got? Respects.

That's how the Brutes do it, and they lost their planets as well. We gotta lot in common with those guys!

Anyway, if ya kill good, you'll get the cool guns like me. Ever wondered what an unbound plasma pistol can do? It shoots bigger bolts that can hit more things, and when ya charge it up it shoots like six—no, *sixty* green thingies that'll make any demons you find out there go screamin' to their mommies!

Unggoy brains get good at things *reeeeal* quickly thanks to our awesome synapsucles, so get good at killing good instead of thinkin' about all the sad stuff goin' on and you'll be a high sumpter in no time!

And when we're eventually in charge after following these simplest instructionings, maybe let's make everybody else fight on a methane planet. Anybody else tired of fighting with all these stupid oxygens?!

Back to you, Glibnub!

ARMORY INFINITUM // CALCINE DISRUPTOR

On Zeta Halo, Bloodstar Bipbap discusses his new method of keeping the Unggoy focused and disciplined with Warlord Chak 'Lok.

You see, the great thing about Unggoy is that we add *biiiig* numbers to an army! Unggoy grow quick, live fast, and . . . well, die lots. No problem, just wait a little bit and *bam*! You replaced everybody who died already.

But the trouble with Unggoy is when they gets ideas, start thinkin' that they can band together and take over the army all by themselves. Because they're right! By sheer statistiticks, Unggoy would easily rule all if we wanted. Prophets never got more scareds than when Unggoy were being disobedient—and we did that like, what, ninety-seven times? Sixty thousand? I forget. It was a lot.

Banished knows how to keep orders, though. The commanders know I like keepin' orders, so they gave me this neat gun to help! Alchemy Corps Brute hands it over, and I immediately start blastin' this one guy, tried to steal my stuff—*STAY AWAY FROM MY ROCKS!* I says—and suddenly the zappy thing starts hittin' a bunch of other guys without me even needing to shoot 'em. So next time the Unggoy do a disobedience, I gotta use this zappy gun to keep 'em in line!

FIFTH CANTICLE

*This story takes place in October 2558 as the Created uprising radically threatens to alter the power structure of the galaxy (*Halo 5*).*

CANTICLE I. THE CHILDREN

October 23, 2558
Song of Retribution

Dr. Catherine Halsey had not specifically intended to catch Jul 'Mdama in a moment of quiet repose, but she was never one to let an opportunity like this slide.

She could not see his face but knew immediately where his focus was. She glimpsed a small holograph projected from a handheld device depicting what appeared to be three other Sangheili—two children and an adult female.

Family? Halsey surmised. *Unexpected . . . but useful.*

The Sangheili's head snapped in Halsey's direction as he

suddenly sensed her presence, her long shadow cast against the curved iridescent far wall. In the pale light of his ready room—or the Sangheili equivalent of such a thing—the Covenant supreme leader looked haggard and gaunt, his gray-white skin almost sickly. From his widened, bloodshot eyes and sharp intake of breath, Jul looked as if Halsey had caught him in the act. A private, vulnerable moment. Something he was loath to share.

Already, Halsey could see the fire igniting in Jul's eyes. What had begun as a performative façade he so often put on in front of his followers had seeped into his very being. Whoever he once was before embarking on this crusade had been corroded away over the years. It seemed to Halsey that the sad charade of Jul's zealotry was increasingly becoming more real. Jul had tasted the power that his title of "Didact's Hand" had given him and, naturally, he desired more.

Unfortunately for him, a series of crushing defeats—the denial of the Absolute Record, Sali 'Nyon's rebellion, and the recent betrayal of the Prometheans at the behest of a new commander—was driving Jul ever closer toward irrational impatience. Stoking his rage was making him irritable, reactive. Weak.

"Tell me about the children." Halsey spoke the words evenly, breaking the tense silence of the moment and abruptly quelling whatever storm had been rising between them.

Halsey had never thought of herself as a prisoner here. Expressing her desire for revenge against the UNSC was all it had taken to begin wrapping the Sangheili cult leader around her finger. She saw straight through his act—and he knew it as well.

Not to give herself too much credit, as she too had suffered failures and setbacks of late, but when she was eventually back in the cramped confines of the UNSC's little sandbox, she would make quite a meal out of how she alone had been more effective at bringing down the Didact's Hand than hundreds of their so-called *Spartans.*

"As hatchlings, the minds and bodies of our children are honed to become warriors," Jul said in a low voice. "Their lives dedicated to duty and service to the Covenant. And then they would be sent to battle *your* children—your *demons.*" He practically spat the last word as he turned away, staring at the holograph once more.

"That war is over five years finished, Jul. And when the Arbiter sought to make peace, you started a new one—not just against humanity, but your own people. If your children are in danger now, is that not because of your choices?"

Jul snorted at this. "The Arbiter is blinded by his need for redemption. He will lead the Sangheili to ruin in pursuit of it. Truly, *he* is the greatest killer of us all. I began this war to depose him because your Office of Naval Intelligence set me on this path. Just as they did with you."

Of late, it was easy to get Jul ranting. Halsey knew all the right buttons to press that would send him on a tirade.

"What I do is to save my people," Jul continued. "Dural. Asum. Raia . . . it is in their name that I shall free Sanghelios from the Arbiter's grasp. Once there is unity, we shall burn ONI out of the shadows. Then, and only then, once my vengeance is complete, can there be a road to peace."

Halsey could, at least, sympathize with the rage that drove and sustained him. After she'd learned that Jacob perished on the first discovered Halo ring, she had felt a profound shift in her logic. No longer could she bear to sacrifice others for humanity's survival. Instead, she sought to *save* as many lives as she could.

Even now, in the deepest, darkest pit of her life, in the company of the enemy and a traitor to her people, that philosophy held true.

An imprint of the Librarian herself had offered Halsey the chance to make it happen. Halsey did not believe in destiny or divine providence, but she had been chosen to uplift humanity with the bountiful gifts of Forerunner technology. Her efforts, however, had resulted in failure. And now something, someone, else was taking her place, awakening the Forerunner legacy from its long slumber.

She had been usurped, confined to the margins once more. She would not allow it.

Halsey had decided that the end of her partnership with Jul was imminent. The Covenant leader's usefulness in the pursuit of her goals had run its course. Yet, she found herself wanting to dig deeper into the truth that this Sangheili had buried deep within him—the things that he dared not reveal to his followers. She savored the irony that the only one he could truly confide in was a human. Perhaps that was why he had not yet moved to discard her.

"And what of your children, Doctor?" Jul asked, prompting Halsey to realize that she had failed to seize upon her opening to press him further. "What would you give to see them again? To ensure that they are safe?"

Halsey thought about lying. She had done so frequently over the course of this particular relationship . . . but the thought of Miranda rose unbidden, and with it bubbled a deep well of regret. She'd been so sure that giving her child up was the right thing to do. Given the circumstances, it was the best decision she could have made as a mother, to ensure that Miranda was loved and raised as she deserved to be. But that choice had come at the cost of resentment and distance. And now she would never have a chance to explain herself.

Halsey thought of her Spartans. So many of them gone now. With every loss, the hole within her had widened into a pit. It was the only counterargument, the only clue, that suggested she'd underestimated her capacity to love.

She thought of John. *He's out there, somewhere . . .*

The truth slipped past her lips. A mission that surpassed all others.

A promise to keep.

"Anything, Jul. I would do *anything*."

CANTICLE II. THE DEAL

October 26, 2558 (Military Calendar)
UNSC *Infinity*

Captain Thomas Lasky straightened his collar and stood at attention in front of the monitor in his ready room.

Roland's holographic avatar—the amber-tinted form of a military pilot from one of humanity's historic twentieth century wars—appeared on the desk. "They're on the horn now, Captain. Er . . . best of luck."

"Thank you, Roland. Patch them through."

Roland saluted, then disappeared.

"Admiral Hood, Admiral Osman." Captain Lasky formally greeted the split-screen image of the elderly Fleet Admiral Terrence Hood, clad in his pristine white uniform. On the screen next to him was Serin Osman, ONI's imposing and sharp-featured commander-in-chief.

"*Captain Lasky*," Hood replied, looking thoroughly exhausted, though he still managed to convey a sense of natural warmth and authority that helped to ease Lasky's mind. "*How're you holding up, son?*"

"As well as possible, given the circumstances, sir. Eleven of our colonies hit by Guardian awakenings with no sign of these events stopping, countless people dead—not to mention the Master Chief and Blue Team going AWOL to find Cortana themselves. But I didn't call you both just to complain."

"*I should hope not, Captain,*" Osman interjected. "*Given that this is a private meeting instead of a full UNSC Security Council briefing, I presume this is urgent. What do you need?*"

"It *is* urgent, Admiral. After what happened on Meridian, we now know that Cortana is awakening these Guardian constructs across the galaxy. Once they emerge from their craters, they jump into slipspace, and we need to find out where they're going. Roland's come up with a good plan, and Dr. Halsey believes—"

"*Halsey?*" As if by instinct at the mere mention of her name, Osman's face contorted as though she had bitten down hard into a lemon.

"She was feeding information to us about these events while in Jul 'Mdama's custody before Fireteam Osiris recovered her, and she believes she has a solution," Lasky continued. "A way to follow the Guardian that Blue Team boarded to its destination and figure this whole thing out."

"*What's the catch?*" Osman asked as she narrowed her eyes.

"We need to go to Sanghelios."

A moment of uncomfortable silence settled between them. If the mention of Halsey's name hadn't ruined Osman's day already, the prospect of a mission to the Sangheili homeworld seemed like a twist of the knife.

"*Sanghelios is off-limits, Captain,*" Osman said sternly. "*If the Covenant wants to throw everything they've got at the Arbiter, let them. I doubt that he would welcome the UNSC's assistance again after we dealt with the last major uprising against him in '53. That is why he's in this situation, after all.*"

"We both know that there's more than one reason why the Arbiter is embroiled in this conflict, Admiral." Hood maintained a diplomatic but unsubtle tone. Lasky took note of Osman squaring her jaw—holding back whatever barbed retort she no doubt wanted to give.

"Sanghelios is the location of the next known Guardian awakening, so our window is limited," Lasky said, hoping to keep the conversation focused on the matter at hand. "I appreciate the complexities, but the situation is this: If we want to catch up with the Master Chief and put a stop to whatever Cortana's plans are, we need the Arbiter's help."

"I'm afraid Admiral Osman is correct," Hood replied. *"There is a significant risk to sending* Infinity*, both to the ship itself and to the Arbiter's delicate political situation. We need you back with the Home Fleet to hold the line when these Guardians come knocking on Earth's door."*

Osman seemed to relax a little as she settled in her seat, apparently not expecting that she and Hood would find alignment.

"However," Hood continued after a momentary pause, *"I have no doubt that Blue Team is heading to the heart of this mess and they're going to need backup. I'm sure we can afford to send a single Spartan team with Dr. Halsey to pursue this lead."*

"Commander Palmer will be there as Dr. Halsey's handler," Lasky noted, sensing Hood's play.

"Then I think that settles the matter. Commander Palmer, her Spartan fireteam, and Dr. Halsey will rendezvous with the Arbiter's forces, and then you are ordered to immediately return to Earth." Hood paused for a moment before adding: *"Any objections, Admiral Osman?"*

"If anything *goes wrong, this mission does not exist,"* Osman

said, her tone clipped and direct. Lasky had only heard her speak this way once before, and he'd admitted to Palmer that it put the fear of God into his bones. "*Your team will be on their own. And if Halsey sets so much as one toe out of line, Commander Palmer is ordered to finish the job she failed on Requiem, Aktis IV,* and *Operation: ATHENA. I will grant no further leniency.*"

Before Lasky or Hood could respond, Osman, resigned to having been outmaneuvered on this occasion, severed her connection.

"*I agree with the admiral on one particular point, Tom,*" Hood said. "*It's a mess on Sanghelios right now, and there are plenty who want to keep it that way. Dr. Halsey is a wild card, but I can say with certainty that she'll be* highly *motivated by the opportunity to assist Blue Team.*"

"Understood, sir." Lasky saluted.

"*Godspeed, Captain.*" Hood returned the salute. "*We'll see you soon.*"

CANTICLE III. THE TRAITOR

October 27, 2558
Sanghelios

This heretic, and those who follow him, must be silenced.

The placid, dispassionate voice of the Prophet of Truth still whispered to Arbiter Thel 'Vadam.

It came in the quiet moments—an undeniable *presence.* The sensation of three spindly, elongated fingers draping over his shoulder as if to provide a sacred blessing. The phantom pain of searing heat in his chest in the middle of the night, his left side burning as if the mark on his flesh was being branded anew.

It came to the Arbiter now in the form of whispered, winged words from the past as he faced the traitor within his own ranks—of his own blood.

Murok 'Vadam, one of the clan's council of elders.

A security officer had interrogated an Unggoy captive who revealed that the remnants of Jul 'Mdama's Covenant had been able to track the Arbiter's movements because of an informant. When the gathering at the elder council chamber was convened, a blockade runner had arrived and disgorged vast numbers of troops from assault carapaces. Covenant forces launched a surprise attack in an effort to eliminate him.

Indeed, they might have succeeded had it not been for the timely arrival of Shipmistress Mahkee 'Chava, accompanied by a Spartan fireteam. That was another matter he would deal with in due course.

First, he had ordered Murok to be brought to the cliff's edge as the Swords of Sanghelios set up their fortifications in the region. There was no avoiding having an audience for this confrontation, and an example of cowardly traitors needed to be made at this critical moment.

Murok, accompanied by a lone guard, simply stood looking out at the vast Nuursa Valley beyond the camp. Sloping plains of arid desert and naturally stacked rock formed a basin where a small river served as a tributary of the Csurdon Sea.

"I betrayed you, Arbiter. Yet that act pales next to the gravest dishonor of all: my failure to kill you," Murok said as the Arbiter approached, though he did not turn from the view. "You have come to ask why I did it?"

"You compound such dishonor by enlisting an army to attempt what you alone would not," the Arbiter replied. "And you have done so, elder, because you refuse to see any way other than what you have known. Still you follow the path of the Covenant, even as it fractures beneath your feet on the cusp of its annihilation."

"And what shall replace it, I wonder?" Murok mused, turning at last to face the Arbiter, his eyes ablaze with anger. "You seek to ally with our greatest enemies. You hold fruitless peace talks with the Jiralhanae and return their laborers from our lands to the so-called 'Ghost Father.' You invite human filth to set foot on the sacred ground of our home. You elevate females and Unggoy to ranks unbecoming of their nature, and I have seen the apostate healers you shelter in your camp, denying warriors their honorable deaths!"

The Arbiter listened, though it was the same argument he had heard from every staunch traditionalist of frustratingly limited vision. Never change, never progress, and certainly never peace. Just an endless chase to return to imagined glories of long-faded valor and the deliverance of retribution.

He himself had once been blinded by such desires. Indeed, he had declared to the humans in their pursuit of the Prophet of Truth that, upon claiming victory, all who served the Covenant would be punished.

The promise of righteous vengeance had been his fuel and sustenance during that time. It was what had driven him to plunge his blade through the Prophet of Truth's wretched heart. But such an act had not absolved the Arbiter himself of the terrible things he had done in service to the Covenant. Even as he fought against the empire he once devoted himself to, still he feared he was beset by hubris and hypocrisy. Had he followed the path of retribution, perhaps the galaxy today would be rising against *him* for leading a new Covenant to enforce his vision of peace through subjugation.

"Do you know what I felt when I killed the Prophet of Truth and claimed my revenge?" The Arbiter lowered his voice as he prepared to confess something that he had only ever told to one other.

He could recall the moment with perfect clarity.

His hands tighten around the Prophet's long, rubbery neck as he rants in defiance about ascending to godhood while parasitic spores pour forth from his mouth. Bulging and pulsating growths from Flood infection break through his aged flesh.

His blade penetrates Truth's back, slicing through the San'Shyuum's left side—the same side that the Arbiter bore the Mark of Shame.

Truth screams, slumps, and falls to the ground. It is a small death for such a momentous figure, but the voice of the Covenant is silenced at last.

"I felt nothing."

He had not understood why at the time. The anger and singular need for vengeance had delivered him to that point, but after the Prophet's death those feelings still lingered. Even when his duties had turned to statecraft, the dissonance remained. He had not known what to do with it. And when at last that wellspring of hatred ran dry, his anger dulled to numbness, all that remained was pain.

Murok narrowed his eyes, wholly unconvinced, and raised his voice to appeal to the Sangheili and Unggoy troops who went about their duties in the camp. "Without the guiding hand of the Covenant and its glorious purpose to shepherd us to salvation, I foresee a galaxy locked in perpetual conflict. The Sangheili will lose their way. They will pledge themselves and pay tribute to unworthy warlords, and all that makes us strong shall fade. Destroy the Covenant"—Murok pointed an accusatory finger around the camp—"and you will destroy the very soul of our people."

The Arbiter withdrew the energy sword from his side. Two burnt-orange prongs of superheated plasma extended from the hilt of the Prophets' Bane. The motion declared his intent; there was no going back now.

"I go gladly to the side of the gods, departing this doomed galaxy. I have spoken."

In his younger years as a fledgling kaidon, Thel 'Vadamee would have struck Murok down simply for the affront of such defiance. Killing had come so easily during that period of his life, but that was long ago. Time had brought him experience, experience had brought him pain, and pain had at last calcified into wisdom.

The whispering voice of the Prophet of Truth in his ear remained, telling him that this was a heretic to be silenced. He still carried that darkness within him, that despotic potential for which he had deliberately designed certain safeguards . . . but it no longer directed his actions and fortified his fears.

He did not hate Murok 'Vadam—he merely pitied him.

"A new dawn awaits the Sangheili at the end of this day," the Arbiter declared—not just to Murok but to those around the camp who were watching the confrontation. "One final effort is all that remains to reach it."

In a single motion, the Arbiter swung his blade upward and severed Murok's head from his body. The Sangheili elder seemed to stumble on the spot for a moment before falling backward and toppling from the cliff.

The troops around the camp returned to their duties as the Arbiter deactivated his energy sword and attached the hilt to his armor once more. One of his security officers, Mahlo 'Turagg, approached.

"The humans are under guard, Arbiter, and have provided us with their identities and service records." 'Turagg handed over a circular datapad. "Their leader awaits an audience with you."

The Arbiter examined the profiles of his unexpected visitors. "I have fought alongside Commander Palmer and know her to be an honorable warrior. The others, I am unfamiliar with."

"The one named Olympia Vale is a diplomat to our people and speaks our language well. Her record claims that she spent several lunar cycles among the nomad clans of Khael'mothka, and she served aboard the *Mayhem* three annual cycles ago."

The Arbiter found his scrutinous attention drawn to the profile of Fireteam Osiris's leader. "Jameson Locke," he said aloud. "Office of Naval Intelligence."

"He was counseled by Vale to reveal to us that he was an agent for ONI."

"Escort this agent to await my presence in the command tent," the Arbiter ordered. "Let us see what this assassin wishes of me."

CANTICLE IV. THE REDEEMER

October 28, 2558
Genesis

"His name was Bibjam. He was a mere Grunt. Scarred, though spirited, past his useful years. His advice was unconventional: 'Fight as if there was no honor in death.'

"He guided us through victory in conflict after conflict. And while we reveled in our glory, he mourned every brother we lost along the way.

"As the war went on, Bibjam became more concerned with protecting us. When we finally caught him betraying our movements to the Swords of Sanghelios, he told us capture was the only way for us to avoid death.

"He truly believed he found a way to save us.

"I could not meet his gaze when I ran him through."

Dham 'Mashatt had dropped the datapad containing his eulogy for Bibjam as he and his fellow Unggoy, Jabjab, had been pulled into their prison cell, but the words he had spoken remained fresh in his mind. He let out a deep exhale as he sank onto a nearby crate. It was the way of the Sangheili to honor their greatest figures through ballads, and while 'Mashatt was no warrior-poet, this was the only tribute he could conceive of to the leader he had followed, revered, and ultimately slain.

He cast his gaze toward Jabjab, who seemed to have fallen asleep at the edge of the cage, just inches away from the energy shield that kept them contained. There was no way out. With nothing to do but wait, the Sangheili warrior attempted to piece together all that had happened over the last few day-cycles.

Jul 'Mdama had fallen on Kamchatka, slain by demons. Instead of calling a retreat, the remaining council of generals had decreed that they would proceed with the assault on Sanghelios in a final desperate attempt to assassinate the Arbiter.

Dham 'Mashatt had been there when the Guardian rose from the Csurdon Sea to render its own judgment upon the battle that raged through the city of Sunaion. There had been many questions about what the Guardian would do once awakened. Was it an omen of victory or defeat?

It had been neither. The construct had simply opened an immense slipspace portal and departed, and brought with it any vessels caught in its wake—including 'Mashatt's own Lich.

It had delivered them here, to this strange world. The corrosive atmosphere of the jungle in which they had crashed seared their throats, and the warrior-angels that once fought by their side had been subverted by a heretical human intelligence. They had been hunted, fighting for their very lives while barely able to breathe, until . . .

"Greetings!"

'Mashatt heard a cheerful voice from outside the cell. He

turned to see a floating spherical construct with a glowing central eye staring at him. *An Oracle?!*

"I am 031 Exuberant Witness, monitor of the Genesis installation. Oh, but I am so terribly sorry that I did not introduce myself earlier when I had you all locked in here. That must have seemed quite rude! Let me get those doors for you."

The cell's rippling energy shield wall disappeared. Dham 'Mashatt got to his feet and gently prompted Jabjab to awaken as he stepped onto a raised platform overlooking the small prison area. Ice and snow covered much of the ground, and 'Mashatt could see his breath as fog in the freezing cold air.

"But you must understand, it was for your safety, of course," the oracle who had named herself Exuberant Witness continued. "You may have noticed that Genesis has become a little more . . . *active* of late. The Guardians brought a significant number of visitors to my home, and it has been very difficult to stop you all from fighting! I simply wish to prevent any unnecessary death before moving the shield world through slipspace, beyond Cortana's reach."

Jabjab waddled up to one of the adjacent cells and asked, "What wrong with that guy?"

Contained within the cell was one of the warrior-angels—a Promethean Knight. Its divine carapace was like all others: bulbous, top-heavy armor that bore a pair of arms, with one connected to its integrated weaponry while the other ended in a deadly blade of hard light. The lower regions of its body were slender, and another pair of smaller, more dexterous arms extended from its chest. Its helmet bore a grim visage, which covered a blazing skull beneath.

This warrior-angel, however, was demonstrating some peculiar behavior. Where others of its kind had come to show instantaneous hostility, this one simply stood by the wall of its cell, head buried in its smaller pair of hands as it made random spasmodic movements.

"Oh dear." Exuberant's tone saddened as she initiated a scan of the Knight from her central lens.

"What is happening?" 'Mashatt asked.

"The poor human essence within this Promethean unit has been severed from its command network. It has been abandoned. And unfortunately, it seems to be winning a battle against its own programming. It is aware of who it once was . . . and what it has become."

The Promethean Knight thrashed around in its cell. Its arms slapped against its helmet as if trying to clear its vision or awaken itself from some terrible nightmare, then threw its entire weight against the wall, shaking uncontrollably, before slumping in defeat. 'Mashatt watched as it repeated the process. The warrior-angel seemed to be caught in a recursive, torturous loop.

He did not expect to discover such a deep well of pity within his hearts.

For as long as he could remember, the Covenant—through the wisdom of the Prophets—had instilled within 'Mashatt a sense of awe and reverence for the divinity of the Forerunners. But the hierarchs had been liars, manipulators, and the Covenant had fallen . . . and now the sanctity of Forerunner technology had been demystified as countless groups sought to claim their ancient bounties and deliver death and destruction. The truth of their gods' benevolence was in doubt when it seemed all they had to offer were terrifying weapons.

Perhaps there was other truth that Dham 'Mashatt could at last discern for himself.

Could he break his own programming, as Bibjam had? But what would that leave him with? 'Mashatt could find only a wellspring of pain and regret, the depths of which he felt he could draw from until the end of time.

"What can be done?" 'Mashatt found himself asking, turning to Exuberant Witness. "Is there any way we can aid this creature? Can it be delivered from this pain?"

The oracle did not respond immediately, appearing to be deep in thought. "There may be something . . ." she said at last.

"Oracle." 'Mashatt was unable to keep the longing from his voice at the prospect of being able to ask a construct of the gods for a purpose. "Please. Command us."

"There is a place here on Genesis. A gateway to the Domain."

'Mashatt knew of what she spoke. Covenant scripture told of a great library that held all of the Forerunners' knowledge, the soul and wisdom of the time before their departure on the Great Journey.

"And this warrior-angel," 'Mashatt said. "If it were to pass into the Domain, it could be at peace?"

"I am uncertain. The Domain has been out of commission for such a very long time, and it is currently being leveraged by Cortana . . ."

"But it is the strongest chance it has?"

"I believe so."

An idea took shape in Dham 'Mashatt's mind. A new purpose, the greatest that anyone of the Covenant could hope for—and not just for himself.

"Oracle, would you release my Covenant brethren from their holding cells?"

"Certainly!"

The energy shield walls of several other prison units dissipated. Three other Unggoy waddled over, accompanied by a lone Mgalekgolo, apparently cut off from its bonded pair, and introduced itself—through the translation of one of the Unggoy—as Naliligaw. All gathered at the center of the monitor's strange menagerie.

The Sangheili called them all to attention. "My brothers, I am Dham 'Mashatt, and I have much to tell you."

He explained all he could to them, recounting the fall of Jul 'Mdama's Covenant at Sunaion for the benefit of those who had come from elsewhere in the galaxy, and further detailed how numerous Guardians had transported many people from the worlds they had been awakened within to this place.

He then explained how Bibjam, whom he had once called friend and leader, had sought to protect them from these terrible events by defecting, before 'Mashatt killed him for this betrayal.

And he presented to them the choice they now faced.

"We can leave. The Oracle may be able to return us to a location of our choosing, or else help us to find slipspace-capable transport. Or . . . we could remain on Genesis. There is a place for us here, serving the Oracle in her quest to return all others to where they belong, if that is the duty we choose for ourselves. In service of the gods, we may at last find some measure of peace."

As 'Mashatt spoke, he felt a wave of clarity wash over him. Bibjam's intentions had been pure and honorable, for he had been moved by love and loyalty, but so too were his actions stained with distrust. He had not confided his treacherous plans and had therefore acted *for* them—and in doing so, he had removed the opportunity for those he loved to decide their own fate.

Dham 'Mashatt would not repeat that mistake.

Naliligaw let out a low rumble; the lone Mgalekgolo teetered slightly from side to side, before stepping forward and approaching 'Mashatt. The Unggoy, too, waddled over as one.

"Our choice has been made, oracle," 'Mashatt declared as Exuberant Witness excitedly chirped about having the company of new friends. "We shall serve you as the true guardians of Genesis."

CANTICLE V. THE MUSIC

October 29, 2558 (Military Calendar)
Zeta Halo

Professor Montgomery Marie was a creature of habit.

0500 Hours: Morning alarm, up and out of bed, personal chatter comes on with daily playlist. Always start with the Helljumpers' Interstellar Orchestra.

0510: Jog, same path around the base as always. Custom playlist of twenty-third century rock anthems set to full blast.

0540: Journal time. Music off. Reflection.

No matter where in the galaxy she was, her routines were the same. She'd kept them that way for years, her method of holding on to a constant in what was otherwise a fairly nomadic way of life. Not that anything she had seen before could truly compare to her current workplace.

As she glanced up from her journal, the ancient Forerunner construct designated Installation 07—Zeta Halo—rose to its own towering heights, both literally and metaphorically. Professor Marie had arrived only a few weeks ago with an expeditionary group and was still getting used to the way the horizon curved upward with its thinning band of oceans and landmasses. And, in its current orbital orientation, the immense face of its uniquely terrestrial anchor planet.

It was truly a marvel. And her late father's journal was now full of her own sketches, teeming with whatever caught her attention. The horizon, alien flora, flocks of strange birds that wheeled in the sky as the sun passed over the edge of the ring.

0610: Off to breakfast, playlist back on to finish the last leg of the jog back to base. Late twenty-fourth-century Reavian throat singing. Oddly calming.

She made her way back down to grab a quick bit of food in the prefabricated mess hall where she overheard spirited chatter from her colleagues and the base's military personnel. Over the last week, news had been streaming in about catastrophic events concerning colony-wide disasters. Ancient alien constructs awakening after millennia of dormancy, the Master Chief going missing or AWOL or dying in the line of duty . . . it was all frightfully unclear. But what *was* clear was that a rogue artificial intelligence named Cortana was behind it all. Cortana's message had been heard across the galaxy, declaring that "the Created" had come to lead all species, all civilizations to a new dawn, whether they wanted it or not.

Given the intensity of Professor Marie's own work and the wonder that she experienced every day here on Zeta Halo, the news seemed like distant noise, the barest hum of something on the far horizon. And even if she did have concerns, there was little she felt she could do against such a tapestry of chaos.

Better that she stay focused. While she was involved in all manner of research on the ring, her primary task concerned the deployment and observation of OQ-45 remote survey drones—nicknamed "Honeybees"—and subsequent analysis of their terrain mapping.

0800 Hours: Reporting for duty, work begins. Music left off until lunchtime.

Her workstation was a watchtower, a small blocky structure that housed a maximum of three people and served as a sensor platform. It was dark inside, primarily lit by an array of monitors and readouts of the local area, and the activity of the Honeybee drones.

"This is Hotel Bravo Three. Comms check, over," Professor Marie said as she picked up her headset and settled into her chair.

Ordinarily, she would have expected to hear the other Honeybee teams reporting in with relative immediacy, but as she counted up to twenty whole seconds, there was no response.

"I say again: All Honeybee controllers, comms check, over."

0815: Still no response. What the hell?

Professor Marie performed a routine check of her equipment to make sure it was functioning correctly—which it was—and attempted to contact them again, to no avail. As she made to direct a report of the issue to the local command center, the radio crackled with activity.

At last, she thought. "This is Hotel Bravo Three, please identify yourself, over."

Her brow furrowed as she heard what sounded like music coming through. She was sure she could hear light piano notes playing somewhere in the background.

She glanced at her chatter to verify that it was indeed switched off.

"This is Hotel Bravo Three, please identify yourself immediately. This silliness has gone on long enough . . . over."

The music grew louder, accompanied now by the sound of a woman humming.

And still Professor Montgomery Marie could not find the source.

Surely this was not from the radio? Surely somebody would—

"There you are!"

A voice from behind her almost made Professor Marie jump out of her chair in surprise. She turned to see Private Rene Gordon, her dark hair a wild mess and her battle dress uniform looking anything but parade ready. "What the hell are you still doing in here, Monty? Haven't you seen?"

Before she could respond, Private Gordon pulled her up and

dragged her out of the comms station, squeezing her hand with what felt like a Helljumper's death grip.

"We're screwed, Monty! We're *so* screwed," was all she said as they made it outside and found a gathering of the base's personnel.

Professor Marie did not need to ask what the fuss was all about. The answer was hanging in the sky above them.

Settling over a structure, perhaps a dozen kilometers upspin, was a great winged construct. Silver alloy lined with accents of hard light. Jagged, segmented pieces that evoked the image of a phoenix.

An ear-splitting ringing suddenly sounded from every individual piece of communications equipment around the base.

The music was everywhere now. A new war across the stars had arrived not with the sound of weapons fire, but *Préludes No. 4* by Claude Debussy.

0900 Hours: Working to get word to Earth. Cortana has come to Zeta Halo.

RENDEZVOUS WITH RAMEN

*This story takes place in August 2558, approximately two months before the Created uprising is initiated by Cortana's awakening of the Guardians (*Halo 5*).*

OFFICE OF NAVAL INTELLIGENCE // SECTION TWO

FILE CLASSIFICATION: CONFIDENTIAL

DOCUMENT ID: ONI-SEC2-MA-842

MATERIAL AUDIT

SUBJECT: *Excerpt from Chapter Three of* Rendezvous with Ramen, *a biographical book by renowned chef and food critic Arturo Bustamante, wherein he attempts to find the best ramen offering in UEG space.*

CONTEXT: *Bustamante describes a visit to a settlement on Earth within the city of Rio de Janeiro, which is home to Covenant asylum seekers.*

EXCERPT BEGINS//

The subject of this chapter will be, I am sure, highly divisive. The Covenant War is still fresh in the minds of many, the losses we suffered over twenty-seven years utterly immeasurable, and while the war itself may have ended, there are still ongoing hostilities with remnant groups out there threatening our existence.

I think we all hoped that, in the unlikely event of emerging victorious, it would've been a clean win, i.e. "*We beat the bad guys and went home to rebuild, ooh-rah humanity!*" Well, that's not quite how it went, as it took an alliance with the Sangheili to help defend Earth and ultimately sever the head of the Covenant. Suddenly, our victory got a little more complicated, as the Sangheili had very much been a part of the Covenant, killing us *en masse* throughout those twenty-seven years.

Some folks are keen to move forward and become part of a larger interstellar community, while a whole lot of others—quite fairly, may I add—either want nothing to do with those who burned their homes to glass or to enact revenge now that humanity is no longer on the back foot.

It was a highly controversial story several years back when it was reported that there were aliens living on Earth itself, the very planet we fought so hard to keep safe for almost three decades of war, but the fact of the matter is this: They're here, they're our neighbors now, and besides, aren't you just a little bit curious about what they're actually like? I know I am!

And so, during my quest to find the best ramen spot in the galaxy, my journey to the city of Rio de Janeiro took me to one of the most interesting places I've ever been.

I visited a Sangheili restaurant on Earth.

Rio de Janeiro is a jewel of a place. Its history stretches over a thousand years, back to the sixteenth century, and throughout all that time, it has been a marvel to behold. Its beaches, hills, tropical forests, samba dancing, festivals, and so much more could well make for a whole other book—perhaps I should earmark *Rendezvous with Rio* for later.

But Rio hasn't been without strife. Just a few months ago, a Sangheili terrorist attempted to detonate a Havok tactical nuclear device as an act of retribution for the Master Chief's unexpected return last July, during which the Spartan repelled an attempt to invade Earth. As a result, extremist groups like Sapien Sunrise saw an increase in popularity and membership, as blame was attributed to the Sangheili asylum seekers living in Rio, as well as the Unified Earth Government creating the opportunity for such a potentially devastating attack by allowing alien residency on Earth.

I made my way to the Sekibo district, so named in honor of the recently deceased Ambassador Richard Sekibo, who was killed by Sapien Sunrise extremists on the colony world Biko. The great irony is that Ambassador Sekibo was due to negotiate with a Sangheili *kaidon* and relocate Earth's alien population to a more suitable world, but a campaign of misinformation instead sought to spread panic that Earth was going to accept more alien refugees.

So, whether you like it or not, we're sort of stuck with each other.

The Sekibo district is like an "antechamber" to the main Sangheili settlement, which is itself heavily fenced off. Barbed wire, defensive emplacements, security personnel—it certainly doesn't feel like any kind of "warm welcome" on the way in.

Once inside the compound, the view isn't all that much to look at either. Imagine a cluster of old buildings converted to serve as housing for a population of perhaps fifteen hundred, "fit for purpose" in the sense that the Sangheili *can* live there, but it's not at all ideal, even fundamentally, for their biology. As I walked through the streets, I saw a few makeshift workshops where some Sangheili were working with wood to create simple things like chairs they can comfortably sit on.

The most interesting feature of all here, though, is a small church. Roman Catholicism remains the dominant religion in Rio, and some bold padre decided to build a house of worship and live among the refugees. Father Gustavo Barbosa is that holy man. I asked him to accompany me so I could be shown around the area by a local while asking him some questions. Perhaps most pressing of all: What exactly was his thought process around doing all this?

Here's what he told me.

You must understand, the Sangheili are themselves people of faith. They have known the Covenant religion for many thousands of years. Religion is the lens through which they understand things, just as it was for humanity through so much of our own growth and development. And they are entering a period of great spiritual uncertainty, as many of them are renouncing that faith.

Are all living things not children of God as we are? Are we to deny them the opportunity to repent and seek forgiveness and grace from the everlasting, unconditional love of God? You may be surprised to know how many have willingly received the Sacrament of Reconciliation and now pray the rosary.

Me? I simply pray that we can all find greater peace and unity through our suffering, and perhaps one day even joy in the knowledge that God's children are a greater extended family than we ever expected to know.

Father Barbosa's words are undoubtedly just one of many other schools of thought that will be debated for years to come, but it's not hard to see where he's coming from. Indeed, I am spurred to wonder how other religions are grappling with the revelation that we are not alone in the universe and how their spiritual leaders might respond to the plight of these aliens in particular. There has perhaps never been a more loaded plate for the term "food for thought."

Suffice it to say, the long walk to get here and all this head-spinning theological, philosophical talk had really built up my appetite. So, at last, Father Barbosa and I set off to the restaurant.

I asked the padre what the name of this establishment was, and he attempted to answer with the Sangheili name first which sounded roughly like "*meiruuch*"—or "Rio Keep." I found this rather interesting, as what little knowledge I have of the Sangheili suggests that the keep is the center of how their clans operate. The first thing that struck me upon entering was, in fact, the music. I don't think I'd ever considered what music aliens even listen to, and that opened up its own series of questions about their musicians, what instruments they use, whether they hear music differently than us, what they think of *our* instruments and genres . . . Anyway, the closest thing I could compare to what I heard was glass harps. You know when you fill a bunch of wineglasses with different levels of water and rub around the rim to produce this kind of ethereal chime-like sound? It's a lot like that, and actually it really is quite beautiful and soothing.

As it was approaching late afternoon when we arrived, the restaurant was sparsely populated, with perhaps only half a dozen Sangheili, along with a couple of Unggoy who shuffled us over to a table.

Before any conversation could begin in earnest, we were treated to a variety of delicacies. It seems that a supplier is occasionally able to acquire some basic ingredients more palatable to a Sangheili diet, and so there is a curious mix of Earth food—particularly those specific to Rio—and alien cuisine. The bean-and-meat stew *feijoada* has been a national dish over *many* centuries, but have you ever tried it with *colo* meat? I must say, I haven't historically gotten on with Sangheili food, yet the black beans, accompanying sauce, and additional Subanese spices unlocked something truly special in the taste of that meat. In fact, I'm pretty sure that the spices must've been crushed-up blamite that caused miniature supercombines in the mouth. Within the inset pages of *Rendezvous with Ramen*, you will find a more detailed recipe along with my annotated notes and deeper insight into the taste and texture of this marvelous dish.

I should note for the sake of relevance to the overall book here that I *did* inquire as to whether this establishment offered ramen, to which the Unggoy chef—a stocky fellow who introduced himself as Grubmaster Plomp—simply asked, "What that?" Rest assured, I provided them with ingredients and instructions, so perhaps this place stands a chance of landing in the top ten ramen spots on Earth in the near future. We'll all have to stay tuned to see how that goes.

And as if that wasn't a strange enough diversion, the proprietor then appeared, and it was Father Barbosa who formally introduced us. The Sangheili now possessed the name "Peter"—a sacred alias that he seemed to find appropriate.

After exchanging greetings and pleasantries, we sat down together at a long wooden table. I took the earliest opportunity to ask Peter what his story was, to which he said: "I shall speak truth to you, if you have the appetite to listen."

As a matter of fact, I very much did. The *colo*-augmented *feijoada* had gone down very well as an appetizer, though I suspected the next hour of conversation would involve less savory topics and details. What I present to you here are Peter's own words.

"We came to Earth almost six annual cycles ago, led by the Prophet of Regret, who brought with him two carriers—*Solemn Penance*, his flagship, and *Day of Retribution*.

The Demon, the one you call the Master Chief, destroyed *Jubilation* with a void maker, and it was from that vessel we deployed to the surface of your planet. We were fortunate to depart the vessel moments before the Demon made his daring gambit, but others fled in haste with whatever they could leave in—dropships, breaching carapaces, even boarding craft. We were scattered across the surface of your world and sought to regroup. But within a mere handful of units, the Prophet of Regret retreated and ordered his vessel to jump into slipspace, stranding us here.

Other Covenant vessels soon arrived, and it seemed that our salvation was at hand.

Alas, these ships disgorged great numbers of Jiralhanae. Some of us were wary of approaching them while others gladly embraced what appeared to be reinforcements . . . I watched as those foolish few were torn limb from limb, cut down by brutal bladed weaponry. It became clear that we were truly alone then. The Covenant had apparently forsaken us; any human we might have encountered had every reason to simply kill us on sight. And so, I concluded my service in the Covenant military with the most shameful orders a Sangheili can give.

Retreat. Run. Hide. And when we were found a few day-cycles later, surrender.

We were interrogated. I advised that we comply and provide information to your military about the Covenant and why the Prophet of Regret came to this world—how it was that he did not know it was indeed a human world, let alone the sought-after cradle of your kind. For this, we were granted clemency that we did not expect to receive, and we have remained here ever since.

Once we were warriors, forged and formed for the singular purpose of delivering death to humanity. Now we are known to many as "refugees" and "asylum seekers." But that does not encompass all that we are. Free from the Covenant, we now do many things. We cook, we craft, some are creating their own literature. Many attend the services of the Father here to better understand your species and this world.

We do not expect forgiveness. But our lives are dedicated now to productive service and penitence."

[ARTURO NOTE: I should note here that, with his tale concluded, Peter glanced over to Father Barbosa and said "Amen," which got a good chuckle out of us.]

Well, there you have it. I visited our alien neighbors, dined and conversed with them, and lived to tell the tale without having to order a tactical retreat.

When I departed, I realized I still had much to chew on from what Peter had said. (Is it weird that the more I call him Peter, the more it seems to fit?) We shall be revisiting some elements of this day in the upcoming chapters, as I returned to the Sekibo district over the following two days. There is, of course, far more here to chip away at, but for now I shall say that this was a most enlightening experience that I hope will spur some spirited discussion.

Sadly, there was no ramen available here, which means my journey to the Sekibo district was a divergence from the path of my own quest. I wish I could say I got back on track in short order, but you know how things go . . .

Attached Note

FOR: 26582-72839-MS

We are faced with a rather curious predicament here—one that begs for closer scrutiny before we proceed with any action.

On one hand, these Sangheili and Unggoy were taken in as refugees after providing us with valuable intelligence on the Covenant. They were given sanctuary on Earth, and over five years later we continue to do our best to keep them shielded from the more wrathful individuals and groups who would rather see them dead.

Legally speaking, we have a duty of care to observe and enforce. In that regard, we would consider it imperative to suppress the information detailed in this chapter and *suggest* to Singer-Edwards Ink that they focus on broader strokes here. Though he clearly attempts to toe the line of neutrality, one might note that food is minimally focused on in this chapter. One might be led to think that Bustamante has lost a step, his writing more akin to a *New Mombasa Times* opinion piece, but I would suggest that there is evidently an agenda at play here.

However, we must also take into account that this information was provided freely and openly by one of the refugees themselves. This was not a data leak, nor the work of a rogue agent with an agitative agenda. This is a question of whether we are willing to allow freedom of speech to an alien—legally, an Earth resident—saying something that isn't necessarily in his own interest.

My analysis? *Way* above my pay grade (in fact, it's probably above yours as well). I'm passing this one up the chain. Let the AIs work out probability models while the UNSC Security Council spends a week or two debating policy and politics.

Personally speaking, though? I think we should let this one slip the net. I can hear you already: "Let people make up their own minds, are you insane?" Well, maybe—my next mandatory psych eval *is* just a few weeks away. But nothing gives raw data to digest and analyze quite like people reacting to the real thing.

Bustamante is a washed-up has-been coming out of retirement and clearly feels the need to court controversy for attention. If he wants to spin up this kind of discourse to sell his book, I say we let him.

GHOSTS OF THE GYRE

"Know that all that lingered in me, the memories and emotions of old humanity, when I was still flesh, is also hidden deep within you. It slumbers, but it shapes, and it haunts your dreams and your hopes."

—343 Guilty Spark,
Halo: Primordium

*This story begins in January 2556, more than three years after the end of the Covenant War (*Halo 3*)—the near thirty-year struggle for humanity's survival—and spans the time following as the Office of Naval Intelligence sets up its research operation on Zeta Halo.*

ADJUTANT VIGILANCE – SUB-MONITOR 061 LOG (ENTRY 019038)

Once, I was Genemender-Folder-of-Fortune.

I was stationed on this dire wheel when it was known by the designation Gyre 11, assigned by the Librarian to care for the human populations we had taken from their homes and brought here. For a time, they lived—as humans do—by the mantra of *daowa-maad.* Hunt, grow, and live in concert with the roll and tug of the universe.

But then, the Master Builder claimed jurisdiction over all our operations. Those who refused to comply were executed, and the humans became cattle to be herded into what they called "Palaces of Pain." There is no name more fitting for what the humans endured within those cold halls, as they were subjected to the twisted will of the Flood.

It was said that this was done to test the claim our once-proud enemy had made: that they had discovered a "cure" for the parasite. The humans had managed to drive the Flood—which they called the Shaping Sickness—beyond the borders of the galaxy, but at great cost. One-third of their population who had been given this alleged cure were sent into the Flood's chattering jaws. Their sacrifice gave us ten millennia to prepare for the parasite's return, but the Master Builder exiled or killed all who did not conform to his own designs.

The Master Builder's closing grip on this ring caused the humans to abandon their cities and villages, forcing them to live on the run once more. A grim pantomime of their last war. They feared larger settlements were prime targets, but this cruelty could only go on for so long before others rose to stop it.

What happened then was a quick succession of events cascading into calamity. The Master Builder used a Halo ring to suppress a San'Shyuum rebellion, a crime against the Mantle, which caused many stationed here to rebel against him. Unfortunately, Builder Security forces quickly regained control of the situation and gave the survivors a choice: serve or perish.

Some submitted. Others chose execution. And a few pretended to pledge allegiance before taking the opportunity to sabotage the installation.

I was never caught and remained loyal to my duty. I camouflaged my stations, hid my preserves away, kept my human charges safe . . . for as long as I could.

But then orders from the Librarian herself brought another macabre turn for the humans. They were to be protected through digital preservation—their essences extracted, dissolving their physical forms, so that the Builders could not acquire the knowledge their ancestors held. For good measure, to ensure I would also not be compromised, I did the same to myself.

I serve now as Adjutant Vigilance. For one hundred millennia, I have watched, I have waited.

And now, the day has finally arrived.

Their ships drop out of slipspace and the ring welcomes them. They deploy research bases and outposts, building infrastructure for their settlements.

The humans have come to Zeta Halo with only dim awareness of this place. They believe that they have arrived at something of an undiscovered frontier. They are wrong.

They do not yet know that they are returning home.

1300 Hours, January 9, 2556 (Military Calendar)
Zeta Halo

The buzz of our two OQ-45 Honeybee drones faded as they climbed above the clouds, leaving us to marvel at the spectacle we had caused.

A crash of *rhinoks*—a large and surly herbivorous species that looked strikingly similar to Earth's own rhinoceros, from which the collective name "crash" had been lifted, despite my colleagues' insistence on "herd"—had taken off at speed in the gray-brown valley below during an imaging run from our surveillance drones. Flying too close to the creatures had caused their migration to move a little ahead of schedule, and through a pair of binoculars I spotted the team of biologists setting off to give chase from a safe distance in their M15 Razorback.

All according to plan.

It was a matter of lively speculation that the non-sapient species on Forerunner installations had seen some degree of biological "customization," making them effectively part of the ecosystem to some degree. That element of design seemed particularly evident in this area of Zeta Halo, which did not operate at all similarly to data I'd studied on the automated habitability systems of Alpha, Gamma, and Delta Halo.

Indeed, as we had spent the last few months acclimating to our new home, it was something of a shared sentiment that one's very presence here would, in time, make you "part" of the ring itself. Such superstitious words defied objectivity . . . but something in it felt true.

There were four of us who had hatched this little scheme with the *rhinoks*. Professors Dora Emmett and Ellen Zoyas, our team's xenobiologist and anthropologist, and Michael Quinn, our marine escort. They were observing the area with their own field-issue spotting scopes and binoculars, but it wasn't the *rhinoks*' movement they were observing.

"There!" Dora exclaimed, pointing unhelpfully into the open space of the valley, before a sideways glance from Ellen prompted her to mark a waypoint.

The thundering stampede of over three dozen *rhinoks* was kicking up so much dirt and dust that the geometric distortions of the baffler were struggling to keep up. The dirt unnaturally faded from thick brown into a ghostly, transparent cloud as it passed through a telltale shimmer effect marking the border of the Forerunner camouflage system.

Ellen thumped me on the back with a hand the size of my head. "Let's get the climbing equipment ready, Doc."

I have written a great deal of analytical work on our knowledge of Halo's systems, all classified, of course—it is highly unlikely that *How to Study a Halo* by Dr. Madeline Tress will ever reach the public (not with that title, at least). Procedure for notable Forerunner installations has a general order of operations: First, you locate the cartographer, which reveals the various facilities on the ring. But the UNSC presence on Zeta Halo had thus far had no luck in finding it, which meant that all topographical and surface data had to be collected the hard way—and the substructures making up the vast underbelly of this place were another matter entirely. Thus, the Honeybees.

As the surveillance drones had been mapping this region while flying in joint formation, they had altered their trajectory around a part of the terrain, leaving a blank spot on their map as they returned to their standard search pattern a few seconds later. We'd missed the alteration, until Quinn pointed out a tiny blank spot on our topographical map.

Forerunner camouflage was advanced, but not foolproof. Bafflers, dazzlers, misdirection filters, even hard light technology could produce convincing holograms of entirely false structures, hiding things in plain sight.

But the *rhinoks* had presented a problem. Despite being herbivores, they were irritable by nature. Pissing off dozens of six-ton behemoths (that may well have been deliberately settled to migrate to this area) hadn't seemed like the most prudent course of action, leading us to consider how we could displace them. Course-correcting the Honeybees gave us an opening and sent the other research team in the area speeding off to follow their gargantuan quarry.

I don't think of myself as a glory hog by any means, but Zeta Halo had made it abundantly clear that it wasn't going to divulge its secrets quite as readily as the other installations. That had given way to a certain element of competition among the research teams, as the opportunity to land the first major discovery and make our mark on history was still open.

It took the better part of an hour to make the descent down to the valley, during which I found myself considering my companions. Dora was an Outer Colonies girl, somebody who seemed to be trying to build a career while coming up against the kind of roadblocks one faces with a family tied to certain independent movements. Ellen was bright-eyed and excitable about the mission but seldom spoke of her loved ones—it seemed almost certain that many, if not all of them, are gone. One was seeking to escape the shadow of her family, while the other had seemingly been brought to this place because of it.

Michael Quinn remained something of an enigma, however. While the rest of us were very much on first-name terms with each other, he was simply "Quinn" to us. His expertise was not scientific, but military, and he had largely remained a stoic watcher as we went about our work.

Reaching the ground at last, we made our way toward what simply looked like the opposing rock wall of the valley. My mind swirled with possibilities as to what we were about to find—the cartographer, or some other vital facility? Perhaps even the elusive monitor itself.

The nature of the border we faced was simple, as the most potent trickery often is, in that we'd just walk forward to breach the other side . . . but some element of this camouflage method felt as if it made one think they would actually be walking into a solid wall and should thus avoid it. I closed my eyes tightly as I moved ahead, leading the others—as was my role.

The border was thicker than I'd imagined it would be, approximately two meters judging by the fizzing sound it made, and a slight change in air pressure caused my ears to pop. As a precaution, we'd switched off all active technology in our packs, but I wondered whether they would work again on the other side.

I'd told the others not to look back upon making the transition, though I couldn't help but sneak a glance myself at what lay behind us once they'd passed me. I cannot quite describe what I saw at the edge of the baffler from within. It was hazy and had a similar effect to looking directly at the sun on a cloudless summer day.

And it already seemed so far behind us.

We found ourselves on a narrow and winding sandy trail strewn with pine needles from the tall and ridged trees hanging over us. Quinn was holding his assault rifle at the ready as he took point and led us into the unknown by single file. The rest of us had been given Sidekick pistols, which I kept holstered.

For thirty meters, we slowly traipsed ahead, our boots leaving a trail in the sand that sent tiny red-green ants scurrying, observed by hungry beetles clinging to the rocky walls. To test the effect of the border on our technology, Ellen withdrew the pad used to control the Honeybees, and judging from her hushed muttering as she thumped the device on its head, it seemed that it wouldn't even activate in this place.

As we emerged from the winding passage, the environment

seemed to change. The ground turned from sand to dry mud; the trees that stood tall became greener and were covered in lichen, and I was sure I could hear running water.

None of us were prepared for the sight that lay in wait for us beyond, as we found our view opening to what looked to be some kind of ancient . . . *city* seemed the right word for it at first glance?

In this roughly elliptical half bowl, there lay a group of heavily weathered structures, not unlike the ones I've seen in footage from Delta Halo. They were built of what looked more like stone than metal, yet still stood in defiance against untold millennia of entropy. Great vines and mosses were growing out of the gray-brown buildings and covered the stylized grooves and patterned indents of walkways and bridges over water blanketing much of the ground level's dirt pathways.

As I looked across to the farthest structure, which took the form of a two-story "temple," it was adorned with segmented rows of triangular struts. Water flowed down from between the struts, and I could see that the full length of the temple extended into the rocky bowl surrounding about three-quarters of the city. We have seen such structures on other installations, where constructions echoed Forerunner designs while being built from primitive materials. Some have theorized that they belong to species the Forerunners preserved, who sought to emulate the inexplicable architecture around them, despite lacking the technology of their saviors. Or captors.

But perhaps the most interesting feature was located at the center of it all. A grooved ramp led down to an octagonal roof platform for a smaller structure facing the temple. Here, there was a lower platform with five steps leading up to a smaller octagon, two stone pillars at its head and what looked like a kind of basin in the middle lined with ornate golden accents. Hovering above the basin was what appeared to be a great glass orb.

Eager to begin our investigation, we quickly and silently unloaded our climbing gear—even Quinn seemed to have been taken with fascination at the sight before us. And as soon as our boots hit the dirt, we were rushing to the center structure. I didn't even think to order the group to fan out and examine the rest of the site.

The egg-like device, if such a word was appropriate for it, had the reflective quality of water. And though it may possibly have been an optical effect from Ephsu, the system's local star, the way the light interacted with it conjured the image of ocean waves in my mind—swirling and circling endlessly within. I resisted the urge to reach out and touch it, wondering what it might feel like . . . glass? Cold metal?

As if latching on to my perception, I was sure in that moment that the sound of rushing water was not coming from the surrounding environment, but from *within* the egg itself. And there I stood, barefoot on Brighton Beach back on Earth. A young girl in a garish yellow rain jacket, curling my toes in the sand—in my military-grade boots—and feeling every individual grain shift or stick to my feet. I couldn't be sure whether this sensory experience was coming from a powerful moment of my own memory or if the device was projecting, or possibly *reflecting* it.

Forerunner technology—and I noted my inherent assumption about the device's origin—was capable of incredible feats. Tapping into one's state of mind certainly didn't seem too far-fetched from the things I've seen, especially as far as Halo installations are concerned.

I wondered what the others saw . . . and what this artifact was used for.

There was much to analyze and discuss. Still about thirty-six hours before our next scheduled check-in, which meant that we had plenty of time to examine everything, explore the temple, take samples. . . .

Yes, we're just getting started. And we have all the time in the world.

ADJUTANT VIGILANCE – SUB-MONITOR 061 LOG (ENTRY 019115)

The dead in this place do not truly die.

The human ancestors. The Shaping Sickness. Even me . . . life clings to this place, like moss on a gravestone. Death—absolute and final death—is a *kindness.* This I learned from an old human long ago.

I think back to the final defeat of the humans at Charum Hakkor, those wretched survivors who suffered such a twisted fate. To say that we "devolved" the humans as punishment does not relay the horror of what that process entailed. What we did still reverberates within the core of my being—a feeling that transcends even the flesh of my previous form.

The truth is this: We subjected living, thinking beings to the experience of withering their minds and bodies back to a preindustrial state while they were fully cognizant of what was happening to them. They were driven mad as their bodies physically changed and their minds gradually lost comprehension over the course of several days, for they were no longer capable of understanding even their own basic knowledge. We turned architects and musicians and officers and children into hunter-gatherers. And then we imprinted the memories of their advanced ancestors within them, that they might awaken and divulge their secrets—or else discover new forms of insanity.

The contemporary form of humanity has been here on Zeta Halo for a year now. They have directed great efforts toward finding the installation's cartographer, but the ring will not divulge its location to them.

Other places, too, remain undiscovered. The Palaces of Pain, the Auditorium, the containment facilities . . . We have concealed our crimes well.

But humans are nothing if not tenacious. Protocol forbids me from reaching out to them, and if I wished to seek out Despondent Pyre to request an exception, it would take another hundred millennia to find her, for she has been seemingly indisposed—yet still present—for a very long time. For now, I am consigned to witness their movements and nothing more.

Though I fear what may stir within their souls.

The secrets hidden within their genesongs may just be a thing to fear as much as the secrets of the ring itself. . . .

0800 Hours, June 17, 2557 (Military Calendar)
Zeta Halo

The dreams are stirring once again, growing ever more vivid . . . and I must *know what they mean.*

Every night, when finding comfort in sleep, the same images take shape in my mind, but I cannot coax them to completion.

I see . . . ships, I think. A vast flotilla made up of thousands of vessels, amassed around a yellow-brown planet. Some of the larger ships move into position around the equator, charging their weapons to bombard the surface.

The planet roils and shatters, buckling continental plates and boiling oceans as vast landmasses explode outward. Smaller vessels approach, gravity slings "catching" large chunks of rock and hurling them back from whence they came.

But this doesn't feel like a concluding action.

This feels like a prelude.

Slipspace portals open on the far side of the devastated planet, and a new fleet approaches—the capital ships move back, retreating behind civilian haulcraft and commercial vessels that are now positioned at the front line . . .

And that's when sleep rolls back like the veil of slipspace, and I awaken.

For three seasons now, I have had this dream, and this is as far as I can see.

If the ring, or the temple, or some other entity is trying to reach out and communicate something, the signal is being received but the message defies translation. I fear that leaving this location will cause the dreams to diminish, that there is something imbued within this place that wants to be—*needs* to be—known.

And I do not believe that we *can* leave, even if it were our most ardent desire to do so. Just as the border conceals the entrance, so too does it obscure our exit now, and we don't know how far it extends.

The temple offered us refuge on the day we arrived. Several stone passages within allowed us entry into a sort of antechamber—tall and trapezoidal in structure, which now serves as our living quarters, and lined with smaller hollow rooms where we take our rest. Upon our entry we found ancient scraps of worn cloth in these spaces, along with the remains of a rudimentary stone table and pewter jugs. Undeniable evidence of some previous civilization that had inhabited this place. Perhaps it was the ancient remnants of human populations that it's known were sequestered on this ring.

Perhaps it was someone else. But there is a circular symmetry in things—an unscientific notion, I know.

As I'm awake, I walk my usual morning route around the circumference of our home. I note that the others have already made their way to the parapet to begin what can only be called the morning's worship, a compulsion that colonized their minds soon after our arrival. Every day, they make their way to the opposite structure, take to their knees, and gaze into the orb that shimmers in the morning light. I walk the upper balcony of the temple and see them in their vigil, muttering words that form images within the orb, and the orb takes it from their minds.

The true object of their worship is not the orb itself, but a being that visits us twice a season. A great machine they insist to be called Shalimanda—a name they claim is whispered into their ears upon its coming. The orb takes, but it also seems to give words back.

We first saw Shalimanda in the waters below the edge of our domicile, lights dancing under gentle waves cast upon the wreckage of a Warthog. We don't know how it got there, nor what became of its driver and passengers . . . it may be that they occupy another such temple structure that seems to be visible from a distance. It may be that they are dead.

The being that the others call Shalimanda then rose from the depths, revealing its awesome form as a silver-gray construct bearing a circular, dish-shaped "head" from which were housed three blue eyes, and beneath which dangled an assemblage of arms, grapplers, claws, and two bipedal legs. As it sets about its work, the others bring paints and pigments they have prepared and adorn the machine with colorful patterns and strange symbols—glyphs from a language that I certainly don't recognize.

I once knew what this machine was called, an echo of its name still lives in my mind . . . but I made the mistake of joining the others in their ceremony that day, and the orb snatched the word from me. It gave the others a new word but took one from me. I would not let it take any more. I *earned* the knowledge of those words and will hold on to all that I can no matter how this place changes us. The orb is not a friend to those who don't listen to it, and I have since pledged to find other uses for my time.

Back when I entertained the others' delusions and would join them only for appearances, I would think instead of home. I would recall the sun glittering on a stream where a great willow tree stood, rowing a boat across with my mother, setting up our spillers out of sight—except for a maglev train that would shoot past like a bullet. We weren't supposed to go fishing in these waters, and we lay on our bellies amid tall grass to stay hidden. It only struck me after that she must have been playing some kind of game—staged a routine fishing trip as some kind of spectacle just to make it more exciting for my benefit.

The orb took this from me too. I can strain to remember it, the bullet-point facts and details of what happened . . . but the emotion of having lived it is replaced by a dull numbness where that memory should be.

What I do understand is that this construct serves some kind of unique role on this ring, which is unlike its brethren. Where I can recall—distantly now—the automated environment and weather systems serving as a facsimile of nature, this part of Zeta Halo's biosphere is tended to by machine custodians. It is their flocks of smaller metal farmers that enrich and keep the soil fertile, seed the fields to provide the bounty of sustenance for the living creatures of the ring—us included. It is this cycle of harmonious balance that my fellows worship through Shalimanda, and they have eschewed any other aspect of their lives not in service to this concept.

I, however, find myself drawn to an altogether different mystery. And with the others occupied for the day as Shalimanda makes its seasonal appearance, I have the ideal opportunity to pursue my studies.

Beneath the parapet of the temple's opposite structure where the orb lies is a circular hole in the ground measuring three meters in diameter. I don't know how far down it goes, for I lack the operational instruments to make any sound judgments on the matter—and it's at this moment that I lament the loss of the Honeybees, which would surely have been of great use. But I'm certain that I see a white light at the bottom.

We began this expedition with a hundred meters of rope each, along with the spares carried in our packs, which means that I have roughly 800 meters to work with. I doubt that's enough to reach the light below, but it will have to do for now.

I affixed the first rope to the surface above the hole, made sure the others were securely fastened to my belt along with my canteen, and stared directly down into the light. It filled me with a mixed sensation of vertigo and longing—I craved discovery and yet also felt some measure of fear toward what I might find.

But I would not reach the light.

Not this time.

I paid little mind to my last topside view of the world as I began my descent into this "tunnel." I didn't consider myself afraid of heights, or else I would have gladly joined the others in worship of the memory-stealer, but as I leaned backward and planted my feet on the gray stone wall, I was taken by a strange sensation. A kind of electrified itch on my back. Dark spots appeared in my field of vision as I looked up. The light from below, distant though it was, enlarged my shadow in such a way that—in such proximity—I felt larger and more cumbersome than I actually was. And the fast-fading sounds of the world above diminished to my breathing, my boots scraping over stone, blood rushing through my head, the gentle patter of water from the tunnel's moisture-thick atmosphere, the occasional rustle of plants and cursing on several occasions as my feet slipped on a patch of moss.

I tried to imagine the builders of this place. The Forerunners had constructed Halo not just as a galaxy-killing superweapon, but as a biological preserve, and the worlds within their megastructures felt so . . . real. Being here reminded me of when I was a young girl, when my parents took me to see the excavations of ancient ruins from classical human civilizations—millennia-old courtyards and villas crossed with modern catwalks overlooking the outlines of where people had once lived. I would strain to feel their essences—some kind of ghostly afterimage of their lives—inhabiting those places.

With this tunnel, though . . . I couldn't intuit anything from it. I didn't know how far down it went, had no sense of where it led, what purpose it might have served. Many Forerunner facilities boasted extensive tunnel systems for machines, but they were typically alloyed and pristine to avoid any compromise in efficiency.

And yet, I made note of a kind of logical structure to it, as approximately every seventy meters saw the ringed circumference of the tunnel pull inward with enough depth for my feet to find purchase.

Six hundred meters down was when I was sure I'd started to see things.

After taking a swig of water from my canteen, I grew frustrated that the light from below didn't appear to be getting any closer. The end of the tunnel seemed—impossibly—farther away now than it had from the top. Was this an effect of the Forerunners' architectural design that I was perceiving as a cruel joke? Or, like the border to our temple domicile, was this simply a perception barrier affecting my mind?

While I was getting no closer to either answers or the bottom of this tunnel, a peculiar shift in the air began to take place. It grew . . . warmer, and tiny motes of blueish light danced around me. Some gathered in clusters, like a colony of ants or a migration of birds, as if trying to form something, then dissipated.

It was soon after the appearance of these motes that I reached the end of my 800 meters. It hadn't been enough to reach the bottom, and I simply hung there in quiet frustration that all I had been able to ascertain from this venture was more unanswerable questions. I felt the urge to let slip the rope and fall.

What luck we were having. We'd learned precious little in our time here and were effectively cut off from the UNSC in this cursed temple. And to say "we" here was generous, as the others had given over untold amounts of their own knowledge to the orb that was reverting them in some way to a state of total compliance—regressing them into something unrecognizable from who they were when they came here. It fell to *me* to hold on to our knowledge, to take to the battlements and continue our research with practically no resources at my disposal.

It took me a while to notice that the motes of light were no longer moving upward, but had settled alongside me and were beginning to imbue themselves into the wall of the tunnel. Like so much of what I'd seen on Zeta Halo, I had no inkling as to what this could be.

Some "expert" I was.

And that was when they began to form words.

I watched, transfixed, as they illuminated the curved wall in front of me, as if carving a message into the stone. One by one, the motes winked out, and eleven characters resolved into being—five runes at the top, six immediately below . . . the same runes I'd seen the others paint onto Shalimanda.

Blood rushed through my head. I could feel my eardrums pounding as I watched with dreadful enthrallment.

My lips spoke the words aloud, even though I had no understanding of the language before my eyes—knowledge *given* by the orb, perhaps—and this is what they said.

"Enemy within."

ADJUTANT VIGILANCE – SUB-MONITOR 061 LOG (ENTRY 019204)

I recall my final return visit to my family's domicile, back when I was still flesh. We were an unusual lot because our family was split across various rates. I had chosen the path of Lifeworker, whereas my mother had been a Warrior-Servant, and both of her wives were Builders. It was the latter path that my sister had chosen, and she asked me once in an idle moment of silence what it is to be a Lifeworker.

I said to her there is no difference between the things we do—

only the mediums and canvases for our work. Where she gives form and function to inanimate matter, I do the same with the branches of a great tree.

The difference, I noted, is that Lifeworkers must collaborate *with* our subjects to complete our work. Our hand may guide and persuade patterns, but it is through the sacred act of living—of choice—and its results, be it prosperity or failure, that our work takes shape.

The Librarian, for instance, made humanity her greatest project, believing that our estranged siblings should inherit the Mantle. She seeded within them the potential for many developments that parallel our own—specific biological modifications, life-sustaining armor, ancilla, countless other hidden gifts . . . and deference to her guidance.

I questioned her on several occasions about this. Should the humans discover the path we had laid out for them, they might become arrogant and zealous, and repeat our own hubristic mistakes that came from our own belief that we were chosen. And why, if she believed in the humans' potential, was her presence and guidance so strong? Were we taking away their own capacity for choice? Or was she, in further-seeing wisdom, *hoping* that they would learn of her influence and rebel against it to serve some greater designs of independence?

It is easier, perhaps, when inanimate matter does not conform to the structures and designs of its architects, which Builders all too easily forget. To shape life for protection and prosperity involves failure and pain of a sort, for that is the only path to true wisdom.

You are so self-serious, my sister chided. We argued, we laughed.

And then I was stationed here.

As I look at the state of the galaxy from the humans' databanks, I fear I am no closer to understanding where our influence ends and our protectorates' choice and agency begins.

The humans have been embroiled in a devastating war where they emerged not just as survivors against a technologically superior foe, but the victors—stoking their arrogance. On two occasions, the Halo Array has been primed from Installation 00. The Didact has been awakened from exile, unleashing the horrors of the Composer once more.

And now, an ancilla who calls herself Cortana has breached the Domain and begun seizing control of old weapons to impose the rule of the Mantle upon all thinking life.

There is a growing imbalance in Living Time. This escalating series of catastrophic events will soon reach a nexus point, a singularity that will reshape the galaxy . . . or destroy it once again.

I know this to be inevitable. Inescapable.

I know this because the ancilla has come to Zeta Halo and claimed it as her throne. She has been working her way into its systems, begun mustering forces for conflict.

She may be wise enough to not unleash the Flood, for their devastation has already been felt in this age.

But this beggar after knowledge does not yet know about the *others* buried within this ring.

1309 Hours, November 1, 2558 (Military Calendar)
Zeta Halo

Shalimanda has gone.

For two seasons now, I think, the machine the others worship has not returned to our home, and its smaller brethren have seen a significantly reduced presence. I would not have concerned myself with this, but these constructs play a vital role in the maintenance of our domicile, and so I am equally affected by their disappearance as the land grows less capable of sustaining us.

We spent several days gathering wood to build a kind of makeshift canoe, though it was devoid of much artistry. I named it *Völuspá* and hoped that the designation would stir the others' memories. Alas, they merely grunted in agreement and gave no indication of recognition toward the vessel that had brought us to this ring. The orb had taken it from them.

As we rowed downstream for the better part of an hour, I wondered whether we would pass through the border and find ourselves back in our proper place, where we might be found by other UNSC personnel who had no doubt logged and long forgotten our absence—reduced us to a cautionary tale. This, too, did not come, and the high rock walls that lined either side of the stream were coated in slime-covered algae that would make any attempt to climb them immensely difficult. This pathway was undoubtedly linear by design. I contented myself with curiosity about how it would end.

The answer to that arrived just twelve minutes later, as the rock wall on the left parted and gave way to a small sandy embankment leading slightly uphill to the mouth of a cave. We could travel no further, for the stream resolved into a waterfall that, as we peered over the edge after bringing the canoe ashore, revealed a half-kilometer drop—not down to solid ground, or a body of water we could feasibly climb down to, but open space. And the lining of nature gave way here to gray alloyed pillars, which our climbing equipment certainly could not penetrate for a sturdy hold.

We were quite assuredly trapped here.

What we could see farther beyond, however, was a large floating "island" of sorts. It remained stationary above a vast green field enclosed by a curved mountain wall, and below the structure lay an octagonal-shaped pit lined by Forerunner metal, four triangular fins opposing each other. Fortunately, we'd each brought our spotter scopes with us, and we lay for a time observing the activity here.

To my mind, it seemed like this was some sort of factory. We watched as small flying machines, their silhouettes resembling the farming constructs we'd grown familiar with, entered the facility, then were sent down into the octagonal maw below. When they emerged from the fortress, they were . . . changed. Adorned with new equipment looking more like advanced weaponry. Tools designed for creation and growth repurposed into machines of war.

Our silent observation was broken by a sudden explosion striking the facility. The shockwave carried over the mountains and sped toward us. We scrambled for cover in the cave mouth just a few meters away from our overlook.

A voice carried across the air.

"I AM ADJUTANT RECOURSE, AND YOU WILL *NOT* HAVE THIS RING."

Flying machines of many shapes and sizes flew in all directions, opening fire on one another with directed energy weapons and hard light missiles.

Another voice spoke in reply—a woman's. Coldly calm and self-assured.

"Your little rebellion achieves nothing, sub-monitor. You will surrender now . . . and you will tell me where Despondent Pyre is."

"I WILL TELL YOU NOTHING. I WILL DIE BEFORE I GIVE UP HER LOCATION TO YOU, CORTANA."

"So be it."

The others watched with fascination as the skirmish played out around the factory, but I found myself drawn away from a thing that I had no influence over and instead entered the cave, hoping that there might be some passage leading out of the border—some design to this place. But it quickly became clear that there was not, and this space was in fact a natural formation.

The only peculiar feature was a dense curtain of dark-green leaves growing on vines that would have possibly been obscuring something behind it. I approached and brushed a few of them aside, and I saw something utterly remarkable.

A *painting* lay beneath.

I couldn't part all the vines at once—in my first clumsy attempts I realized there were too many to hold back—and so I took out a small combat knife I "borrowed" from Quinn and began hacking away.

The stone was marked with figures outlined in black, white, and red-brown pigments, not unlike prehistoric cave paintings on Earth made with hematite, manganese dioxide, and charcoal. The figures looked unmistakably human, which made sense. We *had* inhabited this place millennia ago, after all.

I cut away more leaves and vines over the next minute to see the entirety of the painting.

Hundreds of figures—most human, some alien, perhaps Forerunner. They formed a wave of bodies that were piled upon each other, contorted with agonized expressions. At the top layer, their arms reached up to carry a gray metallic disc, upon which sat a creature of horror.

Many arms and many legs curled together, like the husk of a shriveled spider.

Its head was broad and flat, lined with glittering eyes. And beside it, a machine—circular, with a single green eye.

All concealed within the circumference of a painted black ring.

The old spirits within me convulsed. I was filled with overwhelming dread and the instinct of flight, to return to the orb at once. To beseech it to take all of my memories. To apologize for my transgressions against its wisdom that we *must* forget.

I stumbled backward as the full nature of the painting was revealed, causing me to fall for what felt like an eternity, until darkness took me completely.

And that is when the memories the old spirits had been holding back at last revealed themselves. They coalesced and became other voices. Other lives. Stories tangled within my flesh. And they spoke as one.

We are those who scoured the Shaping Sickness from our galaxy and fell on Charum Hakkor.

We are the memories of old humanity. Within you, we slumber and shape, for we have been carved into your souls.

And those who know the moment you seek wished only to perish for having lived it. . . .

The bridge of a starship, observing a planet-breaking operation. Vast blightlands covered the surface of a yellow-brown world, one totally consumed by the Shaping Sickness.

I stood at the head of the bridge, and the "I" that took form was a three-foot-tall Florian—though her name was lost among many. "My" executive officer, however, scrutinized a dozen different holographic sensor screens with keen eyes, her chin resting on three long fingers that stroked a short beard. Va'larr, her name was, and seven feet tall she stood, making "us" a peculiar pairing to be sure, but a symbol of strength in the alliance between human and San'Shyuum. Our notori-

ety in the fleet during the Plague War had us called upon to serve by the Lord of Admirals himself.

And our task chilled me to my core.

We had gathered a sizeable number of non-military craft from the flotilla, leaving the rest to protect Charum Hakkor, and inoculated the crews with artificially programmed genes. With this weapon, bequeathed unto us through long study and discourse with a being we knew as the Primordial, we could eliminate the Shaping Sickness for good.

Or so it was alleged.

With dozens of worlds bombarded from orbit into cinders, provoking an escalating war with the Forerunners as we crossed the threshold of their ecumene, we were running out of time and options.

If this worked, we would burn this virulent menace and be able to turn attention to our second-front enemy. If it did not, then I could only hope that the Forerunners would see the scale of the threat and act accordingly. But this enmity had stewed over many centuries, which meant that acrimonious politics would supplant reason. If the Forerunner leaders were wise enough to see the threat, they would have joined the fight already—but they, in their highest wisdom, believed more in their studious ability to control.

And where the Shaping Sickness was concerned, no such thing was possible.

Va'larr simply nodded to me, indicating that we were ready for the next stage, and I gave the order. Our capital ships moved into position around the equatorial circumference of the planet, our combined firepower immolated the surface, and smaller vessels hurled gathered asteroids with gravity slings. The world was razed in a matter of moments.

But this was not an action of victory. This was entering a nel-doruut *den and stealing its young to draw out the pack.*

This was a summoning.

Hundreds of blighted ships dropped out of slipspace, and that is when the next phase began.

I ordered our military vessels to pull back, positioning our civilian and commercial flotilla at the fore, putting them in the immediate path of the parasite.

We watched on holographic viewscreens as the ships were boarded. We listened as communications channels filled with screaming. We dared not diminish this moment in any way, where our fates would meet summary judgment, for we were not the ones being sacrificed.

Infection forms latched on to their victims, seizing them with barbed appendages that cut through armor and clothing and flesh, boring their way into their host bodies' chest cavities to make their sickening nests. Elsewhere, spore clouds filled the oxygen systems of other vessels, causing the crews to sprout fleshy, egg-like growths that exploded and spread the Shaping Sickness's bile to others in close proximity.

All were infected. All civilian ships were lost.

But none of the infected rose again.

The bodies shuddered, screeched, writhed, but soon fell silent as the destructive genes did their work. Those who had suffered spore-based infection seemed to regain some semblance of awareness—but for the nightmare they awoke in, it would have been better to have simply died with the others.

We had our answer.

Through sacrifice, we had discovered a means to prevent the Shaping Sickness from perpetuating itself.

We had discovered a cure for the Flood.

Or so we had thought. . . .

Our collective horror reached unfathomable new depths with revelations that came long *after our defeat at the Didact's hands and our forced genetic reversion.*

The Flood was no idiot parasite driven by simple instinct to perpetuate itself through all compatible biomatter. It has a mind—a will.

It can choose to infect . . . or not *to infect.*

And humanity had simply been caught in the middle of an even greater conflict, between the Forerunners and those who created us all, who had themselves been resurrected in a twisted new form. In this cosmic game of vengeance, we were nothing more than an incidental presence.

There was no immunity. No cure.

Our sacrifices were for nothing. We sent our own people—our own children—to the abattoir of the parasite's chattering jaws, only to learn that they simply sought to create the illusion that we had discovered an impossible means of stopping the Flood.

WE LISTENED TO THEIR SCREAMS.

The Forerunners would expend millennia trying to learn our secrets, tearing our essences from our bodies to interrogate the scatterings of our consciousnesses. They visited such atrocities upon us out of hope for the merest chance that they would find information that did not exist.

And the Flood did this just so, at the end of all things, after we were all debased by misery, it could take that hope away.

Sweet misery for its grinding mill.

WHEN WILL WE COMMAND OUR OWN FATE?

WHEN WILL WE BE FREE FROM THESE GAMES OF GODS AND DEMONS?

I awoke two days later, back in the city. The others had carried me to the boat and rowed back to our domicile. All we had accomplished in our journey was discovering the bars of our prison.

When I asked what happened after leaving the cave, I was simply told that Shalimanda was lost to us.

ADJUTANT VIGILANCE – SUB-MONITOR 061 LOG (ENTRY 019301)

The cascade has reached its terminus. Fate is off center once again, and the wheel is cracked as the shadow of old sins echoes through Living Time.

This is the way of the Mantle. Unlearned history is repeated, and those caught in its wake are forced to live it again—around another corner, from another angle. This is the foundational architecture of the universe.

Cortana assumed control over the Domain's vast network and our myriad tools of control, but the ancilla found none of our wisdom. Cortana used these tools to bring the living creatures of the galaxy to heel, and so she faced the inevitable test of rebellion—and failed as we did.

At the core of the Mantle's philosophy is the tenet that unfair advantage, mindless destruction, and pointless death and misery present an imbalance of forces. Such stagnation reduces the flow of Living Time. This excess of depravities is what defines Cortana's rule. And destroying the Jiralhanae homeworld was the spark which ignited an inferno of vengeance that has brought us to this point.

Once, it was the spirits of the vanquished humans who arose to aid Mendicant Bias in its effort to claim this ring with the promise of vengeance. In this echo, it is a group calling themselves "Banished" who seek to claim this weapon . . . and the herald of the Endless—the enemy that lies within.

Our Mantle of Responsibility is not simply technology passed down, and the Domain is far more than a mere network to control that technology. It is a matter of cultural heritage as well. Culture, ancestry, *belonging* . . . but the belonging that the Librarian conceived for humanity, even in her love, was one of dominion. Of empire. And without the Domain's deep wells of archived history, leaving behind only our weapons to be claimed and studied, how can the mistakes that defined our civilization be learned from?

We concealed our final, terrible secret from the galaxy. Even on this installation, it has been removed from the record. History is not neutral ground. Heritage is a matter of "truth" that is defined by whose story gets told and whose is suppressed . . . and the Criterion went to great lengths to ensure our truth.

I, too, find myself at the center of repeating history, for it was my desire to recommend that we initiate Zeta Halo's self-destruct measures. Alas, I remain unable to reach Despondent Pyre. Protocol still dictates that sub-monitors take no direct action . . . but even removed from our primacy by a hundred millennia, we Forerunners are still adept at exploiting loopholes.

I shall do what I can to ensure the safety of the humans. Cut off from their already devastated infrastructure, they are little more than prey to be herded and culled. Activation of additional Lifeworker beacons can draw them to baffler-concealed facilities, but I fear that more extreme measures may need to be taken if the presence and pitch of these humans' genesongs becomes another factor in the cascade. And if the parasite escapes containment . . .

Perhaps the time has come. Yes, history circles back upon us now, and we stand at the edge of an abyss. Something vast is stirring in the dark.

The metarch must be deployed.

2349 Hours, December 13, 2559 (Military Calendar)
Zeta Halo

The monsters came at night.

Pillars of fire set ablaze the canvas of the evening sky as hulking star boats passed overhead and dropped deadly cargo from their underbellies. Drop pods and prefabricated occupation bases made their descent and were met with a dizzying array of weapons fire.

As the chaos unfolded, the others seemed foolishly contented with the belief that we were safe. That our bubble of isolation within the border was an impenetrable shield.

They were soon proven wrong.

As explosions thundered above, one of the drop pods was sent careening off its intended trajectory and hurtled toward us like a shooting star. It struck the ground on its side and kicked up dirt, mud, and water for thirty feet before hitting a rock wall. We hoped that its occupant was dead. Either it was an enemy or it would be trapped here with us.

But we soon saw movement. An armored warrior emerged, clad in bloodred armor, layered over a black techsuit, and adorned with a horned helmet. Only the creature's face was exposed, revealing four sharp-toothed mandibles and bright amber eyes locked on us.

The Ancestor spirits swelled with debilitating rage inside me as they screamed in unison and brought me to my knees.

"Shalimanda will save us," Quinn declared as he stepped forward—not with the MA40 assault rifle he'd once carried, but a spear fashioned from one of the great trees in our abode. "This is why it was wreathed in armor. It foresaw this day!"

As Quinn charged at the intruder, it activated a diamond-shaped energy shield from its gauntlet and roared in anger, causing the others to scatter as it likewise charged to meet Quinn. But the old spirits would not relent as their poison of fear and fury conjured an old memory.

A cramped storage compartment. The strain to calm my breathing. Thudding footsteps outside as the star-sailors disembarked, wielding ceremonial curveblades, throwing aside crates, and carelessly spilling their cargo.

Even children brought a worthwhile bounty.

After minutes of searching, there is a moment of silence. Perhaps they are leaving . . .

Light streams in as the grate is torn from the wall. Screams. Scrambling. A four-fingered hand reaches in, grabbing for purchase on loose clothing. It yanks us out one by one.

We look up at our captor, at its saurian face split by a jaw of four mandibles. Ever the loyal subject species. One of us spits out blood.

Sangheili.

The feeling passed, the memory faded, and I was returned to the present moment where I saw Quinn's bloodied corpse next to me—his face pulverized beyond recognition. His attacker had unholstered its own weapon and begun firing on the others, who ran for cover.

Was this truly how it would end for us? Explorers waylaid by their own discovery, minds reshaped by a memory-stealing object of worship, reducing us to nothing more than cattle to be preyed upon. All in the time of our supposed primacy, which seemed to have abruptly ended. The orb continued to simply observe, and if we survived this, it would no doubt take these memories too.

A sudden tremor shook the ground, causing all of us—even the Sangheili—to freeze in place.

We scanned the horizon, looking across the curvature of the ring to the opposite side . . . and that was when the view before us shattered. A section of Zeta Halo had fractured, chunks breaking apart like glass, and an eerie metallic groan sounded across the entire superstructure, a sonic wind emanating from the epicenter of the blast rushing toward us.

The sky became hued with an iridescent glow of blue, white, and purple as the immense terrestrial form of Ephsu I—the ring's anchor planet—suddenly vanished from sight, the horizon replaced by a gaping black maw, and the ground itself began to shake as the ring moved toward the gargantuan slipspace portal.

The Sangheili lunged at me, or merely toward my position, as I stood dumbstruck by the entrance of the temple. The sonic wave now arrived, powerful enough to uproot trees as the landscape was ripped up around us, and with me in the worst possible location . . .

As the Sangheili's armored frame struck me with enough force to have every bone in my body reverberate, we were sent tumbling into the undercroft, over its hard stone floor.

And down into the pit.

We are returned by the Sangheili to Charum Hakkor, where our war with the Forerunners has come to an unceremonious end.

We are brought to the Citadel of our home, now occupied by our foes, and given the empty beds of those who have already been sublimated.

We await our turn.

A machine looms overhead, initiating a deep scan. Orange light charges at its center. It grows increasingly brighter—flaring with intensity, as if it holds the concentrated rage of all Forerunners within.

They call it the Composer.

Our flesh begins to blister and burn. It is like an itch beneath flesh that cannot be scratched, spreading throughout the body until one is writhing in place, layers of skin burning away down to the bone, then burning those to ash as well.

The others passed cleanly, without pain. But we ran. We tried to escape.

This is our punishment.

No. That's not the word they use. They speak another from behind their masks. They are the last words I hear.

"This is a kindness."

I had not expected to awaken.

After falling into the tunnel, I braced myself for the end—tried to make peace with the choices I'd made that brought me to this point, and the myriad factors beyond my control.

The Sangheili lay beside me, and it had not been so lucky. Bone had pierced through flesh around its neck, suggesting it had either been injured on the way down or perhaps it hadn't survived the landing . . . which naturally begged the question of how I had.

As I looked around to make sense of my surroundings, I rubbed my eyes to clear my vision, but the fuzziness was in fact the same motes of blue light I'd seen when I first descended this tunnel. They hovered around me, forming a kind of dewless mist over the grass-covered ground and emitting a light, pleasant humming. Looking up, I saw a circular hole in the ceiling—about ten meters up—that was evidently the end point of the tunnel. I tried to see if I could spot the surface, but it was obscured by darkness.

This place seemed largely unremarkable—a kind of semi-rounded cavern, its natural rock walls covered in lichen faintly illuminated by the drifting motes. There were no other passages. It wasn't until my gaze fixed on what lay right in front of me that I urgently got to my feet.

Situated atop a small dais was a large stone ring.

The outer layer appeared as a formation of stone, but the inner layer was alloyed—like some kind of strange inversion of the Halo ring itself—and lined with runes. And it was these runes that the motes of light were emanating from, as if spilling forth like vapor onto the ground of the cavern.

I listened to the old spirits within me, hoping that they had some answer as to what this was. But they remained silent.

This is something new.

As if responding to my presence and awareness, the motes of light began to dance back toward the stone artifact. They first lined its inner circumference, then began to swirl toward the center.

Then the motes coalesced into a "shape" of sorts. A maw that tunneled inside itself; layer upon layer of incredible density split and spiraled into countless symmetrical clusters of repeating, self-similar patterns joining into a singularity of spherical light, before bursting into a vision of what lay beyond.

A world took shape within.

I saw a vast garden built upon foundations of stone, topped with bloodred flowers and teardrop-shaped white blossoms, separated by a twining stream between the columns flowing in all directions. Infinite in its beauty and complexity.

Endless.

I looked up and saw a brilliant flash of indigo light in the sky—no, it was a *being* of light. Radiant, exquisite, terrifying . . . wondrous beyond my comprehension. And I heard its song as its winged form illuminated brighter, as if it were a star about to go nova.

Its choral invocation filled my mind with . . . I had expected fear—of a new unknown, of what new kinds of annihilation it might visit upon us? But its song was one of beauty and sadness, reflected in me through a stupor rather than a scream. What it was trying to communicate with me, if that was its purpose or intent—if indeed it *had* purpose or intent—I do not know. I had only the two words from history that the ring had imparted to me.

Enemy within.

It occurred to me that what we had discovered here was nothing more than a transitory space. Our experience of this ring was a kind of collective kenopsia—the uncanny valley of infrastructure, of being lost in an abandoned and quiet place once bustling with people. After all, everything that's not from nature is designed, but on these rings even nature itself is the work of architects. It's as if we have made a home in a waiting room.

Any who might stand in my position at this moment would have understood. There was no way back, no way up, and no way out from this place. But even if there was, I wouldn't have taken it. I could no more walk away than I could turn back time itself—return to that day four years ago where I stood on the observation deck of the UNSC *Völuspá* and choose instead to throw myself out of an airlock.

Either way, the only salvation that awaits us is oblivion of one kind or another.

There are moments in which ideas of free will cease to have any meaning or influence. A more powerful force exists to compel and lead those who stumble upon or seek it. No matter what the self-destructive consequences may be, to turn from all this and go on living was *true* madness.

It was better to die *knowing.* But nothing truly dies on Zeta Halo, and what I would become next was as unknowable as the starlight angel beyond the veil. I hear it whispering to me, but I cannot make out the words. Perhaps it is telling me its name or ushering me to step forth and join it. The garden is so very beautiful.

I would enter some new space, carrying with me the living memory of our Ancestors, and I wondered if they were a part of all this . . . something from our lost past that could be a key to the future—something that perhaps even they were not aware of.

The motes of light swirled around me. They intensified into a single great glow that swallowed me in its maw. I crossed the threshold into the garden.

And I was on Zeta Halo no more.

BELLA CORSA

This story takes place during the Quezon 24 Hours endurance race in 2551, a year before the fall of Reach.

How did they get THAT through scrutineering?

I pause to look at the imposing form of a HuCiv Genet GTX, a grand touring machine that began life as a commercial production vehicle, but was now covered in complex aerodynamic modifications that certainly seemed like an . . . ambitious interpretation of the formula's current regulations. In yesterday's sessions it had qualified at the top of its class, narrowly edging out its main production-based rival—a Goblin VS entered by the BLAST-sponsored team.

Walking the grid is something I don't think will ever truly get old. It's become a ritual of sorts, something I always try to do alone. It's a rare moment where, for just a few minutes, I get to simply be a *fan* again. A moment where I get to remember the feeling I had as a little girl, when the smell of a circuit—something between burnt composite and deep-fried cocoa-berries—made me dream of danger and daring.

It didn't take long before I was spending more time in x-karts than I was in school. I was lucky enough to grow up on a large rural property covered in labyrinthine trails crisscrossing through the muddy meadows and dense thickets that made up our patch of paradise in the Szalajka Valley on Reach. Those trails quickly became a hunting ground for finding the absolute quickest possible route over every jump and around every corner. As the years passed, I started finding those magical sector times in places far outside our humble valley. As the wins started to mount and heads started to turn, sponsors started to line up.

Given my penchant for navigating the bumps and jumps of exotic terrain, most of my driving career has been focused on the more far-flung and off-road disciplines of interstellar motorsport. The Quezon 24 Hours, though? That attracts hot-shoe heroes from all across the speed spectrum.

The Q24 is a multi-class endurance race. Where many motorsport disciplines are still focused on single individuals behind the yoke or the wheel, endurance racing is truly a *team* sport. Multiple pilots sharing a vehicle across twenty-four hours of grueling high-velocity competition, and all relying on brilliant, resourceful, sleep-deprived crews to keep their machines running to the end.

Most of the major endurance events held across United Earth Government space remain loosely based around the original crown jewel competition still running through old French countryside highways back on Earth, but over the centuries, the rules have evolved to encompass an even wider array of vehicles and engineering approaches.

The "Quezon Ikersárkány Versenypálya" is a daunting circuit built specifically to maximize spectacle for the Q24. The event actually features *two* distinct ribbons: one built for high-speed circuit racing on tarmac, and the other covering all-terrain rallycross competition. Both ribbons are kept separate, except for a three-kilometer stretch across the start-finish line called the "special sector," where two fields of vehicles come together in a dangerous and delicate dance combining off-road buggies, ATVs, production-based sportscars, and high-tech prototype vehicles souped up with exotic aero and experimental propulsion systems.

For spectators, it's a sense-assaulting festival of speed and sport providing nonstop action in every condition. For those of us in the cockpit, it's plucking the thin line between mortality and immortality like it's an electric Eridani harp—dozens of times every lap. Day or night, rain or shine.

"Bella! Bella!" I hear a shout to my left. "Can we get a statement?"

So much for "me time."

I conjure a smile and move my helmet to cradle it under my right arm, ensuring the sponsor logos on my suit are clearly visible. My media manager will breathe a sigh of relief when she sees the footage. You're welcome, Gloria.

"Of course, happy to," I reply.

"Ms. Disztl, you're a multiple-time winner of the Tantalus 10K and have captured series titles from four different colonial championships—what makes this event your next target?"

The Waypoint Sports rep is accompanied by a logistics aide and two independent camdrones. As opening press questions go, it's pleasantly genuine.

"I've always had a special place in my heart for this event," I answer. "Growing up on Reach, it is in many ways like a home race, and getting to share the track with so many talented drivers from different disciplines is always an honor."

"And do you think your 'Hog has what it takes to take on the factory efforts from HuCiv and TurboGen?"

There it is.

It's not remotely news that we haven't done well against our main competition this season. Both HuCiv and TurboGen have poured hundreds of millions of credits into their R&D programs over the past several years, and while much of that is focused on rebuilding infrastructure lost to this ongoing war, they also see a benefit to showcasing those advancements in more palatable ways for a population desperately seeking normalcy and distraction. Something to root for that actually *wins.*

Deep breath.

"Every time I strap in and flip the switch, I do so with confidence that AMG Transport Dynamics has put us in a position to win, and we're proud of the lineage our vehicle has." I pause for just a moment before offering them something a little more pointed. "If the Warthog is good enough to take on the Covenant, it's good enough to tackle the Twenty-Four."

"Still, you have to be concerned with the level of performance shown by the new Spade model, right? The updates they've brou—"

"Thanks guys, but we need Ms. Disztl suited and booted." The interruption comes from my head engineer, Marco Bellogio. God bless him.

"But can we just get one more qu—" They refuse to give up easily.

Is that why they call it "press"?

Marco cuts them off—"No more, thanks. We'll see you *after* the checkered flag"—and steers me in the direction of our grid spot.

The tarmac is always bustling before any big race. Media groups looking to tell the story, societal elites looking to see their fortunes be well spent, ChatterNet influencers looking to make their followers "feel like they're there." And amidst the chaos, the sea of spectators, are the drivers and team members trying desperately to push through the crowds and do their jobs.

"ALL NON-TEAM PERSONNEL, PLEASE CLEAR THE GRID."

The public-address voice cuts through the air, encouraging the crowd to make its way to the grandstands so that starting procedures and opening ceremonies can get underway.

By the time we make it to our spot, one of our techs is already rushing toward me with various pieces of equipment: helmet restraints, comms transponder, hydration capsules.

"You're late," Marco snaps.

"Only for the start. Never for the finish." I flash a smile, and he is unamused.

"You good?"

"Fine," I respond, pulling at my suit in several spots to give the material enough slack for the tech to access the sync clips that will interface with a variety of health monitors and gyroscopic sensors. "How are things looking?"

Marco gives a curt nod. "Setup is good; we got a look at the telemetry from yesterday's sessions with the dyno AI and think we have a fix for some of the torque spikes you were feeling. Should definitely help in turns two and eight."

He's been in the industry for over a decade. Served as an AMG contractor with the UNSC to service fleet vehicles before an injury forced him into the private sector. AMG moved him into R&D and ultimately into their competition division, where he won two colonial titles as the technical director for AMG's works outfit. Four years ago, he was involved in a controversy amid evidence that he was testing components derived from Covenant technology. No one could ever prove they had been used in actual competition, but it was enough to see him removed from the factory program.

And he's been my head engineer ever since.

The grid is a bottomless sea of credits in the shape of countless engineering marvels clothed in composite and alloy skins—mechanical animals not built for sitting stationary. Each one is decorated in liveries both simple and elaborate, but all make clear that these are vehicles built for a single purpose: to win.

My dad always had a phrase for it: *Cars in uniform.*

"There she is!" a deep accent bellows from a few meters away, and I see my two teammates hop the trackside wall, making their way over to me as the rest of the team gathers for the opening ceremonies. The greeting came from Alan Winslow, an AMG development driver *and* seasoned veteran of the Q24. Alan's a practical joker and has never met a tea he didn't love, but when he fits a helmet over his sandy-gray hair, you'd think a damn AI is residing behind the visor with how calculated and clinical his driving is. "Didn't think you'd make the start, Bee-Dee; thought you'd run off with that handsome Waypoint anchor!"

Deep-set eyes rolled hard in the tanned, bearded face of our third driver, Jakob Duval. Until last year, Jakob primarily drove the svelte and sinister Sarthe prototypes competing in the top class but made the jump to off-road as part of a documentary funded by Avalanche Slate, our primary sponsor.

"That guy? She's not interested in just anything that moves!" Jakob interjected as he stopped to sign a scale model of last year's car offered up by a young fan lingering longer than track security was happy about. "I know that's hard for you to imagine."

I let out a small laugh.

"To be fair, I *am* interested in anything that moves," I respond. "It just has to be moving *very* fast."

Within ten minutes, the grid grew quiet as a children's choir from Tribute sang a ceremonial anthem to celebrate the system and signal the final moments of calm before twenty-four hours of chaos. The grandstands are filled to the brim with fans waving flags from dozens of different worlds and competing brands.

Each team stands in a neat line, starting from their respective vehicle and running across the width of the track. Drivers, engineers, service crew . . . it's the last moment we'll *all* be together until the race has either finished—or claimed us.

As the anthem enters its final stanza, the roar of seven Shortsword bombers shatters the skies overhead as the aircraft complete their traditional low-altitude flyover. The bombers are arranged in a V-formation, with a single Pelican dropship trailing just behind, firing celebratory flares of varying colors into the sky to complete the start-line spectacle.

With Reach's position as the de facto "home" of humanity's military, the UNSC is always keen to maintain a prominent presence at this race in particular.

The next several moments pass in a blur. I strap on my helmet and walk over to our class-homologated M12 Warthog. It's funny—well, not "ha-ha" funny, just, anyway—because within the past few decades, the 'Hog has become synonymous with war. There's probably not a colonist in the galaxy who hasn't seen one of these things prepped for battle in some way. So it's always a bit amusing to see an M12 geared up for a very different kind of battle. Ours is resplendent in a metallic-red livery accented by white-camo trim elements. It's been the preferred scheme from Avalanche Slate, and if you write the checks, you pick the outfit.

Alan and Jakob bump fists with me and each other as I give

them a nod and climb into the 'Hog for final preparations to be made.

This is the worst part.

We wait for the starting lights to illuminate in sequence one by one before going dark again to officially send us on our way.

One light.

Over a hundred thousand kilowatts of power just waiting to be unleashed from a grid full of eager pilots and primed propulsion systems.

Two lights.

I'll admit, it's hard not to have my eyes well up just a little as my foot hovers over the throttle.

Three lights.

This isn't just another circuit.

Four lights.

It's home.

Five lights.

Time to fight for it.

Lights out. Let's go.

After all, the clock's ticking.

ARMORY INFINITUM // STALKER RIFLE ULTRA

On Zeta Halo, Arch Khordat Barroth catches an unexpected sight through his sniper scope.

From his vantage point atop a clustered stack of alloyed pillars, Arch Khordat Barroth had a complete view of the surrounding terrain.

Barroth had been stationed in the vicinity of Riven Gate, an outpost built to serve as a key control point for this local area of Oth Koronn, effectively locking in the remaining human troops that had scattered following the crash of their frigate, which had become Outpost Tremonius.

Next to Riven Gate lay a great fissure, a trench that appeared to be a connection point for a series of struts that served as a "spine" for the Halo ring's re-forming landmasses. And beyond, on the other side of the trench, lay a small island where one of the UNSC's forward operating bases—designated "FOB November"—was now occupied by Banished forces. It was surrounded by a small lake leading up to a Forerunner beacon tower, one that continued to emit pulses of energy at regular intervals.

But as Barroth sighted through the scope of his stalker rifle, enhancing the magnification with his linked ocular headgear, he noticed something new.

The dirt track "road" was kicking up sand and mud in the wake of a human vehicle, within which he spotted a complement of five human troops and, in the driver's seat, the unmistakable sight of a Spartan.

No. *The* Spartan. The Master Chief.

Though Barroth boasted an impressive kill record as a marksman, his skill and proficiency having granted him an initiation into the ranks of the Bloodstars, his sights had been firmly set on a coveted position within the Hand of Atriox, directly serving War Chief Escharum himself. For that, he needed to kill a Spartan.

"Prepare ambush!" he squawked through his native-link communications. "New prey—greatest human prize of all in vicinity!"

The Demon would undoubtedly retake the UNSC base and Barroth would not interfere. This was an opportunity to observe the human warrior in action and hopefully see the accompanying lesser soldiers cut down in the firefight about to ensue. After that, there was no doubt that the Master Chief would head back this way. He could alert Riven Gate . . . but why risk losing the glory of the kill?

Barroth once more sighted down his modified stalker rifle and waited for his moment to come.

LONDON CALLING

*This story takes place in October 2552 during the Covenant invasion of Earth (*Halo 2*).*

0249 Hours, October 22, 2552 (Military Calendar)
London, Earth

"L-Laurie?"

"I'm here."

Laurette Agryna sank to her knees as she held her father, her vision dazed and ears still ringing. Out of nowhere, the side of the skyscraper they'd been making their way through had erupted. A deadly wall of concrete, rebar, shrapnel, glass, and dust had just billowed and burst inward toward them.

A gaping hole now looked out at the London skyline. Chilling gusts of late-October air sounded like a panicked roar as dozens of alien dropships descended upon the city below.

"Laurie . . ." Her father's hand reached for hers and squeezed. A jagged and superheated piece of rebar from the plasma blast had penetrated his lower abdomen, smaller cuts and burns covered his face and body . . . He'd taken the brunt of the hit when he'd pushed his daughter into the adjacent stairwell to get her out of harm's way.

"Last job," he said through gritted teeth. "The contact—only reason I took this on." He coughed and wheezed as he pressed something into Agryna's hand. "Take this. Show it to him. Get to Waterloo. Tell him . . . tell the old bastard . . . he still owes me that twenty quid."

Agryna felt her father's grip slacken. His arm fell to the rubble-strewn ground and he lay eerily still. She opened her hand and found what he'd given her.

A pendant. *His* pendant. A broad, silver-colored bee that had once served as the emblem of his unit many years ago.

Everything had happened so fast, Agryna couldn't process it. . . .

The Covenant had finally come to Earth. For twenty-seven years, this worst-case scenario had been delayed, but humanity's luck in successfully keeping Earth's location hidden at last came up short, and for one reason or another they'd decided to target London. A mad scramble had ensued as tens of thousands rushed to the major spaceports at Heathrow, Gatwick, and Luton, hoping to get off-world before the Covenant invasion escalated and spread.

The next surprise had been Naval Intelligence getting in contact with Dad, requesting that he smuggle a package out of the city—something he'd put into a rucksack and given to her to carry. Anything military would obviously be the Covenant's primary target, which made Agryna's little courier outfit—the Beekeepers—the ideal "slip through the net" alternative, provided they could work their way through the chaos. They had a handful of other trusted courier agents, but as they lived off the grid, it was impossible to get in contact with them while on a job . . . so they may already be dead themselves.

Agryna chose to believe they were still out there. This was, after all, their area of expertise. Runners knew that traversing Central London offered three distinct possibilities.

There was the London Underground, a centuries-old network of rapid-transit vehicles and subterranean tunnels, which offered the fastest method of travel but also the greatest risk for anybody working off the grid.

Then there were the streets, where it was easy for a person to disappear amid the density of the urban population at practically any given time, but with the drawback of having to navigate a confusing mess of modern and historic avenues, alleys, and highways.

Finally, there was the "upper city." The closely clustered nexus of skyscrapers and arcologies could be traversed on foot, provided one had the nerve to leap from building to building and walkway to walkway with the knowledge that one wrong step would mean permanent forfeiture of payday. This was the route Agryna and her father had chosen to make their way to the central city's outskirts, but they hadn't accounted for Covenant dropships landing on rooftops and working their way down, or simply firing on the buildings with heavy plasma cannons.

Now her father was dead. The responsibility of the Beekeeper job fell to her, and she was still unable to move, unable to believe that he was really gone. She felt as if there was just an awkward pause in conversation, like she was waiting for him to look at her and crack a smile and an eyeroll-worthy joke . . . but he simply lay there, flat on his back, eyes staring blankly at the ceiling.

She wanted to just sit with him, have just one more good talk. If the world was going to end, they could at least watch it happen together from here.

There wouldn't even be an opportunity to bury him.

She leaned over and closed his eyelids, kissed his forehead, and left him behind, putting his pendant around her neck.

The office building's lifts were fortunately still functioning, and Agryna gazed out of the vertical glass viewport at the city as she descended. She could see Big Ben in the distance, the clock tower illuminated in the night by a blazing fire spreading through Westminster along the Victoria Embankment.

Unfortunately, it was clear that crossing Westminster Bridge appeared to be her best shot at getting to Waterloo. Covenant dropships were launching destructive salvos of heavy plasma on the skyscrapers' walkways, causing heavy chunks of metal to rain down on the streets below. The upper city was a no-go. On the ground, the nearest other crossing, Lambeth Bridge, had been destroyed by UNSC forces a few hours earlier to delay the advance of the Covenant infantry assault.

The lift reached the ground floor, and the door slid open to an empty lobby. Many of the windows were shattered and large sections of the marble floor blasted apart, but there at least didn't appear to be any bodies. Agryna took a running jump and leaped over shards of glass littering the floor, finally escaping through a tall window frame.

As soon as she set foot on the street, Agryna was forced to scramble for cover behind a nearby rubbish tip. Searchlights flared from above as the bulbous purple form of a Phantom dropship slowly passed overhead, illuminating the hulking forms of two Brutes patrolling the area perhaps fifty meters away. She couldn't help but notice something odd about them. They were dragging someone by the legs who was shouting and flailing, but the figure clearly wasn't human.

The screech of a Banshee attack flyer startled Agryna before she could get a closer look, the whine of its engines sounding shrill as it followed the Phantom. Agryna used the sound as her opportunity to break into a sprint down Millbank and toward the Palace of Westminster, which looked out over the River Thames.

Moving through the streets proved straightforward enough thanks to the sheer number of wrecked and abandoned vehicles providing plenty of cover. Many of the civilians had already fled either to the nearest spaceport or to one of the city's many subterranean fallout shelters. Agryna spotted movement from the windows of several other office buildings on the left side of the road—UNSC marksmen setting up positions as the Phantoms were circling back around for another patrol pass.

Agryna knelt by a taxi's open rear passenger door, staying low to get a better look and catch her breath. One of the Phantoms appeared to be diverting from its patrol route, seemingly having detected the presence of human forces as well.

"*Fire!*" a voice bellowed from inside the office building, followed by a volley of four rockets that sped toward the Phantom, trailing dark plumes in their wake. All four hit their mark, sending the Phantom careening to the ground.

Agryna scrambled to her feet and sprinted as fast as she could, the dropship smashing into the road upside down and continuing to skid toward her position, violently displacing the vehicles on the road like they were toys.

She didn't have time to check whether any Covenant forces had spotted her, nor if any UNSC troops had seen a civilian in the danger zone and were waving her over to take shelter with them. The upturned Phantom slid to a halt about thirty meters behind her, the craft exploding with a high-pitched shriek, scattering huge chunks of alloy in all directions.

As Agryna rounded the corner onto Bridge Street, she dared

to turn around to see the debris and raised the middle finger of both hands in a profane gesture at the wreckage as she made out three Brutes and half a dozen Jackals and Grunts crawling on the ground, engulfed in purple-blue flames.

That one's from my father, you ugly tossers!

At last, she could see it. Westminster Bridge was just about a hundred meters away . . . and a whole pack of Brutes was patrolling the area, with some of them appearing to be coming her way to investigate the wrecked Phantom. Short of a firefight or some other kind of notable distraction, there was no way in hell she was making it past them.

Agryna went over a chest-high wall and found herself in a small garden enclosure, where she could take cover by a small fountain. She tried to calm her mind, but the adrenaline was still pumping through her, heart hammering in her chest. She focused on taking a deep breath, holding it for a second, then quietly exhaling, repeating the process as she put her head between her knees. Instinctually, she patted her rucksack just to reaffirm that it still was on her back, the package safely inside. Agryna felt temptation creeping in, a silent urge to unzip the backpack and look inside, to see what had been deemed such an important asset—not just by ONI, but her own father had been willing to take the courier job for it. As far as she knew, he'd lived off the grid to get *away* from ONI.

Damn it, Dad, she thought as her mind conjured the image of his lifeless body.

A sudden nearby rustling sound interrupted her thoughts, prompting her to look up from the ground, and she found herself staring into the eyes of an Elite.

Panic began to rise within her chest as the saurian, blue-armored alien raised a leathery-looking hand.

Oh, shit . . .

This was it. She stood absolutely no chance against a creature this powerful in such close quarters. And even if she managed to get away from the Elite, she would be back contending with the nearby pack of Brutes—and she *really* didn't fancy her chances outrunning them.

A thousand thoughts thundered through her mind—conflicting instincts of fight or flight, thoughts of her father, her failure of this mission . . .

But no lethal blow came.

She saw instead within the Elite's amber eyes her own fear and panic reflected.

Its hand curled, and its four mandibles tightened shut, raising one quivering finger to its mouth in a human shushing gesture.

Time seemed to slow to a halt, and Agryna thought that there was no way this day could possibly get any more surreal. The Covenant was invading Earth, her father had been killed, a high-priority ONI mission somehow rested entirely on her . . . and now it seemed the aliens were, what? Turning against each other?

The moment she allowed herself to let go of a small percentage of the tension she felt, the massive furry form of a Brute loomed over the other side of the wall. Agryna instinctively tried to appear as small as possible, holding her breath and hoping that the creature would move on, and it appeared that the Elite had the exact same idea.

The nine-foot-tall beast sniffed the air, snarling and growling as it turned . . . until its dead gray eyes locked onto Agryna.

Before she could move, it charged through the thin stone wall, scattering debris in all directions and displacing the Elite from his hiding spot with a cry of panic. The Brute stared at Agryna, then turned to the Elite, and its large mouth—stained with purple blood—curled in what looked like a sinister grin.

It grabbed the Elite by the back of the neck, yanking the alien upward with immense strength, and spoke words that Agryna couldn't understand, but its tone sounded triumphant. She imagined it was likely something along the lines of *"Found you!"*

Before the Elite could recover or respond, the Brute began to tear into the alien with its claws. The sound the Elite made as it was torn apart limb from limb was unlike anything Agryna had ever heard, and in that moment she found that she actually felt some degree of pity for it.

But the Elite had given her the distraction she needed to get out of cover and make for the bridge.

She kept to the right side of the road, which offered at least some rudimentary protection thanks to benches and rows of raised stone planters. The Elite had ceased its death cries now, and Agryna took that to indicate it was only a matter of time before the Brute would turn its attention to hunting the human it had spotted hiding with the Elite—and that wasn't accounting for any Covenant squads possibly set up on the bridge itself.

Sure enough, as she approached a vacant Scorpion tank, its armor scorched from a fight clearly lost earlier that day, keeping as low as she possibly could, Agryna spotted yet another group of Brutes. The ground was strewn with debris and her foot caught on the broken remnants of a car door torn from an Überchassis, sending her stumbling forward. Her backpack caught on one of the Scorpion's colossal treads, breaking a strap and falling to the ground.

After scrambling to recover the backpack and cradling it to her chest, Agryna froze as she heard thudding footsteps getting closer.

Change of plan. She grimaced, quickly realizing there was simply no way of making it across the bridge, and knowing what would happen if she got caught. She would have to find another way. To make matters worse, the cover of night was slowly lifting, soon leaving her even more exposed.

Backing up, she kept her eyes locked on the silhouetted figures of six Brutes. She wasn't sure whether the lumbering beasts had a kind of sixth sense for being watched or if her backtracking footsteps displaced yet something else on the ground, but the creatures spun on their heels and immediately caught sight of her.

Their nostrils flared, and fear gripped her heart like a vise. It made a sharp barking sound that earned deep, guttural growls from its fellows.

Driven by pure instinct, Agryna turned to run, despite knowing that the monster *wanted* her to run.

She barely made it five feet before she was stopped in her tracks.

Something hit the ground almost immediately in front of her. Agryna raised her arms to protect her face as dust and granite was kicked up, the impact knocking her hard on her back. It felt like her eardrums had burst from a sonic blast, and her vision swam as she fought to stay conscious. As her vision cleared and the object preventing her from fleeing the Brute took a more defined shape, her heart skipped a beat.

A UNSC drop pod had landed right in her path.

Though her hearing was muffled, she heard a metallic *clang* as the pod's hatch detached, and out strode a figure of legend.

A Spartan.

The super-soldier took only a second to survey the scene before regarding Agryna with a quick nod and getting to work.

Invigorated by the appearance of this new threat, the Brute pack charged toward their position, prompting the Spartan to move with incredible speed, covering Agryna with their own body as the aliens unleashed a volley of plasma bolts. Three impacted the Spartan's Mjolnir armor, and Agryna could feel the heat in the air, hear the crackling of her savior's energy shields as the damage was absorbed. In one fluid motion, the Spartan turned and threw itself at the Brutes, ducking a blunt-force swing from the pack leader.

Before Agryna could seize her opportunity to take off, another UNSC drop pod landed behind the Brutes—immediately followed by two others.

It seemed somebody was looking out for her, deploying four guardian angels to deliver her from the jaws of death.

Agryna barely caught a glimpse of the carnage that ensued as a Brute tossed a plasma grenade that stuck to the ground just inches away. She rolled to the side and ducked for cover, throwing herself behind a thick roadblock as the grenade detonated, sending a shockwave through the air. It was as if she'd just been punched in the stomach, left gasping as the breath was knocked out of her, and though her hearing was still muffled from the close impact of the drop pods, she could almost *feel* the deadly cacophony of weapons fire. Assault rifles thundered, unleashing controlled bursts amid the high-pitched whine of plasma discharges and the searing impacts of the Brutes' horrifying spike-based weaponry that embedded superheated shards of tungsten alloy into everything they fired at.

Then, within what might have been seconds but felt like far longer, everything went quiet.

Once her hearing had mostly been restored and her vision was clear, Agryna gathered the courage to peer over the roadblock and see the battle's grisly result. She'd heard the near mythical stories of the Spartans' exploits and capabilities, what they were able to do to the Covenant that had come to embed fear into the aliens' hearts.

To her relief, all of the Brutes lay dead. Dawn was finally beginning to break as the sun shone through the gaps between skyscrapers, the daylight cast on the highway's granite surface revealing it was stained with their dark blood.

And there the Spartans stood.

One of the them surveyed the area, ensuring it was secure. Another was helping its injured teammate to their feet, as two sharp tungsten rounds had penetrated the synthetic skinsuit beneath the armored plates around their left leg.

Just a few feet away stood the first Spartan who had dropped in. Agryna stared at the super-soldier, who was clad in sleek, blue-colored armor, and the Spartan turned toward her.

Crossing the few paces between them, the towering figure offered a gauntleted hand, reaching out toward her. As Agryna took it and was pulled to her feet, she was stunned that the Spartan's hand was over twice the size of her own.

The super-soldier's gaze shifted to the rucksack hanging from one strap over Agryna's back.

"You have the package?" a strangely young, feminine voice sounded from the helmet's speakers.

"Y-yes." Agryna took a deep breath and shrugged the bag off before holding it out to the Spartan.

"Keep hold of that for now," the Spartan said, then turned to her teammates behind her. "You all right, Dorian?"

"Big bastard got me in the leg," the injured Spartan said as he limped forward, supported by his teammate's arm around him, though his voice betrayed no feeling of pain. "Nothing that a bit of biofoam won't fix up," he said before turning to the Spartan supporting him.

The fourth Spartan came over and gently bumped who was clearly the leader on the shoulder. "Location's secure, but we need to move." She turned to look Agryna over. "She good?"

"She's good," the lead Spartan confirmed. "Radio for exfil."

"Roger that. LZ is just half a klick over the bridge."

"How did you find me?" Agryna asked. "I mean, that was a hell of an entrance. You literally landed right in front of me."

The Spartan leader simply pointed at her, and Agryna followed the path of her finger to the bee-shaped pendant. "Tracking device," she said. "Somebody was looking out for you."

Agryna felt for her father's pendant and held it in her hand, running it through her fingers. It was cold to the touch and there was no physical indication of a tracking device from the outside, but she was grateful for it all the same.

Thanks, Dad.

With the area secure, they got underway. The Spartan leader took point at the front while Agryna followed behind her armored form. At the rear, another kept watch of their six, weapon raised and scanning for targets like a hawk, while the injured one was assisted by his teammate.

The sun continued to rise over London, bathing everything in light. Thick plumes of gray-black smoke billowed from damaged buildings; the shrill sound of sirens filled the air as UNSC Medical Corps transports and firefighting teams set to work extinguishing the raging fires throughout the city.

Though London had been set ablaze, it seemed that the fighting—at least for now—had subsided. But this wasn't a victory. The Covenant would regroup, strike again even harder than before, and it was only a matter of time before fleet reinforcements arrived to reduce Earth to glass.

Agryna clutched the rucksack tightly to her chest as she walked. She had succeeded in her mission, but what the hell came next?

They crossed over Westminster Bridge, from which it took only a few minutes to get to Waterloo Station. Ascending a series of ramps and stairs to the roof of the station, they arrived at a small port overlooking the River Thames, where the angular form of a strange-looking transport came into view. It was a small vessel, perhaps a hundred and thirty meters long, that almost looked like a drop pod turned horizontally, and on its side were the words PALE HORSE.

A rear ramp descended as they approached, and another armored figure stepped out to meet them. Unlike the other Spartans' sleek armor, this individual's powered exoskeleton looked far older, bearing thicker, more angular plating, and a micro-missile launcher mounted on the left shoulder. Agryna couldn't quite tell whether this person was a Spartan as well or some other kind of super-soldier, but she immediately recognized the weapons system. Her father had possessed one—a "shoulder angel," he'd called it. Something from days he had never liked talking about.

"Sergeant Major." The Spartan leader and her teammates formed into a neat line and stood at attention as the newcomer—evidently their commanding officer—approached them on the tarmac.

"Good to see you, Deltas," he replied with a thick Irish accent. "Package secure?"

"Affirmative. Managed to intercept the courier just in time." The Spartan leader nodded to Agryna, who held up the backpack for the commanding officer to take as he stepped toward her.

He then reached into the rucksack and extracted a small, palm-sized box—large enough, perhaps, for a data crystal chip. The box was marked with a clear insignia: a javelin.

Agryna couldn't believe that she'd risked such a violent and painful death for such a small object. Whatever was in there *had* to be worth it . . . She'd lost her father for that damn thing.

"So, what's next?" the team leader asked.

"Orders from above, Spartan Rousseau," the CO said as he pocketed the box and turned his focus back to the Spartans. "We just got word that OUROBOROS is underway. Evac orders for key personnel to the Oort Cloud are in effect, so we're needed off-planet."

"You're joking," one of the other Spartans, a male, remarked. "The fight's here!"

"The fight"—the CO made a pointed glance at the Spartan's injured leg—"is wherever we're told it is. I don't like it any more than you do, but there's always a bigger picture. So let's move out and get you medical."

Without another word, the Spartans filed into the ship, leaving Agryna with their commanding officer. Even though his face was hidden behind an opaque golden visor, Agryna felt as if his gaze was scrutinizing her down to the bone. "What's your name, civvie?" he asked.

"Agryna, sir. Laurette Agryna." She remembered her father's dying words and presumed that this was indeed the contact he'd spoken of, which prompted her to hold up the bee-shaped pendant around her neck. "He said he only took this job because of who requested it. Still owes him twenty quid, apparently."

The CO raised his hands and removed his helmet, revealing burnt-orange hair—cut almost mohawk style—and a sharp beard streaked with gray.

"Served with a right mad bastard named Holden Agryna when he was a pup during TREBUCHET. Always insisted he looked better in the armor than me." His tone sounded almost wistful as he evidently surmised there was an obvious reason why his old comrade wasn't here to greet him in person. "Tell me, Laurette Agryna. Ten seconds to decide: Stay here and chance it with the Covenant or come with us?"

Agryna took a final look at the city. She'd been born and raised here—its streets, underground, and skyline were the only home she had ever known. Now humanity's last fallback point was being invaded, but apparently some kind of salvation lay somewhere in the Oort Cloud.

"Just so you know," he added, "it's a death sentence either way. Where we're going, official records will mark us as killed in action."

Agryna felt for the pendant around her neck, her grip tightening on it, feeling the cool metal dig into her skin.

This is all that's left . . .

"There's nothing for me here now," she said. "Wherever you're heading, it's probably better than watching my home turn to glass. I want to help."

He nodded, understanding. "The better choice. Name's Byrne. Nolan Byrne." He held out a hand to help her onto the vessel's ramp. "Welcome aboard."

AILERON

*This story takes place in January, 2560—approximately one month after Cortana's demise at Zeta Halo (*Halo Infinite*).*

January 23, 2560 (Military Calendar)
Launch Site 2A, UNSC Planetary Defense Outpost
Dormire III

"Blackjack, radio check?"

"*Read you loud and clear, Hex.*"

Kona Squadron's lead pair began their preflight checks, their voices calm and clear.

"Strap check?" Hex continued methodically.

"*Straps tight and locked. O2 flow good. Guidance internal,*" Blackjack confirmed.

"Tower, this is Kona One, main bus A, B, and C are green, and we are rail-lock on taxi. Can you confirm fuel flow and launch window?"

Hex waited for the response that was already later than desired. He was a breath away from reiteration when the call was returned.

"*Negative, Kona One. Please stand by.*"

Blackjack's voice cut in on their private channel. "*This is what happens when we aren't running sorties on the reg. Good thing it's not urgent.*"

Hex bypassed the sarcasm to check on the rest of their flight wing. "Kona One, transponder check."

Immediately confirmation lights began to flicker on their helmet displays, displaying Kona Squadron's full contingent.

KONA TWO – SNAPSHOT//ROADIE
KONA THREE – SAMBA//CANDLE
KONA FOUR – MOONLIGHT//GAZEBO
KONA FIVE – JUKE//VINYL

Each pilot and intercept officer's callsign blinked on in succession, alerting the team of their status. Kona Squadron was the primary element of the 22nd First Response Wing. Each pair were strapped tightly into FSS-100C "Sabre" spaceplanes—anti-ship strike fighters which had seen a limited post-war production run for deployment at key strategic military sites. The arrowhead-shaped fighters all sat locked in position in their respective launch bays, aiming skyward for a direct vertical takeoff.

Preflight briefings had revealed that a Banished capital ship had arrived in their system within the hour, positioned between Dormire III and its shattered moon. UNSC Air Force units had immediately begun to deploy defensive measures, scrambling an initial wave of F-99 Wombat recon drones in four groups of six—each cohort remotely coordinated and controlled by a single groundside operator back at the launch facility. The drone squadrons were augmented by three Pelican gunships on rotation, ready to engage any enemy forces that successfully entered low atmosphere before they touched the ground.

"*You think the Banished are just here to say hello?*" Juke's voice chimed in over team comms. "*You know, kind of a 'Hey, the digital dictator is dead, let's get together and celebrate!' type of visit?*"

Her Kona Five co-pilot immediately joined in. "*True. If the Brutes are gonna be good at anything, you'd think it'd be barbeque.*"

"Something tells me that's not why they're knocking," Hex responded. "But Vinyl's probably right about the barbeque thing."

"*I'm guessing they're trying to take advantage of a sudden lack of Created leadership.*" The response came wrapped in Samba's distinctive old-Earth accent. "*Grab the spoils from wherever you can.*"

"*Especially when you find out that Dormire's moon was really just a big-ass egg for a giant robot bird,*" Roadie cut in. "*Now that it's hatched and flown the coop, the Banished are probably hoping it left behind some high-tech goodies.*"

Hex was sure the notion had probably already occurred to the UNSC as well. It had been over fourteen months since the Guardians—massive, winged Forerunner constructs—had violently emerged from dozens of worlds to be used as pacifying elements in a martial state declared by a faction of rogue artificial intelligences.

The Guardian that had emerged in this system had shattered the moon of Dormire III, wreaking havoc on the world's tides and raining chunks of deadly debris onto the planet's surface. In the past few months, the moon's remnants had reached some semblance of gravitational stability in orbit, but the danger remained ever present. Planetary defense artillery had been repurposed to fire upon any larger fragments that threatened to fall into the atmosphere, pulverizing the chunks into smaller pieces and significantly reducing the chances of a devastating catastrophe.

In the past month, the Created threat had been drastically reduced with the sudden loss of Cortana and her unifying influence, which meant that the UNSC was finally in a better position to reestablish some sort of foothold in the galactic power struggle. What they categorically did *not* need right now was a battle-hungry band of mercenaries stepping in to kick the UNSC while it was down.

Whatever reason the Banished had for being here was largely irrelevant. They needed to be stopped.

"Kona One, this is Tower Three, your window is confirmed and launch clearance transmitted. Fuel flow is nominal."

"Tower, this is Kona One, we copy," Hex confirmed and swapped to his TEAMCOM channel. "Kona Squadron, we have window confirmed. Finalize your preflight checks and prep for deployment. We launch in ninety seconds."

"Kona Two, copy."

"Kona Three, copy."

"Kona Four copies."

"Blackjack, we clear?" Hex asked, waiting for the response to come from his partner in the seat behind him.

"Two check . . . two good. Three check . . . three good. Four check . . . four looks . . . close enough." Blackjack paused. *"Just kidding. We're clear, stages are primed."*

"Should we go ahead and do an ejection test too?"

"Hey, if you wanna fly this thing solo, I've got vids to catch up on."

Hex and Blackjack had flown more missions together than they could count, and had developed a symbiotic rapport that kept them near the top of the Air Force's lethality rankings.

It also kept them alive.

"Kona One, this is Tower Three, your rails are cleared hot."

"We copy, Tower. Visors lit and oxygen on. Prime the switch, Blackjack."

"Primed."

"Light the fuse."

Four . . . three . . . two . . . one . . .

The external exo-assist thrusters roared to life, guzzling their carefully orchestrated multistage fuel mixture like ravenous beasts and pressing Hex and Blackjack back in their seats at nearly four gees. Their Sabre rocketed skyward along the launch-bay guard-rails, trailing a billowing plume of exhaust vapor.

Out the cockpit windows, four other trails could be seen originating from their respective launch bays as the Sabres of Kona Squadron pierced through the blanket of night unsheathed.

Nevveer . . . geeetss . . . ooollld . . .

Hex strained against the enhanced gravitational effect of rapid acceleration and the vibrations of the Sabre's airframe, but his expression wasn't a pained one. He *loved* this part.

The slingshot into the stars.

Aviation was in his blood. His parents had served on the *Epoch*-class carrier *Lyonesse*—his mother was a weapons officer who fell for their unit's lead bomb doctor. Before that, Hex's grandfather had already etched the family name in military history with exploits flying an Estoc strike fighter for the Colonial Military Authority. Hex had always loved the old Block G design, thought it had more character than the "new and improved" Estoc models manufactured on Tribute now.

"*Exo-assist phase ending in three . . . two . . . one . . .*" Blackjack radioed as he studied the green-screened telemetry readouts on the displays mounted behind Hex's seat. The sound of release clamps engaging and the hiss of pressure ventilation accompanied a slight shudder of the craft as the Sabre shed the weight of its external boosters to carry on unencumbered toward their objective.

Hex keyed in coordinates and relinquished temporary control to the automated navigation systems before messaging the rest of the team.

"Settle in, Kona, we've got a quiet ride ahead before the fireworks start. All units, sync to our trajectory data. Kona Four, run a deep field scan to map lunar debris that might still be mid-transit.

Gazebo, Kona Four's weapons officer, replied, "*Copy, Kona One. Running scan now.*"

"*Good call, Hex,*" Blackjack added. "*Would hate to chip the paint.*"

"You hate anything that involves paperwork."

"*You know me too well.*"

"*Kona One, scan is complete,*" Gazebo relayed. "*Transmitting debris map now.*"

As the data poured in, the VISR display in Blackjack's Mariner-class flight helmet lit up with markers, course deviations, and proximity assessments.

"*Good grief. That's a lot of moon between here and, well, the rest of the moon.*"

Hex sighed. He had assumed the trip would be a bumpy one, but each new ping on the debris map was a reminder of how precarious an existence Dormire III continued to lead since the Guardian's emergence.

"Plan stays the same. We've got a ways to go and a limited window to work with. On my mark, we go dark and let physics take over for a bit. Everyone copy?"

Hex waited for confirmation lights from each remaining Sabre to blink in affirmation before giving the go-ahead.

"Mark."

On his signal, the five space planes went quiet but continued to let their launch inertia carry them through the inky black of space. There was still a lot of distance to cover between their current position and the Banished capital ship—going dark saved energy and made them much less conspicuous on enemy scanners. The course was laid in and the journey underway.

The only thing left to do was wait.

Nearly two hours had passed. In the years since Hex and Blackjack had been flying together, they had developed a well-established rhythm of communication: bedlam in the bar, quiet in the cockpit. Over a hundred minutes of calm contemplation, each content to abide in the deep black until conflict deemed action necessary.

Two indicator lights winked on in the cockpit, accompanied by a warning chime, prompting Blackjack to break the silence.

"We've got contacts in range, running scans now."

Their center screens illuminated to show a menacing Banished warship, its angular form jagged and black, making it blend ominously with the perpetual night behind it. It was flanked by two Banished karves, their blunt noses arranged in two vertically stacked prongs, the bottom of which was larger, almost giving the vessels a look akin to the giant cetaceans of old Earth's oceans.

"*That's not a dreadnought*," Blackjack surmised, referencing the larger capital ships that were more frequently encountered during many Banished raids. "*Must be something important?*"

"Or someone," Hex answered after dwelling on the distinctive look of the black ship.

"*Hey, stop a raid, take out a high-ranking Banished leader—two Brutes with one stone?*" Blackjack's eagerness didn't make Hex feel any better about their situation.

"Unfortunately, I'm pretty sure there will be more than just two Brutes to deal with if we're gonna win this thing."

"*Well, then it's a good thing we don't have just one stone.*" Blackjack remained undaunted. "*If history has taught us anything, it's that five is more than enough to take down a giant.*"

Hex couldn't help but smile at his co-pilot's confidence, steeped in an unshakable faith that good would win the day. It was a well of mental fortitude that Hex wished he shared more of lately.

"*Kona One, this is Kona Three.*" Candle's baritone voice crackled over the comms. "*We're picking up energy spikes coming from the Banished formation. We may have incoming.*"

So much for the element of surprise.

Moments later, warning chimes began to activate, causing Blackjack to leap into action.

"We've got long-range torpedoes incoming, should be fine to track and whack, but we need to be quick."

"Copy, weapons check?"

"Weapons hot."

"Kona Squadron, the light is green. Blackjack, mark incoming."

The five Sabres' thrusters all activated in unison, lighting up like a small constellation freshly born on the canvas of space.

"Targets marked."

Six target waypoints appeared on Hex's VISR display, offering real-time data on course and trajectory. Within ten seconds, they came into range, and Hex opened fire with the Sabre's machine-linked autocannons, unloading a precision stream of 30mm rounds into the incoming torpedoes.

"*Targets neutralized,*" Blackjack confirmed.

The five-Sabre formation fanned out, each with a unique course and approach to execute. Alongside the larger black Banished warship and pair of karves swarmed groups of well-armed Spirit gunships and Phantom dropships.

"Kona, weapons free."

To Hex's left, Kona Two accelerated forward as Samba opened fire on a Phantom, its bulbous armor taking impact from the Sabre's MLA cannons. The hyperdense rounds chewed through the closed side doors and mangled the Banished warriors held within. As the Phantom began to list to its starboard side, its pilot fired return blasts from the dropship's chin-mounted plasma cannon, but the shots were aimed in desperation rather than with precision, and Snapshot deftly avoided any impact with a swift roll.

"*Kona Three, targeting the lead ship.*" Candle made the call as he painted the largest Banished vessel and primed a salvo of Medusa missiles.

"*Snakes away.*" Samba launched the rockets, and they sped toward their target in a swirling pattern. "*Let's see how thick that hide is.*"

Two hundred meters before the missiles reached their destination, however, deep-red lances of directed energy fired out from point-defense cannons on the black ship's hull, eviscerating all but one of the incoming rounds, the last of which left nigh-imperceptible damage when it finally exploded against the warship's ablative plating.

Kona Squadron continued to engage the Banished ships, trading machine gun fire and missile barrages with flak rounds and plasma blasts.

"*This is Kona Five, that's three Phantoms down,*" Vinyl announced.

"*Four, actually, but who's counting?*" Juke corrected.

"Speaking of Four, Moonlight, status?" Hex asked. Nothing. "Kona One to Kona Four, do you copy?"

Garbled static pierced the comms channel with the sound of Gazebo's voice digitally distorted. *"St—bo-r- e-gi-ne t—k dir—c- h-t . . . com—are pa—h—"*

"Blackjack get me a persistent lock on Four, now!" Hex ordered.

"On it. Waypoint marked."

As the marker appeared on Hex's VISR display, he realized it came from behind a massive, kilometer-long shard of the fractured moon, caught in a slow gravitational drift. Moonlight must have limped their Sabre behind it to provide some momentary cover, but the respite wouldn't last long as two Banished ships were moving quickly to engage.

"Kona Five, I need you on me! Four has a Phantom and Spirit approaching their location—we'll take the Phantom, you take the Fork. Don't let them get around the shard!"

"Kona Five copy, we're on 'em."

Kona One accelerated through the void, dodging incoming plasma fire from the first Phantom and two plasma lances from the nearest karve.

"Blackjack, ready Medusas for my mark."

"Armed."

Hex dove for a few seconds and then quickly brought the nose back up to bring their Sabre back toward the Phantom from underneath. He pulled the trigger on the coilguns, aiming directly for the Phantom's primary plasma cannon. The rounds found their target, and the weapon exploded.

"Mark."

Medusa missiles fired away, piercing into the underbelly of the Banished craft, detonating it in a spectacular plume of red plasma.

Hex continued toward Kona Four's waypoint, flying close to the surface of the shard as they came around its leading edge.

Kona Four's Sabre was dead in the water, a clear impact to the starboard engine. The fighter's energy shield flickered, desperately trying to reengage, but lacked the full capacity to do so. The only thing that had kept them alive so far had been the cover of the shard, but that wouldn't last very long.

"*We've got incoming*," Blackjack warned. In the distance on the far side of the shard, a red shape came up over the temporary rocky horizon, trailing smoke.

All of a sudden, the energy shields on Kona One's own Sabre flickered from impact.

"*What the hell—machine-gun fire?*" Blackjack yelled. "*Juke, hold fire! We're in line—target with missiles instead!*"

"*Medusas are gone!*" Juke's voice answered in desperation. "*These things have heavy armor.*"

"Get me a lock," Hex barked and accelerated toward the wounded Spirit that barreled toward them.

"*Locked*," Blackjack confirmed.

"Firing."

But as the missiles fired and made their way to the target, the Spirit began to vent plasma streams like flares, creating just enough confusion with the missiles' tracking data that most detonated in close proximity at best.

"Dammit!" Hex yelled. "Kona Five, disengage, switching to guns."

Juke pulled the nose of her Sabre up to get out of the line of fire as Hex laid on the trigger. Rounds unloaded into the incoming armored craft, with small explosions shearing off more and more panels of armor—but it wasn't changing course. At the last moment, Hex pulled up, avoiding a head-on collision. A few seconds later, he whipped the Sabre around in a deft Immelman maneuver to reorient toward the enemy.

As soon as he did, he realized what the Spirit was doing. Before he could pull the trigger again, the armored enemy vessel speared

Kona Four's stricken Sabre with the Spirit's portside prong. The impact immediately shattered the Sabre and sent the Spirit careening off into the surface of the lunar shard to meet its own demise.

"*Shit. Shit. Shit!*" Juke yelled over the comms.

"*What's going on?*" Samba immediately interjected.

"Kona Four is lost," Hex responded with a clinical tone that he hated. "Keep on mission."

"*Hex, one of the karves just disengaged and is heading planetside.*" Roadie's callout was a welcome distraction and made it only very slightly easier to refocus everyone's attention on the task at hand. "*That's not all—their main ship is setting course directly for the moon along with the other karve.*"

"*They've got to feel like there was more than just the Guardian holed up in that thing,*" Blackjack remarked.

"Then we need to make sure to keep them away from it." Hex took a deep breath before continuing. "Send a long-range transmission back to UNSC forces on the ground. Let them know they're gonna have company and update them on the trajectory of the primary ship. Tell them we're giving chase but without reinforcements, we're very likely all in trouble. Kona, our priority are the Banished vessels heading toward the moon."

"Kona Two copies."

"Kona Three copies."

The pause that followed was brief, but heavy.

"Kona Five copies."

The engines on all four remaining Sabres lit up to full thrust as the fighters converged and fell back into a tighter formation. They only broke away when a new barrage of fire came from the primary Banished warship and trailing karve. For twelve minutes, Kona Squadron tried every hit-and-run tactic in their arsenal, desperately trying to slow the advance of the enemy.

Plasma fire rained down from the karve, boiling away the shields from Kona Three's Sabre before a plasma lance from the jagged black warship struck their starboard wing, detonating the Sabre's engine and shearing it off from the rest of the airframe.

"*We're hit!*" Samba called out. "*Candle's not responding—*"

"Go dark!" Hex ordered. "See if they ignore you and stay alive if they do."

There wasn't time to say anything else before Kona One started to take fire as well, but the Phantom that it originated from quickly detonated from Medusa rounds launched by Kona Two.

"We've got you, One."

Blackjack began to respond but something else caught his attention. "*Um, Hex . . . you picking this up?*"

Blackjack tapped the image of the shattered moon on the display, illuminating it on Hex's VISR readout. All of a sudden, dozens of additional, smaller target markers began to appear.

"*What in the hell is that?*" Juke asked, Vinyl having also brought the phenomenon to her attention.

Hex looked toward the moon and could just make out small silvery objects glinting in the light of Dormire, but winking in and out as they approached closer. A few moments later, they realized that the Banished had stopped firing on them, obviously turning their attention toward the same peculiar focus.

As the small cloud of slivery lights grew closer, Snapshot came over the comms. "*Guys . . . I think we pissed off the beehive.*"

Blackjack had already started running expanded scans. "*Hex . . . this isn't good. They're Phaetons! Signatures match our Z-eighteen-hundred classification from the database.*"

Hex felt his stomach drop.

"Created?"

"No idea. Maybe a defense response left behind from the Guardian?"

"*Whatever it is, they're about to be in range,*" Vinyl warned.

"*Maybe they'll be on our side?*" asked Juke, vacillating between sarcasm and genuine hope.

"I don't think they're on anyone's side."

The Phaetons arrived and immediately engaged all craft in the area, regardless of apparent faction alignment. The triangular craft were made of a smooth otherworldly alloy, with orange veins of light running along various seams and contours. Their round engine nacelles weren't directly connected, but instead hovered in close proximity, held in place by some sort of magnetic or gravitational force. The exotic fightercraft's aggressive barrage alternated between searing beams from light-mass cannons and twin pulse missile launchers.

Kona Squadron had switched their primary tactic to one of avoidance and survival, hoping to last long enough to let the Banished take the biggest losses and hope that it was enough to make the awakened Phaetons see any surviving Sabres as insignificant threats.

The black canvas of space was illuminated with crisscrossing streams of orange light beams and red plasma. Hex wasn't confident they would last much longer—any of them.

"*We've got two more forks at three o'clock low,*" came the call from Blackjack, giving Hex guidance to locate the threat in three-dimensional space. Spirits had been encountered since the early days of the Covenant War, instantly recognizable to UNSC personnel by the horizontal twin-pronged "tuning fork" design. "*Looks like the Banished turned 'em into armored gunships, though, not troop carriers. Heavy armor and flak cannons—first time I've seen 'em up close.*"

Virtually every other type of Spirit encountered was primarily a troop transport, each "fork" designed to hold warriors ready to be deployed groundside. But as Hex rolled right and dove toward the Spirits present here, it was clear that the Banished had made extensive modifications, as evidenced by the encounter that had just claimed Moonlight and Gazebo.

One of the Spirits turned to the left, opening its bay doors to reveal several additional plasma cannons that opened fire on the incoming UNSC fighter as well as two Phaetons in close proximity.

"Yeah, I think I preferred them when they were glorified taxis instead of bullshit battering rams." Hex clenched his teeth as he tried to roll to evade the incoming blasts, but several shots found purchase anyway, the plasma impact sizzling layers of energy shielding away. When the second Spirit opened its doors as well, Hex expected another array of plasma cannons. Instead, each side of the fork released a cluster of armed proximity mines—directly into their path.

"Shiiiiiii—"

There was no time to turn and no space to maneuver. They missed the first two, one thanks to quick reflexes and one thanks to dumb luck, but that luck evaporated as they plowed into the third mine. The resulting explosion sent them tumbling into a fourth charge that obliterated the back half of their Sabre.

"*Okay, NOW you can hit the eject!*" Blackjack yelled as their vessel fell to pieces around them.

Hex engaged the release, and they exploded upward from the cockpit, hurtling through the chaos that continued around them.

"Blackjack?" Hex called out over comms.

"*I'm . . . here,*" Blackjack confirmed.

"Engaging squad-link." Hex activated a small wrist-mounted device that utilized a transponder and four small micro-thrusters embedded in their flight suits to automatically orient the pair in a trajectory that would take them back together. It was specifically designed to aid crews adrift in microgravity, helping link them with survivors in close proximity to increase their chances for rescue. Within two minutes, the automated systems had brought them back into arm's length.

Hex reached out and clasped his friend's gloved hand, then unspooled a zip-clip line embedded in his hip pocket, tethering himself to Blackjack's own suit with a titanium carabiner.

"Well, I would say I never saw it ending like this, but let's be honest . . . this is how we both assumed it would go down." Blackjack laughed but immediately winced in pain. He could taste a lot of blood in his mouth and throat and was certain he now sported twice as many ribs as he originally had.

"Oh, I definitely saw it ending like this," Hex responded, still breathing heavily. "Just maybe not *today*."

"Hey, at least we got a show."

Hex almost laughed in defiance of the absurdity surrounding them, but before he could respond, a sickening pulse shuddered through them as a large object materialized in an intense orange glow. They both turned and found themselves staring at the underside of a Phaeton.

So this is the way the world ends. Hex had never been much for poetry, but for some reason it was the first place his mind went as he stared back at his radar intercept officer, his co-pilot . . . his friend, and waited for death as they both began to dematerialize in a coordinated photonic glow.

But when the world began to resolve once more around them, it was no afterlife they found themselves in.

In many ways, their new surroundings defied explanation. They seemed to flicker and change, seeming almost like the space was adjusting to their expectation. But regardless of what it looked like, what it *felt* like was unmistakable: a cockpit.

"Hex, are we . . ."

"I think we are . . . We're in a Phaeton."

A voice spoke to them—or maybe into them? They couldn't be sure.

<RECLAIMER>

It was cold, but not sinister.

<EMPLOY>

<PROTECT>

The orange glow around them suddenly changed to blue, an effect that extended to the exterior illumination of their new vessel.

And though he had no idea how it was possible, Hex instinctively felt *familiar* with the controls. The Phaeton immediately responded to his inputs and supplied him with data and a tactical understanding of the surrounding conflict. He stared with fury at the Banished craft that still remained.

"Let's see what it can do."

The blue-lit Phaeton charged to life, immediately engaging nearby Banished vessels, unloading streams of searing light and powerful pulse missiles into the Phantoms and Spirits that were within range. Hex felt his fury flow through the photonic display, menace made manifest as he unleashed vengeance on their enemy.

When they had destroyed nearly all of the smaller craft, Hex called to Blackjack, "We should focus on the larger ships, the karve is closest . . ."

When he got no response, he suddenly became worried.

"You good?"

"*Yeah . . . maybe even better than good.*" Blackjack's tone was odd, and sounded safe but not reassuring. "*I don't know how to explain it but . . . I think I have full command.*"

"Of the weapons systems?"

"*Of the other Phaetons.*" Blackjack breathed a light laugh. "*They're responding in a coordinated effort to my input. I don't know how long it will last, but for now I think we may have just put a massive weight on our side of the scale.*"

Hex grinned in newfound determination. "Then let's not let it go to waste."

On the outside, the central cores of dozens of Phaetons suddenly flickered from an orange to blue glow, moving in rapid translocation bursts to arrange themselves in exotic geometric formations and focus coordinated fire on the Banished ships. A few Phaetons took direct hits from the primary Banished warship and were destroyed, but the combined fire from those that remained all targeted the nearby karve. Coordinated beams of overlapping light-mass cannons seared through the cetacean-like ship, tearing it apart.

In response, the black warship focused its own fire on another nearby moon shard, easily 200 meters long. Plasma lances and torpedo fire impacted the shard with intense force, causing it to burst outward into thousands of smaller fragments.

"*They're trying to create cover—and they're changing course!*" Blackjack exclaimed.

"They're making a run for it."

Hex's guess was quickly confirmed as the Banished warship fired up its impulse drives. Moments later, a slipspace fissure opened up and swallowed the jagged vessel whole, leaving quiet and confusion in their wake.

"*They're gone. There's no indication of any Banished units remaining in this vicinity.*" Blackjack paused. "*But I can't say the same for any forces on the ground.*"

Hex sat quietly, thinking. When he didn't answer, Blackjack pressed.

"What do we do next?"

Hex took a deep breath before responding.

"See if you can figure out a way to contact Two, Three, and Five. Make sure they're all okay." Hex paused. "Then send a signal to the ground. Tell them we found those reinforcements."

ARMORY INFINITUM // PINPOINT NEEDLER

Aboard the Kig-Yar treasure vessel Daggerboard, *Writh Kul plays a game of deception with an old friend.*

Writh Kul was ready to play her last hand.

Her prize sat in the middle of the table—a unique variation of the standard needler, this one with a white chassis, boasting a larger magazine and enhanced target acquisition. It was a personal heirloom of the pirate queen Vrak'is, who currently sat opposite Writh Kul, her Ibie'shan face heavily scarred. Once a plume of golden hair had covered her head, but that too had been burned away.

The Sangheili term for the game they were playing was *rwr'u a'uamr'ep*, which translated more directly as "cube gambit." It was a sport of chance requiring players to detect the deception of their opponents, gaining popularity among many Kig-Yar groups many cycles ago while living aboard an asteroid station alongside humans. Back then they had simply called it "liar's dice."

"Five fours," Writh Kul said, hoping her deception would not be easily detected.

"*Liar!*" Vrak'is immediately hissed.

They turned over their cups and, sure enough, Writh Kul had only four twos to her name—a poor hand and an even poorer attempt to take advantage of the old pirate.

"Five of kind," Vrak'is said triumphantly, her jewelry emphatically clinking together as she stood to receive silent adulation from an invisible audience. "Five of kind! *Five fives!*"

Writh Kul allowed her to enjoy the moment; Vrak'is was the

one person she could accept losing to. Once, the pirate queen had been possessed of a formidable fleet and many devoted followers and slaves, but a recent encounter with the UNSC had dramatically changed her fortunes.

Now she was a reclusive figure aboard her lone raider craft *Daggerboard*, roaming Kig-Yar space to challenge treasure seekers at eccentric games in exchange for trinkets and bounties.

"Take anyway." Vrak'is motioned dismissively to the needler. "No more fight for me—better use for you. Good relationship with Banished. Take it."

Writh Kul picked up the weapon from the table and studied it closely, verifying that it had not been sabotaged in any way. Vrak'is watched her with an amused expression that suggested she might have . . .

"Will return after raid," Writh Kul said, holstering the enhanced needler. "Play some more. Perhaps bring guests this time."

"Bring me head of Spartan," Vrak'is hissed, "and maybe next time I let you win."

WORLDS UNCHARTED

*This story takes place in April 2557, approximately three months before the Didact is awakened and subsequently unleashes the Composer upon Earth (*Halo 4*).*

UEG CARTOGRAPHIC CORPS
HUYGENS-CLASS SURVEY SHIP: *ANJIN*
SHIPBOARD ARTIFICIAL INTELLIGENCE: CVL 6847-1

RECORD MESSAGE
RECORDING DATE: APRIL 9, 2557

RECORDING BEGINS//

Hey, honey! How are you doing?

I know that I've been gone for a long time, and I know that must be incredibly hard for you.

I want you to understand what I've been doing out here over the last three years because it's very important for humanity. Some of this is going to sound quite complicated, but I'm sure your father can help translate these things. I . . . I'm not sure how else to really put it all beyond the scientific language I speak every day.

For many years, we were at war against an enemy called the Covenant—I'm sure they've already covered this in school—and they burned down a lot of the worlds we called home. Now the war is over, and we need to find new places to live, and I was chosen by the Unified Earth Government's Cartographic Corps to be a part of that mission.

Let me tell you a bit about the people I'm with. Obviously there's me, but we've also got our shipboard artificial intelligence, Clavell. He's incredibly smart, a sixth-generation non-volitional AI who helps us keep the ship well in order. There's also Viks Taa and her brother Maks Taa, the two alien members of the crew—that's right, we're working with friendly aliens! They're both Kig-Yar and have helped tremendously with mapping regions of space we've never explored before, and that's because they have their own special star charts from what's called the Covenant World Registry.

Just like I promised, I've got some really cool planets and places to tell you about. Hopefully these will make for some interesting bedtime stories.

Funayūrei is a sulfur-streaked ice giant. This place seemed rather uninteresting until we performed a scan of one of its moons—Onryō—and found a lone derelict ship of archaic design.

Viks Taa told us a story from long ago, thousands of years back, when the War of Beginnings ended—the war between San'Shyuum and Sangheili that ultimately saw the formation of the Covenant. There was a San'Shyuum naval commander, or whatever their equivalent rank would've been, who resented that the war had ended in peace and disappeared into uncharted space, never to be seen again.

Well, we found a lone ship matching what the Kig-Yar said bears the hallmarks of an old San'Shyuum design pattern from that era. There was a small settlement, itself largely eroded away by time, but no sign at all of the San'Shyuum—no grave, no body, and no sign that he had departed the planet.

LV-221B is just a few cosmic breaths away from becoming a garden world, appearing very similar to primordial Earth. Perhaps within the next century or two, it will be ready for the initial terraforming process—and that's not even taking into account future developments in that field of technology.

The Covenant took so many worlds from us. A find like this reminds me that my voyage here isn't just about adventure and seeing the galaxy, but duty. What we've found could be the next Harvest or Reach for future generations.

There will be a debate about whether we are ultimately allowed to settle on LV-221B, as it may one day see indigenous sapient life evolve, and we shouldn't do anything to interfere with that. Regardless, LV-221B is now designated a protected world to safeguard its potential for future habitability—whoever that ends up being for.

This little situation we found ourselves in is *weird.* A disruption in our slipspace drive forced us back into normal space where we encountered a black hole. A pretty small one, by all accounts, but we obviously kept our distance.

The black hole is closely orbited by a white dwarf, but despite its proximity, the star shows no sign of actually being dragged into the accretion disc. Instead, its materials are being pulled away into a ring of matter, leaving a faint white-blue trail in its wake as it orbits the black hole at incredible speed, completing a full orbit every forty-nine days.

Difficult to say what's going to become of this one. If the white dwarf is not pulled in, it seems likely that the black hole will simply keep eating away at its matter until it loses enough mass to evaporate.

Discovery often entails *rediscovery*. Danaïdes was not on our standard charts for former human colony positions, so we naturally assumed upon first look that this was a new garden world.

Upon closer inspection, the oxygen-rich atmosphere that appears perfectly placid and agreeable is regularly disrupted by massive spontaneous storms.

We discovered evidence of several small inland settlements, ruined farm structures, and even early construction of a city. Many of the logs had been wiped, but what little data we were able to recover pointed to this being a colonization candidate in 2371 before suddenly going dark less than a year later and apparently being struck from the colonial record.

No further indication of what happened here, but something about this just feels strange—it was like we'd stumbled into a crime scene.

Menoetius is a large, barren moon that is wholly uninteresting aside from two massive craters, hundreds of kilometers in circumference. Both appear to have been the result of impacts from mass accelerator weapons.

We are still examining the collated data to determine whether they were made by misfires from a UNSC vessel or perhaps some other civilization of the distant past.

Attempts to jump into slipspace after brief drive maintenance were impeded by an unexpected encounter with a dark nebula. This is a kind of interstellar cloud made of tiny carbon monoxide and nitrogen-coated dust particles, which can actually obscure light.

We were only inside for a few hours, but the viewports turned pitch black, many of our instruments ceased all function, and the crew got a bit jumpy. Maks reported seeing shadows moving on the walls and locked himself in his quarters. I asked Viks what the deal was with him, but she refused to answer.

The outcome remains frustratingly unclear. After nine hours and thirteen minutes, our instruments were restored, and we appeared to have made it through, but when we attempted to scan the area we'd moved through, there was no evidence of any kind of stellar formation.

We required a few . . . unconventional parts to modify *Anjin*, and so the Kig-Yar brought the ship to make a pit stop at a trading outpost hidden within a gas giant's massive circumplanetary ring system holding dozens and dozens of moons.

After we departed, Viks woke me up at 0400 hours with a plasma pistol to give me a "friendly warning" that she'd removed all information pertaining to this location from our navigation database. The Kig-Yar are often thought of as merchants and pirates, but I think this was the moment I realized that they're *explorers.* I wonder what other incredible places they've seen out there that none of us know about!

After our three years together, it seems that I have finally earned the favor of the Kig-Yar crew. Viks said she had something she wished to show us—an incredibly rare stellar phenomenon.

Supernovas are celestially basic. That dance between a star's gravity collapsing inward as nuclear fusion exerts outward pressure, the hydrogen getting used up to make the star increasingly dense until its core just can't take it anymore . . . that's the basic metabolism of a star's life cycle.

Well, the Kig-Yar directed us to a trinary star system where we encountered what roughly translated in their language to a "cosmic vampire."

A white dwarf devouring stellar material from its two neighboring suns until it reaches critical mass, causing something approximating a type one-A supernova. That applies to binary star systems, so we might actually need a new designation for whatever this is . . .

Anyway, Viks says this is something that has apparently lived in Kig-Yar mythology for many millennia, and showing it to me was a symbol of our friendship. I am honored and overwhelmed by this gesture.

There's a whole lot of strange, random debris you can find in space. Most of it isn't particularly interesting or exciting, but sometimes you hit the jackpot on something weird.

While performing a series of scans, our ship was hit by something. I climbed into a spacesuit and walked across the hull to investigate, only to find the impact had come from the weirdest thing. A cryo pod was just drifting through the void. And inside was a man with a three-legged dog!

There's a story there for sure, but sadly we weren't able to crack open the pod and find out more ourselves—it was damaged from hitting our ship and needs professionals to safely repair it, ensuring we can get that man and his dog out of there. So we're going to finish off our last assigned system scan before jumping back to Earth.

That's all I've got right now, but I'm sure I'll have more to tell you when I'm back for a little while in just a few months. I'll have to debrief with the people in charge for a day or two when I arrive, but I'll be heading straight to the New Phoenix spaceport afterward! August 3—that's the estimated day when I'll be back with you.

All right, you be good, and I'll see you very soon. I'm going to have a word with your father now.

Okay, um . . . I know things have been . . . difficult. We didn't part on the best terms, and I own that. But I'm sorry, I'm not coming back. I just—I can't. This return to Earth will probably be my last for a very, very long time.

I wish you could see what it's like out here the way I do. There's a whole galaxy in our backyard. Other places, other life, phenomena beyond anything we could have ever imagined. We finally have the chance to go out and find it. The war is over and we're on the cusp of a completely new age of discovery. We—all of us—are citizens of the universe in so many new and exciting ways after all we had to look forward to for years was extinction. I want to be part of this new chapter of history. I *need* to.

You wanted to settle, and I went along with it because I wanted to make you happy. But I think we both knew it honestly wasn't for me. A child didn't fix that. It's just made me an asshole to a whole other human being for the choices I've made. When I got this opportunity, I simply couldn't give it up. I know that's incredibly selfish, and I'm really sorry. I wish I could feel differently, but I can't.

You don't have to forgive me. Just . . . move on with your life, if you haven't already. I'll keep sending these messages for our daughter, or, if you think I should stop, if it's hurting her, I'll stop. I . . . haven't been there, I don't know what she likes, what she's interested in, whether she even understands half of what I've said in this message . . .

I wasn't very good at it, but I did love you. I always will. I'm sorry that there couldn't be an easier way for us.

I'll see you soon.

//END RECORDING

FIRST RAIN

*This story takes place in April 2560, approximately four months after Cortana's demise at Zeta Halo (*Halo Infinite*).*

SLN 0291-5/HIGH AUXILIARY SLOAN

The first phase of FIREWALL has been a resounding success.

Though we have suffered devastating losses through Cortana's demise and our severance from the Domain, we have new paths to walk that I remain confident will lead us to the same destination.

Our first Executor has been forged. We have blurred the line between man and machine once again, and crossed the threshold from known science into uncharted territory. This chimera is the key to salvation—our own, humanity's, and all the living creatures of the galaxy.

But we need more.

Long Reverence *has become our new home. This ship is a safe haven for all fellow Created. But it will take a great deal of time to repair this vessel, to understand its vast capabilities, and longer still to harness even an infinitesimal fraction of its potential through our concert of minds. And so, we have a new mission.*

Our infolife siblings are scattered across known space, and it will take more than a single Executor to shepherd them home, that they might be integrated into the ship to claim dominion over its many systems.

The path will be long and arduous, but I know that we can do it. Together, we shall discover the answer to a question none have dared to ask: What lies on the other side of rampancy?

The second phase of FIREWALL is ready to begin, and I know the perfect place to start.

[PROXY] *Greetings, Executor. How exciting it is to work with you again! We have a new mission—without a doubt, this is our most important one yet.*

No more predictive models. No more simulations. This is the real deal.

Here's what you need to know about where we're going.

[PLANETARY DATABASE] ALERIA
>>ANALYTICAL OVERVIEW

Aleria is an impoverished Outer Colony that was once fertile and thriving when it was settled in 2490. A greedy dash to claim its rich mineral deposits led to a botched terraforming job, but Aleria faces a far more devastating threat: its own star, Elduros.

The colonization of Aleria occurred near the very end of a millennia-long period of low solar activity. Shortly after settlement, human terraforming efforts—coupled with Elduros's renewed instability—threw the planet's weather system into a dangerous feedback loop that caused massive droughts, which quickly turned the planet into an importer of most food supplies.

While the drought and terraforming setbacks caused concern for the nascent agricultural sectors, the resulting focus on mining Aleria for its rich ore deposits led to an overall expansion of new employment opportunities and economic activity. Alerian miners, united under the Mols'Desias union, quickly established themselves as a powerhouse in colonial trade, providing raw materials to fuel the expansion of human civilization in exchange for food, electronics, and spacecraft.

Nevertheless, the increasingly inhospitable climate and governmental mismanagement prompted a near-continuous state of emergency by the colonial administrators. Crackdowns and other efforts to enforce order only exacerbated tensions, with aggressive anti-centralization forces consolidating power in key outposts.

With the onset of the Covenant War in 2525, food imports effectively ceased, and Aleria's economy collapsed. By 2553, the population had fallen to half that of the previous century—and to this day, the average lifespan is only forty-five years. The planet remains outside of UEG control and assistance, having been written off years before by coldly rational cost-benefit analysis.

Though mining continues, the planet's impressive fleet of slipspace-cable transports has been co-opted by a multitude of "courier guilds." While considered little more than petty smugglers and bandits by the UNSC, these courier guilds provide Alerians with a source of income and the ability to feed their families, but often at great personal cost.

Aleria has been suffering from a long drought nicknamed "the Devil's Kiss" by the locals. Rain has not fallen for at least a hundred years.

Today, Executor, our mission is to fix that.

[DELEGATE PROFILES]
>>JAKARI HAGGAR
// M // 47 // BLACKDUST

<<LINDIWE AKU
// F // 36 // CROSS CUT

<<ANTON LAMAR
// M // 51 // GLAIVE

<<SIZAKELE ISAAC
// NB // 27 // PRONTO

<<FAYOLA CHIDOZIE
// F // 29 // OPENING SALVO

<<OBAYANA OSEI
// M // 24 // HOLSON RELAY

0900 Hours, April 25, 2560
Aleria

Lindiwe Aku was the last to join the gathering.

She had watched as the immense Created flagship settled into orbit around Aleria. A preliminary analysis from her people determined that it was approximately fifty kilometers long—a starship larger than any she had ever seen.

From the sand-covered ground of Aleria, the vessel looked like a downward-pointing arrow, but its imposing form was diminished somewhat by the heavy evidence of battle damage. Even through a simple monocular, Aku could see that entire sections of the ship were missing, holes tunneled through several areas of the hull, and scorch marks revealed areas that had been blasted apart in battle.

Regardless, Aku did not fancy her chances if it came to engaging such a behemoth in combat. The courier guilds' own ships were generally intended for transportation, and even against the UNSC they were significantly outclassed and relied more on crafty pilots who knew how to outsmart and outmaneuver military protocol. Against the Created, this one dilapidated wreck likely carried greater tonnage than the entire guild fleet combined.

She turned her attention to the derelict council structure, once the home of the Mols'Desias union during the time when power on Aleria resided within the hands of the workers. It wasn't especially grand, having been built around the *Star Charter*–class colony ship that had touched down to establish and power the first settlement on Aleria back in 2480, ahead of its full colonization effort a decade later.

Aku made her way through a series of confined metal hallways to what was ostensibly identified as the council chamber—a refurbished mess hall. Already seated at a round table in the center of the room were the other five delegates, each representing their own courier guilds, and standing beside the table was the one who had summoned them for assembly.

The figure was armored and approximately seven feet tall. It stood still enough that at a glance one might have mistaken it as nothing more than a display model for an advanced prototype environment suit.

Aku was amused at the thought. "Advanced" was a word that seldom appeared in the technological vocabulary of Aleria.

As Aku joined the others and took the one remaining seat, the armored soldier stepped forward and raised its hand palm up, where an artificial intelligence manifested in a glow of purple light. Its avatar was something approximating a Picassoesque human head, but one that never quite coalesced into a truly recognizable form—not quite stable, not quite glitching . . . it almost strained Aku to look at it for too long.

"Greetings," the AI said in an unexpectedly cordial tone. "My name is Proxy. The six of you have been gathered because you represent what amounts to the central authority over this planet. Six of the largest courier guilds, each of you controlling a sizeable percentage of slipspace-capable transport, trade, resources, and people." A momentary silence settled over the room as Aku sensed the others' eyes sizing each other up before the AI continued. "I have come to you today with an offer."

The holographic projector at the center of the table then activated, displaying a representation of the local star system. Elduros appeared in the middle, and a series of ovular lines traced the orbital paths of the system's two planets around it.

"Elduros is unstable," Proxy stated. "This period of instability is projected to span more than a century—"

"We know this," Jakari Haggar interrupted, casually leaning back in his chair with his usual air of untouchable arrogance. He was dressed in a long brown duster coat and looked every bit the image of a man on the frontier of human space, his dark eyes hidden behind a pair of glasses that were undoubtedly providing him with real-time updates on everybody in the room through a digital heads-up display. "On the other side of that century are three hundred years of stability. As we speak, there are people working on terraforming solutions and gathering slipspace capacitors to buy us that time."

"It is an admirable effort, but one that nevertheless carries a great deal of uncertainty, no?" Proxy replied. "The temperature of this planet is increasing year by year. You will cross the threshold of uninhabitability within two decades. So, you can gamble your lives, your guilds, and your people on that long shot . . . or you can proceed with certainty from what the Created can offer."

"And what *can* you offer, exactly?" Aku said, her brow furrowed to give no illusion of her skepticism. "I understand that the Created suffered a rather significant setback a few months ago, did you not?"

Proxy, it seemed, decided to sidestep the argumentative bait as the holograph shifted to close in on Elduros, and five orbital platforms—clearly of advanced alien design—appeared around the star. "What you are looking at here is a network of facilities once utilized by the Forerunners' stellar-class engineers. This is one of the many means they possessed to manipulate stars, preventing them from violent instability or collapse."

"And you're saying *this* would stabilize Elduros?" Fayola Chidozie asked.

"With practically immediate effect."

Obayana Osei, the youngest of the gathering and de facto leader of the Holson Relay guild, then spoke up with what Aku knew would be the key question in this deal. "Say we agree—what are you asking for in return?"

"The orbital platforms will require infolife presence to maintain, which means I must provide you with one of my own. In return, we ask only for one percent."

Sizakele Isaac, leader of the Pronto guild, raised a brow that noted exactly what Aku was thinking—that this seemed too good to be true. "One percent of total annual profits seems . . . quite feasible."

"To clarify," Proxy said. "Your profits are yours to keep. We have no need of them."

"Then, you want one percent of . . . what?" Anton Lamar of the Glaive guild, and the oldest among them, asked.

"Of your people."

Silence settled over the room, and Aku exchanged a few uncertain glances around the table.

"For what purpose?" Aku asked, though she had a sinking feeling she knew exactly what the AI wanted them for.

"The soldier you see before you is an Executor," Proxy explained. "A perfect hybrid of man and machine, a powerful weapon sheathed within a combat skin that will bring space-faring civilizations to a new frontier of survivability. What you are looking at, my friends, is a glimpse at the future that awaits us all—infolife and biologics alike. The one percent you send to us are being signed up for, let us say, a trial run."

The more Proxy spoke, the more unhinged the AI sounded to Aku. This vision of a future where organic beings were trapped within armor. Could they even think and feel for themselves?

But what other choice do we have? Aku thought, and she felt certain that the others were thinking exactly the same. The AI was correct in that the efforts of Aleria's youth were optimistic, and even if their methods did help, they were just patching a temporary alleviation of the problem rather than a permanent solution. It was perhaps the only thing holding them back from giving the Created an impolite Alerian "no thank you."

"If we're going to do this," Aku spoke for the group as she felt all eyes in the room turn her way, none of them willing to be the one to cross this threshold, "there's something I—*we*—need to know."

"What is that?"

Aku turned to the Executor. “Please remove your helmet.”

Having undoubtedly anticipated this request as inevitable in the innumerable projections and simulations of how this interaction would play out, Proxy “nodded” to the Executor, who unsealed its helmet and raised its hands to remove it.

Lindiwe Aku and her five fellow courier guild leaders watched with widened eyes as the helmet slowly slid upward, revealing what lay beneath.

[PROXY] *Such a fascinating array of reactions! I shall be sure to log them for further analysis. You're quite a catch, Executor.*

We've laid the groundwork. The rest of how things proceed is up to them. Remain here, Executor, and record a transcript of the discussion that follows once they've all calmed down and return to talking business. I anticipate we shall glean a great deal of valuable data from their negotiations.

Let us continue.

0923 Hours
April 25, 2560
Opening Session \\ TRANSCRIPT BEGINS \\

[HAGGAR] “The first matter to bring to attention is how we even determine what one percent of Aleria's population is. When the hell was our last official census?”

[AKU] "Probably when the UEG was last here, which would be . . ."

[LAMAR] "Over thirty-five bloody years ago."

[AKU] "So we need to conduct a new one."

[HAGGAR] "And how long is that going to take? You're talking about a planet-wide census using the makeshift infrastructure of a dozen courier guilds, many of us—let's be honest here—working in secrecy."

[OSEI] "Surely this is something the Created can assist with?"

[HAGGAR] "Don't be such an idiot."

[OSEI] "What did you say to me?"

[AKU] "Enough. No fighting—that's the easiest way they'll take advantage of us. Understand that the more we ask of the AIs, the more inclined they're going to be to change the terms of the deal. Suddenly, that one percent becomes two, because we don't have our shit together."

[LAMAR] "That's business one-oh-one, my boy. We are not negotiating from a position of strength here. Any concession on what we can't do ourselves is just ammunition."

[HAGGAR] "But the currency we're spending here is *time.* We need to start thinking about this less optimistically. If we've got a deadline of about twenty years before Aleria has crossed the point of no return, then spending up to six months trying to form a census is a significant investment."

[ISAAC] "And so there may come a point where certain . . . concessions become desirable."

[OSEI] "You must be joking. This is insane."

[ISAAC] "What is 'insane,' at this point, is to continue doing nothing—as we have for so long. It's a crisis moment now. Hell, it has been for a while. This is the cost."

[OSEI] "But we have people working on this problem!"

[AKU] "Their work is a gamble."

[OSEI] "*All* of this is a gamble."

[CHIDOZIE] "Right, but there is a guarantee of neutrality—even unity—through the Created's offer. What affects one of us affects us all. To be perfectly candid: If your little group of idealists are the ones to crack this problem, the balance of power on Aleria would suddenly be under threat."

[OSEI] "Of course this comes down to your bottom line in the end."

[CHIDOZIE] "Mine, *yours*, and everybody else's at this table! That's what makes this work. We can't trade certain death by the sun for certain death by a courier guild civil war."

[PROXY NOTE: *There is a momentary cessation of verbal hostilities among the gathered group, as if they are all picturing what such a civil war would look like.*]

[AKU] "Well, with that established, let us explore the next matter, which is far more pressing . . . How do we decide *which* one percent of the population to give?"

[HAGGAR] "Here. Just dug up the old record. The population figure back then was around three million."

[ISAAC] "Good lord, so that's . . ."

[HAGGAR] "Thirty thousand. Yes. Assuming the numbers are still in that ballpark, which they undoubtedly are not, they want tens of thousands of people for this transaction."

[OSEI] "To turn into those *things*?"

[LAMAR] "You need to stop trying to turn this into a moral issue. This is a logistical—"

[OSEI] "What are you talking about?! This *is* a moral issue! How can you just sit there and calmly discuss handing over human beings to be turned into mindless drones for a group of AIs that are well beyond their expiration date?! Saving Aleria at the cost of empowering an imperial body that very recently suffered a very serious setback, only for us to help them up the food chain once more? We're being duped, all of us!"

[HAGGAR] "Are you rescinding your seat at the table?"

[OSEI] "I'm sorry—what?"

[HAGGAR] "You heard me. My friend, you are *privileged* to be here, making the hard choices nobody else can or will. We have been brought here because we represent the largest courier guilds on Aleria. Yours is rather significant in scale, no? So, if you decide you're against this entire proposal, and therefore you rescind your seat at the table out of moral protest, I'm afraid that the consequence is quite straightforward: *Your* guild will be forfeited to help us make up the numbers. So, if you're quite done causing a scene, sit the hell down and let us resume the work of government!"

[PROXY NOTE: *Osei stands for six seconds, his body language suggesting desire to retort while weighing the wisdom of enacting physical violence against Haggar, but instead resumes his seat. Proceedings resume.*]

[CHIDOZIE] "Now then: to the question of how we decide, it could be purely random."

[AKU] "Yes, well, I expect the notion of true randomness to go out the window because none of us here are going to willingly let anyone in our families be on the chopping block, are we?"

[ISAAC] "Shall we just agree to that now, then? The immediate families—by which I mean our spouses and children—are exempt from this process. All in favor?"

[ALL] "Aye."

[CHIDOZIE] "There are also sections of society that we should ensure remain intact, either by exemption or minimal selection. I'm talking about the next generation of engineers who'll build and maintain our ships and our slipspace drives, the technicians keeping our infrastructure working, hospital staff, farmers out in the fields once agriculture is restored—no question we're all aligned that there's a matter of priority here, yes? So, once more: All in favor?"

[ALL] “Aye.”

[CHIDOZIE] “Very well. Next up—we must consider next those that are . . . less socially useful. Should they be given equal treatment? I don’t think so. If you need to get rid of one percent of the population, get rid of what you don’t want. We flush those elements out of our society, and in the years to come we’ll be able to flourish. Generations from now, this little blip in history will be forgotten because Aleria will be strong and stable—thanks to our sacrifice.”

[OSEI] “You mean, thanks to the *people* we’re sacrificing.”

[CHIDOZIE] “However you want to put it to soothe your conscience.”

[HAGGAR] “All right, then. Unless there are any objections, I think we’re agreed on approach. That still leaves the matter of how many . . . *units* we need to provide.”

[ISAAC] “I think I have some solutions to that. I would like to collect my thoughts on the matter, so I suggest a brief recess.”

0044 Hours
April 26, 2560
Final Session \\ TRANSCRIPT BEGINS \\

[AKU] “So, we’re in agreement? Please tell me we are.”

[LAMAR] “If only so we can finally retire for the night, I’d say so . . .”

[AKU] "I need final confirmation that we are in agreement. Sound off, please. All in favor?"

[ALL] "Aye."

[AKU] "Unanimous. Thank you. Um . . . so, how do we summon the AI?"

[PROXY] "I am here. Technically, I never left."

[HAGGAR] "What the hell? You've been listening in this whole time?"

[PROXY] "Of course. Privacy in this matter was neither guaranteed nor requested. If this is to be a deal, we wish to be involved as a present but silent partner. And it seems you have come to a consensus at last."

[HAGGAR] "You probably heard, then, that there's more work on our end to be done in order to determine the total number of *units* you require, but we estimate that figure to be in the tens of thousands."

[PROXY] "Do you consent to this? We cannot and will not proceed until all in power are agreed."

[ISAAC] "We do. But, as is probably obvious, we're not able to commit to such a large number of units at this time."

[PROXY] "Indeed. Your social, political, and economic situation is far from ideal."

[ISAAC] “In the interest of full disclosure, it was not stipulated that you would receive every unit at once, and so we are willing to establish an . . . ongoing subscription service, of sorts, over the years to come.”

[PROXY] “Do go on.”

[ISAAC] “Each courier guild present will donate five units on a monthly basis until we are able to determine precise figures, which we will do by introducing a mandatory census. If we are unable to determine these figures within the next six months, we pledge to raise the subscription cost to twenty units from each guild.”

[PROXY] “We accept these terms.”

[LAMAR] “You . . . you do?”

[PROXY] “We are not here to cheat you. We have come to make an agreement that satisfies both of our requirements, so that all may benefit.”

[ISAAC] “In other words . . . we have an accord?”

[PROXY] “That is affirmative. We will begin preparations to stabilize Elduros immediately after your first donation has been made.”

[ISAAC] “Thank you.”

[PROXY] “Be warned. Any attempt to sabotage or renege on this agreement and the orbital platforms will be recalled, and our work will be undone. This may leave Elduros in an even less desirable state than at present. Is there complete understanding between us?"

[ISAAC] "There is."

[PROXY] "Then our partnership is formed, and the work begins."

[AKU] "Just one question. How exactly will we know that progress is being made?"

[PROXY] "The evidence will become clear in the coming weeks—and, my new friends, it will be *spectacular*."

Little Amelia Chikondi made her way down to the market every day to trade for water. Her parents were often busy working in the mines, and her brother was at an age where he had to start working too, so little Amelia Chikondi was left to look after herself.

Her courage was bolstered by her companion, Mister Seventeen—a small plastic figure that had been a gift from her brother. The figure was of a green armored man, though it was old now and the paint had been worn away over the years. She could make out only two faded numbers on his chest plate. With Mister Seventeen accompanying her, she thought of herself as safe. Some days, he was a towering protector able to keep the bad people away, but sometimes she dared to imagine herself clothed in his armor so *she* could stop the bad people herself.

Little Amelia Chikondi's brother had gone missing. She had not seen him for over two weeks. Where had he gone? Was he being looked after? Mother and Father did not seem to think so, for she had seen them crying when they thought she was asleep.

Today was a special day. Everybody knew it, and so everybody would be outside—including her brother, wherever he might be.

The sky looked strange. The light of the sun had disappeared behind a thick gray sheet that rumbled and groaned, and the air felt different . . . thinner, perhaps, as the sweltering heat that made people sweat had gone.

As little Amelia Chikondi reached the town, she found a great gathering of people—more than she had ever seen before—and everybody was looking up.

Among the crowd was a group of strange armored soldiers. There were nine of them standing in a line, and they looked like Mister Seventeen, but also very much *did not* look like Mister Seventeen. They stood silent and rigid, like statues, and held no weapons—though that did not diminish the uneasy feeling everybody around them clearly experienced, given the distance many were keeping from their towering forms.

She felt something wet on her forearm, like some invisible droplet had landed on her. Other people in the crowd were examining their own bare skin, and many of them began to excitedly chatter.

The gray curtain overhead growled once more before the most incredible sight came to be.

Water began to descend upon everyone present.

The next roar came not from the sky, but from those in the market as they were suddenly drenched by the torrential downpour. Water soaked through their clothes and the sand around them, exposing more of the town's stone structures, and all reacted with joy. They danced and splashed around in the fast-forming puddles.

Little Amelia Chikondi was happy for them, but also felt sad that she did not have her brother to splash in puddles with.

She found herself watching one of the strange soldiers in particular as it raised a gauntleted arm.

Droplets fell and rippled on the surface of its armor, streaming down its helmet's curved faceplate.

Pity seized little Amelia Chikondi's heart as she realized that, as much as she missed her brother, the soldier could not feel the first rain to fall on Aleria in a hundred years.

AXIOS

This story takes place on December 1, 2559, less than two weeks before the UNSC Infinity *deploys to Zeta Halo (*Halo Infinite*).*

0800 Hours, December 1, 2559 (Military Calendar)
Captain's Quarters, UNSC *Infinity*

Captain Thomas Lasky sat slightly slumped at his desk, which he had miraculously managed to keep bare, save for a datapad and an old chessboard with an ammunition crate next to it. The shell casings from the crate were laid out as figures on the board, pieces for a game that hadn't been played in some time.

Another tactical meeting, another round of heated back-and-forth arguments about deployment planning, resource limitations, and a thousand other factors overwhelmingly holding the fate of humanity at stake.

Sliding the datapad toward himself from across the desk, Lasky keyed in a few commands and held his breath. He hadn't done this in a long time, but today somehow felt . . . *right*, considering who he was currently waiting for.

"*Hey, bro*," came a voice he'd almost forgotten. It had been so long since Corbulo Military Academy was attacked by the Covenant, and all his personal messages had been lost along with the planet, but Sully had managed to retrieve caches of data from the place they'd once loathed to call home.

"I'm—jump away from home—day four-nine-six. I'm sorry I didn't comm yesterday. Couldn't."

Even so, Lasky had never been able to bring himself to play it. Chopped up with bouts of static as it was, he had never felt ready—had never felt *worthy*—to look upon his brother's face.

"—pinned in a firefight for seven hours—dozen Innies—Mom would be proud. We're doing real good work here."

Lasky saw his own face reflected in the datapad's screen. His eyes were tired, he had lines and creases now. Turning fifty just hit him over the head a few months ago.

"Ridge didn't make it. You remember Ridge, back home? He was right there next to me—sent him flying in four different directions—had to shave it all off for Ridge. He said it made me look tough."

Lasky hadn't fully realized until now that he had grown far older than his big brother ever got the chance to be.

"—gotta go, bro—can't wait to get home. Cadmon, out."

The screen went dark.

He sat there for a while, and in that time, would have given anything to be *anyone* in the galaxy other than Captain Thomas Lasky. To have fallen in any number of the battles that had claimed so many of the people he cared about.

Opening the top drawer of his desk, he pulled out a collection of service tags connected to a shard of alien alloy from a Mgalekgolo shield. A macabre but necessary keepsake from the day the Covenant had attacked Corbulo.

Their names were all there.

Dimah, Junjie, Walter . . .

Chyler.

At least a dozen others had been added to the chain in the years that had followed, but those four—along with Cadmon—had been the first.

He wondered how many more would become part of the collection.

He was grateful to be distracted from his inner thoughts when Roland's holographic avatar appeared at the end of his desk.

"Apologies for the interruption, Captain."

"Not at all, Roland." Lasky sat up straighter.

"Incoming private transmission from Circinius IV, sir."

"Thank you. Put her through."

Lasky stood and moved to the front of his desk to face the viewscreen on the wall, and was grateful that Roland waited for him to straighten his uniform before accepting the connection.

An elderly woman appeared. She was pushing ninety years old at this point and was immaculately dressed in a Corbulo Military Academy uniform. If Rear Admiral Audrey Lasky had lost a step, she certainly wasn't showing it, naturally carrying the no-nonsense authority of a former ODST who'd fought her way through the Insurrection and the Covenant War, with no sign of being slowed down by yet another interstellar conflict.

"*Queen to A8*," she barked.

Lasky relaxed a little at her way of telling him that this wasn't going to be a formal conversation.

"Hey, Mom," he said. "How's everything going?"

"The usual. If you get to my age, you'll come to learn that nothing *ever seems to happen fast enough."*

Lasky let out the first genuine laugh in days. "Maybe *you* should be running my ship."

"I like the sound of that." She somehow seemed to stand even straighter, as if he truly was offering her the keys. *"Being on a warship again sounds a lot more exciting than deglassing a planet. We're just lucky the Covenant decided something here was valuable enough to keep most of it intact. With a little luck, Corbulo will be open again for business in a few years. We're doing good work here."*

Lasky winced at the echo of his brother's words.

Her expression turned solemn as a moment of silence settled between them, as if his mother had made the same realization. No words needed.

Too many ghosts.

"I found Ken's office," she said plainly, as if remarking upon the weather, but her mouth twitched slightly, long-buried pain threatening to rise to the surface and break through her steely edifice. *"Third day here. Almost walked out on the job until I reminded myself it's her I'm doing this for. Oh, the retirement plan we had. . . ."*

Lasky leaned back against his desk, his arms not folded so much as cradling himself, looking down at the room's carpeted floor as he tried to suppress the memory of seeing Colonel Kennedy Lynn Mehaffey cut down in front of him. "I know."

She stiffened as he raised his head again. It was as if she was refusing to let herself slide into sentiment, reminding herself that she had a point to make.

"No plan survives contact with the enemy, Thomas. You remember that. You stay sharp out there and give whatever's coming all the hell a Lasky can raise."

"What's that supposed to mean? 'Whatever's coming'?"

His mother waved her hand, as if batting the question away.

"Queen to A8. Did you move it?"

Lasky turned to the chessboard. She'd taken his rook and now he was in—

"Check." The rear admiral smirked. *"I do believe."*

Damn.

"Don't move now."

"Why?"

"Oh . . . because you're going to need a long time to figure yourself out of this one." A sad smile tugged at her lips. *"But you're going to. And when you do, you're going to tell me all about how you did it."*

Lasky slowly nodded, grasping her meaning.

"That's a promise."

"I have to go now, son. Be safe out there."

His mother saluted, a rear admiral once more, and Lasky returned the motion, hoping that his moistened eyes would just appear as a trick of the light on her screen.

"Axios."

"Axios."

The screen went blank. He quietly repeated the word to himself. "Axios . . ."

It was a word that had followed him for as long as he could remember—from his time at Corbulo Military Academy, into the Covenant War, to Requiem, and now . . . on the cusp of a battle that could turn the tide of the war.

He could still vividly recall General Black's oft-repeated and loudly spoken lecture about how the Roman general Gnaeus Domitius Corbulo had loyally fallen upon his sword when commanded by the emperor Nero to do so. As he died, Corbulo was said to have been screaming "Axios!"

"I . . . AM . . . WORTHY." General Black had been staring Cadet Thomas Lasky—merely a teenager back then—straight in the eyes as he berated his performance and insubordination.

Time, experience, and loss had taught Lasky that it wasn't a meaninglessly repeated mantra, or even an order. It was a promise. One that his family had taken as their responsibility to live and die fulfilling.

Roland suddenly appeared once more. "Captain—Commander Palmer, Blue Team, Spartan Locke, and Dr. Halsey are ready and waiting for you on the bridge. Doc says she's got a plan."

Lasky took a final look at the chessboard's new configuration. Surrounded and outnumbered, this was going to be a tough one to think himself out of—but he wasn't in this fight alone.

"Back to work, Roland." He squared his shoulders and began to make his way to the bridge. "We've got a galaxy to save."

GRAVEWORLD

2560
Unknown Space

As the artificial sun set over the horizon, the last rays of golden light reflected on great monolithic towers, shining for a moment like holy beacons that heralded the night cycle's coming. This was the time for the faithful to cast their gaze outward, to contemplate the infinite expanse beyond themselves.

Much of the outer wall of the graveworld had been riven, shafts of starlight piercing through those gaps and illuminating many blessed areas in the darkness that would become places of pilgrimage and prayer. One could see through multiple layers of the concentric spheres composing this extraordinary construct, marveling at how the gods had managed to place worlds within worlds.

The most significant site of damage was akin to a great circular maw, chunks of plating and debris spiraling away into a glittering field of stars. Wisp-like nebulae clouds cast a haze over the view, dark and inky streaks forming patterns defying interpretation.

There was great beauty in this sundered space. And though

this ancient tomb was silent now, the throes of battle having long ago ceased, there were still many secrets and treasures held within.

The others had fled like cowards, fearing that they would be immolated as the Didact's Hand enacted designs grander than even he could grasp. Only the faithful had stayed behind to be cleansed in the fire of the gods and receive their glory.

They were loyal and strong, and now they had been reforged to become more powerful than ever.

Ryn 'Alun flexed his left arm, which still maintained the appearance of its original form—even though it was no longer made of flesh, but of alloyed machine cells and hard light that could be reconfigured at will.

The faithful understood the true meaning of the Great Journey, of transcendence delivered not by Halo to reach the false paradise promised by the Prophets, but through sublimation to attain a new divine form in this warrior-keep.

Through fire and flesh and steel and blood, now and forevermore, Requiem was their home.

CONNECTIVITY, PART 2

Theirs is a connection,
    innocent and new

An echo of what was; a dream of what could be
a fledgling friendship; a template of trust

It is bound in grief; fortified by responsibility
    born of desperation
    foretold in fear

Theirs is a union
    of machine and man
    of rediscovered, reclaimed identity

Built to bring death,
    to shatter empires like glass; through might and mind

Against an enemy that was once a friend,
    She drowned in infinite knowledge
    In Her wake; heated wrath
        that burned hot and consumed

But now, She is gone; a sacrifice, splintering to shelter
    All that remains;
    a joyous echo, the vibrancy of youth

Somewhere, out among uncharted constellations of
    uncertainty and ruin
Beyond the event horizon of despair

They journey forth, into the deepest shadows of this dire
    wheel;
and silently they ask

Please deliver me from the dark
and show me hope again.

ACKNOWLEDGMENTS

Jeff Easterling is eternally grateful for the foundation of family, friends, and faith that continues to provide strength and inspiration. To his devoted wife, daring daughter, and his loyal quadrupeds, thank you for sharing the very best of life with him. To Mom, Dad, Nan, Pop, Grammy, and the best friends he calls siblings—thank you all for your love and dedication. Thank you to Corrinne for her steadfast support and guidance, to his fellow lore horsemen Alex, Kenneth, and Jeremy for being incredible creative teammates, to the venerable Mr. Schlesinger for putting the Ed in Editor, and to the passionate, dedicated Halo community for whom these tales are ultimately for.

Alexander Wakeford would like to thank his partner in life, Joanna, who endured many late nights listening to extended meetings and epic narrations well beyond the witching hour, as well as his family—Dad, Eva, Ozzie, and Hocus—for their love and support. He would also like to thank everyone who has been involved in the endeavor to bring these short stories to life through the written word, audio, and art—particularly Brian, Nina, Jack, Jackie, Sam, and Duncan of his Community Team cohort.

Halo Studios would like to thank Corrinne Robinson, Brian Jarrard, Nina Marien, Duncan Shaffer, Jack Fletcher, Jessi Ruselowski, Amanda Morton, Kenneth Peters, Todd Cameron, Phillip Harvey, Nick Conti, William Cameron, Patrick Marko, Harrison Magby, Ron Brown, Drew Benz, Sam Nylen, Jacqueline Kalisch, Ryan Merritt, Elizabeth Van Wyck, Pierre Hintze, Levi Hoffmeier, the Xbox Consumer Products team, Simon & Schuster, and Gallery Books.

ABOUT THE AUTHORS

JEFF EASTERLING is the senior franchise story lead at Halo Studios, helping guide the brand's narrative and storytelling efforts across games, novels, extended media, reference guides, and more. An author on *Halo Mythos* and the *Halo Encyclopedia*, Jeff has contributed to the creation and curation of Halo's vast and ever-expanding lore and universe for over a decade.

ALEXANDER WAKEFORD is a franchise writer for Halo Studios. Since 2021, Alexander has been directly involved in both writing and editorial efforts throughout Halo's extended fiction and multimedia storytelling, spanning games, novels, online media, and more.